Soul T

by K. J. T. Carr

Cover art by Neil Rankin.

For Emma, for believing in me when I did not.

PART I

CHAPTER ONE

The morning sun shone through the curtains of Takket's waystation room. By the time the sun rose again, either he'd have proven himself to be the greatest thief in the Imperium, or he would have been burned to ash.

A hundred thieves, some Mages, most Mundanes, had tried to steal the bones of the angel of Southreach. All had been immolated. The Soulshards left in the ash now adorned the temple that housed the bones—a warning against other thieves foolish enough to repeat the attempt.

His predecessors had all failed for the same reason —lack of patience. They tried to break into the temple in a single night, or brute force their way through the guards. They opted for the exact methods the priests expected. Takket had a different plan. Today, the priests would invite him inside.

Staring into the mirror, Takket neatened his elegant beard. He would miss it when he shaved, but it was too memorable to keep. High Priest Innavonus was well known for his exquisite beard, and, for today only, Takket would become that man.

The previous evening, he had arrived in this waystation with a beard bushy, and dirty in the battered tunic and riding boots of a horse messenger. Now, the neat beard was matched by slicked back hair. His clothing had been replaced with the immaculate red cloak of a Circlist priest. He had completed his transformation by smearing a pigment through his greying brown hair, turning it a pure white. Annoyed, he realised these days there was no need to accentuate his wrinkles.

The time and expense he had invested in this day astonished him. The cloak alone had cost a year's wages in Soulshard flakes. The investment would be worth every Shard. No one would doubt his disguise. No one would remember his average build, brown eyes or fair complexion. No, they would remember the grey hair, the beard, the fine clothing. Give people something remarkable yet replaceable to remember, and the trivial details would be forgotten.

Casting one last glance to the mirror, Takket shouldered his leather travelling bag—now containing the plain clothes he had arrived in and a long length of rope—and strode out through the door into a hallway of varnished mahogany floorboards and wall panels, flanked by oil paintings exhibiting religious and historical scenes—all lit from above with the ever-shifting red glow of Shard chandeliers. So close to the city of Southreach, this waystation must attract many important guests.

He descended the curling staircase at the end on the corridor, running a hand down the banister, to the main reception hall. The early morning light was just breaking through the stained-glass windows at the front of the building, the images of angels and demons scattering the room with multicoloured light. A lone attendant snoozed at the desk.

Takket strode towards the man, his riding boots thudding over an extravagant maroon rug, startling the attendant. The man's face fell as he saw Takket's cloak.

'Pardon, sir,' he stammered apologetically, straightening his brass-buttoned jacket. 'They didn't tell me we had a high priest staying with us.'

Takket raised his nose imperiously and lied in his best high-class Indspire accent. 'Yes, well I don't like having to deal with the...' he waved a hand towards the man '...help. My driver booked us in yesterday. During my mediation last night, it seems the dullard decided to help himself rather freely to your bar here. He's sleeping it off upstairs.'

The attendant's smile was quickly hidden as he caught Takket's glare. 'My apologies if our staff encouraged him in any way. I'll have words with restaurant manager. Is there anything I can do to help you today?'

'Yes. I have an appointment in the high temple in an hour, and it seems I am in need of a new driver. Can you organise one for me? I'll settle the bill when I return—demons know how much I already owe for that man's bar fees.'

'Of course, sir. Horse or Shard?'

Takket glared at the man as if he had just spat on his cloak. 'Shard, of course.'

'Right away.' The man scuttled towards the main doors. Takket followed at a more sedate pace. He took no joy from tormenting the poor man, but it was good to get into character. Besides, lying was a skill like any other, and to hone a skill you had to practice. He made sure to lie at least once a day, warming up with an easy falsehood.

Takket heaved open the stained-glass doors and was greeted by the brisk southern wind, which carried a metallic smell. The low sun glared through the Sharddust kicked up by the wind, casting a red hue over the cobbled driveway of the waystation. The dust was thick here, so close to the major city of Southreach. Fine red particles mixed with the morning mist to surround the waystation like soup. He could barely see to the end of the drive, let alone the landscape beyond. The only indication that anything existed within the all-concealing haze was the muffled call of unseen birds.

The crunch of a cart rolling over dust-caked cobbles drew Takket's attention. A tall horseless carriage pulled up—its wooden frame layered in black paint—and its driver hopped down from his seat in front of the enclosed passenger cabin.

'Where to?' The man lowered his red-stained woollen face covering to give Takket an obviously forced smile. All Mages were terrible at covering their emotions.

'The Circlist Temple of the Angel of Southreach,' Takket replied with an air of authority. 'As quick as you can.'

'As you say.' The driver pulled open the carriage's door for Takket to climb aboard. The passenger cabin was plush, red velvet cushions overlaying the blackened wood frame. Clear glass windows looked out at all angles into the red haze. Not the cheap kind either, these were modern Mage-crafted windows that barely distorted the light at all. If this was the class of carriage in the waystations, Southreach really was trying to compete with the capital for luxury.

The driver tugged a set of riding goggles over his eyes and slammed the door. Just the other side of the front window, he climbed onto his perch.

Takket set his bag to one side and took a seat along one of the benches inside the cabin. Yanking his woollen scarf back over his face with his right hand, the driver reached down with his left. From a compartment below, he drew out a Soulshard about the size of a finger. The Shard responded to the Mage's gloved touch by amplifying its glow from a dull twinkle to a radiant red.

Its brightness increased further as the carriage lurched into motion. Takket settled back into his surprisingly soft bench as the coachman guided the vehicle out of the driveway, the Mage steering with one hand while drawing on the Shard's power with the other. The cart creaked and shook its way over the cobbles. Thankfully, it was not long before they joined the smoothed main road leading to Southreach.

No sooner had they cleared the drive than the Soulshard in the driver's hand disintegrated into fine red dust, its power exhausted. The driver cast the dust to the side, the handful joining the sea of red Sharddust floating in the wind.

The cart slowed little in the time it took the driver to retrieve a new Shard, this one the size of an adult's hand. The cart began to accelerate rapidly to speeds faster than a horse in full gallop.

The large Soulshard rock would probably have enough power to reach Southreach—assuming the driver was a competent Mage. Even then, the price would be exorbitant. Shard carriages were a luxury afforded only by the very rich, far less efficient than the Shardrails, but travelling on a train packed with passengers would just draw attention to Takket's disguise. Besides, it was not like he was actually going to pay for this journey.

A murky landscape whipped by. Fields of root vegetables braced the road, interspersed with ramshackle pig farms and the occasional hamlet. As the sun burned off the morning fog, the view became clearer, but the red persisted. Sharddust hovered near the ground, slowly settling into piles by trees and houses, only to be kicked up by the slightest breeze. The rivers that crossed the road under stone bridges were stained blood red. The dust was a constant in the world, but it was always thicker this close to major cities.

By the time they reached the outskirts of Southreach, the sun was high enough in the sky to no longer be completely filtered by the layer of Sharddust. Although a general redness still dominated, other colours now became visible—bright yellows of tree leaves, deep purples of hedgerows along the roadside, dark greys of buildings.

Those buildings grew ever more frequent. First they were single-floor cottages at the very edge of the city, the hovels of the poorest of Mundanes. They steadily rose in height to two, three, then four storeys, the space between them constricting into only the narrowest of alleyways. Traffic increased at the same rate, horse carts and pedestrians rapidly filling the road, forcing Takket's driver to slow to a crawl. Mundanes of all ages packed the streets. Their heavy woollen cloaks were tucked tightly against the bitter southern cold, the drab fabric decorated only in the unwanted dusting of the red haze. Muffled through the cart's windows came the cries of shopkeepers, shouts of men and women dodging carts, and screams of infants.

Eventually, Takket's cart clattered its way to the old city walls, passing under the archway that had once stood as a battle-ready gatehouse, now nothing more than a marker for the wealthy core of Southreach. Once through, the houses were more widely separated, and were constructed in an archaic style. One or two levels at their base, each had a narrow tower rising up to various heights, imitations of the ancient Magetower that loomed high above the rest of the city.

That tower dwarfed the rest of Southreach. At least thirty storeys high, and as wide as a hamlet at its base, it gently narrowed to a crowned peak. Far above the layer of Sharddust, the view from the top would be breathtaking. It still stood as a wonder, centuries after its creator had died. Takket had to give the long-dead man grudging respect—few knew the name of the Magelord who had constructed the tower, but his legacy stood the test of time.

They rolled their way towards its base, moving much faster now that the traffic had thinned to only a scattering of Shard carts.

The driver guided the carriage around the corner of a mansion and their destination came into view: a red-stone building that would have been imposing had it not sat at the foot of the much larger Magetower. The structure—the Circlist Temple of the Angel—was fronted with two small replicas of the Magetower, each about four floors high. Between them hung a massive black granite ring, through which the morning sun now peeked.

10

The cart stopped by the stairs leading up to the temple. Hopping from his perch, the driver pulled down his face mask and opened the door. Shouldering his pack, Takket was greeted by the stench of the city. The coppery tang of Sharddust was almost overpowering, contrasting with the background odour of the waste of thousands upon thousands of people. Unfortunately, he frequently had to endure major cities in his profession. Priceless artefacts were seldom found in hilltop monasteries.

With the smell came the gentle sounds of the inner city. Carts crunched over the Sharddust on the roads, birds chirped in gardens, and people engaged in pleasant conversation. All of this was muffled by the red haze, the Sharddust filtering sound and light alike.

Turning his attention to the matter at hand, Takket began making his leisurely way to the temple. The hem of his cloak dragged over the smoothed marble staircase, picking up the fine red Sharddust that collected on the edges of the steps.

At the top of the stairs, he was greeted by a young acolyte in a rough-spun black cloak, who—on seeing Takket's clothing—bowed low, hand over heart.

'High Priest Innavonus,' the young man greeted. 'We are honoured to have you here.'

'I am here to meet High Priest Instantino,' Takket said regally.

'The High Priest is expecting you in the angel's shrine. Follow me, please. May I take your pack?'

'No, thank you,' Takket replied. 'Sloth is the ally of the demons. I will not allow myself to become pampered.'

The young man nodded thoughtfully and pushed

open the two great doors to the temple. Takket
followed him into a vaulted hallway, lit from above
with Soulshard chandeliers. A gaggle of acolytes
hurried to the entrance, sweeping the polished stone
floor to clear Sharddust that drifted in from outside.
Keeping a building this large free of the red haze was
a full time job for the lowest ranked in the temple.

Takket's guide took a right at a branch in the
hallway, following a gently curving corridor. The
temple had the same layout as all Circlist temples, the
bulk of the building forming a large ring enclosing a
circular courtyard. The scale of this temple, however,
put most others to shame. The ceiling towered so far
above that there was a notable delay between footstep
and echo. The glass windows to the side stretched up
to meet the ceiling, alternating between stained glass
masterpieces and clear panes to allow natural light to
bathe the hallway.

Through the windows, Takket could see the
ceremonial courtyard. Not the simple gravel or stone
courtyards that most temples made do with, but a lush
green paradise, with tall trees and even grass. Takket
had to admit he was impressed that they managed to
cultivate the grass with so much Sharddust outside the
temple walls, but the tall building surely kept the
majority of the low-lying dust at bay. Set against the
green background were red marble statues of angels
and demons engaging in their unending battle.

The building was meant to impress, to show the
power of the Circlists, demonstrate the skill of their
Mage architects. Takket would have been overawed,
had his mind not been focused on his impending
crime.

The acolyte pushed aside a polished mahogany door and ushered Takket into a darkened chapel. As the door creaked shut behind him, the only natural light filtered through a stained glass window high on the far wall. His attention was drawn to a pool of flickering red light in the centre of the room, where an object rested on a pedestal made of interlocked Soulshards. Silhouetted against their combined light, a figure rose from a crouch.

'High Priest Innavonus, I presume,' a strong voice called out, echoing through the expansive shrine.

'Yes.' Takket crossed to the man. 'High Priest Instantino, it is good to finally meet you in person.'

'It is.' Instantino gave a bow, which Takket returned. 'Though it feels as if I already know you better than I know some of my colleagues.'

'It does.' Takket flashed a fond smile as he walked up to the other man in the uneven light of the Soulshards. He looked older than Takket had expected, only a few strands of hair clinging to his head. Small eyes looked out under bushy eyebrows. The man wore an identical robe to Takket, the bright red glittering in the unsteady light.

Takket really did feel he knew Instantino, though their relationship was rather more one-sided than the priest suspected. Takket had been intercepting the messages between the two high priests for the past year, and editing the responses for three months. The real High Priest Innavonus had no intention of ever making the strenuous journey to visit Southreach, but so far as Instantino knew, this was a lifelong dream.

Playing the part, Takket turned to gaze at the object atop the pedestal. There, illuminated by the

Soulshards, suspended in a cylinder of solid glass, rested the bones of an infant. Not just any child, this skeleton proudly displayed a pair of wings rising from its shoulders. As Takket approached, he could see other abnormalities: the skull was disproportionately large—even for a child—the forehead strangely grooved, the limbs too short.

'The Angel of Southreach,' Takket breathed.

'Stillborn from a human woman,' the priest intoned. 'Proof of Circlist doctrine.'

Takket suppressed a smirk. It proved nothing, certainly not circular reincarnation. It could be a natural malformation. It could be an elaborate fake. It mattered little. The bones were famous across the globe, priceless, sought after by collectors, fanatics, Circlists and Scalists alike. Wars had started and had been ended by these bones. Magelords of old had died in their pursuit. Empires had crumbled, and the Imperium had risen in their name. They had sat here in this temple for almost a century, guarded by the Mages that filled this building.

Tonight, those bones would belong to Takket.

It was well into the night by the time Takket extricated himself from Instantino and the rest of the priesthood. Shortly after meeting the High Priest, Takket had been whisked away on a grand tour of the temple. His parade through room after stuffy room had given way to a roast lunch with the senior priests, most of whom quizzed him about life in the capital and the health of Arcane-lord Venning Indel.

The afternoon had proved the most challenging part of the day, as Takket was expected to deliver a sermon to the temple's resident priesthood. Takket had never been an overly religious man, and he viewed the various sects with equal scepticism, so he doubted a lecture on religious doctrine would be convincing. Instead he spoke of politics. He had spent more than enough time infiltrating high society to have become adept at discussing taxes, the authority of the Arcane-lord, the rights of Mundanes. Takket had launched into a tirade against the New World across the seas, urging action to spread Circlism to replace the dominant Scalist views there. If it was the one commonality to all people, it was the love of having their views reinforced publicly. His speech was met with a standing ovation.

Takket had spent the banquet dinner asking questions that he knew would illicit lengthy responses. He nodded along quietly, sampling the range of parsnips, carrots and pork on offer, speaking only to draw more information from his companions. Long ago, he had found that the easiest way to avoid giving away a disguise was to allow others to do the talking. Thankfully, talking was a favoured pastime of priests. After the meal, Instantino had granted Takket permission to pray privately before the angel's bones.

Exhausted from a day of lying and play-acting, he now finally stood alone in the angel's shrine. The sun had set long ago, and only the occasional flicker of a street lamp highlighted the lone window. Otherwise the only source of light was the pedestal, casting its ever-shifting light over the room.

Takket crossed to the pedestal and examined the bones. The glass encasement was strong, formed by a Mage to survive rough handling. The pedestal itself looked stronger still—imported Soulshard batons, each the size of a forearm, banded together with lead and driven into the ground. They would be worth a fortune, but Takket could not hope to lift them all, and prying apart the lead lining would cause too much of a din.

No, he could not steal the pedestal, but he could use it to aid his escape. He set his travel pack to one side and hauled out the length of rope. Made of modern artificial fibres, forged by the latest advances in Mage-crafting, the rope was strangely soft yet more than strong enough to hold his weight despite being the thickness of his thumb.

He wrapped the rope around the pedestal, tying his best knot in the dancing light. Satisfied, he shifted the contents of the bag—now only his cheap travelling clothes—and turned to the bones.

He would have given a quick prayer to the angels, but somehow doubted they would aid him in this task. Instead, he asked the demons to help him with this act of mischief, and hefted the cold glass block containing the bones. Not as heavy as he feared, though he still felt a strain in his legs as he lowered the bones into his satchel.

He secured the loose end of the rope around his waist and shouldered his pack. Hurrying over to the far wall, he looked up to the reflected light of the window. The lower window sill was a good fifteen feet high, but thankfully the gaps between the red marble wall sections were large enough to use as handholds.

The climb was not easy, the sharp marble corners cutting into his fingers, his heavy pack dragging him down, the polished surface giving poor grip, but it was hardly the most difficult climb he had ever attempted. Scaling the ancient tower of Iggranious had been far more challenging. Getting down again had been worse.

With a grunt, he pulled himself onto the narrow window sill, the marble platform icy to the touch. The stained glass twinkled with the glow of street lamps and the reflected Soulshard light. He could try to twist away the lead lining holding together the panes, lower them softly to the ground one by one, but that would take time—time enough for a passer-by outside to notice the disappearing window and sound an alarm.

No. Takket would go for the direct approach. He untied the rope around his waist and secured it to the bag. With a quick plea to the demons, he closed his eyes and flung the pack through the glass. The heavy block within his pack made short work of the decorative panes, punching a sizable hole through the window.

Takket grabbed the rope to slow the bag's decent, as the sound of glass on cobbles echoed across the city. After lowering his pack to the floor, he flung himself out into the chilling wind and rapidly descended the rope to the street below.

Takket shivered as the wind buffeted him, smells of coal fires and gas lanterns carried in the night's breeze. Hands already beginning to shake, he untied his pack and sprinted towards a nearby alleyway. Gas lamps stood as pools of red light in the haze, acting as markers for the streets rather than giving any real visibility. Sharddust persisted through the day and night alike, swallowing the city in this persistent fog.

As shouts of alarm chased from behind, he lost himself in the maze of houses.

Allowing himself a grin, Takket sprinted in the direction of the old city gates. He had done it. He had stolen the sacred jewel of one of the Indel Imperium's great cities. Now all he had to do was escape.

Takket's cloak billowed as he sprinted towards the gatehouse, leather satchel weighing heavily over his shoulder, the strap creaking with each step. From behind, shouts of alarm had given way to a bell summoning aid from nearby watchmen. The guards at the gate were already peering curiously towards the noise, their monotonous duty finally interrupted by excitement. There was no way they would simply let Takket pass through, not when a chance to fulfil their role as law keepers had finally presented itself. They would search Takket's pack, question him for hours, anything to avoid going back to dully monitoring the gate.

Takket would have to offer them something more intriguing.

'Demons below, what are you doing?' he shouted. 'Can't you hear the alarms?'

The tallest of the guards straightened, the buttons on his high-collared blue uniform glistening under the gatehouse's gas lamps.

'We can hear it,' he replied sternly, 'but we have a duty to guard this post.'

'For the sake of the angels, this is an emergency. Vandals are attacking the temple. Didn't you hear the smashing windows? Scalist zealots, I'm sure. The priests are in danger. Demons below, the *bones* are in danger. They need all the help they can get.'

The watchmen shared a look, worry giving way to anticipation.

'We should go to the barracks to raise more men,' the shorter guard said reluctantly.

'No use soldiers delivering a message when I can,' Takket persisted. 'I'll run to the barracks, you get to the temple. Hurry, before it's too late.'

The taller watchman nodded once. 'With me, Harling. We'll teach those Scalist demon-puppets to stay in the New World.'

The two sprinted away, gripping their ornate flintlock rifles. Takket took off through the gatehouse, heading towards the barracks further up the main road until the two guards disappeared into the Sharddust. Satisfied, he darted into the narrow alleyways.

The further he ran from the city walls, the more decrepit Southreach became. Arcanes and Mages kept to the old city, their wealth supporting pleasant gardens, fine structures and expert sewage systems. Here, where the Mundanes lived, the locals made do with what they could put together. Rickety houses showing signs of multiple amateur repairs leaned precariously against one another. The paving under his feet turned from stone to gravel and finally to bare mud. Every wall was lined with thick Sharddust—the city cleaners were paid only to keep the Mage's areas clear. At least the grime was harder to see with the lack of gas lamps, the only light coming from the stars overhead. The reek was the worst of it—without a decent sewer system, waste was just tossed into the alleyways, covering the area in a choking stench.

Despite the late hour, the alleys echoed with noise.

Screams of children. Drunken conversations. Shouts of rage, passion and fear. The sound of a thousand families crammed into the buildings around him contrasted sharply with the inner city's tranquillity.

Takket turned into a particularly dark alleyway, thankful that he could not see exactly what the soft, sticking floor was coated in. Finding a relatively clean section of gravelled street, he threw down his pack and retrieved his small wash bag, drawing his razor. Shivering in the darkness, he hacked off his beard, then shaved the stubble down smooth, gritting his teeth at the occasional cut.

Once finished, he threw off his cloak and pulled out the travelling clothes from his pack. He changed as quickly into the scratching cotton tunic and trousers, the cold stabbing into his arms. He wrapped his cloak around the glass block containing the angel's bones and strapped his bag shut. The cloak would be as incriminating as the bones, but at least it would provide padding.

Finally, he reached into a pile of what he hoped was Sharddust resting against a wall. He rubbed the fine powder through his hair, leaving it stained and dishevelled. For good measure, he patted more dust over his face and clothing. To any passer-by, he would look like an overworked courier, too poor to afford shaving cream, a regular bath or even a change of tunic. Just another Mundane, like the thousands of others packed into the surrounding tenements.

Shouldering his satchel, he headed downhill towards the waterfront. He stuck to the side streets and alleyways. The theft would have been discovered by now and, although they would likely be looking for an elderly man with a long beard, Takket did not want to take any chances. By now, the Mage sergeants would be out assisting the Mundane watchmen, and Mages needed no excuse to hassle a lone Mundane. Sticking to the poorest areas would keep him relatively safe—what Mage would want to pick their way through this squalor?

His progress was slow through the winding streets, but he was in no rush. The Shardrail would not be opening until dawn, and he would need its speed to put enough distance between him and the city before the thief hunt intensified.

He had always considered himself to have a good sense of direction, but even he repeatedly got turned around by the mismatched buildings and seemingly random arrangement of alleys. Thankfully, whenever he became truly lost, he just had to follow his nose. The fresh wind from the harbour brought with it blessed relief from the waste around him.

Eventually, the tenements began to give way to warehouses and factories as he reached the waterfront. Ships sat in the harbour, their lights bobbing with the gentle waves. To one side lay the Shardrail station, its lines stretching away into the distance, to freedom.

Turning into a darkened alleyway between a textile mill and a Shard-cutters, he lay down against a set of empty crates. Leaning back, he felt the weariness of the day settle over him. All that was left was to wait until dawn, and pray he would next be sleeping in a Shardrail cabin, not a dungeon.

Takket woke to sounds of hammering. The sun had barely risen, but the industrial area was already alive with activity. Mage-driven machines began to wind up. Men and women shouted back and forth, calling over the din. The thud of crates being moved was punctuated by the sound of chisels striking Soulshards.

Takket stretched, immediately regretting the action as his leg cried out in pain. Once he had been able to sleep in a cobbled alley and rise feeling spry and ready to face the day. Now his every joint complained at the uneven surface. It took a conscious effort to avoid limping as he strode out of the alleyway, dusting off the fresh layer of Sharddust that had settled on him overnight.

Outside the alley the red haze filled the street, the mist and Sharddust dancing in the wake of the horse-driven carts shuttling their loads between the factories, Shardrail station and harbour. Takket dodged between the carriages and foot traffic, steadily making his way towards the station. The odour of the harbour was strong here, the smell of salt water, seaweed and fish a welcome change from the stench of the city.

He reached the row of houses adjacent to the station and looked through the billowing red haze to the fence at the rail yard's edge. He swore to himself as he noticed the watchmen at the gates pedantically sifting through bags. They were stopping every male coming through, thoroughly searching their luggage.

Peering through the haze, he could see lines forming at the waterfront. No doubt more watchmen were searching passengers leaving on the morning ships. If this was the response here, the roads out of the city were certain to be monitored. He had hoped it would take the city longer to block off the exits, but

Southreach clearly did not take the theft of the bones lightly.

Takket looked around for other options. The rail yard was surrounded by fencing, there to keep away the fare-dodgers. The fence was some eight feet tall, topped with sharpened points. Still, he could climb it. In the thick haze, it was unlikely anyone would spot him.

Taking a step towards the fence, he was quickly brought to a stop by the cry of protest in his leg. He was having a hard enough time walking after his uncomfortable sleep. Even his arms ached from last night's climb. As much as he wanted to deny it, his age was taking its toll. He was in no shape to vault a low wall, let alone this fence.

He chewed his lip in growing frustration. The longer he lingered here, the more time he gave the watchmen to notice him. A man hovering at the edge of the station was bound to draw suspicion. Still, he needed to get out of the city. The watch would be out in force as the news spread. Bounties would be offered. It would take just one person to notice a foreigner lingering in the city, and Takket's life would be forfeit.

Stealing this relic was meant to be his greatest heist. With all routes of escape blocked, he feared this theft would be his final failure.

CHAPTER TWO

Takket turned from the station and headed into the shadowed alleyways, the layer of Sharddust crunching underfoot. The sounds of workers, passengers and industry faded as he contemplated his predicament. Panic rising, he began to plan. He had once bluffed his way into the Indspire treasury. He had once stolen the Necklace of Irrasa right from the neck of a sleeping Arcane. He would find a way to leave this demon-infested city.

Perhaps he could hide the satchel. Come back when it was safe. But he did not know the city well enough, so any hiding spot he found would be obvious to the locals. Maybe he could book himself into an inn, wait until the guards stopped searching. No, the inns would be some of the first places searched. He had no safe house here, no backup route. He had foolishly believed that removing the bones from the temple would be the greater challenge, and it would be a simple matter to leave the city.

His thoughts were interrupted—the alleyway before him was blocked by a man and woman, their eyes locked on him.

'Takket,' the man said in a heavy New World accent. Shocked at the sound of his real name, Takket searched the man for recognisable features. He had light brown hair—neck length—and the full beard common to Mundanes. Takket guessed the man was

Soul Thief

about ten years younger than himself, putting him in his mid-thirties. Sharddust powdered his worn tunic and stained his leather boots. His companion looked strikingly similar, her hair the exact same shade, lightly dusted red. Her ankle-length coat matched the man's tunic with its dark grey fabric, thickly bundled against the cold. Just another pair of Mundanes, neither familiar to him.

Preparing to run, he took a step back when she called out, her voice matching her companion's accent. 'We're friends. Antellok sent us.'

Takket paused at the name of his fence. The man had introduced him to the buyer for the angel's bones and set up a dozen more contracts during their long career together. He had never misled Takket. Yet.

'He told you what I'm doing here?' he asked, aghast.

'No,' the man replied. 'Just that you might need help getting out.'

The woman gave a grim smile. 'Though given your reputation, where we are, and how furious the city watch seem to be, I'd hazard a guess at what's in your pack.'

Takket again stepped back, ready to break into a run.

'We don't want the bones,' the man replied. 'We need your help, and your arrest would harm our cause.'

'What cause?'

'We'll explain later. The city watch are calling in everyone they have for this search. Soon the chance of getting you out will be gone. Do you want help or not?'

'What's the price?' There always was one.

'A few minutes of your time,' the man replied. 'Hear out our proposal, that's all. We'll get you onto the Shardrail. We can talk on the journey north. A small price to pay for freedom, no?'

Takket doubted his escape would come so cheap, but knew when he was in a corner. 'Fine.'

'Give me the satchel,' the woman ordered, extending an arm.

'You've got to be joking.' Takket pulled the leather bag closer to himself, the strap creaking at the shifting weight of its heavy burden.

With a weary sigh, she replied, 'We've got far more important things to worry about than some old bones. Look, they're searching for a man. They're not even glancing at the women travelling alone. I go through, you follow a few minutes later and we'll meet on board —we've booked a cabin. My brother here will take you there.'

'What's to stop you running off with the bag?'

She rolled her eyes. 'Well not only will you have my brother, but I don't doubt you could tell the guards I have the bones before the train leaves. Now are you going to take a chance with us, or wait for the watch to find you?'

Cursing, Takket looked around. He doubted his fence would have sent him untrustworthy contacts. But then, before this, he would have doubted his fence would send anyone. Still, he was hardly overloaded with options.

'Fine, we talk on board. No promises.'

'That's all we want.' The woman grabbed the satchel and sauntered down the alley.

Takket and the man followed some distance

behind, watching as she reached the station's entrance. Takket chewed his lip. If they caught her, he had no illusions that she would keep her silence. He needed to be ready to run the moment anything looked amiss.

The woman strode through the gates, barely earning a second glance from the watchmen.

'There,' the man said. 'Now follow me.'

Takket complied, approaching the gates. They joined a queue of passengers without luggage, who were thankfully moving faster than those with bags. Mundanes and Mages alike were being pulled aside, their belongings thoroughly searched. Threats, pleas and hinted bribes were shrugged off by the watchmen, diligent in their duty. Takket had seriously underestimated the reaction of the watch.

He approached two guards at the front of the line, their blue uniforms neatly pressed. One was holding up a paper scroll, checking it against the faces of every passer-by. A wanted poster. Angels above, the printing presses here worked fast. Unable to see the image, Takket had no idea how good a likeness the artist had achieved. Described images were rarely accurate, but so many had seen him in the temple. He had shaved his beard, but what if they anticipated that? His disguise, a common courier, now seemed obvious.

He was going to be caught. A legendary career ending in embarrassing failure. Not brought down by a team of Mages or a skilled Arcane, no—Takket would be taken in by some junior watchman.

The guard waved him past.

Takket walked by, letting out a breath he had not been aware of holding. Looking up, he felt a chill as he realised he had lost sight of the woman with his satchel. He could see the sleek, black-painted form of two waiting trains through the red gloom. Dozens of people walked back and forth. Children laughed. Passengers hurried along family members. Conductors blew whistles and called to porters.

No sign of the woman or his bag.

Had she already boarded a train? What if she had just disappeared into the gloom? Had he just given away one of the most priceless objects in the Imperium? Had he finally fallen victim to a ruse? Handing her the bag had been a needless gamble. He was losing his touch.

'This way.' The brother headed towards one of the waiting trains.

Takket followed cautiously, eyes darting around for possible escape routes. If they had just fooled him into handing over his prize, they would not let him live long enough to alert the watch. He had been in this business long enough to know what happened to loose ends.

They passed the elegant front carriage of the Shardrail train, light from the wealth of Shards within shining clearly through the driver's window—enough Shards to allow a Mage to propel the vehicle to blistering speeds, crossing a continent in mere days. Armed guards stood around the carriage, their embellished rifles resting against their shoulders. They were Mundanes, employed by the Shardrail company to protect the valuable store of Soulshards, which were particularly vulnerable while the train was in station. There would be Mages too, but they would be snug inside the vehicle, not out here in the biting cold.

The brother kept on moving, footsteps crunching

over the layer of Sharddust coating the platform. The first few carriages they passed were opulent—the luxuries glimpsed through the windows were the kind that most Mundanes could only fantasise about. Arcanes would occupy those carriages, if they wanted to slum it. Most took airships these days.

After the Arcanes' carriages, came those of the Mages. Each carriage had a communal area with its own bar, soft chairs and elegant tables, all separated from the private cabins. The cabins had facilities for two people, but were still larger than the main rooms of most Mundanes' houses.

Then they came to the carriages of the Mundanes. Gone were the polished exteriors and fine decor of the Arcane and Mage's carriages. The Mundane cars were boxy and cramped. Paint peeled from the outside, revealing rusted ironwork. The windows, frosted over, were often cracked or poorly fitted, allowing the frigid wind to whistle through. The front half of each carriage contained row after row of benches, packed as tightly as possible. The cabins in the rear section for the richer Mundanes were no less claustrophobic, with four people sharing an area smaller than a Mage's outhouse.

It was not fair, was not just—but what was in this world? Takket had seen the injustice at a young age, but unlike most, he had done something. The Mages his parents served gave their children finer food than he received. Well he had just raided the kitchens. They had more extravagant toys than he could ever hope for. Well, those would simply go missing. As he had aged, his targets had changed, but his habits had not. Food and toys gave way to the parties of fine society. So what if he was not invited to a social function. Door servants were easy to bluff past. Who cares if no honest Mundane could afford to buy his teenage crush the jewels she deserved. It was not like locks were that hard to pick.

The brother led Takket into one of the rearmost coaches. The air inside was barely warmer than on the platform, and held the cloying odour of aged sweat and vomit. Takket tried not to let his distaste distract him. If the man intended to make an attempt on his life, it would be now.

Giving Takket a small smile, the man opened a battered door to one of the private cabins and waved him inside. Takket ducked through the doorway to the small room, hand curling into a fist. He had never been a fighter, but he would be damned if he would go down meekly.

The woman sat on one of the two low bench-cum-beds inside, Takket's bag on her lap. Promising, but Takket did not let down his guard. He stayed on his feet, putting his back against the window, the icy surface leaching warmth through his tunic. The man stepped into the cabin, closing the door behind. There was barely enough room for the two of them to be standing. If this was an ambush, it was going to be a most awkward struggle for dear life.

'Please sit,' the woman said as her brother joined her on one bench. Takket checked the opposite bench for signs of hidden needles or similar traps, then cautiously sat. Despite doubling as a bed, the bench was overly firm. Takket could feel the hay stuffed inside, reluctantly shifting under his weight.

The cabin was even smaller than it appeared from

outside. Above each of the benches were a set of fold-out beds, currently stowed to make ad-hoc headrests. Above these lay shelves for luggage. The room was designed for a family of four, though Takket felt it was overflowing with just the three of them.

'The bag,' Takket said sternly. The woman held it out, rolling her eyes at how cautiously he took it. Still heavy. Good. Not daring to open it fully while at the station, he slipped his hand inside. He felt the soft material of the priest's cloak, and within it, the cold firmness of glass. It was here.

Takket could not let himself relax. This could still be a trap. The moment you stopped looking for deception was the moment you lost everything. They sat in strained silence. Takket tried not to jump at each person passing by the ice-frosted window, seeing watchmen in every eddy of the red haze.

Finally, the train jolted into motion, slowly at first, but soon building speed. It shot out of the station in an eerie silence, the Mage driver causing no noise, the polished rail giving only the slightest groan at the weight. The only sounds were the gentle creak of the car's suspension as it rocked back and forth, and the faint howl of wind through the window's poorly sealed edge.

The looming silhouettes of factories and warehouses ripped passed the windows, quickly replaced by houses and fields. Takket turned to look in the direction the train had come. Through the morning mist and persistent haze, he could see the shadow of the great Magetower. They had made it.

He had escaped Southreach.

As the red-stained landscape whipped by the window, Takket regarded his two saviours, refusing to relax. He could not see their build under the baggy clothing, but they held themselves with an air of confidence—perhaps from skill, perhaps from an inflated opinion of themselves. Either way, they were clearly not afraid.

'The price, then.' Takket hid his nerves with contempt. 'You wanted my attention. Now you have it.'

The man gave a small smile. 'I'm Yelleck. This is my sister, Enara. We're from the New World, in the Arcanedom of Varsen.' He spat out the last word. Their accents were New World, but Takket had trouble distinguishing between the various lands of that fractured continent. They certainly appeared related. So far, Takket could not spot a lie, but that did not mean they were being honest.

'A long way to come for a train ride,' Takket said simply.

'A long way to meet you,' Enara said.

'I'm flattered,' Takket replied dryly. Had these two been sent by one of his enemies? He had certainly made enough of them in his career as a thief. He hoped his fence would not have willingly sent assassins his way, but he wouldn't have put it past the old man. Especially if he had faced coercion...or a large enough bribe. Takket had no delusions about loyalty in the underworld. If his contact stood to profit in the long run, he would sell Takket to the demons in a heartbeat. Antellok knew this was to be Takket's last grand heist. Had the old man decided that Takket was no longer valuable?

'Your legend has spread wide,' Yelleck said. 'The theft of the baton of Iggranious is talked about in drinking rooms across the New World. A Mundane stealing prized possessions of Arcanes...your story is inspiring.'

'Inspiring drunks in the New World wasn't at the centre of my mind when breaking into that vault, but thank you.' Takket kept his voice level. Hearing how far his accomplishments had spread did fill him with pride. Not that he would let it show.

'Nevertheless, your actions *have* inspired,' Enara said firmly, 'and it's not just drunkards that are listening. You've demonstrated that Mages and even Arcanes are not untouchable. Mundanes can fight them, if we try—if we follow your example.'

'So glad I could be uplifting.' Takket shifted in the hard seat. 'If you're here to avenge some idiot who tried to emulate me and paid the price, that failure is on them.'

'Nothing of the sort,' Yelleck said, leaning forward. 'We're here to hire you.'

Takket drummed his fingers impatiently on the bench, only to stop once he noticed how much dust he kicked up.

'Antellok didn't tell you? He could have saved you a lot of time and effort. This is my last job. Yesterday, I did the impossible. The payment for this will set me up nicely. I'm going to get a fine house somewhere in the Thousand Isles and let some new fool steal the trinkets of Arcanes.'

'Your fence told us this already.' Enara waved a dismissive hand. 'But he also said you'd change your mind when you heard what we're proposing.'

Yelleck learned even closer and whispered conspiratorially, 'We need you to steal the Pure Shard of Varsen.'

Takket barked out a laugh. Their steady expressions implied they were not joking, which just make him laugh all the harder. They were insane. Brilliant—he had been saved by two lunatics. Antellok would never let him hear the end of this.

'We know it's not going to be easy,' Enara started before Takket cut her off.

'Easy? It's suicide. You want me to steal a Soulshard carried by an Arcane.'

'Not just any Shard,' she persisted. 'A Pure Shard. It has the power to turn a Mundane into a Mage, or a Mage into an Arcane.'

'And gives an Arcane nearly unlimited power.' Takket shook his head. 'Ever seen an Arcane drawing power from a large Shard, a baton? I saw one move a building—an entire building, foundations and all—just to get a better view from his porch. I don't even want to imagine what an Arcane can do with one of the most powerful Soulshards in existence. He could kill me a thousand different ways before I got within spitting distance.'

'That's why we've come to you, Takket,' Yelleck said. 'For anyone else, this would be impossible. For anyone else, stealing those bones in your bag would have been impossible.'

That gave Takket pause.

'What are you even going to do with the Shard? Burn it, to make one of you a Mage?'

Enara shook her head. 'Nothing so selfish. We're from the Free Circle.' When Takket stared blankly, she

34

explained, 'We fight for Mundane rights in the Arcanedom of Varsen. We've had minor successes, freeing Mundanes sentenced to death and the like, but lately we've been failing. While the Arcanes have the Pure Shard, they could wipe out every Mundane in the land. Without it...they would be vulnerable. They would have to listen. They would have to respect us. United, the Mundanes might even be able to overthrow them. A land ruled by Mundanes...can you imagine such a thing?'

Takket snorted. 'Fighting for Mundanes' rights? I've heard that before. People begging for a handout. Wishing their houses were as nice as those of Mages. Wishing they could afford foreign food. You know what I did when I realised Mundanes didn't get our share? I took from the Mages. I even took from the Arcanes. I live better than most Mages nowadays. Angels above, when I sell these bones, I'll live better than some Arcanes. I didn't cross seas to ask someone else to improve my lot. I did it myself.'

'We're not talking about lack of luxuries,' Yelleck scowled. 'You Imperium Mundanes are all the same. You think you've got it bad because your houses aren't as nice, your train carriages are more crowded. Mundanes in Varsen would give anything to live like you do, even if just for a day.'

'Can't be that bad,' Takket said dismissively.

'Really? When was the last time a Mundane was immolated here?'

'Last year,' Takket said, indignant. 'A man attacked a high priest. It's not like it doesn't happen in the Imperium.'

'Last year?' Yelleck gave a condescending smile

and turned to his sister. 'Let's see, last year our count was fifteen thousand. Give or take. They don't keep the greatest records of that sort of thing.'

Takket frowned in confusion. 'Fifteen thousand what?'

'Fifteen thousand Mundanes burned to death. All to generate Soulshards. Keep the economy alive, keep the Mages fuelled with enough power to continue their lifestyle. Fifteen thousand men, women and children incinerated alive. That was a quiet year.'

Takket sat back, letting the words sink in. It was an exaggeration, no doubt. But even if it was...he shook his head. He had heard stories, everyone had, but they had never seemed so bleak, so extreme. Of course, the only people he had spoken to from the New World had been magic-users, and they would hardly be concerned about such matters. Mundanes only made the trip on trade vessels, and they were not the sort Takket would associate with during his infiltrations.

'So the demons have their way with your continent.' Takket shrugged to hide his shock. 'You really think stealing a single Shard will make a difference?'

'Not just any Shard,' Yelleck said firmly. 'A Pure Shard. Throughout history, every discovery of a Pure Shards has changed the world. The first led to the original Mages, the end of the Mundane era. The second shattered the First Imperium. The third ended the Devastation. But now? The last seven have fallen into the hands of Arcanes and are used only to reinforce their rule. Those Pure Shards give them their strength, the power to wield unchecked authority. Those Pure Shards make them untouchable. When a

36

Pure Shard arrives, Arcanedoms rise. When one changes hands, Arcanedoms fall.'

Takket looked outside, unsure how to respond. Fresh air now whistled through the window, diluting the lingering odour of cramped bodies. The Shardrail had climbed to run across a ridge, lifting them out of the worst of the Sharddust. The view extended to the horizon, a sight only found uphill and away from cities. The low-lying red haze blanketed the landscape, dancing in eddies kicked up by the wind. Hilltops and mountains rose like green and grey islands out of the red sea of Sharddust. Otherwise, the only features of the landscape were the crumbling ruins of ancient Magetowers, and the odd tall pine stretching high enough to clear the dust and allow their green branches to bathe in sunlight.

Birds flitted back and forth, hovering over the red haze, diving down to strike at prey in the murk below. A handful of airships made their lazy way through the clouds, so high up that their bloated forms appeared as mere specks.

The view always calmed Takket. It brought clarity, perspective. It was all too easy to be lost in the fog, focused on the details. You had to rise above it to see what lay ahead. Focus on any one plan too long, and you would never notice greater opportunities.

'Nice as your goals are...'

'You'd be paid, of course,' Enara interrupted. 'When you pull off the theft, we aim to take control of Varsen's treasury. Without their supply of Soulshards, they'll be exposed. We don't need all the Shards there, we just need them out of the hands of the Mages and Arcanes. You can have half of what we find.'

Takket held her gaze. Half of an Arcane family's treasury? Forget an island to retire on. Takket would be able to buy an archipelago. Angels above, with that number of Shards, he could set himself up as a lord here in the Imperium. Joining the ranks of the handful of Mundane-lords in existence—now that would be quite the retirement.

He turned back to the window. In the distance, dark towers rose out of the Sharddust layer, capped in jagged tops or overgrown with vines. At one time, Magetowers filled the landscape from shore to shore, built by the Magelords of old. Now only these crumbling relics remained. All their demesnes had come crashing down. Each had pushed their luck that little bit too far. Never satisfied with what they controlled, they had tried for greatness, and lost everything. Instead of going down in history, they had been forgotten. Such was the fate of all who overreached.

'Nice as your goals are,' Takket repeated, 'they are unachievable. Mundanes who work at court are carefully selected in every Arcanedom. Too much fear of each other's spies. Sure, I could get into Varsen's tower for a day, for a party. What you are asking would need weeks. Months. Time to assess security. Plot an escape. There's just no way.'

'That's just it,' Enara replied. 'We have a way in. A way that requires you. The Imperium's new diplomat to Varsen was killed in an airship crash days ago in the Crater Desert. We've managed to keep it secret so far. We have an opportunity here. We can replace him. Think about it—a Mundane new to the land but with unbridled access to the court. We'd need an expert at

38

impersonation, someone who can move around court for months without raising suspicion. Someone who can see chances that all others miss. Someone who can do the impossible. Someone like you.'

Takket sighed as he gazed out on the tranquil scene below. Today, the view brought him no clarity. He had thought that the next time he would be looking over this view, he would be grinning from ear to ear, but he felt no sense of accomplishment. He had stolen the bones, sure, but too much had gone wrong. He needed help escaping the city. Demons below, he had not been able to scale a fence. Takket knew now that he was getting old. It really was time for him to retire, to let younger men climb buildings and deceive Arcanes. His chapter was coming to a close. That was alright. He had left his mark on the world. When he presented the bones to their buyer, no one would doubt his skills. There was no better way to crown his career.

'No,' he said finally. 'My time is done. I wish you luck in your efforts, but I can't be the one to help you.'

Enara opened her mouth to respond, but Yelleck rested a hand on her arm. They met each other's gaze for a while, then both sighed in resignation.

'We'll leave you alone to think,' Yelleck said as they rose from their bench. 'We know it's a lot to ask. In the end, it will all be worth it. If you change your mind, your fence knows where to find us. Angels bless you, and demons be blind to your passing.'

Takket merely nodded as they left the cabin, leaving him with only the gentle creak of the carriage's suspension for company. He was glad to be free of the foreigners. His choice had been astute. This way, he would go out a success, not end up as another

Mundane executed for taking that one step too far. He had achieved his greatest feats. Now he could simply relax and enjoy the spoils of a life outsmarting the more fortunate.

CHAPTER THREE

Takket had seen no sign of the siblings during the two-day journey north. A few times he had poked his head through the doorway, but found only Mundanes with exhausted faces, cloaks pulled high against the persistent chill. Tempted as he was to track the pair down, he was loath to leave the bones unattended, and carrying around his satchel would only draw attention. Besides, if they really were used to a life fighting Mages and Arcanes, they would be adept at remaining concealed.

In their absence, he had spent the journey locked in his cabin, passing the time fitfully sleeping or gazing out of the window. He purchased lukewarm soup from a porter whenever the man knocked on the door, though he had to force down the over-boiled vegetables within. The train spent most of its time running along ridges to protect the front carriage from the abrasion it would suffer ploughing through the Sharddust. For much of the journey, this gave Takket a sweeping view over the landscape. The endless sea of red haze dominated the Imperium, broken only by tree tops, mountain ranges and crumbling Magetowers.

Occasionally, as it approached a city, the Shardrail was forced to descend into the haze. Each time, the view was obscured by Sharddust twirling in the train's wake. As the train hurtled across the landscape, dark objects would lurch from the gloom—houses, forests, factories, people.

The waits within the stations were strained. Shardrail was the fastest form of transport, so Takket *should* be keeping ahead of the news of his heist, but even so he feared that a fast messenger train had overtaken them. He would spend the painful minutes in stations staring at the door to his cabin, half-convinced it would be kicked in at any moment, watchmen pouring in to drag him to his execution. Whenever the train pulled away he let out a sigh of relief.

By the time the sun rose on the third day, the red haze had begun to thin. As they approached the coast, Takket started to see a familiar landscape emerging. Fields filled with low-lying crops flanked the Shardrail, broken by small farming towns built in the shadows of fragmented Magetowers. Trees became more common, as did grass, both able to thrive where the Sharddust was less dense. On the horizon, the sunlight reflected off the red-stained Demon's Ocean. At the water's edge there hunkered a scattering of warehouses and red-brick hovels—Drakenport.

Takket was home.

He stood, grimacing at the ache in his legs, which had spent too long on the solid bed. Eager to be free of the confines of the cabin, Takket shouldered his satchel and walked down the length of the carriage as the brakes let out a squeal. He waited impatiently at the door as the train grudgingly slowed to a halt at Drakenport's single platform. A handful of Mundanes waited with him, likely looking for work among the trading town's ships now that the worst of the winter winds had died down.

He pushed open the door while the train was still braking, the handle grating with rust. Embracing the fresh sea air, he stepped out the moment the train stopped. The smell of salt water, fishing boats and brine pools made a welcome change from the stagnant odours he had endured for the last three days. Even though winter was just ending, the air was warmer here, so much farther north than Southreach.

The platform filled with Mundanes disembarking from the carriages. Drakenport was rarely visited by Mages, most of its population being made up of seasonal workers. The lack of magic-users was part of what fuelled Takket's fondness for the town.

The crowd drifted towards the city centre and its job offices, where they could sign onto a trade ship for a few months. Takket searched the shuffling masses for Enara or Yelleck, but around him he saw only the Mundanes, their faces grimly set at the prospect of months of hard work sailing around the Thousand Isles.

Takket left the crowd, heading through a row of weathered brick houses towards the waterfront. Blood-red waves lapped at the cobble beach, washing over discarded fishing nets and the odd scattering of flotsam thrown free from trade ships during winter storms. The water swallowed the Sharddust, leaving the air clear to the horizon. Takket allowed himself a smile as he stared out across an ocean broken by the hundreds of islands that gave this archipelago its name. Some were small, barely large enough to fit a lone fisherman's hut. Others were counties in their own right. Between them ships of all sizes—from one-man fishing boats to Mage-powered cargo liners larger than most warehouses—navigated the treacherous waters. Their captains followed the few narrow channels that were free of the underlying boulders that would pierce wooden and metal hulls alike.

As the clean air washed over him, Takket became all too aware of his coating of grime. He had slept in the same dust-stained tunic and trousers for the past three nights, and one of those nights had been spent in an alleyway. The Mundanes' carriages rarely saw a cleaner, and the only washing facility was a shared bathroom in the rear of the cart—more of a closet with a hole where one could relieve oneself onto the track.

Antellok could wait. Takket needed a proper bath and fresh clothes. Maybe then he would finally shake this malaise. He told himself that it was just the anti-climax of having finished his final heist. Just ennui at a career coming to an end. It would pass. If not after cleaning himself, then certainly when he presented his fence the bones and recalled the heist's tale.

Takket set off along the beach, picking over the shingle on his way to the edge of town. He was careful to avoid the larger boulders, which were slick with seaweed and had turned his ankle many a time. Walking across the smaller stones was uncomfortable, the pebbles grinding against one another with every step, but it was safer. It would have been faster to walk through the town's streets, but after days cooped up inside the cabin, he was glad to be truly out in the open.

At the far end of the beach he came to a familiar cottage, resting in the lee of a large boulder, which protected it from the worst of the winter winds. His home. It was not a particularly imposing structure, just a single floor, faced with the local dark rock. Thick bars of wrought iron caged the few windows, nominally to protect the glass against stones thrown during storms, but truly there to prevent theft during his long absences.

He walked along the overgrown path to his front door. The wood was banded with iron bars, coated in a thick layer of black paint to stave off corrosion that was all too easy on the coast.

Taking a large set of keys from his tunic pocket, he set about the laborious task of opening the door. Three locks, two traps, and a bar that he had to reach through a small gap to slide clear. If he were to set his mind to it, a thief as skilled as Takket could still break into this place, but who would think to burgle what was clearly some poor dockworker's cottage? No, the security was to protect the place against vagrants and local teenagers, to whom a disused house might seem quite attractive.

Inside, the cottage was as humble as its exterior. The hardwood floors were scuffed, and creaked with every step. The interior walls were simply whitewashed stone. Most of the cottage was taken up by this main hall, which served as a living room, bedroom, kitchen and dining room combined. Even so, it was sparely furnished, with only a straw bed, handful of stools and a cooking range. Despite the insulating hay packed between the ceiling beams and tiled roof, the house was no warmer than the beach outside.

Takket slid shut four heavy bars to secure the door and made his way to the wrought iron burner in the centre of the main room, his heavy footfalls startling some creature under the floorboards, sending it squeaking away in panic. Opening a nearby chest, Takket put a handful of coals into the burner and struck a match. Mages and Arcanes would heat their homes magically without a second thought. Mundanes had to resort to more rudimentary methods.

As the fire built, Takket collected a bucketful of rainwater from a tank in his washroom, and set it atop the burner. It would take some time to heat, but he could at least put the bones somewhere secure while he waited.

He walked to one of the side rooms, a small space that at first glance would appear just as a barely stocked pantry, only containing a few of the new canned foods that would last through his long trips, and three sacks of baking flour.

This room, however, concealed a secret.

He pulled the sacks to one side, then dug his fingers through a gap between the floorboards. Pressing the latch hidden underneath, he pulled upwards, opening the trapdoor over a pitch black stairwell. He took a gas lantern from one of the pantry's shelves, leaving behind a clean circle in the thick dust that had built in his absence. Striking another match, he lit the lamp and began to descend into the dark.

The boards were far grander than the house above, varnished and with no wear and tear. At the bottom of the staircase, his feet met the softness of the fine carpet. He followed a path from memory, lighting the series of lamps to bathe the basement in light. Turning around, he smiled at his true home.

Compared with the simplicity of the cottage above,

the basement was luxurious. Mahogany panels lined the walls, surrounding the lush red carpet. Elegant chairs and benches stood around a delicately carved table, their silken upholstery not far removed from pieces found in many Mages' front rooms. Flanking the master bed, with its mattress of the most expensive duck-down padding, were a pair of steel safes, the hardest design to crack that Takket had encountered.

The room was a lifetime in the making. The basement had been carved out by his own hands over years, passing the time while he had to lie low after one heist or another. The decor had been paid for by a career of taking baubles owned by the richest men and women in the Imperium. Only a handful knew of this place's existence, and all worked directly for Antellok —who made sure his employees knew their lives depended on keeping his secrets. To their credit, the workmen had done an outstanding job. Takket would use them again soon, to build his retirement mansion.

He knelt by the right-hand safe, the carpet joyfully soft against his knee. With a series of keys and combination dials, he unlocked the safe. Inside glowed half his fortune: Soulshards ranging from splinters and grains—small denominations useful for haggling with Mundanes—to flakes the size of a thumbnail, all the way to gems, rocks and even a few two-foot-long batons, all casting their swirling light over the room.

He nestled his satchel inside. In comparison to the Shards he would gain from sale of the bones, the contents of these two safes seemed no more than a child's allowance.

Takket closed the safe and hurried up the stairs as the bucket of water began to boil. He emptied it into a metal tub in his washroom, then refilled it to set the next bucketful heating. Often, he had considered having a tub of higher quality, like the ceramic baths that Arcanes popularised, but such extravagance would not fit in with the cottage's humble aesthetic, and might alert someone peeping through the windows that the house contained more finery than its exterior suggested. As it was, even having regular baths was a luxury most Mundanes would not comprehend, but if it was one aspect of high society that most appealed to Takket, it was good personal hygiene.

A few years ago, he had toyed with the idea of having a bathtub in the basement, but the thought of carrying several buckets of steaming water down the stairs hardly thrilled him. It would be possible to install plumbing, but the logistics would be a nightmare. It had been a harrowing enough exercise having the safes fitted. No, the most comfortable baths would have to wait until his island home was complete.

For now, he filled the iron tub and settled in, feeling the grime of the past days come free in the hot water. He was glad the ground floor had such poor lighting—he did not want to imagine the colour the water was turning with the mix of dust and dirt.

After a relaxing bath, he carefully shaved and trimmed his hair. Out of habit, he left it relatively long, halfway down his neck. It was always better to cut hair to fit into a disguise than to have to wait to let it grow.

Feeling himself again, he returned to the basement, fishing out his clothing in the gilt armoire there. He pulled on a black silken shirt and matching trousers, the fabric a welcome change from the scratchy clothing he had been stuck with since the heist.

He wrapped himself in a dark linen cloak, a softer material than the wools most Mundanes made do with, but not too extravagant. It would mark him out as a wealthy trader, or perhaps a Mage's favoured servant, but nothing more.

He retrieved his satchel, locked up the cottage and set off.

Time for his final act as a thief.

Time to get paid.

The afternoon sun was low in the sky as Takket walked back to Drakenport. Instead of trudging across the beach, he took the narrow footpath between his cottage and the town. Few used the path, so it was perpetually overgrown on either side with tall grass. Takket ran his hand along the tops of the stalks, feeling the soft blades against his hands. Legends spoke of a time when grass had covered the continent, back during the Mundane Era. Millennia of Sharddust had since driven the plant to cling to the edge of the coast or the tops of hills.

At the edge of town, the path joined the packed gravel and dirt road. Takket strolled along the firmer surface, gazing at the familiar workhouses, lodges, taverns and grocers that made up Drakenport.

The town had changed little in the two decades he had lived here. It served as a minor trading hub, a convenient port to link the Shardrail from Southreach to the shipping lanes between the Thousand Isles. Few lived here permanently, most were seasonal workers following the shifting winds to work on board ships when the weather permitted. A few wealthier Mundane traders would come from time to time, overseeing the transport of their goods. Only a handful of locals stayed to run the workhouses and taverns to support the transient population. People were always coming and going from all walks of life, but too few stayed to recognise faces. It was a perfect base for someone in Takket's profession. No doubt, this was the reason Antellok had chosen Drakenport to set up his operation.

Takket made his way through the crowds near the city centre. Ship crews staggered along towards taverns and workhouses, shoulders slumped from a day of hard work on the sea. Grocers were closing their shops, pulling down wooden shutters and barring their doors. Tavern keepers were opening in preparation for the evening, lighting gas lamps outside their buildings to attract customers. A few of the local youths loitered in the streets—too old to be minded by their parents, too young to work.

Takket focused on keeping a relaxed expression as he walked, all too aware of the fortune in his satchel. For those bones, people would literally kill—they certainly had in the past.

At the heart of Drakenport, Takket came to an open plaza, the only paved section of the town. Enclosing the plaza were warehouses of various sizes, all built from darkened wood, all severely weathered from the winds and the spray of salt water. Takket set off towards one that proudly displayed a painted sign naming it as ANTELLOK & SONS, IMPORT & EXPORT.

Takket found the doors already open. The entrance to the cavernous building was wide enough for two carts to easily pass each other. Rows of stacked crates stretched the length of the hall, some piled high enough to almost reach the thick beams criss-crossing the ceiling. Towards the rear, the warehouse opened to the ocean, allowing ships to dock directly inside. Even in the late afternoon, the space was teeming with activity. Workers ran back and forth or carried crates between them. Lines of men and women carried boxes on and off of the waiting boats while clerks watched them critically, counting the transfers on pads of paper. The smell of fish and seawater that dominated Drakenport had given way to a hundred overlapping odours: spices from the far north, dyes from the east, dried meats from the south.

Takket turned from the bustling activity, and started towards a hut built against one wall, the sound of his footfalls lost in the din of thudding boxes, creaking mooring lines and authoritative yells.

The guard outside the hut was new, as was the fresh lick of yellow paint on the door. It seemed Antellok's business was healthier than ever.

Takket gave his name to the guard. 'I'm here to see Antellok.'

Nodding, the weathered man opened the door. 'He's expecting you. Go on.'

The hut's interior was larger than Takket's cottage, but felt oppressively small compared to the warehouse outside. The clutter did not help its cramped appearance—stacks of paper lined the many desks, ledgers filled innumerable bookcases around the walls, writing materials, maps and open records covered every available surface.

From behind one particularly overflowing desk

there rose the familiar face of Antellok. The old man grinned at Takket and strolled over to pull him into a tight embrace. The man's stubble scratched at Takket's neck, and the smell of Thousand Isle musk was overpowering. Some things never changed.

Antellok stepped back. 'Angels above, you did it.' The man hurried towards the door to bar it, waddling a little more than normal. When they had first met, Antellok had been a bulky man, broad shouldered and thick armed. Now most of that mass had settled around the man's gut. 'Let me see it.'

Takket cleared a space on one of the desks and set his satchel down. He carefully lifted the bundled cloak within, and set it on the desk. In the flickering light of the room's gas lantern, Takket revealed the glass block, and inside it, the bones of the angel.

'Magnificent,' Antellok breathed. 'The buyer will be pleased. I've sent him word already. He should be here in a few days with the payment. You still want me to keep a hold of it to pay for that retirement house of yours?'

'Yes,' Takket replied. Antellok would do many things, but he would never steal money entrusted to him. He was a middle-man—his business relied on the faith of all parties. He would send others to lie, swindle, steal and murder, but if he said he would take something for safekeeping, you could rest easy.

Antellok turned from the bones to regard Takket. 'Probably for the best.'

'What do you mean?' Takket frowned.

'I heard quite the story from our mutual friends from the New World.'

'They've been here?'

52

'Arrived this morning, straight from the train. They're staying at the Sunken Mage Inn while I organise your replacement. Said you turned down their offer...?'

The word 'replacement' stung. 'Yes, I turned it down. As I told them, it's suicide.'

'Like I said, probably for the best.' There was a twinkle in the old man's eye that Takket could not decipher. 'It seems you were right—it may be time for you to retire.'

Takket's frown deepened. 'What's that supposed to mean?'

The gleam in the eye was joined by a mocking grin. 'Oh, something about you getting stuck in Southreach and needing a couple of New World amateurs to save you.'

Takket glowered at Antellok. 'I got the bones, didn't I? I did what no thief in history has managed.'

Antellok gave a patronising smile. 'That you did. That you did. I'm just sorry your big last heist ended up being a disappointment. I mean it would have been a fine epitaph, being the man who singlehandedly stole the bones of the angel of Southreach. "The man who stole the bones with help of a pair of foreigners" doesn't have the same impact. Eh, I suppose it depends on how you spin the tale.'

'Come on, Antellok, you know me. I could have found a way out of there. The baton of Iggranious. The Indspire vaults. You know what I've done.'

The old man raised his hands in supplication but that damn glint refused to leave his eye. He was enjoying this. 'Hey, I'm not saying you weren't a great thief in your prime. I'm just agreeing that it's time to retire. The Takket I met twenty years ago would never need help getting out of a jam like that.'

'Then why did you send them? Why not have them wait here for my return?'

'Because you're not the Takket I met twenty years ago.'

The words hit home, sudden rage twisting Takket's gut. He turned to hide his face. He would not give the old man the satisfaction of knowing he had got under Takket's skin.

'I did my part,' he said gruffly as he strode towards the door. 'Don't screw up the sale. I'll be back in a week to discuss the payment.'

Takket stormed out, slamming the door. He was outside the warehouse before he paused to think. Why had the old man's words irritated him so much? Antellok was always teasing and taking jabs, but normally such comments rolled off Takket's back. Today, however, those barbs had sunk deep. Was it just lingering reluctance to retire, not wanting an era to end? Or did he know that there was some truth in the words? Twenty years ago, Takket would have pulled off the heist without incident. Twenty years ago, Takket would have been far from the city before anyone even realised the bones were missing.

Sighing, Takket looked out over the plaza. The sun had passed below the horizon, casting the last orange glow of twilight across the sky. The few gas lampposts in the town were being methodically lit by a lone attendant. Laughs came from the various taverns. Takket knew it was just the drunken jests of men relieved to be finished work for the day, but part of him felt targeted by those laughs. Antellok had been right. His last heist, his greatest achievement, was tainted with failure.

He would not be remembered for taking the baton of Iggranious, or breaking into the Indspire vaults. He would not be remembered for stealing the bones of the angel of Southreach. He would be remembered as the aging thief who almost got arrested because he was too old to scale a fence.

His head told him that it was time to retire, that the details of the theft would be forgotten, that taking any more jobs would just lead to greater disaster. His heart pulled him in another direction. His final theft would be the one to go down in history, but it need not be the theft of the bones of Southreach.

Conviction building, he turned his back to the path that led towards his cottage, and instead set off down the road to the Sunken Mage Inn. Perhaps he still had enough left in him for one last heist.

A heist to shake the world.

CHAPTER FOUR

Takket strode down the gravel street, lost in thought. He barely registered the strengthening wind blowing from the Demon's Ocean. His resolve had weakened as, at the outskirts of Drakenport, he approached the Sunken Mage Inn. He had, at least, managed to steal the bones. His last heist had not been a complete disaster. Stealing this Pure Shard would end only in greater catastrophe. Surely it was better to go out alive and marred with a minor failure than to be killed seeking to outdo his younger self. Surely travelling to an unfamiliar continent would just increase the chances of tragedy. Surely it was madness to trust two strangers with his life.

Despite his apprehension, he kept walking. He had to find out exactly what the siblings had planned. Once he knew for certain that their scheme was impossible, he could walk away with confidence. Maybe he could dissuade them from their suicidal goals, prove that Antellok's faith in the heist was misplaced. If nothing else, while humouring them, he could talk the pair into buying him a drink.

The Sunken Mage Inn stood on the far side of Drakenport from Takket's cottage. The ground floor was built from the same rough stonework as Takket's home, but the upper two floors were constructed from wind-battered wood. The flickering light of a roaring fire escaped into the night through lead-lined windows, accompanied by raucous laughter. The inn was popular among the sailors, many of whom thought the painted sign out front—featuring a Mage being pulled underwater by a sack of Soulshards—would bring them luck. Takket had never understood maritime superstitions.

Takket approached the oak double doors, ducking past a staggering man who stood a good foot taller than Takket, the smell of cheap alcohol on his breath. Slipping inside before the doors could swing shut, Takket was greeted by the stench of stale liqueurs, sweat, vomit and urine. He descended the short flight of stairs leading to the main drinking room, feet sticking with each step.

The room was notably warmer than the chill outside. In a hearth to one side, a large fire raged. The chimney was struggling, and the room was choked with woodsmoke. Mundanes were packed into the drinking room, a few sat around worn wooden tables, most simply stood in groups. Judging by the lingering salt stains coating their hair and woollen cloaks, most had spent the day on the seas, repeatedly drenched by seawater kicked up by the winds.

The crowd sounded jovial enough despite their haggard appearance. Men and women bellowed and filled the hall with laughter. Glasses of cheap local liqueurs made every jest hilarious, every story gripping.

Takket navigated around tables to find the bar, where he waved to the gnarled innkeeper.

'Hallden,' he called out over the drunken conversation.

'Takket.' The man grinned, twisting the scar that

stretched from his forehead to his chin—a memento of a bar brawl in his youth. 'Been a long time.'

'That it has. I've been kept too busy to visit,' Takket lied. He hated this inn, and came only when business forced him into the dive. 'I'm looking for two friends of mine, New Worlders.'

'Man and woman? Mid-thirties?' Takket nodded. 'Far booth.'

Takket followed the innkeeper's gesture and caught sight of Enara and Yelleck huddled over a table. Muttering a thanks that was lost in the din, Takket set off towards the pair.

Near the lead-lined windows, Enara and Yelleck sat across from each other in a booth. The upholstery had once been grand—leather dyed red, held in place with brass pins—but had long since become worn. The dye had faded, the leather tattered, the pins had become scuffed and were caked in years of dirt.

As Enara shifted over to make room, Takket almost stormed out at the sight of Yelleck's self-assured grin. They had been expecting him. Demons below, they had probably been saving the booth all day.

Taking a deep breath to settle himself, Takket sat down, trying to hide his distaste at how his cloak stuck to the bench.

'You're back,' Yelleck said, smug.

Takket shrugged, then started to lie. 'Antellok begged me to hear you out a second time. The old man seems to be pinning a great deal on your plan succeeding. I figured I at least owe him a few minutes of my time. So I'm here, as a favour to him, just to listen. No promises. Demon's below, your scheme seems deranged at best—you're going to have to do a lot of convincing, and fast, if you want me to stay for long.' He paused to look around the room. 'Speaking of which, we *are* meeting in an inn after all, and I could certainly use a drink.'

'Of course.' Yelleck spread palms that seemed a little too soft and uncalloused for a Mundane. 'Anything you want.'

Takket decided to push his luck. 'Anything? Then I'll have a mountain whisky.'

'Expensive tastes,' Yelleck grumbled. Still, he stood and crossed over to the bar. They really must have been determined to hire Takket if they would spring for such an expensive drink. The grains only grew at high altitudes, far from the layer of Sharddust, and always attracted quite a price. Most Mundanes made do with local liqueurs, fermented from various scrubs and roots. Passable, but always filled with a metallic aftertaste from the dissolved Sharddust.

'I'm glad you came back,' Enara said earnestly, 'even if your fence did have to twist your arm.'

'I'm not promising anything,' Takket reminded her. 'I just said I'll hear you out once more. That's all. I still think your plan is suicide.'

'Yet you're still here.'

'I'm still here. What can I say? I've never been one to pass up a free drink.'

Enara smiled uncertainly. 'Well, if a drink is all it takes to bring down the Varsen dynasty, then it's a small price to pay.'

Takket was about to say more when Yelleck returned, plopping down a full bottle and three glasses. Takket frowned with suspicion—he had expected a shot, maybe a double if they were feeling generous, not this *extravagance.*

'A *bottle* of mountain whisky?' he asked, checking the vintage—couple of years old, but still likely this inn's most expensive drink. 'I thought you said you were from a Mundane resistance group. How can you afford this sort of thing?'

'We are.' Yelleck filled the glasses. 'But there are a lot of us. Together, we have funds, we have manpower, we have connections. We're far from some gaggle of grumbling farmers. We've been at this for as long as you've been thieving.'

Takket took a glass, breathing in the oaky aroma before taking a sip. The drink was delightful, the kind he had become accustomed to at balls and high-ranking dinners. The innkeeper must have been grinning ear-to-ear.

'Sounds like you have everything you could possibly want,' Takket said. 'Why do you need me?'

'Even if every Mundane in Varsen rose up together, we'd be wiped out. Even if we had rifles for every man, woman and child, we couldn't face down an Arcane equipped with a Pure Shard. Mundanes can fight Mages in great enough numbers, especially with firearms. We'd just need to force them to burn through their Shards—as they create and destroy energy, their Shards disintegrate. Once they run out, they're mortal just like us.

'Arcanes pose a greater challenge, but are not unassailable. Arcanes don't burn through the Shards as long as they are just transferring energy from one form to another. They can last a long time, drawing heat around them to hurl projectiles, drinking light and

60

using it to boil the blood of their foes. Still, they run out, especially at night. In prolonged fights, they freeze the area around them, snuff out all lights, burn all combustible materials. They can fight for a long time, but not indefinitely.

'But an Arcane with a Pure Shard? They can draw energy from such a distance that it's almost impossible for them to run out. And even if we were to exhaust all nearby energy, they could just burn the Pure Shard. Last time someone did that, it created the Crater Desert. If by some miracle, we fight Arcane-lord Haddronius Varsen down to the last of his energy, he could just level the city out of spite.'

Takket took another thoughtful sip. While he had never quite fathomed the intricacies of magic use, Yelleck's claims matched with Takket's experience. Mundanes had risen against Arcanes in the past. Never ended well. 'So you need someone to steal the Pure Shard. Turn the Arcane-lord into just another Arcane. Powerful, but vulnerable.'

'Exactly,' Yelleck replied. 'Now you see why we need you.'

'No.' Takket shrugged. 'I see why you need a thief. I don't see why you crossed the ocean to seek me out. You telling me you don't have thieves in the New World?'

'None like you,' Enara said fervently. 'Few thieves survive long enough under Haddronius Varsen's rule to gain any skill. Most are caught and immolated at a young age. Those who do live? They're burglars, robbers, window-men. They either avoid being seen, or show up with a cudgel and take what they want. Neither is going to be possible here. We need an actor, an impostor, someone who can take on the role of the diplomat and stay under Haddronius's nose for weeks, worming their way closer until it's time to strike. We've searched the New World and the Imperium for someone capable. We found you.'

Takket allowed himself a smile as he topped up his glass. It sounded like he was far harder to replace than Antellok had indicated. To find him, this pair had scoured continents.

'So you need me. Great. But that doesn't make the plan any less suicidal. The disguise will only last until someone who knows this diplomat meets me.'

'That's just it,' Yelleck replied. 'Nobody on the continent would recognise him. He has no family— only child, parents died a few years back. He's known around the Imperium's court, but he's never set foot in the New World before. We can get you his official documents from his crash site, forge any that need replacing.'

Takket took another sip. 'And the Imperium won't be at all suspicious when one of their diplomatic airships goes missing along with its crew?'

'We can hide the wreckage until you board the airship to the New World. If we dispose of the diplomat's corpse, and any of his belongings are too damaged to salvage, they'll just assume the ship crashed on its way back from delivering him.'

'How are you going to dispose of a corpse out in the Crater Desert?'

Yelleck held his gaze. 'Trust us. We've had plenty of experience getting rid of bodies.'

The intensity in the man's eyes sent a shiver down Takket's spine. Still, the pair seemed to know what they were doing. Takket mulled it over. Their plan was not terrible. It would likely end up with everyone involved burned to ash, but there was a chance it could succeed. If it had the right thief. If it had him.

But that was not going to happen. He had come too far to throw away his life seeking glory. Still, the whisky was good. He could string the pair along for a while yet.

'Fair enough,' he said after another sip, 'but a diplomat from the Imperium is going to be expected to have extensive knowledge of the court. The dealings, the Imperium's past agreements. I've dealt with politicians before, but wouldn't say I'm an expert in international relations.'

'Much of the diplomat's personal effects survived the crash,' Yelleck said. 'That includes all the official records he had to prepare him.'

'And in court,' Enara added, 'you'll have us with you. We can pose as your assistants, natives of Varsen to guide you. Between us, and our contacts, we should be able to answer any questions you have.'

'And getting us there? If the airship crashed, how do we cross the Angel's Ocean?'

'Varsen is sending their own airship,' Yelleck explained. 'They plan to pick up the diplomat at Portspire. We can take a Shardrail to the edge of the Crater Desert. We'll ride krilts to the crash site and back, Shardrail to Portspire. I'm sure you can make some sort of excuse as to why you didn't arrive by airship. After all, you are a professional liar.'

Takket gazed across the crowded drinking hall. Men and women laughed and shouted over one another. Glasses and bottles containing the local liqueur filled the room—some would be terribly bitter, others sickeningly sweet. The smells of various beverages mingled with the thick smoke. The open hearth to one side kept the room pleasantly warm, helped by the density of bodies.

'You never gave me a straight answer before,' Takket said, watching the crowd. 'If you're not going to use the Pure Shard to make one of you a Mage, what *are* you going to do with it?'

'There are Mages that sympathise with us,' Enara replied. 'Mages that believe Mundanes should be treated as equals, peers. There are many who have converted to Unism or Circlism in recent years, most of which believe in making Mundane lives better, whether to protect their future incarnation or prevent the creation of demons. Other Mages are just decent people, who don't like to see suffering. These sympathetic Mages are in the minority, and couldn't stand up to an Arcane if they tried... but what if we made one an Arcane? A Mage can burn a Pure Shard to become Arcane, start a new Arcane dynasty. Not one built on self-aggrandisement and oppression, but one that is a partner of Mundanes, a protector. We could change the world.'

Grand words, spoken with conviction. These two really believed they could accomplish their goals, topple an Arcane dynasty. Takket had a feeling similar words had been spoken by the leaders of every Mundane uprising...before they and their followers were burned to ash.

Takket's attention drifted beyond the boisterous crowds to a table at the far end of the room. Three elderly men were sharing a bottle of thorn-brandy.

They talked little, seeming content to be enjoying each other's company. Their clothing was humble, all wearing tattered wool cloaks, pulled tight, and leather boots that had seen better days. They would not be remembered after they died, their deeds fading as their children's memories waned, yet they seemed happy. At peace. Perhaps Takket should look to their example, worry less about legacy, and simply enjoy his retirement. If they could be this content with whatever meagre charity their children could provide, imagine what his life would be like with the fortune he had amassed.

Takket gave a soft sigh. The whisky was good, but Takket had no intention of getting drunk tonight. His house took enough effort getting into while sober, and spending a winter night outside was not how he wanted to start his retirement. It was time to call the evening to a close. Time to make an excuse that these two would not be able to avoid.

'The payment.' He drained the last of his drink. 'Half the Varsen treasury. That's a staggering number of Shards. Seems awfully generous. Too generous to believe.'

Yelleck leaned forward, topping up Takket's glass. 'Shards are the tools of Mages and Arcanes. We want to build a nation for Mundanes. We can use Shard-grains to keep our riflemen supplied with ammunition, use some of the larger denominations for explosives or trading with the other Arcanedoms. But the rest?' Yelleck shrugged. 'Batons are too unwieldy to use for explosives, too rare for common trading. Having a vast treasury would just make us a target. Besides, without you, we'd have nothing. Half of a treasury is a damn sight better than no Shards at all.'

Takket smirked. 'And you just expect me to believe you'll keep your word? That when you take over, when you have it all under the control of your army of Mundanes, you'll not put a bullet in my back and keep the fortune for yourselves?'

'Of course,' Enara said, adamant. 'We couldn't betray you even if we wanted to. Angels above, Takket, you'd be the man who brought down the Varsen dynasty, the man who freed a nation. You would be a hero.'

A hero.

Enara continued, but her voice faded as the words echoed in Takket's mind. He had been looking at his legacy all wrong. Sure, the greatest thieves were remembered, spoken of in taverns, their names becoming a legend in the underworld. But heroes? Heroes had epics written of their feats. Their tales were told to children at bed time. They were emulated by Arcane-lords, praised by priests. Randok the Reformer. First Priest Inastin. Magelord Grethin. Their names had been repeated for centuries, from the cheapest tavern to the highest Magetower. Could Takket really join their ranks?

When Takket looked back over the crowd, he saw a very different scene. Hidden with forced smiles were the bloodshot eyes of men and women pushed to their limits. Holding glasses of liqueur were hands scratched and bruised from day after day of backbreaking labour to make ends meet. Boisterous laughter shook Sharddust from hair greying before its time. Embellished tales were interrupted by grating coughs, men and women too sick to be working, too poor to take a day's rest.

Was the New World truly worse than this? Takket could only guess at the plight of those Mundanes. What if they could be saved? What if *he* was the man who saved them?

Antellok would eat his taunting words. Takket was not past his prime—he was just getting started. Takket would not simply carry out the greatest theft of his life —he would force the most significant change in history. That would be his legacy: the thief who saved a nation.

He turned to Yelleck, feeling a smug smile of his own.

'I'm in.'

CHAPTER FIVE

The krilt under Takket lurched up the fractured granite cliff, edging its way towards the ridge-top high above. The six chitin-coated legs of the ash-grey creature were splayed wide. Every leg was divided into three segments, each as long as Takket was tall, dwarfing the central horse-sized abdomen on which he rode. Mandibles on its flat head clacked and chittered to the krilts ridden by Enara and Yelleck. Their strange calls blended with the creak of worn leather saddles.

They had been riding for most of the morning, and Takket was slowly becoming used to the ungainly motion of the krilt. It moved a single leg at a time, its footfalls unsettlingly quiet—the large bone-like feet made only the occasional grate over gravel. The creatures, imported from the New World, were unparalleled when it came to traversing difficult terrain, but were exhausting to ride. The last few hours had been tense, Takket constantly adjusting his balance while clinging onto the leather harness for dear life.

Five days had passed since leaving Drakenport. After making final arrangements with Antellok, the trio had departed on Shardrail towards the Crater Desert. The train could only get them so close. There were no stations in the desert—too few people visited the desolate basin. The cracked and broken terrain made even through-routes impossible, so the rail lines avoided it entirely. There were no cities, just scattered farms on the hillsides hugging the crater.

Instead of rail, they had made their way on horseback to Issel, a small village at the base of the Crater Desert's surrounding ridge. There, they had traded in the horses—and a substantial down payment —for krilts. The village used the beasts to collect the rich Sharddust within the desert, and rented the creatures to occasional curious Mages visiting the crater. The Sharddust may have been a blight that choked most of the world, but for these farmers it made surprisingly good fertiliser.

Throughout the journey, Enara and Yelleck had insisted he speak for them, dealing with any necessary payments himself. They claimed he needed to get used to taking charge of the group, but Takket suspected they just wanted to avoid being singled out as foreign. Distrust of the New World was common in the Imperium, and became more pronounced farther away from trading cities. The pair had given him a sizable satchel filled with Shards to cover the expenses, so Takket was quite content.

Takket's krilt let out a screech, echoed by those behind, as the rock face crumbled underfoot. The creature recovered rapidly, bracing its other five legs. The first time Takket heard a krilt screech, he had panicked—thinking the animal was in distress—but had soon realised that the krilt was just warning its partners of unstable terrain or falling rocks. Considering their insectoid appearance, the creatures were remarkably social.

With one final lunge, the animal hauled itself onto the ridge-top, chirping in triumph. After readjusting his balance, Takket looked out over the vista. At this altitude, the cold air was free of Sharddust, smelling wonderfully fresh. Before him, the rock face rapidly descended, plunging into a swirling sea of Sharddust that stretched towards the horizon. Barely visible in the distance, it was capped by the far side of the circular ridge.

The Crater Desert.

It looked as if an impossibly large giant had formed the landscape into a bowl and filled it with a blood-red soup. The truth was far more terrifying. This was the work of an Arcane. The crater was the result of the one and only occasion that an Arcane had burned a Pure Shard. Two armies destroyed, an uprising ended, a landscape forever altered. This is what the Mundane resistance most feared. If backed into a corner, Haddronius Varsen could turn his capital and all its surroundings into *this*.

Storms frequently carried Sharddust into the crater, but little ever escaped. Over the centuries the basin had steadily filled with powder. Despite the abundance of Sharddust, nothing grew here. Outside the crater, farms flourished. High enough to be out of the haze, but with ready access to plentiful Sharddust fertiliser, it was a farmer's dream. Inside the crater...nothing. Even after the thousand years since the blast, there were no sprouts, no roots, not even moss. Burning the Pure Shard had not only annihilated all life, it had purged the area into a permanently barren wasteland.

Hauling themselves up either side of Takket, the other krilts gave their own chirps. For a full minute they sat there, catching their breaths, buffeted by the fresh wind. The krilts gently clicked back and forth, showing no sign of fatigue.

'Where now?' Takket shouted, eager to get to the crash site, though dreading the descent. He was already exhausted.

'A mile or so into the Sharddust sea,' Yelleck called back. 'We left markers. Ready?'

Takket sighed. 'Ready as I'll ever be.'

Yelleck laughed, then urged his mount forward. Takket tried not balk at the sight of the creature taking off down the near-vertical cliff.

Taking hold of the steel barb fixed under the chitin plating at his krilt's neck, Takket pushed. The creature chirped contentedly as it followed its companion. Abandoning the barb, Takket gripped the front of the harness as the creature's torso angled sharply downward. He pushed his back into the rear of the saddle, bracing his weight on his hands and the stirrups.

He gulped. The ascent had seemed bad enough, but riding downward was terrifying. Not only did he have to constantly battle to keep balance, he was forced to look out over the drop. He was one slip away from plunging down the sharp incline, skidding over the several hundred feet of sharpened granite into the murky sea of Sharddust.

He longed to be able to look away, close his eyes, but he could not take the chance. Watching the creature's movements gave him his only warning of its jarring motion. It, at least, seemed to have no qualms about climbing head-first down the cliff, but he supposed he would feel more secure if he too was encased in thick armour.

The krilt continued to make its way down the

shattered rock face, probing fissures and ledges one leg at a time. Takket was relieved that the creature was intelligent enough to require only minimal instructions —he did not relish the idea of releasing the harness to manipulate the steering barb.

The beast planted its right foreleg onto a rock shelf, contentedly chittering as it shifted its weight to lift the next. A crack resounded from below—the ledge gave way.

They fell.

Takket's krilt shrieked as it slid uncontrollably down the rock face. It splayed its legs wide, but nothing could stop its spin. They flashed past another krilt, Takket meeting Yelleck's stunned gaze. All Takket could do was grip the leather harness, his knuckles whitening, and pray.

The creature, at least, managed to stay upright, its legs skidding across the ground. If it rolled over, it would certainly crush Takket.

His surroundings whipped by as the krilt spiralled on its feet, kicking up clumps of dirt soaked with Sharddust, leaving a blood red cloud in their wake. His ears filled with the rush of air, the rumble of breaking rock and chitin, and always the krilt's piercing scream.

A gloom descended as the creature skidded into the billowing haze of the Sharddust layer. The dust irritated his skin and scoured his eyes. He could feel it clumping onto him, soaking into his fearful sweat.

Their descent began to level as they came to the base of the crater. Finally, the krilt managed to lock its legs into fissures criss-crossing the ground. Takket almost lost his grip, something jarring in his shoulder as he fought to stay on the creature's back, but kept his balance.

They had stopped.

Takket panted, his terror giving way to the joy of survival. Despite the aches in his legs, the shrill cries of the krilt, the pain in his hands from leather abrasions, he laughed.

His chortle ended in a coughing fit—the Sharddust was thick here, thicker even than Southreach. Every breath drew in the metallic taste of the abrasive dust. Through force of will, he brought his breathing back under control, spitting out a blood red glob from his Sharddust-filled mouth.

Shattered ground surrounded him—plateaus a few paces across separated by deep fissures, partially filled with dust. The world was stained red by the haze, which obscured everything further than a dozen feet away. The entire desert was like this. It was no wonder the Imperium had not found the crash site. He had no idea how Enara and Yelleck planned to rediscover the airship.

He yelled a reply to muffled shouts through the Sharddust. The shadowy form of a krilt lurched into view, with Yelleck sat atop it looking relieved.

'You're alive,' he called out.

'Just about.' Takket inspected the gouged chitin at the end of his krilt's legs. 'Will he be alright to continue?'

'Of course.' Yelleck shrugged. 'Krilts are tough.'

Takket nodded. 'How do we find the crash site?'

'Follow me. We saw one of our markers while trying to find you.'

Yelleck turned his mount around and started to

disappear into haze. Takket took hold of the control barb again, pushing forward to urge the krilt into motion, guiding it with gentle tugs to the side. The animal was well trained, responding to the slightest prompts.

Over the level ground, Takket found the ride much easier. The krilt still moved in sporadic lunges, but at least its body was no longer near-vertical. If the skidding fall had hurt the beast, it gave no indication, easily stepping from one broken plateau to the next. The krilt followed the silhouette of Yelleck's mount through the suffocating red clouds.

They found Enara and her krilt waiting by a metal pole driven into the ground. An unsteady light shone from a Soulshard atop the pole. A distant glow caught Takket's attention. Barely visible in the haze, the shifting light of a Soulshard lit the redness. Takket urged his krilt to follow Yelleck's as he headed for the flickering light. After a minute of riding, they came to another metal rod holding a Soulshard. Further ahead, the next light marked the way.

Takket prodded his mount forward alongside Yelleck.

'How did you find this crash in the first place?' he shouted through the haze.

Yelleck shrugged. 'We have a base nearby. The Crater Desert may be a wasteland, but it's a fantastic place to hide.'

'Hide from what?'

'From the Imperium. You're far kinder to Mundanes here than in the New World, but you have close relations with Varsen. If a fugitive from Varsen is captured here...well, Imperium Arcanes don't like immolating Mundanes, but they have no qualms about shipping them back to Varsen to be burned alive.'

Takket nodded slowly. 'And your people saw the crash?'

'Exactly. The angels are with us. While returning from outside the crater with supplies, one of our people saw the airship in distress. Looks like the pilot's Soulshard failed. The airship turned into a falling sack of metal and canvas in the blink of an eye. We scoured the desert and found the wreckage. When we realised what it was, we knew our prayers had been answered. The angels had sent us our chance at freedom.'

'Won't any of the locals follow the markers?' Takket asked as they passed another.

'We're on good terms with the nearby farmers. Rather a necessity for us to live in this area. We can't grow our own food here, can't afford to risk the authorities finding us. The locals know not to follow the markers. If anyone else does...well we have people guarding the site.'

'I'm sure they'll be glad to end that particular duty.' Takket could barely imagine spending one day in this oppressive gloom, let alone several.

'Ask them yourself.' Yelleck pointed ahead. Figures emerged from the haze, stepping over the twisted metal remains of an airship. The canvas hydrogen container, still partially draped over the passenger cabin, had completely deflated. The cabin had survived the impact remarkably well. About the length of a train carriage, it had half buried itself on impact, but the fragile ground had softened the landing, assisted by the deflating canvas balloon. The glass windows had shattered, but the frame mostly held its shape.

The pilot's cabin had suffered far worse. It was barely recognisable, just a haphazard series of metal pipes, blackened and twisted. No wonder the Mage or Arcane piloting the ship had not managed to slow the descent: the failing Shard must have blasted the entire crew section apart. It was a small miracle that the canvas balloon had not ignited. The angels really must have had their hand in this. Or else the demons really hated Haddronius Varsen.

Takket clambered down from his krilt, Sharddust crunching underfoot. The creature gave a few contented clicks before lumbering over to a fissure. Its long tongue lashed out, fishing around for the rich supply of Sharddust caught between the plateaus.

Focusing on the matter at hand, Takket turned towards the passenger cabin. He had a lot of work ahead if he was going to stand a chance at succeeding —and surviving—this heist. A missed file, a forgotten personal trinket, a broken official seal—any could mean the difference between being the greatest thief in history, and yet another Mundane burned to death in the Arcanedom of Varsen.

Takket perched on a hardwood table inside the passenger cabin, flicking through the stack of papers he had collected. The interior had fared much worse than the frame. On impact, the furnishings had been launched into the air. Engraved wooden chairs had splintered into shrapnel. Crystal drinking glasses has slashed the upholstery, scattering the duck down stuffing to mingle with the intruding Sharddust.

Coating it all was the dried blood of the cabin's former occupants, shredded by glass shards, wooden splinters and cracked porcelain.

Thankfully, the bodies were gone. Takket doubted anyone would be able to identify what was left, but Yelleck and Enara had insisted they should be removed. They had set off with the five crash site guards, dragging the bodies. They had not explained exactly how they were going to dispose of the corpses. Takket doubted he wanted to know.

Besides, he had to focus on his own task.

After nearly an hour scouring through the debris-filled cabin, he had amassed a pile of documents belonging to the late diplomat. Most were stained with blood or caked in the dense Sharddust that had crept in through the smashed windows—the copper smell of the latter at least covered much of the stench left behind by the corpses. Still, the documents were legible, a few sheets printed using the latest typewriters, most scrawled by hand.

There was too much to take in in a single sitting, so Takket flipped through the pages, trying to identify the most critical documents. Some were official papers: diplomatic orders, a letter from Arcane-lord Venning Indel to Haddronius Varsen, a pair of signed treaties— most of which were so damaged he would need to forge copies. Other sheets contained notes on Varsen, detailing senior members of the court, New World protocol, spy updates. No doubt, it would all prove invaluable in the coming months, but it was not what he was searching for.

He needed to know more about the man he was to become.

Takket turned to a leather-bound book under the stack of documents, brushing a layer of Sharddust from its cover. It had clearly been well used—the spine cracked, the leather cover scuffed and dented, the pages dog-eared, showing only the barest hint of the gold trim that once adorned the tome. Takket opened it to the front page and read the flowing script.

The Journal of Khantek Fredeen.

The diary of the diplomat. Perfect. Takket chewed over the name, *Khantek Fredeen.* He needed to memorise that. He would have to answer to it for weeks, picking it out in distant conversations. The name itself spoke highly of the diplomat. Only those born to Arcanes or Mages were permitted to use second names. Khantek must have been a Mundane child of Mages. It was unusual, but not unheard of. What was notable was the fact he had made something of himself. Most Mages' children born without magical talent were ostracised—disappointments to their parents, distrusted by regular Mundanes. That Khantek had overcome this burden to reach such a senior position indicated he was remarkably driven.

Takket flicked over the page and started to read the first entry.

Mother insists I use this book to keep a journal, and I trust her. She always did look out for me, always there to listen to my concerns. I suppose I will have to get used to bringing my concerns to this book instead. Tomorrow I leave for Indspire, half the Imperium away. Two thousand miles from home. Two thousand miles from everyone I have ever known.

Takket smiled as he turned the pages. Perhaps this expedition was not a fool's errand. This tome contained Khantek's inner thoughts, his way of speaking, his handwriting, his worries and desires. Judging by the wear and tear, Khantek had poured significant time into this book. Someday, the information here might save Takket's life.

He skimmed several pages, wanting to get an overview of this man.

The letter I have long dreaded arrived this morning. Mother is dead. She has never been the same since Father's passing, and we all knew this day was coming, but I still feel lost. Her letters are all that has kept me sane these long years in Indspire. Her advice has saved me from more than one scheme at court, as you well know. Now I am truly alone.

The Arcane-lord has given me permission to take a leave of absence to attend the funeral. I will return home tomorrow, though Rakenspire no longer feels like home. Without Mother, it's just another far-flung town in the Imperium. Indspire is my real home now. Demons below, when did that happen?

The tell-tale smudge of teardrops marred the page. Strange for a Mundane child to have such a good relationship with a Mage parent. Perhaps that support had helped him achieve so much in life.

Takket looked through the cabin's empty window frames into the billowing red haze. There was no sign of the resistance members. They had barely walked a few feet when they were swallowed by the Sharddust smog. The breeze was light here, but there was still enough to knock the dust into dancing eddies.

At the edge of his vision, he could make out the forms of the krilts, happily gorging themselves of the feast of Sharddust. Their contented chirps and the grate of Sharddust blown against the wrecked airship were the only sounds. The crater was strangely peaceful. Ordinarily, Sharddust-thick areas were located around busy cities, bustling with activity at all hours. Farther from the cities, the Sharddust became less dense, allowing sounds of birds and animals to travel long distances, creating a din of their own.

Here though, in the heart of the crater, there was almost nothing. The Sharddust dampened all but the nearest sounds, filtered all but the purest red hue of sunlight. It felt isolated. Safe. No wonder the Free Circle had chosen this place to hide their fugitives.

A glow in the red haze drew his focus.

It seemed distant, out in the direction the others had taken the bodies. The shifting light indicated a Soulshard as its source, but a single Soulshard could never be bright enough to cut so far through thick smog...unless it was being burned, but the resistance group had no Mages. It seemed doubtful an intruding Mage had happened upon the group out here in the middle of nowhere. Was it one of the sympathetic Mages they had mentioned, here to help? Or just a pile of Soulshards, perhaps a set of those markers they had used to find this place?

Takket sighed. He knew so little of these people. He was used to taking months to research his marks, his employers, his assistants—anyone involved in a heist. This time, he had a scant few days. If all went well, he would be in Varsen in just over a week. He would have to allocate some time for investigating his new partners, but for now, his focus was Khantek.

He flicked through to the last gnarled page in the journal, turning to Khantek's final entry.

At last, the time has come. Years of work. Years of scheming, keeping the right allies and losing those falling from grace. I have finished settling arrangements at my family manor. It will be at least a decade before I set foot in Rakenspire again. This morning, we began our journey west. We are to meet with the Varsen delegation in Portspire.

Then to Varsen itself. The New World. A land of strife and constant border wars. There I will represent the entire Imperium. Me. A Mundane, rising to such a high position. Mother would be proud. If only she were still with us. She would love the view from this airship.

Leafing back and forth through the pages, Takket picked out fragments of Khantek's life, slowly building up an image of the diplomat. Over the next few days, he would read the journal cover to cover, collating every last detail. Even this cursory glance brought Takket closer to the man.

In Khantek, Takket saw a peer. A Mundane bitter at the restrictions imposed on him at birth, but unlike most, a Mundane who truly strived to make his life better, rather than wallow in self-pity. The more Takket read, the more he respected Khantek. He had manipulated, schemed, bribed and deceived almost at much at Takket, worming his way ever higher in the Imperium's court. He had the same fears of growing old, of losing his edge before realising his greatest achievements.

Takket had to pity the man. The journey to Varsen was to be Khantek's crowning accomplishment. He had come so close to achieving his dream. If it had not been for some freak Shard failure, he would likely be there now, living his fantasy. As it was, the demons had put a stop to his plans. All Takket could do was make the most of the man's unwilling sacrifice. He would accept this blessing, secure his own legacy. Maybe then, there would be some justice in Khantek's death.

CHAPTER SIX

Takket's Shard carriage bounced its way down the worn and patched flagstone highway. Traffic stretched into the red haze ahead, horse-drawn carriages rattled along, overtaken by those powered by Mages. By the roadside, Mundanes trudged through the mud. The highway leading to Portspire was one of the busiest in the Imperium. The city served as the gateway to the New World, its wealth attracting merchants, officials, nobility and always the streams of impoverished Mundanes.

Takket and the two Free Circle members had spent four exhausting days travelling from the Crater Desert. By krilt, horse, Shardrail and now carriage, they had made their way westward across the Imperium—snatching only fitful bouts of sleep. The night before, they had stopped in the wealthy town of Fenspire. There they had acquired their disguises: the silken shirt, trousers and fine maroon cloak worn by Takket, and hard-wearing black linen clothing for the others. With a bath, a haircut and some new travelling bags, they began to truly resemble an international delegation.

The bath had left Takket's skin feeling clean for the first time in a week, but had done nothing to rid his sinuses of the copper tang of Sharddust. Every breath seemed saturated from their stay in the Crater Desert. Coughs stained his handkerchief red. When he tried to sleep, Sharddust grated in his nose.

If the invasive dust bothered Enara and Yelleck, they showed no sign. They sat opposite him, leaning back into the plush velvet upholstery. The cart was not quite as splendid as the one he had taken to Southreach—the black paint flaking, the windows partially abraded by Sharddust—but it would pass for a diplomat's transport.

A sharp jolt rocked the carriage as it passed over a pothole on the overused highway. They were nearing their destination. The Sharddust rapidly bled off as the carriage followed the line of traffic towards the coast. Through the front window, the coastal landscape emerged. Roads and rail lines crossed over innumerable streams that divided the grassy plain, all converging on a bay hugged by the white limestone buildings of Portspire.

At the heart of the bay, on an island scattered with white marble mansions of Arcanes, there loomed the city's tower. It was not truly a Magetower—the original Mage's residence had shared the same fate as so many Magetowers, and had been destroyed during the Devastation. Over its ruins, the Imperium had constructed this modern marvel. Ninety storeys high, it was the second tallest structure in the world, outmatched only by the Arcane-lord's palace in Indspire. For such a large structure, it was strangely elegant—wide at the base, tapering in at its midpoint, expanding out again at its peak. Marble fragments worked into the concrete scattered the light, causing the tower to sparkle before the setting sun.

At its peak, three massive airships hovered. The tower allowed the craft to moor without descending, avoiding ground-level hazards and saving the pilots' precious Shards required to lift the airships back to cruising altitude. The rest of the tower was filled with government offices, apartments for Arcanes, embassies from all Arcanedoms in the New World. Hundreds of windows ringed the exterior, at this distance appearing as speckled decoration. It was a building impossible to construct by mundane means, on a scale even the Magelords of old could not achieve. Only Arcanes had the power and resources to raise such a monument to their own abilities.

The view was obscured by the more humble buildings at the outskirts of the city. Even these were more impressive than any building in Drakenport, faced with white limestone, only lightly stained pink by the haze. Water features and sculptures of angels stood among trimmed grass in lawns and public parks. The wealth of New World trade was evident on every street.

'Are you prepared?' Enara asked.

'I'm ready.' Takket spoke with a confidence he did not feel. A single misstep could lead to disaster. A poorly chosen word in conversation. A minor mistake in a forgery. A forgotten name. Any of a hundred errors could mean their deaths. But the others did not need to know that. Takket, having never seen Enara or Yelleck under real pressure, feared adding to their stress.

'Remember,' Yelleck said firmly, 'from here on, you are Khantek Fredeen. We are your assistants.'

'I know,' Takket replied irritably. 'This is hardly my first job. Just focus on your own part.'

'Of course.' Enara smiled. 'And once again, thank

you for this. A thousand years from now, people will still recall our tale of our heist.'

Or the tale of our deaths, Takket added silently.

The cart's journey smoothed as it reached the long marble bridge crossing the bay to Portspire's main tower. The waves lapped gently at the shore, protected from three sides by the buildings lining the waterfront. Ships of all sizes—from small wooden fishing boats to building-sized cargo liners—poured into the harbour to dock before the sun set. Tugs were out helping the larger vessels into port, intermittent red puffs of Sharddust emitted from the Mages manning their cockpits.

Cargo ships sailed for the horizon. They would be stocked with the finest exports of the Imperium: artwork, marble sculptures, fine mountain whiskies, the latest works of fiction—the products of the cultural heartland of the world.

The ships docking now would be returning from the New World. Some would be laden with common goods such as spices, rare minerals, modern rifles. Most, however, would be filled with Soulshards, particularly batons that could only be formed by burning humans alive. The practice was so heavily restricted in the Indel Imperium that the prices soared. In the Imperium, the methods of producing the batons may have been taboo, but no Mage questioned their merit.

The water itself was a deep red. The sea swallowed the Sharddust generated by Portspire, keeping the air relatively clean—at least for a city—but staining the ocean for miles. With the red sky from the setting sun, the world seemed as monotone as from inside the

Crater Desert.

The carriage slowed to a stop in the shadow of the tower. Enara and Yelleck leapt to their feet and hurried through the door. Yelleck held it open for Takket, who stood, smoothed his cloak, and sedately stepped down.

Takket raised an eyebrow as the pair stood idle. Keeping to his best Indspire accent, he nodded towards the open door. 'My bags?' Yelleck flushed and dived back into the carriage to begin unloading the new leather cases. 'Enara,' Takket continued, 'go inside and inform the Varsen embassy of our arrival.'

She nodded and hurried away. They had decided not to use false names for the Enara and Yelleck. The pair's names were common enough in Varsen, and Takket did not want to pile pressure on the amateurs. They insisted they would be capable of holding to their disguises, but Takket was loath to put more than the bare minimum of faith in their acting abilities.

The carriage driver hopped down from his perch. 'That comes to two rocks and three gems.'

Takket nodded and fished in his leather satchel for the correct Soulshards. Sewn from calfskin leather, embellished with gold clasps and brass fittings, the bag was the finest he had ever owned. Stamped onto its front was the emblem of the Imperium: a Soulshard flanked by angelic wings. He counted out the glowing crystals—plus another gem-sized crystal as a gratuity —and handed them over.

'Will you be needing a carriage back?' the driver asked.

Takket smiled distantly. 'Not for a good decade at least.'

'Staying here then?'

'Going to Varsen.'

The Mage's eyebrows rose. 'Better you than me, is all I'll say. Well, safe journeys.'

'And you,' Takket replied. As soon as Yelleck had unloaded the last of Takket's luggage, the driver climbed back onto his bench and set off, burning a Soulshard to start the carriage's motion. Takket watched the vehicle navigate in a wide arc and roll back down the bridge to the mainland.

Takket looked up at the tower, only to be hit by a wave of vertigo. If the tower was designed to make visitors feel insignificant, its architect ought to have been proud. He could barely make out the windows at its peak. The curved frame just served to throw off any sense of perspective, making the tower appear impossibly tall.

He lowered his eyes as he heard the sounds of approaching footsteps over the white gravel path that stretched to the tower's base. Enara was hurrying back, followed by a formation of half a dozen Varsen soldiers. Leading them was a wire-thin man bedecked in the green-and-black uniform of Varsen. Styled similar to the linen jackets of the soldiers, his was made from smooth silk, a golden sash reflecting the darkening sky.

'Khantek Fredeen, Envoy of the Indel Imperium,' Enara introduced, panting. 'This is—'

The thin man cut her off. 'I'm Constable Hannig Vale, security adjunct to Chief Constable Ensellus Valdera of Varsen. You're late.'

Takket nodded, relaying the practiced lie. 'We encountered issues with our airship over the Crater Desert. I elected to continue by carriage while the airship returned for repairs.'

Hannig's left eye twitched. 'Well, let's hope the Imperium produces better envoys than airships. Follow me.'

The man turned on a heel and marched back towards the tower, his soldiers stepping aside to let him pass. Takket tried not to be phased by the man's curtness.

'Bring my luggage,' he said to Enara and Yelleck, before calmly strolling after Hannig. He would be damned if he was going to run after the man. Halfway to the tower, Hannig paused to wait. Takket told himself his sedate walk was appropriate—no real envoy would run after a mere security officer. In truth, he relished the irritation on the man's face. This might just be fun.

The tower's interior was breathtaking. Takket followed Hannig along a plush carpet dyed Imperium scarlet. The smell of sea spray followed them inside, a gentle wind blowing through the entrance doors. After twenty paces, the white tunnel opened up, revealing the cavernous centre of the tower. The building was hollow, rooms only built along the exterior walls, leaving the central column empty. On every level, internal windows looked out over the drop. Mages levitated across the chamber between the numerous balconies. The scene was lit red by the shifting light of a thousand Soulshards lining the walls.

'You're a Mundane, aren't you?' Hannig did not show the least appreciation for the wondrous building.

'Yes.' Takket tore his eyes away from the view.

Hannig gave an unimpressed grunt. 'This way.'

Takket followed as the man stalked through the maze of statues lining the ground floor. Some were made of local limestone, or red and black rock from elsewhere in the Imperium. Other statues were chiselled from imported New World materials—jade from Varsen, sandstone from Medeth and Santona, obsidian from Kilroth. All bore the styles of their homelands: the grandeur of the Imperium, the abstract representations of Varsen, the stark simplicity of Kilroth.

'We don't have time for you to marvel at these diplomatic gifts,' Hannig snapped. 'You are already well overdue. We need to be on the airship tonight, and we still need to ensure you pose no threat to Arcane-lord Haddronius.'

'Are all Varsen envoys so discourteous?' Takket said, not having to feign the indignation.

'I'm not an envoy, I'm a security officer, and I've been waiting for half a month for your arrival. Now step onto the dais.'

Takket obeyed, following Hannig onto one of the dozen limestone platforms in alcoves along one side of the chamber. The dais hung from heavy chains, which stretched through a vertical shaft running along the chamber's wall. Yelleck and Enara accompanied Hannig's soldier escort onto the platform. Even with the nine of them and all their luggage, there was still plenty of room on the large disk.

Hannig tugged a hand-sized Soulshard from his pocket, the rock glowing brightly at his touch. With a shudder, the platform began to ascend, Hannig's Shard shining brilliantly as he drew its energy to levitate the dais. As they steadily rose, the chains rattled. Halfway up, they passed the descending counterweights, there to minimise the number of Shards used to operate the lifts.

Their way was lit with evenly spaced Soulshards, filling the shaft with a red glow to match that of the larger chamber. The smell of seawater was replaced with incense.

Eventually they came to a stop only a few floors short of the tower's summit, level with a hallway that opened to one side of the platform. There, a pair of men pulled levers. Something grated against the underside of the dais. Moments later, Hannig released the platform, letting it settle onto supports, the Shard in his hand crumbling to form a pile of dust.

'Clean that up,' he ordered the two men as he cast the dust to the side, then turned to Takket. 'Come with me, Envoy, my men will take your assistants to the flight deck.'

Takket complied. The hallway had been painted black, highlighted with a deep green rug running down the centre. Even with the abundant gas lamps lining the walls, the hall was oppressively dark. Abstract statues spaced between the lamps looked alien and foreboding. Even those meant to represent angels unsettled Takket, the abstract shapes lending them a demonic edge.

Hannig opened an oaken door at the end of the hallway and stood to one side, waving Takket into a stark room. Enclosed in a cube of unadorned concrete, the room was furnished only with two wooden chairs facing each other across a simple table, illuminated from above by an uncomfortably bright gas lamp. The room stank of bleach. Takket's apprehension grew—

only hospitals and morgues were this thoroughly cleaned.

'Sit,' Hannig instructed, shutting the door.

Takket edged towards one of the chairs and cautiously sat. 'What's this about?'

Hannig took the chair opposite. 'I am here to ensure that you do not pose a threat to the Arcane-lord. Chief Constable Ensellus wanted to be here himself to conduct this...interview, but he could not spend so long away from the Haddronius's side. You are lucky —he would not have taken your delayed arrival so lightly.'

'Dragging me to an interrogation cell is taking it lightly?' Takket asked sternly, shifting in the chair. The hardwood back rest seemed designed to dig into his ribcage, the seat tilted at just the right angle to feel unbalanced. The table was no more appealing, its edge rough and littered with splinters, daring anyone to rest a hand on its surface.

Hannig's left eye twitched again. 'Not refusing your admittance out of hand is showing you an abundance of latitude. If our ties to the Imperium were not so valuable, you would be back on that carriage to Indspire already.'

'Yet despite those valuable ties, you still feel the need to question me.'

'We question everyone applying for admittance to the court of Varsen.' Hannig extended a hand. 'Now, show me your official papers.'

Takket drew a sheet from his satchel and handed it over. It was one of his finest forgeries, the hand an almost identical match to the original, including the Arcane-lord's signature. He had hand-carved a seal, all

92

the more impressive given the fact he had done so on a jostling Shardrail. Of course, it helped that he had the real document as a basis—albeit tattered and bloody.

Hannig leaned over the document, reading it in its entirety. He paused over the signature and seal, squinting at them critically. Takket's pride in his work faded. Had he made a mistake? Missed an important feature of the seal? Left a tell-tale quirk out of the handwriting?

Hannig pulled out a magnifying glass to inspect the seal, grunting. Takket looked around amid rising panic. This was taking too long. There was no escape. Even if he outran Hannig, there was no way he could get off this floor, let alone flee the building.

He was trapped.

Hannig gave a disappointed sigh. 'This appears to be in order,' he said at last. His chair groaned as he shifted his wiry frame. 'Now to see if you pose any direct threat.'

'You think I'm some sort of assassin?' Takket forced incredulity into his voice. The security measures were even stricter than Yelleck and Enara had indicated.

'In the New World we don't have the luxury of the heedless trust afforded to visitors of the Imperium. Any of the other Arcane-lords would happily see Varsen fall, see Haddronius dead. Assassins come in many forms. It would not be the first time diplomatic robes hid a murderer's blade.'

'The Imperium wants nothing but friendship with Varsen.' That was actually true, so far as Khantek's notes indicated. Varsen painstakingly maintained their close links to the Imperium. Those links gave Varsen some semblance of security in the volatile continent of the New World. The Imperium would not risk the tribute and favourable trade offered by the smaller nation in exchange for political support.

'That remains to be seen.' Hannig pulled a thick folder from a satchel and dropped it on the desk with a thud. Takket caught sight of the name *Envoy Khantek Fredeen* on the cover as Hannig opened the folder. 'Let's start simply. You are a Mundane.'

'Yes.'

Hannig took a thumb-sized Soulshard gem from his pocket, light radiating from the crystal at the Mage's touch. Without a word, he tossed it across the table. Unthinking, Takket caught the Shard. No longer in contact with someone with magical ability, its light faded into a subtle glow.

'Impressive reflexes for an envoy,' Hannig muttered.

'I was a catcher for our spinball team growing up,' Takket lied. He hated the repetitive nature of the ball game, but it seemed a good excuse. He doubted the constable would appreciate being told how useful dexterity was to a thief.

Hannig noted something down on a fresh sheet of paper. 'Well, you clearly are a Mundane.' He nodded to the dimly glowing Shard in Takket's hand. 'That will make things easier. You will not be restricted in the number of Shards you can carry with you in court. Even so, I urge you not to draw a Shard in the presence of the Arcane-lord—my fellows respond to potential threats with deadly speed.'

Takket nodded, beginning to fear how the court's paranoia would impact his heist.

'Family members,' Hannig said simply.

It took Takket a few seconds to realise that Hannig had asked a question. 'Father and...Mother have both passed away.' He let his voice catch upon mentioning his mother. 'I've no siblings. Surely this is all in that file of yours.'

'It is my job to be thorough. You have no wife? Romantic involvements?'

'No. What does this have to do with anything?'

'Family members can be exploited. Now, your business dealings. Do you have any property in the New World?'

'No.'

'Do you own any ocean-worthy trade ships with a displacement over five thousand tons?'

'No.'

'Have you ever received a gift or payment from any New World Arcanedom with a value greater than one Shard baton?'

Takket had to suppress a sigh as he gave another denial. This was going to be a long evening.

Takket was exhausted by the time he returned to the lift platform with Hannig. For nearly two hours the man had probed Takket, questioning everything from his childhood to his eating habits. The journal had been a blessing, and Takket was deeply thankful he had spent so much of his journey here reading through the tome. Even so, he had to embellish many finer details. He could only hope Hannig—or his master, this Chief Constable Ensellus—had no way of verifying the name of Khantek's childhood pets or the details of his teenage love life.

Eventually, Hannig had given in, though he seemed no less suspicious. Every time he met Takket's gaze, he looked like he was caught between anger and disgust, his left eye twitching. Whether caused by Takket's delayed arrival, his nationality or some unintended slight, Hannig made no attempt to hide his contempt.

The lift reached the top floor. They walked down a corridor lit brightly with Soulshards and out through a pair of glass doors. Stepping onto the open top deck of the tower, they were buffeted by a wind strong enough to stagger Takket. It blew in from the ocean, bringing the smell of brine, blessedly ridding Takket of the lingering stench of bleach—another hour in that interrogation room would have given Takket a migraine.

The sun had set during their meeting but the star-filled sky gave adequate light. Both moons shone down brightly, their glow reflected in the waves of the Angel's Ocean stretching into the distance.

'My men and I will escort you on the crossing,' Hannig shouted over the roaring wind. He started down the wooden walkway that stretched towards the largest airship Takket had ever seen. The metal and glass cabin was the size of a manor, two floors high and four times as wide, hanging under an ellipsoid hydrogen balloon that could easily cover most hamlets. The canvas was dyed in the green and black of Varsen, lit by powerful gas lamps fixed to the tower. If the Imperium was trying to impress the New World with this spire, it seemed the New World was responding with magnificent airships.

Takket followed in Hannig's footsteps. He could

feel the wooden beams creak underfoot, but could hear nothing over the wind.

'Such a long journey just to accompany us would take too much of your time,' Takket shouted. 'It really won't be necessary.'

'Yes, it will,' Hannig replied sternly. Of course. Their interrogation was far from over. The man would monitor Takket during the entire crossing, watching for any potential threat from the Imperium's delegation.

Striding up to the airship, Takket was relieved to see Enara and Yelleck waiting inside. The craft's black-painted frame strained against the steel mooring cables. He stepped onto a plank spanning the gap between the airship and the platform, trying not to allow himself to be disturbed by the endless black below.

He hurried across, breathing a sigh of relief as he set foot on the cabin's soft carpet. The airship was luxurious. The metal frame was painted black and panelled with mahogany. Gas lamps burned brightly, highlighting the gold and marble busts lining the hallway, each with a plaque naming the Arcane-lord of old it represented.

Hannig stepped alongside. 'Your quarters are to the right, front starboard cabin. Your assistants will have to share the room to the rear. If you have need of me, I will be stationed with my men in the port side cabins. For your convenience, the dining hall to the rear will be staffed at all hours. There is an observation room to the front if you wish to pass the time. Upstairs is the crew section—off limits to passengers. Questions?'

'None, thank you.' Takket moved aside to allow a

pair of white-suited Mundanes to hurry over and pull in the boarding plank.

'Good.' Hannig headed to a ladder at one side of the corridor. 'We leave at once. I'll alert the pilots. They're both Arcanes, and you've kept them waiting long enough.'

Hannig lunged his way up the ladder. Takket shook his head. He had anticipated deference—after all, he represented the Imperium. He was going to have to seriously adjust his expectations.

Walking to the front of the airship, Takket shivered. The air may be fresh so far above the surface, but it was bitterly cold. He would need to make use of the heavier winter cloaks he had purchased if he was going to survive the journey without losing any fingers to frostbite.

The carpet of the hallway ended at the entrance to the observation room, which was instead floored by a metal grate. Below the grate hung a glass floor, looking down into the moonlight reflecting off the water. The floor smoothly curved up to merge with the glass walls, allowing a panoramic view.

To his left, there was motion at the mooring cables attached to the tower. Mundane workers braved the winds to detach them, allowing the steel cables to swing free.

The room lurched.

Takket quickly caught his balance. The ship drifted away from the tower, quietly turning to face the sea. The silence was soon broken by a mechanical groan from above, the steel cables slowly being winched up.

Takket stared across the speckled blackness of the Angel's Ocean. He needed sleep. They had scant few days to prepare for their arrival at Varsen, and he would need all the energy he could muster. The days ahead would be filled with meticulous examination of the recovered documents, trying to find some way to achieve the Mundane resistance's lofty goals. Still, he lingered for a few minutes, staring into the night. Somewhere, far beyond the horizon, lay the New World, and his chance to become a legend.

CHAPTER SEVEN

Takket massaged his temples.

For most of the day, he, Enara and Yelleck had been shut in his quarters on the airship, and they seemed no closer to a workable plan. Strewn about the opulent room was everything they had recovered from Khantek's wreckage. Histories, security assessments, dossiers on courtiers, all teeming with information. All pointing to a single conclusion.

The theft was impossible.

Takket pushed himself out of the too-soft couch to pace the room, pulling a bear-fur blanket tight around his shoulders—the sun's glare did little to stave off the altitude's chill. Despite the cold, the master bedroom was a delight. Jade decorated every piece of furniture, from the mahogany bed to the gas lamp fittings to the marble sink. The emerald carpet was so soft that it must have been recently replaced, perhaps for this very journey. Sunlight poured through the windows lining the exterior wall, the glass panes stretching from the carpet to the elaborately engraved ceiling.

They had managed to spread the documents over the entire room—the breakfast table, the numerous couches and the abundant floor space. Other than brief forays to the dining hall for meals, the trio had spent the day working through the papers, trying to gain some insight into how they would accomplish their plot. Takket picked his way between military force estimates and biographies of Haddronius's ancestors, eventually reaching a drinking cabinet carved from a single block of jade.

He perused the offerings, a collection of Imperium liqueurs and Varsen root wine. He opened various glass carafes to sniff their contents. Hints of berries, oak, spices and smoke filled his nose, all backed by the strong smell of alcohol. Longing for something familiar, he poured himself a glass of mountain whisky and swallowed a mouthful.

'I don't see how it can be done,' he announced. 'Every report we have says Haddronius keeps the Pure Shard on his person at all times. Every official function, every private dinner, every time he goes to the damned bathroom, he has it hanging from a necklace. I'm good, but trying to pry a Shard from the neck of an Arcane is suicide.'

'He can't keep it on him at all times,' Yelleck said wearily. He sat beside his sister on one of the room's green velvet couches, the siblings bundled against the chill with down-stuffed quilts from their room.

'Really?' Takket asked, gesturing to the documents littering the space. 'I've yet to come across a single account of him without it. Demons below, if he decided not to wear it for an hour, the court would be in hysterics.'

'He can't wear it at night,' Enara responded. At Takket's blank expression she continued, 'No Mage or Arcane can be in contact with any Soulshard while sleeping.'

Takket frowned. 'Not a superstition I've heard of.'

'Well they don't advertise it to Mundanes, but it's no superstition.'

'You telling me Mages are afraid of getting cut by a stone at night?'

Yelleck sighed. 'No. They're afraid of burning down their mansions.'

'Look at it this way.' Enara closed the folder in her lap. 'Have you ever seen someone talk in their sleep? Have you ever bolted upright from a nightmare, shielding yourself from a dream's phantom? Woken up gasping because you've been holding your breath? Well think about what would happen if a Mage cast magic in their sleep. Multiply that a thousandfold, and you'll see why no Arcane-lord dares sleep with their Pure Shard.'

'A bad dream could cause them to destroy the entire city.'

'Exactly.'

Takket breathed in the smoky aroma of the whisky, thinking.

'This is good,' he said slowly. 'So night is our opening. If Haddronius removes the Shard on his way to bed, that's where we need to strike. We just...'

He trailed off as he heard a faint creak from the wooden ceiling panels. Frowning, he paced the room, examining the religious engravings looming above. He had assumed them to be were purely decorative, but as he looked closer, he noticed holes worked into the recesses of angelic eyes and demonic wings. It was probably just an ingenious ventilation system—despite having the three of them cooped up all day, the room still smelled fresh.

'We just what?' Yelleck asked impatiently.

Takket motioned him to silence and crept around the room, inspecting every ceiling tile. It had been hours since Hannig had bothered them. Each time they left the room, he had appeared. He sat with them at breakfast. They had taken lunch well before midday to avoid him, but he had been waiting. Even when they sat at a table for three, spaced to block him from pulling up a chair, the man had sat near enough to overhear even hushed conversation. Three times that day he had walked into the bedroom, enquiring whether they would be more comfortable in the observation deck. The last time, Takket had snapped at the man, demanding privacy to complete their preparations for arrival. Hannig had appeared to obey.

Suspicious as ever, Takket had inspected the walls for spy holes or vents that could allow eavesdropping. He had moved every piece of furniture, checked behind each marble sculpture, inspected every wall panel and even behind the velvet-padded headboard of the master bed. All he had discovered was the opulence of one of the finest rooms he had ever set foot inside. No suspicious gaps, no mirrored panels, no glass peepholes.

He had even gone over the floor, lifting up the carpet only to find solid metal beneath. Besides, the carpet was too thick to allow any sound through. The room had seemed secure. He had allowed himself to relax, had let the others speak openly of their scheme.

He had not checked the ceiling.

Cursing himself for such an oversight, he moved over to clear a space on the dining table, shifting aside documents and folders. He hopped onto the table via a chair, and stooped under the ceiling.

Each square ceiling panel was a yard wide, resting on a gold-painted metal framework. He eased the panel above him upwards, surprised at its weight. Lifting it just clear of those alongside, Takket slid the panel across. Gingerly, he stood, edging his head into the void above the tiles.

He was greeted by a wind howling through a crawlspace between the airship's two levels, bringing with it the freshness of the outside air. Light trickled in through ventilation grates at the bow and aft of the ship. Down the centre of the craft lay a heavy iron beam, no doubt some key structural support, completely separating this side from Hannig's quarters. The only other way up lay to the rear, where the crawlspace stretched back over the siblings' room.

Takket examined the inch-thick layer of dust that had built up over each tile. Other than where he had slid the ceiling tiles, there was no sign of disturbance. No one had been up here in years, whether to clean or to eavesdrop.

He ducked down, dragging the tile back into place. He was rewarded with a face full of decade-old dust. He gagged at the stench of years of mould and decay touched by a hint of Sharddust. He could see why the crawlspace would not be Hannig's first choice. The man would likely struggle to convince his underlings to drag themselves through that grime.

Still, Takket erred on the side of caution. Hannig not having been up there yet did not mean he would not try later. They could pass off the piles of documents as innocent preparation by envoys, but if their conversation was overheard it would mean their deaths. The only question would be whether Hannig would do it himself, or wait to present the trio to the chief constable.

Lowering himself from the table, Takket crept across the room. He pushed aside the varnished door to the washroom he shared with the siblings and hurried over the marbled floor. Sometime during this journey he would have to take a soak in the exquisite bathtub built into the side, looking out over the clouds. Sometime.

He opened a second door in the bathroom and stepped into Enara and Yelleck's shared room. While not as grand as the master bedroom, it was far from humble. Rows of single beds lined the walls, green velvet blankets over duck-down quilts. Separating the beds were mahogany dressers, embellished with gold and brass, topped with jade. Even the servants of Varsen's guests were afforded luxury.

Takket took a crystal vase from atop a makeup stand in one hand and dragged a stool across the carpet to the room's main door with the other. He positioned the vase on the stool's padded seat, slightly overhanging one edge. Unbalanced enough that anyone opening the door would topple the vase, but not so precarious that unexpected turbulence would send the glass shattering. It was a crude alarm system, but such a contraption had served him well in the past.

He crossed back into his room, dusting his cloak and blanket. Enara and Yelleck peered at him expectantly.

'We're safe to speak now.' Takket sat on a couch beside theirs, leaning back into the overly soft surface. 'But keep your voices down.'

The pair nodded.

'You were talking about taking the Pure Shard while Haddronius slept?' Yelleck prompted.

'Exactly. All I need to do is get into his room at night. I'll spend a few days watching guard patterns, working out the best way in. This might actually be possible. You will need to be able to hide us once we make a move, or have your uprising ready to strike. Haddronius will tear the city apart for that Shard.'

'We can do that,' Enara replied hesitantly, 'but there's a problem.'

Of course there was. 'What is it?'

'Even getting you onto the same *floor* as Haddronius may not be possible,' she explained. 'Haddronius's spire is styled after ancient Magetowers. Only the lower floors have stairs. The entire upper section is accessible only through a central shaft. You need to be able to levitate to reach any of it.'

She drew her finger over a rough plan of the tower. The Imperium's Embassy was at the base, with the bulk of the official chambers. The stairwells only went as high as the throne room, a third of the way up the tower. The rest was a series of quarters for Mages, then Arcanes, junior members of the Varsen dynasty, senior courtiers with magical talent. Near the top lay the Mageguard barracks. The royal family's floor was at the very peak of the spire, fifty floors up.

'So I climb.' Takket shrugged. 'I've climbed the exterior of Magetowers before.'

'None like Varspire Tower,' Yelleck countered. 'The outer wall is polished obsidian, same with the inner shaft. No lone Mundane can hope to get into the upper levels.'

'So I need a Mage,' Takket said with a sigh. The siblings shared a look. 'What is it?'

After a pause, Enara answered, 'It's nothing.'

Takket held her gaze until she explained. 'We've told you we know Mages, ones sympathetic to our cause, but...I doubt they would take such a risk.'

'Besides, it would do no good,' Yelleck added. 'To fend off foreign assassination attempts, the shaft is monitored by Varsen's Mageguard. At least a dozen battle-ready Mages keeping watch at all hours, three times that many waiting in the barracks. There's no way to get past without raising an alarm. Haddronius may not be able to wear the Shard while sleeping, but you can bet your soul to the demons he'll have it nearby. At the first sign of an attack, he'll be armed and ready.'

Takket's headache began to return. 'So I need to be invited.'

With another sigh, he stood, turning to look out of the floor-to-ceiling windows. The sight was surreal. Clouds floated *beneath* him, patching over a sea that stretched uninterrupted to the horizon. There was no land, no islands, no rocks. Despite the volume of traffic that crossed these waters, Takket could not make out a single ship. The Angel's Ocean was so vast that even the thousands of ships crossing back and forth seldom encountered one another.

Even the horizon was remarkable. From this height he could actually see the curvature of the planet. Air travel was an alien world. No matter how strange this was, his gaze was drawn ahead. Somewhere far beyond the horizon lay Varsen—a land more alien even than these skies.

'I'm sure you could arrange an official tour of the royal quarters,' Enara said hesitantly. 'But...'

'But I would be watched the entire time,' Takket

finished. 'I don't just need to be invited up there. I need to be left unattended. Not just for the theft itself. I need time to explore for escape routes, watch guard patterns, investigate security mechanisms. I need unrestricted access to that floor for days. Weeks. If this Chief Constable Ensellus is half as thorough as Hannig, I doubt that's going to happen.'

'Ensellus is far worse than Hannig,' Yelleck said grimly. 'He's served Haddronius his entire life. He worships the man. There have been dozens of attempts on Haddronius's life—from rivals in court, to members of the Free Circle, to foreign powers making a move. None have even come close to the Arcane-lord. Ensellus sniffs out threats to the throne like a garrick sniffs out carrion. Hannig is an amateur in comparison.'

Great. For a moment he had allowed himself to believe that this was truly achievable, that he could pull off the theft, change a nation. Change the world. Now they had stumbled back to step one. If he could not get to Haddronius's floor, he could not steal the Shard.

He examined the window panes, trying not to focus on the ache behind his eyes. Ice crystals grew from the corners and bloomed from minute cracks, patterning the smooth glass. Tiny droplets condensed from a passing cloud, only to be blown by the winds into crystallising trails.

Yelleck broke the silence, voice hopeful. 'Ensellus might not allow you onto the floor unattended, but he's not the highest ranked person at court.'

'I don't think I can convince Haddronius to overrule his security chief and let me wander around his bedroom. I'm good, but no thief's that good.'

'Not Haddronius,' Yelleck persisted. 'His daughter. Seduce the daughter, move into her room, and you'll have all the access you could possibly require.'

Takket thought back to the dossiers of the royal family. 'I thought Valena was married. I doubt her husband would look too kindly on her taking a Mundane lover.'

'Not the heir,' Yelleck explained. 'The youngest of the three children.'

Takket took the file Yelleck handed over and read the name at the top. 'Hekaena Varsen.'

'Hekaena,' Yelleck repeated with a sly smile. 'Twenty-nine years old but unmarried. The extra child, not required to produce heirs for the Varsen line, free to pursue her own whims. As a close family member of Haddronius, her rooms are on his floor.'

'Sounds perfect,' Takket said dryly. 'The only problem is, Khantek is a mere Mundane. Hekaena is an Arcane. Few self-respecting Mages allow themselves to become involved with a Mundane these days. An Arcane would not give me a dance at a ball, let alone take me back to her room. Repeatedly.'

'Hekaena's different,' Yelleck pressed. 'She has a soft spot of Mundanes, always has. She spends more time in the city than the spire, building houses for Mundanes, feeding orphans of criminals. She's something of a legend among the Mundanes of Varsen. If any Arcane could fall for a Mundane, it's her.'

'And you're not just any Mundane,' Enara added. 'You are Khantek Fredeen, child of Mages, self-made man, now the representative of the entire Imperium.

109

That's quite the conversation opener. Besides, I'm sure this won't be the first time you've talked your way into a girl's bed.'

Takket just grunted, sitting back down to read through the file. The document focused mainly on the rifts between Hekaena and the rest of her family. It seemed her help of the Mundanes had caused more than a few political upsets over the years, upsets that the Imperium had designs on exploiting. If anyone would spurn the wishes of Chief Constable Ensellus and bring a Mundane to the royal floor, it was Hekaena.

'We still have a problem,' Takket rubbed his head again. 'I'm still no Mage. Once I get the Shard, how do I get out without being burned to a crisp?'

Enara and Yelleck shared another look. 'We may be able to help there,' Enara said. 'While we might not be able to convince one of our Mage allies to help you storm Haddronius's rooms, I'm sure we can persuade one to wait at the base of the central shaft. You let us know when the theft is going to occur, and we'll have them in place. You can't levitate, but you *can* fall. Just jump down the shaft with the Shard. The Mage will be there to catch you.'

'You trust your Mage can slow me in time?'

Enara nodded. 'If it's one thing all New World Mages are skilled at, it's stopping objects hurtling towards them at high speeds. If they can stop a bullet mid-battle, they can catch you.'

'It's perfect,' Yelleck continued. 'We'll convince the Mage by offering them the Pure Shard. When they burn it, they'll become an Arcane immediately. We won't need to hide the Shard, won't need to worry about pursuit. We'll start the revolution right there, at the foot of Varspire Tower. Strike at the heart of Haddronius's power base.'

Takket did not much like the sound of trusting his life to the skills of some Mage, but self-preservation should give the man an added incentive to lower him to the ground gently. If a Soulshard was subjected to too much force, it would shatter. Rock-sized Shards gave a blast powerful enough to level a room, batons could bring down buildings. Who knew what a Pure Shard could accomplish.

He leafed through the file, finding an artist's impression of Hekaena at the back. She seemed relatively plain, long in the face, her hair stretching down to her waist. He was caught by her eyes, the vivid red irises of an Arcane. Still, it would be easy enough to believe that he, a mere Mundane, could become smitten with her. It was a story sappy enough for a romance written in the Imperium—a humble Mundane and a powerful Arcane falling for each other, love overcoming the divide of their birth. Those novels, however, seldom ended in the Mundane betraying the Arcane and undermining her family's power.

'This is our route in,' Takket said slowly. 'I seduce Hekaena, move into her room. I keep the relationship going long enough to plan the theft. Then, I wait for Haddronius to sleep, break into his room, steal the Shard and we flee the tower.'

Yelleck grinned. 'We'll be ready. The moment you hand over the Shard, we can mobilise, strike the spire before they realise what is happening, make them listen to our demands.'

Enara nodded emphatically. 'Sounds like we have a plan.'

The siblings rose to hug one another, then excitedly set about discussing details. Takket stood to stare out of the window. They had a plan. It relied only on him managing to seduce the daughter of one of the most powerful men in the world, keep her trust while he snooped around her father's sanctuary, find a way to gain access to an Arcane-lord's room while he slept, then put his faith in a Mage catching him from a fifty-storey fall.

What could possibly go wrong?

CHAPTER EIGHT

Takket smoothed the maroon silk of his cloak collar in the bathroom mirror. Night had fallen an hour earlier, gas lamps brightly illuminating the white marble tiles. He felt refreshed. Having agreed on a strategy, there had been little left to accomplish during the journey. He had slept in on the plush bed, comforted by the ship's gentle rocking. The bath had been a highlight. He had lain there for hours, soaking in fragrant oils, staring out of the window while he flicked through Khantek's journal.

With nothing left to plan, their preparations for Varspire had shifted to solidifying their cover stories. This mainly involved pouring back over the mounds of files and binders, no longer searching for a security flaw, but simply absorbing the local politics. Khantek was the Imperium's representative to its closest ally. Takket would be expected to have mastered everything from dining formalities to the details of centuries of border wars and assassinations on that volatile continent.

He had spent much of the afternoon updating Khantek's journal. Given enough time, Hannig or Ensellus would no doubt gain access to his private possessions. The entries abruptly ending two weeks before arriving at Portspire would arouse suspicion.

Takket had picked up where the late diplomat had left off, discussing their fictitious tale of the emergency landing just past the Crater Desert, the hassle of finding a Shard carriage—or any civilised transport—in the hinterlands. He had to bend the truth after their arrival at Portspire, but did not hold back when describing his dislike of Hannig—the journal had to be believable, and Takket doubted anyone had written a kind word about the constable.

Takket attempted to match the dead man's penmanship and conversational writing style. If nothing else, it was vital to immerse himself in Khantek's mindset. For much of the past two days, they had managed to sequester themselves away from Hannig's prying eyes, but such privacy would be rare in Varspire. Takket would need to act like Khantek when he rose in the morning, speak like Khantek over meals, negotiate like Khantek at court. He needed to become Khantek.

'Are you ready?' Enara asked, leaning against the tiled wall.

'It's just dinner.' He leaned forward on the marble sink to inspect his reflection, the textured surface cold to the touch. His hair was smoothed back, still partially damp from the bath. A faint cut marred his jawline where he had slipped with his razor. Shaving in this cold was arduous. At least his eyes were not as gaunt as they had looked during the journey to Portspire.

'Just dinner with an Arcane,' Enara corrected. 'It's rare for a ship's pilot to invite anyone to dine with them, let alone a Mundane.'

'But, as you like to remind me, Khantek is no common Mundane.' Takket grinned, satisfied that his appearance had just the right level of dignity. 'I'll be fine.'

Enara smiled hesitantly as he walked into his bedroom. 'Angels watch over you.'

'It's just dinner.' Takket picked his way over the stacks of paper. The piles were better organised now, but just as spread out. It looked a mess, but he knew where every dossier lay, where to turn to find family histories or trade summaries. He could only hope he would have the freedom to lay everything out in the embassy.

Taking a breath to settle himself, he opened the varnished door to the hallway, almost stepping into Hannig's looming form.

'You're late,' the constable snapped.

By one minute, Takket thought with a glance to the ornate clock inside his room. Forcing a smile, he gave a more measured response. 'My apologies. If you're here to guide me, I know the way to the dining room.'

Hannig's eye twitched. 'I'm here to join you. We're both eating with Arcane Annis Varsen.'

Lovely. That explained the freshly ironed creases on the man's uniform. 'Varsen? I was not aware we were being piloted by nobility.'

'A distant relation,' Hannig muttered, leading the way towards the rear of the ship. 'She shares a great grandfather with Haddronius. She's still a Varsen, however, and you will show the corresponding deference.'

'I do not need lessons in protocol from a security officer.' Takket kept his voice level. Khantek would never accept such a patronising tone. Mundane or no, he was the Imperium's representative. Hannig swallowed a retort, and they strode down the hall in silence.

A pair of white-suited Mundanes jumped aside, abandoning their efforts to polish the wooden wall panels, and bowed to the passing Mage. Takket was used to seeing a similar response in the Imperium, but never quite so hurried, so tense. The men stood perfectly still, holding their breaths, eyes downcast towards the green carpet. In his career, Takket had seen enough fear to recognise it in their faces.

The men were terrified of Hannig.

Takket frowned, puzzled at what could merit such a response. Hannig was certainly not an easy man to get along with, even with the title of Envoy of the Imperium to shelter Takket. He could only imagine how Hannig behaved towards Mundanes who lacked diplomatic protection.

Another pair of white-suited Mundanes pulled aside the glass doors to the dining hall. What the hall lacked in size, it made up for in grandeur. Its four round tables were covered in pure white sheets, topped with silver tableware and floral centrepieces. The latter saturated the room with perfume. Three glass walls looked out over the rear of the airship, a mirror of the bow's observation room. A Soulshard chandelier supplemented the gas lamps with its dancing red glow.

Takket walked over the patterned marble floor to the one occupied table, tucked into the rear corner. The woman who sat on one of its plush chairs wore a jacket of black and green silk, trimmed with lapels and gold braids to give her a distinctively militaristic look. Her dark hair was pulled back from her tanned skin into a bun. As he approached, she met his gaze with the bright red eyes of an Arcane.

116

Takket bowed low, hand over heart. 'Arcane, it is an honour.'

She smirked before speaking in a heavy New World accent. 'Please, Khantek, just call me Annis. Hannig's the only one to stand on ceremony aboard my ship. Sit, sit.'

While Hannig flushed, Takket took a chair beside Annis. Like everything on the airship, the chair was overly soft. Takket found himself sinking back into the upholstery and had to adjust himself to gain a halfway respectable pose. His pillows at home were firmer.

'I hope you don't mind,' Annis said once he had stopped shifting, 'but I ordered for us. My chef does a fantastic Varsen roast.'

'I look forward to it.' In truth Takket was not hungry, having done nothing more strenuous all day than walk to the bathroom.

At a signal from Annis, a gaggle of Mundanes marched over from one of the windowed walls. The men and women filled glasses with Varsen root wine, then laid out brimming plates. Takket examined the meal before him. Carrots, parsnips, potatoes—and other root vegetables Takket could not identify— swam in gravy, well coated in sprigs of various herbs and spices. Dominating the plate was a thick cut of meat, its edge cooked to charcoal. He breathed in the complex aroma. Varsen chefs were certainly fond of their spices.

'Beef?' Takket guessed. It was hard to tell under the sauce drowning the meat.

'Right you are,' Annis said with a grin. 'Do you know how hard it is to find a decent cut of beef in the Imperium? Costs us twice as much to stock up for the return journey.'

Takket cut into the steak and popped a chunk into his mouth. The scorched meat was tough, and would have been dry if not for the generous helping of gravy, but it was delightfully flavoured. Takket could only identify a couple of the multitude of spices glazing the meat. The exotic flavours were quickly overpowered by a burning aftertaste, and he was soon reaching for his glass of root wine. The sour liquid only brought sharper pain.

He cleared his throat, trying to disguise his discomfort. 'Yes, most livestock in the Imperium are used exclusively for the Shard industry.'

'Ah, of course,' Annis replied. 'Your ban on human immolation must put quite the strain on the rest of your economy. We, at least, have the freedom to raise animals for the purpose the angel's intend—to be delicious.'

'It's not a ban,' Takket corrected as the woman bit into another chunk of beef. 'It's just rare.'

'Hmm,' she responded, a gleam in her eye. 'And summer snowstorms are not impossible, just rare.'

Hannig narrowed his eyes across the table. 'How many Mundanes *were* turned into Shards in the Imperium last year?'

'Two,' Takket replied, recalling one of the many official files. If Hannig wanted to catch him out, he would have to pose more challenging questions.

'So,' Annis said with a full mouth. Certainly not as refined as expected. 'How are you enjoying my ship?'

'The journey has been fantastic,' Takket replied. 'The view over the ocean is quite something. It's enough to make a diplomat envy your calling.'

She gave him an appraising look, then grinned. 'Good answer. Just don't let that envy twist your soul. Wouldn't want your next life to be as a demon, would you? That is what you Circlists believe, right? Mundanes and Arcanes alike ascend to the ranks of angels and demons when they die?'

'That's what *Unism* Circlists believe,' Takket replied slowly, not liking how Hannig's eye twitched at his response. 'But yes, the Imperium officially follows that doctrine.'

'How you don't lose track of all those sects is beyond me,' Annis said. 'Varsen is easier. Everyone's Scalist. Simple.'

Takket frowned. 'I was under the impression that there is a growing Circlist community in Varsen.'

She waved her hand dismissively. 'Just Mundanes mostly. A few Mages. Everyone who counts is Scalist. No offence.'

Takket bowed his head. 'None taken.' It came as no surprise that an Arcane would neglect to include Mundanes when referring to the entire population.

She smiled, taking a sip of her wine. 'At any rate, I'm glad you're enjoying the flight. Must be better than your journey to Portspire. I hear your airship had some difficulties.'

Takket swallowed another spice-soaked hunk of meat. He was starting to become accustomed to the heat, even if he had to repeatedly blow his nose on the linen napkin. 'Yes. The pilots had to turn back after crossing the Crater Desert. They dropped me off nearby to make my way via less exciting transportation.'

'Sounds like Imperium engineering at its best.'

Annis grinned. 'That's what's wrong with everything from your continent. Too much thought goes into form, not enough on function.' Takket had to bite his tongue not to point out that the beautiful room they occupied was hardly austere. 'What was wrong with the ship anyway?'

Takket shrugged, yet again relaying the fable. 'Something about one of the Shards starting to break down. The pilot was concerned it would fail and explode.'

The clatter of cutlery on porcelain ceased. Annis squinted at him, sucking her teeth in thought. 'The Shards? Your pilots were Arcanes, right?'

'Of course.' Mages would burn through too many Shards getting any but the smallest messenger airships to move through the skies. Most were piloted by pairs of Arcanes, taking shifts to keep the craft aloft. It made the airships prohibitively expensive for all but the richest or most distinguished of passengers.

'That makes no sense,' Annis said. 'When a Shard is poorly cut, it burns to dust the instant an Arcane draws from it. Arcanes don't wear down Shards. That's what makes us Arcanes, not mere Mages.' She waved dismissively at Hannig. 'The Shards on this craft have been going for a good ten years. The canvas balloon or steel frame will give way long before the Soulshards.'

The Mundane servers returned, replacing the half-emptied plates with bowls containing some sort of pastry dripping in syrup. Before Takket could investigate further, he realised his dining partners were staring at him, Annis in confusion, Hannig with eye-twitching suspicion.

'Yes,' Hannig said slowly. 'Do please go over the

story once more. I would love an expert's take on your unfortunate journey.'

Takket kept the panic from his face. He had repeated the agreed-upon lie word for word. This is exactly what Enara and Yelleck had told him to say. Demons below, he would have to improvise. 'The pilot said something about indications on the Shard, I didn't follow exactly.'

'And that was enough to have you abandon the journey?' Hannig probed.

'The pilot was convincing.' Takket's mind raced. 'He said it reminded him of a story from his youth—a friend of his was involved in a similar air crash. Said a Shard had failed, pulverising the flight cabin.'

Annis shook her head. 'As I said, Shards don't fail like that. Demons below, maybe the Imperium really is falling behind in its isolation. What made the pilot assume the crash had been caused by Shard failure?'

Takket thought back to the real crash site. He could still see the twisted metal, shattered glass, broken bodies. 'He said the investigators could tell from the wreckage. The cabin was blown apart from the inside. Metal twisted *outward*, not simply crushed from a landing. Something exploded inside the cabin.'

The other two shared a frown. 'I suppose the pilot may have done it on purpose,' Hannig said thoughtfully. 'Burned the Shard to unleash an explosion. Bit of an extreme way to commit suicide.'

Takket shook his head. Could Khantek have been killed by a suicidal Arcane pilot? That seemed less likely than some freak Shard accident. 'You really think that would happen?'

Annis shrugged. 'Maybe, but I've never heard of

such an occurrence. It almost sounds like...no, that's impossible.'

'What?' Takket pressed.

'Just the description you gave,' she continued. 'The cabin blown out from the inside. That used to happen in the New World, but certainly never by accident.'

'I don't understand.'

'In the New World, we don't have the Imperium's luxury of everlasting peace. Airships make fine targets for foreign powers wishing to make a point. It didn't take long for someone to realise they could magically propel a Shard at the cabin. With some practice, even a Mage can get a Shard on target. They would shatter as they hit the metal frame. If one went through a window before hitting the ceiling, it would blow the cabin outwards. Sounds a lot like what your pilot's friend experienced. In the New World we're all trained for it. Part of a pilot's duty is keeping their senses on the air around the airship, ready to deflect any incoming projectiles.' She jutted a thumb over her shoulder, towards the starlit horizon. 'But in the Imperium, with your centuries of tranquillity, I doubt it's even occurred to your Arcanes. Even Imperium pilots over the New World would be perfectly safe. None of the Arcanedoms would dare risk the ire of the Imperium. Poor bastard never saw it coming.'

'You're saying...'

'I'm saying an airship can be brought down by a Shard exploding, but it's never an accident. Sounds like someone on that airship pissed off the wrong Mage.' A chill descended over Takket as Annis continued. 'Well, mystery solved, I suppose. Someone brought down your pilot's friend. Your pilot got unnerved out and overreacted to some Shard's imagined defect. I'd suggest you send a report home. Angels above, the Imperium's in trouble if your pilots are that naive.'

Takket could only grunt in acknowledgement. The sickly sweet dessert was going cold in his bowl, but his stomach was churning.

Khantek had been murdered.

After half an hour of forcing conversation and choking down dessert, Takket managed to escape the dining hall and return to his quarters. He leaned back on the varnished mahogany door, trying to sort the thoughts that churned in his head.

Someone had brought down Khantek's airship. It was no fortuitous accident, as Yelleck and Enara had claimed. Someone with magical ability had gone out of their way to cause the crash. But who? Why?

The first explanation he had entertained was a political assassination. Over the years, Khantek had made enough enemies in court—everyone did—but bringing down one of the Imperium's airships to exact revenge seemed extreme. If anything would lead to a death sentence in the Imperium, it was that level of treachery. Besides, if someone had wanted Khantek dead, why had they not investigated the wreckage to ensure the target had been killed? Enara and Yelleck had said their contacts had reached the craft soon after the crash, and had made no mention of anyone else approaching the site.

Takket shook his head, pacing his deserted quarters, picking his way over stacks of documents. With the darkness outside, the windows lining the outer wall had become mirrors, reflecting a distorted picture of the luxurious room. He moved around, dimming the gas lamps, plunging the chamber into a peaceful gloom.

The attackers may have simply assumed everyone on board had died, but why had the Mundane resistance's scouts seen no sign of strange Mages near the Crater? They must keep a close eye out for intruders approaching their hideout, or they should at least have noticed a glowing Shard hurtling towards the craft.

Perhaps Khantek had not been the target. The explosion had been centred in the crew cabin. Maybe it was an assassination aimed at one of the Arcane pilots. They were higher ranked than any Mundane, even the Imperium's Envoy. From his limited experience with Arcanes, Takket found it easy to believe one could offend another enough to warrant murder. Annis had indicated that a skilled Mage could have easily picked out the crew's cabin over that of the passengers. At least the theory explained why they had not needed to investigate further—after seeing the crew cabin ripped apart, there would be no need to check for survivors.

Takket sighed, throwing off his cloak. The thing stank of Varsen spices now. Thankfully, his room smelled of the fresh air blowing through the crawlspace, not the pungent perfume of the floral arrangements in the dining hall. As pleasant as it had seemed at first, the smell had begun to wear on Takket, contaminating the taste of every mouthful of food, every sip of root wine.

Even if a pilot had been the target, why had the

Mundane resistance not noticed a battle-ready Mage launching Shards at the airship? Were the people that Takket was working with truly so incompetent that they could spot an airship in danger, but not the glowing rock slamming into its side? Had the scouts falsified their report?

Or had Enara and Yelleck lied?

He turned towards the door leading to the shared bathroom. How much did he actually know about his companions? If their story of how the airship had crashed was a fabrication, what other falsehoods had they been feeding him?

Takket sighed, climbing into the too-soft bed, pulling the heavy covers tight against the cold. Nothing made sense. He had experienced deceptive employers in the past, but none Antellok had vouched for. The man prided himself on knowing everyone's motivations, enabling him to better manipulate people. Surely he would have known if Enara and Yelleck were trustworthy. He had never led Takket wrong in the past. What could he gain from risking his greatest thief with traitorous employers? Antellok played the long game. He would never throw away an asset for short-term gain.

But Takket was not longer an asset.

He stared into the black recesses of the ceiling's carving—angels holding out helping hands, demons tricking mortals with false promises. He should not be asking what Antellok would gain, but what the man had to lose. Takket was going to retire, never again to earn so much as a flake for Antellok. If Takket succeeded in this task, Antellok would get his share of the riches. If Takket died...well, the fence had not lost anything. Demons below, he had Takket's fortune for safekeeping. Sure, the man would not steal anything given to him in confidence, but if Takket died? It was not like Takket had any next of kin who could inherit. No, the money would stay with Antellok. Whether Takket succeeded or died in the attempt, the fence would get his hands on a small fortune.

Takket's mind went back over their conversation in Drakenport. The entire time, there had been that damned glint in the fence's eye. It could just have been the amusement of pushing on Takket's nerves.

Or it could have been joy at goading Takket into one last heist.

It had been all too easy for the man—he prided himself on knowing everyone's motivations, Takket's included. His mocking had not been good humour or frustration. He had known Takket could not live with his final heist being a failure. He had known just what to say to twist Takket to his will one final time.

And Takket had blindly obeyed.

It had taken Takket far too long to realise he could put no faith in Antellok's recommendation. After a lifetime of lying and manipulating others, Takket had allowed himself to be easily played. Now he was on an airship, heading for a foreign continent, his life in the hands of two complete strangers. No longer the master trickster, he was now caught in someone else's web. He would be damned if he would wait helplessly for them to pounce.

CHAPTER NINE

At sunrise, Takket gave up on sleep. The sense of urgency had returned. Once more he had to unearth secrets and concoct schemes, but the targets were no longer in distant Varspire but in the next room. By dawn tomorrow, they would be able to see the rugged landscape of the New World. Between now and then, he had to discover his co-conspirators' secrets.

He had forced his breakfast down in tense silence. He could not question Enara and Yelleck with Hannig skulking at a nearby table. Dread of arriving in the New World without uncovering the siblings' plan was eclipsed by the terror the constable elicited.

Returning to his quarters, Takket faced a different obstacle. He could not simply start throwing accusations. If Enara and Yelleck planned to betray him, he could not reveal his discovery of their plot. If he was to pry into their treachery, he had to be subtle.

After the three had settled onto couches to read through dossiers, Takket spoke up. 'I think we have a good handle on the court for now. I want to know more about this resistance movement of yours.'

Yelleck frowned. 'The Free Circle? Why?'

'I like to know who I'm in business with. Who I'm trusting with my life.'

'Believe me,' Yelleck replied, turning back to his documents, 'the less you know, the better for everyone.'

'Better for you, maybe,' Takket countered. 'But being in the dark doesn't help me in the slightest.'

Yelleck glanced around nervously. 'It may be best not to discuss this here.'

'Why? Hannig? If he's listening in to our conversations, we're condemned already.'

Before Yelleck could respond, Enara patted his arm. 'It's alright,' she said. 'It's a reasonable request. What would you like to know?'

'How about we start with numbers. How many of you are there?'

'I honestly can't say,' she replied. 'We keep membership on a need-to-know basis. We don't exactly have a roster of who's planning to overthrow the government. It's complicated by varying levels of involvement. Some people are content giving us funds or allowing the use of their homes. Others opt for a more direct role, joining raids, smuggling out prisoners. Still, I'd put our number of dedicated members in the thousands. Not a huge number given the millions in Varsen, I know, but enough to lead the revolt. Trust me when I say that every Mundane in Varsen will flock to us once we disarm the Arcane-lord.'

Takket gazed out of the window. The pink morning sky had brightened to a clear cyan, dotted with clouds. Far below, a cargo liner made its way eastwards to the Imperium, the massive vessel barely visible among the waves, just a maroon speck against the ocean. Inside its hold would likely be an Arcane's ransom worth of Shards, guarded by a small army of Mages paid handsomely for their service. Up here, the priceless vessel seemed so insignificant.

'Thousands.' He turned back to Enara. 'Must have taken quite some time to build up such a network. How long have you existed for?'

'The Free Circle or resisting Mundanes?' she asked.

'Both.'

'Well, we've called ourselves the Free Circle for about thirty years now, from when Circlism really started to spread among Mundanes of the New World. But there have been Mundanes resisting Arcanes in Varsen since the start of that demon-spawn of a dynasty. Before the Pure Shard allowed the first Varsen to rebel against her masters, Mundanes resisted the Kilroth dynasty. Before them, Santona. Before them, the Imperium. There have been Mundanes resisting in the New World since Magelord Grethin brought us there a thousand years ago.'

'Quite a history.'

Enara shrugged. 'Mundanes have despised their treatment since the first Mages.'

'And in all that time, you've never succeeded?'

'Before the Devastation, before firearms, there was little Mundanes could do to threaten a Mage. Mundanes achieved some limited success during that chaotic time as Mages tore the land apart killing one another, but then the third Pure Shard was discovered, the first Arcane ascended. By the time rifles improved and technology caught up to the point an army of Mundanes could face an Arcane, all Arcane-lords had armed themselves with Pure Shards. We could wait for the angels to give us some miraculous new technology that allows Mundanes to challenge a Pure-Shard-armed Arcane...or we take their weapon from them.'

Takket could find no flaw in her logic, so let the topic drop—for now.

He turned to the room. Sunlight scattered through the windows lining the outer wall, the thick glass casting rainbow patterns over marble sculptures and varnished wood panels. At its low angle, the sunlight caught motes of dust floating around the room, more slipping through the ceiling vents with each gust of fresh wind. The gusts, at least, kept the air smelling clean, even if he still had to bundle himself with fur blankets to ward off the chill.

He needed to focus his questions on the crash, where he knew they had lied. 'Your base in the Crater Desert, seems to me that getting Mundanes to the Imperium is a hell of an effort to hide a few people.'

Enara nodded. 'It is. We use it as a last resort. We move people there only if there's no other way to save their lives. More often, we move them between Varsen's cities, occasionally to other New World Arcanedoms, but they're not much better.'

'And you're never been bothered by the Mages that visit the desert?'

Enara smirked. 'There are only a handful of Mages that ever visit, maybe a couple a month. It's an arduous trip for those unused to hardship. Mostly, they just look from the encircling ridge then leave. Few ever descend into the crater, and none deep enough to reach our base. You were there. Would you want to linger in that dust?'

The memory was enough to make his skin itch, recalling the sting of Sharddust. 'No, I suppose not. So you don't keep an eye out for approaching Mages?'

'Why would we?' Enara asked. 'It's safer to have

everyone hidden in the base. Dispatching scouts would just increase the chances of someone spotting them and investigating.'

'So it was a complete coincidence that your men saw Khantek's airship?'

'Yes. As we said, it was a group returning with provisions. The angels do seem to bless us. The group caught a glimpse of an explosion, saw the airship tumbling from the sky.'

Takket thoughtfully ran his fingers across the couch's plush armrest, feeling the green velvet shift effortlessly. Perhaps Yelleck and Enara had not lied, but simply been mistaken. A Mage could have targeted the airship, perhaps one with a grudge against the pilots. If they were not keeping watch, the resistance members could have easily missed the flying Shard, their focus on their krilt's footsteps. They looked up at the flash of the explosion, and assumed it to be an internal accident.

Was Takket just being paranoid? It seemed like an easy error to make. Mundanes with little knowledge of airships could easily jump to the conclusion that the crash was some accident, not a deadly plot. Maybe it was time to relax and focus on the heist.

'What made you think the airship was brought down by Shard failure?' he asked offhandedly.

Yelleck frowned. 'A blast that big? From inside the airship? Sounds like a Shard to me.'

'But a Shard failing?' Takket pressed. 'I've never heard of such a thing.'

'Well,' Yelleck replied, 'how often have you travelled by airship?'

'Good point. Does this sort of thing happen often?'

Yelleck nodded. 'More often than you'd think. There was a case just last year in the New World.'

Takket frowned, suspicion returning. 'An airship brought down by Shard failure?'

'Oh yes. Was up in Kilroth. Happens every now and then.'

Suppressing panic, Takket looked between the two. There was the lie. If an airship had gone down last year due to Shard failure, Annis would certainly have known.

'And it was definitely an accident?'

Yelleck splayed his hands in confusion. 'What else?'

'I've heard of instances where airships were brought down on purpose. Mages launching Shards as projectiles.'

Briefly, the two New Worlders' expressions betrayed their fear and anger. There was no mistake here, no simple misinterpretation of a mangled wreck. These two knew that an airship could be brought down.

'Oh, sure, it happens,' Enara said after only a moment's hesitation. 'But never in the Imperium. I've seen debris from such attacks myself. Khantek's airship looked nothing like that.'

Takket nodded and hummed an acceptance, not believing a word. The conversation turned to how to pack the mountain of dossiers for arrival at Varspire, but his mind was elsewhere. They were lying to him. But why? He was ever more convinced that they were behind Khantek's crash—no doubt one of their Mage allies was hidden in their base—but why lie about it? Killing a diplomat seemed a small step compared to open revolution.

What other secrets did they hide?

Half an hour had passed since Takket made excuses to chase Yelleck and Enara from his room. After dusk fell, he had claimed he needed to get an early night ahead of their arrival at Varspire. As much as he genuinely needed to rest, he knew he would get no sleep that night.

Sounds of packing still echoed through the bathroom door. Enara and Yelleck worked away, sorting the documents into boxes, tidying laundry and organising the travelling cases for a quick departure.

Takket sat in darkness, perched on the smooth surface of the wooden table, its cold seeping through his velvet bathrobe to bite at his thighs. He watched the light filtering around the door frame, tracking the passage of the two conspirators by their shadows.

Satisfied that they were both out of the bathroom, he stood and traced his fingers along the engraved images of the ceiling tile above him, feeling the icy breeze creep through. Easing the wooden panel upwards, Takket shifted it to rest on the dust that carpeted the crawlspace. He reached through the opening, his fingers gripping the metal supports that held the ceiling tiles. With a heave, he slunk into the void above.

Settling face first over the thick dust, Takket tried not to gag at the age-old grime under his hands. A shiver shook his body, the fresh cold wind stabbing his skin. He wore only the velvet bathrobe, taken from his room. It offered some padding for his knees as they rested in thick filth, but was too thin to ward off the frigid air. Whatever he wore up here would become caked in dirt. At least the bathrobe was not his, so could easily be washed and left drying in the bathtub.

He edged through the crawlspace, softly placing each hand and knee, careful not to make a sound. If caught, even the great Takket would never be able to explain this snooping.

Despite his efforts, he could not help but to disturb the dust. The fresh breeze was soon choked by the stench of mould. He was surrounded by a decade of tattered threads, rotten food, skin flakes, and angels-know-what. He tried to breathe through his mouth to lessen the odour, only to get a mouthful of the mildew-filled debris.

Pinpricks of light guided him onwards—the air holes worked into each tile allowed through the glow from Enara and Yelleck's gas lamps. He came to the first pool of light, suppressing a grimace as he lowered his eye towards the grime, peering through the hole into the empty bathroom. A minute of breathing ageing mould later, he had edged the next few yards to a hole overlooking the siblings' room, but could not make out either occupant.

He shuffled his way down the crawlspace, careful not to knock any dust through the holes. Hands and knees aching, he reached an opening near the centre of the room and peeked through. Below, he could see Enara and Yelleck, steadily stacking away piles of paper into leather suitcases.

'Have you seen the building plans?' Enara asked, her voice muffled through the wood and dust.

'Second bed on the left, just next to the biographies.'

Enara moved out of sight. Yelleck turned to a pile of clothes, neatly folding them before he tucked them into a case.

'Are we forgetting anything?' Enara asked.

'I don't think so,' Yelleck replied. 'We've got all the documents secured. This is the last of the clothing. Takket has the official correspondence. *Khantek*, I suppose I should be calling him now.'

'Everything seems set for tomorrow. Angels above, this might actually work.'

'Let's not get ahead of ourselves. We've a long way to go yet. This was the easy part of this whole mission.'

'True.' Enara strolled back into view with a stack of papers. 'Still, can you imagine if we succeeded?'

The pair paused to look at one another. Yelleck answered cheerfully, 'It would change everything.'

They shook off the moment, returning to packing. Takket stifled a sigh. What was he trying to achieve? He knew the pair had lied. No good would come from spending the night eavesdropping. They would not say anything incriminating. For all they knew, he could be listening through his door.

He could not become preoccupied with reasons for their deception. The fact that they had lied—repeatedly—made abandoning the heist the only sane course of action. These were precious minutes he could spend planning his escape. If there was ever a time to cut and run, it was now. Getting out of Varsen alive would be a challenge. If he abandoned these two, he would get no help from the Free Circle in returning to the Imperium. Worse, the pair could expose him if they suspected betrayal. He needed to think.

He started to turn around, a laborious exercise while trying not to send grime pouring into the room below.

Enara's voice drifted through the dirt. 'Wait, where are our Soulshards?'

Takket stilled. *Soulshards*? They had already given him all their Shards. Yelleck had been explicit that Takket had to be the one to handle their money. The siblings had not so much as touched a Shard since they met, had simply handed him a satchel to cover their expenses.

'Over by the drawer, here.'

Yelleck moved out of sight. Takket silently cursed, scurrying over the tiles and rotting dirt to follow. He winced at every creak of the metal frame, every scuff of his knees across the muck, sure that at any moment the pair would look up accusingly.

He came to another gap in the woodwork. Below, Yelleck fished in through a drawer in one of the jade-topped dressers. Had they kept back half their wealth? Perhaps they merely distrusted the thief they barely knew. Perhaps they needed funds to flee Varspire after fulfilling their hidden agenda.

'Here they are,' Yelleck called. The pouch he pulled out was surprisingly small, a canvas sack barely large enough to fit two rocks. Takket had imagined a concealed fortune. A pair of Soulshard rocks could buy a month's food for a Mundane, but given the expenses so far, it seemed a pittance.

Unfastening the pouch, Yelleck poured the contents—two Soulshard rocks—onto his palm. The moment they touched his skin, their gentle glow burned brightly, casting a brilliant red light over their room. Takket stared, mouth open in shock. Soulshards never reacted to a Mundane's touch, only to a magic user.

Yelleck was a Mage.

Mind racing, Takket dropped into his room, sliding the tile back into place. Yelleck and Enara had gone to bed shortly after checking on the Soulshards, giving Takket time to make his way back through the crawlspace undetected.

He stumbled into the bathroom, locking the adjoining door. Feeling around the smooth marble wall, he located a gas lamp. He turned its brass knob, a glow blooming over the room. Light reflected from the white tiled walls onto his robes, highlighting the grime he was caked in.

He threw off the ruined nightgown and rushed to the sink, splashing cold water on his face. Staring at the mirror, he watched the liquid drain away, collecting dust in black trails across his skin.

Yelleck was a *Mage*.

Takket tried to get his head around the revelation. The man who had so long railed against the treatment of Mundanes, the man who claimed that his aim was to form the first Mundane republic since the Mundane Era, the man who had sat across from Takket for weeks, was a Mage. Magical talent was inherited. That meant Enara too was likely a Mage. Although it was not guaranteed for a child of a Mage to have magical talent, exceptions were a rare disappointment.

That is, if they *were* siblings. They looked related, but who knew what Mages could do to their bodies? Was there truth in anything they had told him? If they really were part of the Free Circle, they must be one of the group's few Mage allies. Could they be leading the revolutionaries? No, that made no sense. No Mundane resistance fighter would follow a Mage. So they were just allies.

Takket's grip on the edge of the sink became painful, his knuckles whitening as he pushed down on the textured marble. Khantek had been killed by a Mage. It had been no political assassination or accident. Enara or Yelleck had thrown the lethal Shard. Fragments of the puzzle fell into place. The crew cabin had been purposefully targeted. They needed the passenger compartment, with all of Khantek's documents, intact. They had brought the craft down, then set off to search for Takket.

He still could not understand why they would do all of this. Khantek's assassination, Takket's employment, the work over the last few days, it all pointed towards the pair genuinely desiring the Pure Shard. They could be working for the Free Circle, just keeping their role in Khantek's death secret to avoid scaring off Takket.

Then again, they could be two Mages looking to burn the pure Shard to start a new Arcane dynasty. They could be thieves looking to sell the Shard to the highest bidder. All Takket knew was that they were both liars.

It mattered little what motivated their schemes. He had to decide his next steps. The obvious solution was to flee Varsen, head back to the Imperium, retire as he should have done before this demon-cursed expedition. Stowing aboard a cargo ship was possible, but it would be difficult to hide for the weeks the ships took to cross the ocean. He could feign a critical illness, get replaced as the Imperium's envoy, but then he would need to disappear once back in the Imperium. A deathly ill official would likely be rushed straight to Indspire's healers, under constant watch. Simply resigning would not work either. He would have to hand off confidential documents to his replacement, a member of the Imperium's court who would no doubt recognise him as an impostor.

He paced the bathroom naked, the sharp edges of the freezing marble tiles digging into his feet. He shivered in the biting cold. Good. The low temperatures would wake him up, bring clarity to his sleep-deprived mind.

None of the options looked promising, not least because all involved admitting defeat. If he turned away now, *this* would become his final heist—a total failure. He had set off to affirm his legacy. Fleeing now would only prove Antellok's mockery correct, that he was beyond use, that he would never be remembered for his work.

Turning back to the mirror, he watched water dragging dirt in dark tracks down his torso. His hair was grey with the filth, his every wrinkle accentuated by the dust. Yet, when he locked eyes with his reflection, he saw strength. Determination. He was Takket. A legend whispered of the world over. The man who had scaled the spire of Iggranious, talked his way into the Indspire vaults. The man who had spent a lifetime stealing from Mages and Arcanes. What others thought of as impossible, he achieved with ease. He had overcome greater challenges than a pair of dishonest partners. He had never before let others dictate his fate, and he was not about to start.

Yelleck and Enara's plans need not concern him. They could entertain themselves with their lies and deceit. His plan was solid. He would present himself to the court as Envoy Khantek Fredeen. He would steal Arcane Hekaena's heart, use her to gain access to her father's sanctuary. He would steal the Pure Shard of Varsen and free the Mundanes from tyranny. Enara and Yelleck's scheming would be forgotten, a minor hurdle in the tale of his greatest success. Only he would be remembered as a legend. Only he would be known as the greatest thief in history.

Only he would become a hero.

PART II

CHAPTER TEN

The passengers crowded into the observation room. Even with the white furniture pushed aside to accommodate Hannig's escort and Takket, it was still oppressively cramped. Takket stood on the edge of the grated metal floor, braced against the encircling windows. The occasional gust of fresh air through the disguised ventilation system did little to clear the dank odour of so many bodies.

Takket was transfixed by the unfolding view. The endless blue of the Angel's Ocean mingled with the blood-coloured water that gave Red Bay its name— Sharddust saturated waters oozing from the New World. The bay was flecked with countless ships, making their way towards the distant shore enclosing the bay on three sides. Cargo liners from Portspire ended their journey here. They would have followed a similar route as the airship, but their journey across the ocean would have taken weeks, not days. Sea birds flitted around the airship, diving towards the boats in hopes of stealing a fisherman's catch or feasting on the abundance of dusteater eels that followed Mage-powered ships.

Warden Island passed below the airship, the grated floor giving a clear view of the fortress that dominated the land mass. Walls jutted out in an angry star, sections discoloured from repeated repairs. Whenever warfare broke out between the Arcanedoms bordering

Red Bay, Warden Island attracted the fiercest fighting. Its position at the heart of the bay allowed artillery from the island to control shipping throughout these waters. If armies rose to dispute borders, the island always became their true prize. The battle-scarred fortress bore the green and black banners of Varsen. For now.

The menagerie of boats cut their way through red waves to or from the shorelines. To the north lay Kilroth, the oldest of the New World Arcanedoms. To the south stretched the broken shoreline of Octdane, the youngest nation on the continent, its war of revolution still in living memory. The bulk of the naval traffic, however, was bound westward, where three rivers marked the land ruled by the Imperium's dearest ally—Varsen.

They were close enough now to see details of that shoreline. Sharddust billowed down from the highlands, shadowing the landscape with dancing haze. Great rock formations broke from the dust layer, jagged grey-brown boulders the size of mountains jutting out at precarious angles. The wind blowing in from the sea played with the rock formations, forcing Sharddust towards them, only to twist it into red-stained spirals that whirled across the rock faces, scouring the exposed stone.

Passing below them, hundreds of boats converged on Varsen's main port—Brixen. Glass windows reflected the morning light. The city was a wedge hugging the shoreline at the estuary of Tellin River, glittering through the thin Sharddust layer near the waterfront. Seen from above, the roadways of Brixen were a warren, capped at either end with impressive star forts. Shardrail lines cut through the chaotic layout in three straight lines, linking the dockyard to the rest of Varsen.

The airship began its descent once they cleared the shoreline. The fresh air whistling through the room became tinged with the occasional hint of Sharddust, a scent that had been alien these past days. Judging by the thickness of the red haze coating the land, he would have to become re-accustomed to the smell. If anything, the dust was thicker here than in the Imperium. A thousand years ago, this land had been virgin territory, untouched by Mundane or Mage. A green paradise had awaited the first intrepid explorers, using the now-forgotten techniques of sky orbs to cut across the ocean.

That paradise was long dead.

Winds howled below, buffeting the airship as it descended further. The abundant Sharddust hurtled across the landscape as it had since Magelord Grethin first set foot on this forsaken continent. The dust had killed all but the hardiest of local plants. Without plants to hold the soil firm, the abrasive dust had scoured the landscape down to the bedrock, then chiselled away the softer stone, leaving the jutting, alien formations that stretched out of the Sharddust layer.

The sandy brown rocks were mottled in a dark moss and entwined in thorned vines. Here and there, a scattering of greenery stubbornly held on to the top of the taller rock formations. The defiant grasses and bushes, held above the densest of the Sharddust, stood out sharply against the dull brown and red background.

A few creatures that had managed to rapidly adapt to the dust's arrival picked their way across the landscape: packs of Krilts lurching their way over rock faces, hannis goats leaping between gorges, emaciated garricks hovering on their membrane wings to look for morsels to scavenge. On some of the larger grassy peaks, small herds of sheep or cattle grazed, bracing themselves against the wind.

The airship followed the meandering Tellin River, which was visible through the Sharddust only by the sunlight reflecting from its surface. The peaks of the rock formations were now above the airship, lining the edges of the river valley. A scattering of hovels could be seen built into the cliffs, hardy chitin-coated houses wedged into ravines and clefts. Tiny figures of Mundanes climbed the cliffs to tend struggling farm plots atop the rocks.

As they drifted around a corner of the river valley, the billowing Sharddust was broken by a sprawling city huddled in the foot of a jade green tower. Wide at its base, the tower rapidly tapered inwards, forming a vicious spike striking towards the clouds. Small replicas covered the rest of the city, elegant Magetowers stretching out of the Sharddust. At the city's edge, a series of wide platforms balanced on metal pillars. Grass covered many, dotted with people or livestock. Other platforms were topped with grain fields, safely held above the Sharddust. Even the largest of these field platforms seemed insignificant compared with the central tower. The entire city looked like a hundred small pointed creatures, clustered around their mother.

Varspire.

Floating over the outskirts of the city, Takket picked out other houses in the haze. Stone and chitin structures huddled around Magetowers, haphazard dwellings built over one another: homes of Mundanes, spread over the city, separated by bedrock streets. The structures filled all available space, even in the shadow of the field platforms, growing around the supporting pillars. The chitin building material forced novel shapes, rounded houses piled on top of one another like mounds of pale spider eggs laid between the Magetowers.

Those towers now surrounded the airship, the tallest spires reaching well above the craft as it hovered just above the Sharddust layer. Mages levitated between the buildings, Soulshards glowing in hand. Burning Shards was a small price to pay to never set foot in the dust-choked streets of the Mundanes.

Just above the Sharddust layer, they approached a jetty stretching out at the base of the looming Varspire Tower. Mundanes precariously balanced at the edge of the metal pier, reaching out with slender hooks to catch the airship's dangling mooring cables.

The grinding of machinery echoed through the cabin as the steel cables were winched in, dragging the airship towards the platform. The view, once wondrous, was replaced with the dark mass of the Magetower rising out of a sea of Sharddust. As the airship came to a rest against the jetty with a final clunk, Takket could only stare at the polished jade walls, knowing this tower would either become the site of his greatest achievement, or his death.

Takket had barely stepped foot off the airship when Varsen's greeting party arrived. Two dozen riflemen in green and black coats stomped along the metal jetty, the structure shaking with the rhythm of their footfalls. Leading them through the warm, Sharddust-touched air was an elderly man in a trailing cloak of emerald green. His white hair was pleated into a tail hanging over his shoulder. Despite his age, the man moved with purpose, the soldiers struggling to keep pace.

He held Takket's gaze as he approached, irises the burning red of an Arcane. 'I am Prime Adjunct Innisel Drak, chief adviser to Arcane-lord Haddronius Varsen,' he intoned, placing a hand over his heart.

Takket bowed. 'I am Envoy Khantek Fredeen, sent on behalf of the Indel Imperium.'

Innisel inclined his head—as much of a bow as Takket would receive. 'I welcome you to Varsen, Envoy Khantek Fredeen. You will follow me.'

Takket trailed after the man through the column of soldiers, who fell into step behind. Unlike Hannig, this was a man Takket had to hurry after. He was an Arcane. That meant a great deal in the Imperium. In Varsen, it meant everything.

The sun beat down, unobstructed by the billowing haze below, and Takket soon found his forehead beading with sweat. The dry heat was a sharp change from the conditions during the crossing. Still, with Varsen on the equator, it came as no surprise. Never had Takket felt so drawn to the shade of the Sharddust.

Even though the haze churned just below the jetty, its copper tang was still strong. It obscured another smell rising from below, a dank stench of humanity. Sewage, decay, disease—the Sharddust may have blocked his view of the undercity, but the odour would not be so easily contained.

Stepping into blessed shade, they entered a cavernous opening into the spire. The colour scheme continued indoors. Obsidian walls, highlighted in jade, curled into a rounded ceiling. A carpet as soft as those on the airship stretched down the hallway. Gas lamps burned behind green stained glass, casting an ethereal light down the passage. They strode by abstract statues hewed from jade and obsidian, separated by soldiers in their emerald coats standing to attention. This was a world of green and black.

A white light ahead promised respite from the monochromatic tunnel. They ascended a wide set of stairs, so steep they must have been designed to be difficult to climb. Of course—those who wished an audience with the Arcane-lord had to prove their dedication.

At the top of the stairs, the hallway opened into a domed room, furnished in green and black, lit by a multitude of gas lamps. More soldiers stood ready ahead, presenting their rifles to form a tunnel through which Takket was ushered. Beyond the soldiers stood a gaggle of dignitaries in grand silken costumes: cloaks for the men, elegant flowing dresses for the women. At least half stared at him with red irises so bright they seemed to glow—Takket had never seen so many Arcanes.

Innisel led Takket through the onlookers to wait by a set of stairs leading up to a raised dais. On that dais glowed Varsen's throne, the entire piece formed from banded-together Soulshard batons. Other than the fur-lined seat and backrest, the whole throne gleamed in ever-shifting light. Takket could only guess how many Mundanes had given their lives to produce such a wealth of baton-sized Shards. All to give one man a chair.

The angelic call of a choir cut through the murmurs that filled the hall, voices of unseen children heralding the Arcane-lord's arrival. All eyes were drawn upward. Directly above the throne, a circular opening in the ceiling twenty feet wide led to the spire's central column. Countless floors towered dizzyingly above, the glow of a hundred Soulshard lighting the way for the figures drifting between the levels.

One figure was descending, robes billowing as he gracefully drifted into the throne room. The air was filled with the rippling creak of the hundred onlookers and soldiers dropping to their knees, eyes downcast. Even Innisel knelt, leaving Takket standing alone. Takket bowed low, keeping one hand over his heart— he was the one man in this room who did not owe Haddronius fealty, and envoys did not kneel to foreign rulers.

Still, Takket kept his eyes downcast. If he wanted to survive a day, let alone the heist, he had to show respect. Varsen may value its relationship with the Imperium, but they would suffer no insult.

'Rise,' a sharp voice rasped over the room. As the others stood, Takket looked up at Arcane-lord Haddronius Varsen. The man was now sitting on the throne, causing its Shards to glow blindingly bright. As his eyes adjusted, Takket could make out more details. Haddronius looked in his seventies—although Takket knew he had recently turned one hundred—his thinning white hair pulled back to drape behind his shoulders. His wrinkled skin was clean-shaven, his red eyes matching the brilliance of the Shard throne.

The neckline of his emerald and gold silken robes plunged to his sternum to reveal the source of his power. Hanging by a golden chain was a Soulshard the size of a hand, so small for the most valuable object in the country. The Shard's splendour may not have been represented in its size, but its colour separated it from all others. Not the ever-shifting red glow of standard Shards, this one shone with a steady white glare, bursting from Haddronius's chest like a rising sun. The Pure Shard of Varsen.

Takket's prize.

Innisel broke the reverent silence. 'My lord, may I present Envoy Khantek Fredeen, here to represent the Indel Imperium at your blessed court.'

Takket bowed deeply again, reciting words penned months ago by a committee of dignitaries in Indspire. 'It is an honour, Arcane-lord Haddronius Varsen. The Indel Imperium sends kind greetings. Arcane-lord Venning Indel wishes nothing but friendship between our people. I pray to the angels above that I may facilitate the growing strength of both our great lands for decades to come.'

Takket looked up to see Haddronius's red eyes studying him harshly. The moment dragged, Takket's skin crawling, but he refused to look away. Eventually, the ancient man clapped once.

'Welcome to Varsen,' he rasped. 'May the angels welcome you and the demons be blind to your passing.' He smiled a twisted smile. 'I look forward to seeing how you compare to your predecessor. I invite you to a banquet tonight to celebrate your arrival.' He gave a dismissive wave. 'You may leave.'

The room broke into a din of applause. Soldiers stamped their rifle butts against the floor in unison. Following Innisel's lead, Takket stepped backwards, bowing low. As they reached the line of soldiers, they turned and strode away, the brightness of the throne casting their shadows long across the carpet. Followed by the roar of applause, they descended the staircase. Mages, Arcanes, battle-trained soldiers, all showing their adoration of the Arcane-lord, all ready to lay down their lives to protect Haddronius from any threat. A threat such as Takket.

Innisel led Takket back through the hallway to where Enara and Yelleck waited among their stacked luggage. Alongside them hovered a man in a drab woollen cloak, his fair hair greying, particularly in the long beard. He could not have been much older than Takket, yet seemed worn out, his face broken by deep wrinkles, dark bags hanging under small eyes.

'This is Akken,' Innisel explained. 'He will be the servant assigned to you for the duration of your stay.'

Enara flashed Takket a concerned glare. A personal servant would make any privacy almost impossible.

'That won't be necessary,' Takket replied, offhand. 'I don't need any further assistance. I already have these two.'

Innisel shifted uneasily. 'I'm afraid it *will* be necessary. You are a personal guest of his magnificence, the Arcane-lord. You must be treated as such. Not assigning you at least one servant to run your errands would be atrocious hospitality, even if you are merely a Mundane.' It was remarkable how politely courtiers could insult a man. 'Besides, there is much about Varspire that you will need to learn—the layout of the floors, timings of meals, dates of functions. I cannot afford to personally escort you through all the trivialities. Don't worry—I've worked with Akken for many years. He is quite satisfactory.'

Akken dipped his head, acknowledging what was likely a compliment.

Takket cleared his throat. 'Well, if you insist.'

'I do.'

'It's an honour to serve you, Mage,' Akken said with a weary bow.

'I'm a Mundane,' Takket corrected.

The man hesitated, then smiled brightly. 'Still an honour. If you would come with me, I'll show you to the embassy and your rooms.' As Enara and Yelleck reached for the luggage, Akken grabbed the two largest suitcases. 'Here, let me help you with those. In Varsen, Mundanes look out for one another.'

The pair looked pleasantly surprised. Takket wondered if Akken would be as accommodating if he realised they were Mages in disguise.

'I must leave you here,' Innisel said. 'I shall see you at sundown for the banquet. Akken will show you the way. Until then, make yourself at home. I'm sure you have much to do.'

Takket thanked the man as he scurried away, then turned to follow Akken. The side corridors they passed through lacked the scale of the main hallway, but not the grandeur. The abstract Varsen sculptures of jade were joined by several pieces from the Imperium, standing out with their embellished details. Not a single rival New World Arcanedom was represented by the art. These halls were reserved for Varsen and its solitary ally.

Deep inside the structure, the smell of Sharddust had faded. Wind howled through ventilation pipes in the ceiling, but this did little to replace the stagnant background. The tower smelled of cleaning solutions, gas lamp fumes, and air breathed by too many people.

The soft green carpet was replaced with a deep maroon as they turned a corner into a large hall. The walls were formed of white marble, trimmed with rubies and lit with the unsteady red glow of a Soulshard chandelier. The hall was tastefully decorated in Imperium style, red velvet couches separated by white marble tables. At the room's far end, the red and white banner of the Indel Imperium proudly hung above a branching staircase.

'The Imperium's Embassy,' Akken announced, setting the luggage down. 'Offices and formal dining room on this level. Servants quarters upstairs to the left. If you'll follow me, Envoy, I'll show you to your room.'

Takket trailed the man up the stairs, the scarlet rug giving a sure grip over the marble steps. He ran a hand along the railing—real mahogany. It must have been imported from the Imperium. Few trees still grew in the New World.

Akken pushed aside a varnished door and led Takket into a sprawling windowless room. Gas lamps illuminated a sizable writing desk dominating a study area to one side. Fresh stacks of paper sat alongside writing equipment ranging from archaic quills to modern fountain pens, all resting on the desk's leather-topped surface. A four-poster bed lay to the other side, adorned with thin red sheets. Fresh air drifted through the abstract engravings covering the ceiling—no doubt another hidden ventilation system. Through a door Takket could see the white marble of a bathroom, complete with a ceramic tub. Even with the hanging spectre of capture or death, it seemed he would at least be comfortable while plotting the demise of a dynasty.

Takket jumped as a figure emerged from the shadows in the far corner of the room.

'Envoy Khantek,' the man said nasally.

'Yes?' Takket tried to calm his racing heart. The man strode across the room, footfalls silent on the soft carpet. He was wrapped in a black silken coat, seemingly an embellished version of the military uniform worn by the common soldiers, only with far more gold on his lapels and the sash across his chest. His face unnerved Takket. Small suspicious eyes—the colour of cut rubies—peered out from sharp features. Pointed cheekbones and a thin jaw line seemed to give the man's smile predatory intent.

'I am Chief Constable Ensellus Valdera.' The man inspected Takket as one would a spider found in a shoe. 'I have just debriefed Hannig. It seems he is satisfied that you pose no threat to the Arcane-lord.'

Some calm settled over Takket. 'I'm glad. I would never—'

'I don't share his faith,' Ensellus interrupted. 'You are a foreigner, a Mundane.' His face soured at the last word. 'You do not have the Arcane-lord's best interest at heart.'

'I'm the envoy of the Imperium,' Takket replied defensively.

Ensellus began slowly circling Takket, leaving him

feeling like a sheep being eyed by a ykkol cat. 'Yes. An agent of a foreign power.'

'An agent of your ally.'

'An ally, for now.' The chief constable came to a stop behind Takket, forcing him to look over his shoulder. 'Alliances shift. The greatest empires are built from the ashes of those who once called them friend. Some may take the Imperium's benevolence for granted. Some are restrained by political niceties when addressing you. Neither apply to me. I am not above the law in Varsen. I *am* the law. You will obey the law, Envoy. You will obey *me*.'

Ensellus moved around to face Takket, his face close enough to smell the exotic spices lingering on the man's breath.

'What are you implying?' Takket held the gaze of the man's bright red eyes.

'I'm not implying anything. I want to be perfectly clear. I will be watching you. If I so much as suspect that you might be planning anything to harm Haddronius Varsen, you will be back on an airship to your decedent continent before you can utter a protest. If you're stupid enough to actually try something to endanger the Arcane-lord, I will burn you myself. You would not be the first foreign agent to die by my hands.' He narrowed his eyes, his angular nose less than an inch from Takket's. 'I'm watching you.'

He strode out of the room, feet somehow silent despite his haste. Takket turned to stare at the open doorway, a weight growing in his stomach. This was Ensellus's greeting to a foreign diplomat, an honoured guest. He could only imagine what response might await a thief.

CHAPTER ELEVEN

Takket followed Akken through the corridors of
Varspire Tower. The servant scurried along the vibrant
carpets, shoulders slumped, pausing only to bow
deeply to passing Mages or Arcanes. As they
approached a pair of large, black-painted doors,
guarded by two riflemen in dress uniform, Takket was
greeted by a symphony of aromas: spices, herbs,
woodsmoke, spirits, cooking meat. His stomach
growled in anticipation—he had skipped lunch to
build an appetite. The guest of honour at a Varsen
banquet was supposed to sample every morsel on
offer, and moderation was alien to Varspire's court.

Akken pushed the doors aside, the strong aromas
flowing out on a wave of heat. Takket stepped
through, looking around the expansive hall. The far
wall was made of glass, gently curving with the
tower's exterior. Angry red light of the setting sun
flooded through, accentuated by the Soulshard
chandeliers dangling from the vaulted ceiling. The
other walls were obsidian, embellished with jade
sculptures built into the wall. Statues of plants—
common and exotic—ringed the lowest level. These
shifted into carvings of insects, birds, then larger
creatures as his gaze rose. Half way up were
engravings of huddled Mundanes, standing under
Mages and Arcanes with eyes represented by rubies.
At the edge of the ceiling, statues of angels and

demons completed the tableau—Scalist doctrine symbolised in the arrangement: Arcanes over all, closest to the spirits.

At least two hundred people milled around the hall —Mages and Arcanes—waited on by the Mundanes, who wandered the room with downcast eyes. Some faces he recognised from court earlier, others from his stacks of dossiers. The Imperium's artists had done a fine job capturing their likenesses. The guests were scattered around tables laden with meats, sauces, vegetables and drinks. Some attendees lounged on benches, others stood by the tables, eating merrily. At the heart of the room, an upturned krilt roasted over an open fire, its shell cracked with heat, the meat popping and hissing.

'If I have your leave, Envoy.' Akken stared at the jade tiled floor. 'I have much work to do putting your rooms in order.'

'Of course,' Takket said, distracted. 'You may go.'

He had no idea what required the servant's attention—they had already spent most of the day unpacking—but his mind was fixed on the wondrous decor. Polished jade tiled the floor, arranged into an elaborate pattern. Obsidian pillars were wrapped in ribbons of green, black, white and maroon, the colours of Varsen and the Imperium intermingling.

The room hummed with chatter, men and women debating politics, catching up on the latest events and telling lurid jests. The same words could be heard in every Mundane tavern across the world, merely pronounced with less eloquence.

'Envoy Fredeen,' a voice called across the hall. Takket turned to see Innisel hurrying over. 'Welcome to the banquet. I'm glad you could make it.'

'I could hardly miss a meal in my honour.'

Innisel gave a small laugh. 'True. Please, I must introduce you to our host.'

'Haddronius is here?'

Another laugh. 'Oh no. The Arcane-lord rarely partakes in such frivolity. This evening is hosted by his named successor.'

'Ah.' Takket thought back to the dossiers. 'Valena.'

'Exactly. Follow me.'

Innisel cut a path through the crowds. A few curious faces turned their way, Arcanes examining Takket while chewing roasted skewers or sipping root wine. Innisel's pace and focused expression kept any interruptions at bay.

They arrived at the smouldering krilt at the hall's centre. The fumes of burning spices stung Takket's eyes. An imperious woman stood nearby with bright red eyes and long dark hair tied back. She wore a green robe with a plunging neckline, similar to Haddronius's. A Soulshard hung from a golden necklace, but where Haddronius's had been small enough to appear as gaudy jewellery, hers was a baton, the size of a forearm, and stretched from her collarbone to her waist. It glowed brilliantly, casting eerie shadows over her face.

'Arcane Valena.' Innisel bowed low. 'May I present Envoy Khantek Fredeen.'

Takket bowed, hand over heart. 'It's an honour, Arcane Valena.'

'I'm sure.' Valena examined Takket critically. 'So you are the Mundane the Imperium sent as a representative. I still cannot decide if your appointment was meant as an insult or a punishment.'

Takket frowned. 'I'm afraid I do not follow.'

'A *Mundane*, sent here. The Imperium knew how Varsen would respond to such a lowly individual. So, were you sent to insult my father, or is this assignment some torment to punish you for a grand blunder at court?'

Takket drew himself up. 'Neither, I assure you. I have spent my life at court, observing official meetings, negotiating trade deals, ferreting out corruption. I was sent because I am the most qualified. In the Imperium, that counts for far more than whether or not I can draw magic. A diplomat's weapon is his tongue, not his Shard.'

Valena smirked. 'Good answer. Maybe you will survive after all. Come, let us see what kind of man the Imperium has sent us. We always reserve the finest cuts for the guest of honour.'

She extended a hand, the arm gloved to the elbow, towards the krilt. The Shard on her chest glowed brightly, and the krilt's scorched head twitched. With a crunch of shattering chitin, one of the krilt's mandibles broke free, hovering in mid-air. Juices dripped from the broken stump, hissing loudly on the coals below. Takket was hit by the smell of cooking fat, tinged with something acrid. The mandible, blackened with soot, floated into Valena's hand.

'The mandible flesh is considered a delicacy here. The one part of a krilt with real flavour, though many find it too...intense. Here, take it. I have cooled the shell enough for you to hold.'

Takket grasped the mandible, the blackened shell uncomfortably warm to the touch. Out from its broken stub protruded torn greyish meat, dripping with clear juices. Smiling to Valena, he took a bite of the exposed flesh. The rubbery meat grudgingly gave way, trapped liquid bursting into his mouth in a wash of bitter metallic flavour. He had to chew the piece thoroughly, the acrid taste lingering on his tongue. The taste, the texture, the smell, it was truly awful—as many delicacies were, in his opinion. He refused to let his face betray his disgust. This was hardly the foulest thing he had ever forced into his mouth.

He forced himself to swallow the half-chewed meat. 'Strong, unique.' Takket's mouth was filled with a coppery aftertaste. 'Fitting for Varsen's national dish.'

Valena's red eyes sparkled with amusement. 'Another good answer. Perhaps we should not be insulted by your presence after all. Your predecessor only managed to swallow the meat on his third attempt.' She smiled and signalled to a nearby man. 'Antonius, come meet our new guest.'

A tall man with close-cropped black hair strode over, kissing Valena's cheek. Takket recognised the name: Antonius Varsen, Valena's husband. Despite being a few inches taller than Valena, he was far less imposing, shoulders cowed, arms nervously tucked to the side. He briefly met Takket's gaze with his burning red eyes.

'Pleased to meet you,' he said so quietly that he could barely be heard over the crackle of roasting krilt.

'A pleasure,' Takket responded. He had never met an Arcane with so little presence. It came as no surprise—Antonius was married to the future ruler of Varsen, always to be in the background, an Arcane chosen to secure political alliances and sire Arcane

160

children. Even there he had failed to excel, one of their two children being a mere Mage.

Mere Mage. Only in Varsen could a Mage be a disappointment.

'Well, Envoy Khantek,' Valena started, 'please make yourself at home. We have the finest dishes in Varsen on offer tonight. Please do sample everything. The rellik peppered lamb is particularly good.' She turned away. 'I will not take any more of your time.'

Her tone made it clear that he had been dismissed. He supposed he was going to have to get used to Arcanes granting him the bare minimum of their time. The fact that Valena had deigned to actually speak to him was no doubt considered high courtesy.

He paced the room, looking for faces familiar from dossiers. An envoy would be expected to meet all the major dignitaries as soon as possible. Above all others, Takket searched for the face of Hekaena. The sooner he met her, the sooner he could be done with this heist.

He took a plate from a Mundane servant—a small girl in a rough-spun green robe who milled about the room, eyes fixed on the floor's polished tiles—and he picked a selection of the dishes on offer to chew while he circled. The peppered lamb was indeed pleasant, the thick husk of spices compensating for the burnt meat.

Instead of Hekaena, Takket found the second child, Drothinius. The Arcane lounged along a bench in a silken robe, holding a Soulshard baton in one hand while popping sugared pastries into his mouth with the other. He was podgy for an Arcane—quite an achievement given an Arcane's naturally blessed physique. His week-old stubble was similarly abnormal for a dignitary. He might be trying to set a trend, or he might simply not care.

'Arcane Drothinius.' Takket placed his hand over his heart and bowed. 'A pleasure to meet you.'

The man looked up, startled. He frowned, clearly not recognising Takket. A woman on a nearby bench leaned over, her pale blond hair pulled back into a flowing tail, revealing her bright red eyes.

'My love,' she said impatiently. 'This is Khantek Fredeen. The Imperium's envoy.'

'Oh?' he replied off-handedly. At a glare from the blonde woman, he sat up, sucking his fingers clean. 'Oh, of course. Welcome to Varsen, Khantek. This is my wife, Insania.'

Takket bowed again. 'A pleasure.'

Insania narrowed her eyes. Everyone here seemed to size Takket up as one would a cornered rat. 'How does Varspire compare to the Imperium's court?'

Takket thought back to the parties he had attended in Inspire—uninvited, of course. 'Warmer and darker.' He smiled. 'You certainly know how to welcome guests. I thought it was the Imperium that was meant to be ostentatious.'

Insania smirked. 'This? You're just being diplomatic. You cannot honestly tell me your dinners at Inspire are less grand than this.'

'Perhaps you're right.'

'Of course I am. Oh, I can just imagine it. The pageantry. The balls. None of the need to scrim and scrape to pay for bloated militaries. I was born in the wrong continent.'

Drothinius grunted. 'You could have moved, dear. Besides, you like it here. You enjoy the trappings of

Varspire as much as I do.'

'No one enjoys Varspire as much as you do,' she corrected. 'And there's nothing wrong with wanting more. Always strive to improve yourself. You must agree, Khantek. A Mundane here representing a continent—quite the accomplishment.'

Takket bowed his head humbly. 'I will admit that it took a lot of effort to achieve my position. Effort well spent.'

Insania gave him a measuring look. 'Ambition. I like that. You should spend some time with my husband. Maybe some of that grit will rub off on him.'

Drothinius rolled his eyes. Takket was not sure how to respond, so kept his words simple. 'I would be honoured.'

'Perfect,' Insania said. 'That's settled. I'll make arrangements.'

Drothinius groaned, shooting Takket a melodramatic glare. 'Only a day here, and you're already increasing my workload.'

'Apologies,' Takket replied. 'I did not mean to impose.'

'Nonsense,' Insania said. 'You two will get on royally.'

'Don't worry about it, Khantek.' Drothinius plucked another pastry from a silvered plate held by a serving boy. 'My wife has a habit of taking politeness as invitation. I'm sure we will survive whatever she concocts. Hopefully it won't involve leaving the tower.'

'I look forward to it to. I should keep circling. There are so many here I need to introduce myself to.'

'Good idea,' Drothinius said, mouth full of syrup-coated pastry. 'Lingering may end up with the two of us locked into months of appointments. Is there anyone in particular you are looking for?'

Takket kept his voice nonchalant. 'I should start with the royal family. Do you know where your younger sister is?'

Drothinius waved vaguely across the room. 'Oh, Hekaena will be hiding from all this luxury. Hard to believe that we share the same blood. She's probably by the window, staring out at the angel-forsaken cityscape.'

Takket bowed again and set off through the crowd. The voices had increased in volume as the wine flowed freely. No longer protected by Innisel's presence, Takket was interrupted every few paces. Distant relations to the Arcane-lord introduced themselves. Mages pressed him for the most recent news from the Imperium. Arcanes asked for details of the latest fashions. Major and minor functionaries plied him with strange samples of spice-coated food, every person going into detail about why *this* was the best sauce in Varsen, or why *that* wine tasted superior. To him, most dishes seemed the same—variations on charred meat or bland roots, drizzled in a burning sauce. Whether fermented in the highlands or coast, cask aged or brand new, to Takket, every glass of earthy wine simply tasted like wine.

By the time he manoeuvred himself around to the windowed wall, night had fallen. Windows of Magetowers outside glimmered with light from gas lamps and Shards. Glowing specks arced across the night sky, Mages burning Shards to move from tower to tower, going to dinner parties or returning from a day of well-paid work. The Sharddust layer floated below the cityscape, lit internally by a smouldering orange light—wood fires heating the homes of Mundanes lost in the gloom below.

A solitary figure stood to one side of the window, illuminated by a Soulshard baton held at the end of a staff. In the ever-shifting light, he recognised the woman whose file he had studied over and over—Hekaena Varsen. She wore a simple black dress, one of the few people present to be in hard-wearing linen rather than silk. Her long, jet black hair hung loosely down her back. There was a certain elegance to her long face, strong yet welcoming. The artist's portraits did justice to most of her, but not to her eyes. The red of all Arcanes was flecked with a silvery white, seeming to sparkle in the light of her Soulshard.

She turned those eyes towards him and he bowed low, hand over heart.

'Arcane Hekaena Varsen,' he said. 'It is an honour to meet you.'

'It is?' She did not study him as the others had, merely glanced his way before turning back to the window.

'Of course. The daughter of Haddronius Varsen. A member of one of the greatest Arcane dynasties. There are many in Indspire who would sell their own mother for such a meeting.'

She snorted derisively. 'Sell out their flesh and blood to gawk at me? I'm touched.'

Takket shook his head, flustered. 'I just mean, anyone would be grateful to make the acquaintance of such a fabled blood line.'

'Oh?' She sipped wine from a crystal glass. 'And

why would that be?'

He blinked. 'You're a Varsen. This land in named after you. This great tower belongs to your family.'

That only earned him a smirk. 'Built by hands long dead. My only link to them is happening to be born from their great grandchild.'

'That alone is something to be awed. Of all the Arcane families across this world, only a handful hold a Pure Shard, rule a country.'

'And none of that has anything to do with me,' she replied, disinterested. 'You believe being a Varsen is my greatest accomplishment?'

'Well...' This was not at all how he had planned the conversation.

'Being born—the first thing I ever did, the thing I had the least control over, and yet, paradoxically, all anyone cares to discuss. One wonders why you people don't fawn over my father's shits to the same degree. He produced them just as much as he produced me, and we both had the same input in our creation.'

'I just mean...'

'I know what you mean.' Her glowing eyes bore into him. 'You mean what all you Imperium envoys ever mean. You mean that you want to continue trading with my father, that you don't want your supply of batons to run dry, so you keep us on good terms. For my father, you threaten the other Arcanedoms. For my sister, you promise to do the same when she takes Father's place. To the rest of us, you spout meaningless pleasantries.'

Takket tried to regain some control of the conversation. 'I'm sorry if I've caused offence.'

'Oh, don't worry.' She turned back to the window.

'You're doing your job. If Farther—or more likely, Innisel—asks, I'll say you were the epitome of formality and grace. Now that I have done my job, and waited here until I met our honoured guest, I am done for the day. Good night, Envoy.'

'Please, call me Khantek,' he stuttered as she pushed a half-empty glass of wine into his hand.

'I wouldn't worry,' she called over her shoulder as she stalked away. 'I doubt I'll have much need to call you anything.'

Takket watched her vanish into the crowd, staff lighting her path. Groups parted to make way, bowing deeply in respect, but she ignored them, striding to the door. He stood dumbly. This was not at all what he had planned. He was supposed to charm her, impress her, lay the foundations of the seduction. Instead, he had insulted her with a simple greeting.

He drained the leftover root wine to settle his thoughts, the earthy liquid burning his throat. Gazing over the crowded room, he felt his stomach sink, knowing he had to continue to mingle to keep his cover, but dreading the thought of more overcooked food and repetitive conversation. How could he keep his mind on such things when his entire plan was crumbling?

His gaze met a pair of red eyes that stared out of the crowd. Ensellus stood there, glaring at him. Demons below, the man really was watching Takket's every step. Still, if the rest of the plan went as poorly as tonight, there would be no crime for the constable to catch Takket committing. Perhaps stealing the Pure Shard of Varsen really was impossible.

Well after midnight Takket staggered into the embassy, stomach groaning from too much food and far too much wine. He kept silent as he slunk up the maroon carpeted staircase. Enara and Yelleck had asked him to wake them when he returned, to discuss the evening's events, but Takket was in no mood to relay his failure to that deceptive pair.

He eased open the varnished mahogany door to his room, only to be startled by a figure jumping by his desk.

'Angels above,' Akken yelped. 'Sorry, I didn't hear you coming up. Gave me a start.'

'How do you think I feel?' Takket watched the man hurriedly sort fallen stationary. 'Working late?'

'Yes, sir.' Akken still sounded panicked. 'A Mundane's work is never done. Good night, sir.'

'Good night.' Takket frowned, puzzled. He softly closed the door behind Akken, then turned to his bed. He longed to collapse into its soft mattress, sleep until the aftertaste of spice and wine faded, until his befuddled mind became merely hungover. Yet something about Akken's manner held him back. Too skittish. Too eager to leave. What had the man even been doing by the desk at this hour?

He crept over to the study area, telling himself he was just being paranoid. Yet, paranoia was the difference between a successful thief and a corpse. He looked around the desk and chair, first thinking to search for hidden spikes or poison powder. The dossiers urged him to be mindful of political assassination—many Arcanedoms would seize any chance to sour the Varsen-Imperium alliance. He found nothing but the freshly dusted leather of the desk surface.

As he turned towards the bed, his foot clipped a leather document case. Strange. He was sure he had tucked that away before leaving. Perhaps Akken had knocked it accidentally. Favouring caution, Takket picked up the satchel and examined its contents. Dossiers of the senior courtiers. They all seemed to be there, but something unsettled Takket. They were out of sequence. He had arranged the dossiers in order of importance to his plan. Haddronius at the front, Hekaena second. They had been reorganised in order of seniority.

Takket frowned deeply. Someone had rearranged this. Akken? But why? There was a chance the man was trying to help, correcting what he saw as an error in his master's notes. But he had no reason to touch the case, let alone root through the papers. Maybe it had been Enara or Yelleck, studying after Takket had left. Perhaps Takket had simply misplaced the documents.

Logical explanations, but a lifetime of lies, play-acting and intercepting letters led Takket to another possibility: was Akken a spy?

CHAPTER TWELVE

Stepping out onto one of Varspire Tower's balconies, Takket was greeted by a warm breeze and the morning sun peeking above the horizon. Magetowers cast long shadows that stretched across the rolling Sharddust. The wind brought the dust's metallic scent, mixed with the stench of the Mundane houses hidden beneath the haze. Balconies did cling higher up the tower, far above the stink of the city, but they were reserved for those with magical talent. Humble Mundanes had to endure the dust.

Drothinius wandered out onto the balcony, leaning his bulk on the steel handrail. The Arcane wore a sleeveless black robe, no doubt more suited to this heat than Takket's heavy cloak. Insania followed closely behind, wearing a cream and maroon dress in the latest Imperium fashion.

'Ready for our foray into Varspire's economic heart?' Drothinius asked without enthusiasm.

'I've been looking forward to it,' Takket replied. In truth, he was dreading descending into that layer of haze to visit a Soulshard crematorium, but he had to keep up appearances. Besides, it was getting harder and harder to think of excuses to avoid Yelleck and Enara. He had filled his first few days at court meeting everyone from Haddronius's favoured advisors to his head chef to middling functionaries. Each evening, Takket would feign exhaustion and retire early. He knew he would have to face the traitors some day, keeping his discovery of their betrayal a secret while probing for clues as to their true motives. For now, he was glad to put off that painful encounter.

'Let's go.' Drothinius gripped a Shard baton. 'I'll levitate us both. Just try to relax.'

Drothinius's Soulshard gleamed brightly. Takket's stomach lurched. He felt himself being pulled upwards from his chest, his ribcage dragging his body against gravity's pull. His feet lifted from the jade balcony, Drothinius rising with him to come to a hover some three feet above the floor. Insania drifted up to join them, clutching her own glowing baton.

Takket did not have time to become accustomed to hovering above the platform before Drothinius pushed them away from Varspire Tower.

Takket immediately regretted looking down. Beneath his feet, the Sharddust layer danced in twisting eddies. He could make out a handful of lights from taller Mundane dwellings, but saw nothing of the ground. A red void boiled below, only the grace of an Arcane standing between him and a plunge into that nothingness.

They accelerated, Takket feeling the force Drothinius exerted on his ribcage. Wind whipped by, cooling his face and tugging at his cloak. The distant sounds of the city below were drowned out by a constant roar. His heart pounded. He had scaled Magetowers, talked his way into vaults, taken trinkets from the necks of Arcanes, but never had he felt quite so *exposed*.

As they approached a granite Magetower, the roaring subsided and they slowed to a stop, dangling in the air above the swirling red Sharddust.

'Is it here?' Drothinius shouted to his wife.

'Yes,' Insania replied. 'Directly below us.'

'Good. I do not want to have to wander aimlessly in that murk. Honestly—you arranged this just to spite me, didn't you.'

Insania smiled.

Rolling his eyes, Drothinius allowed them to drop into the billowing red mass. The metallic smell of Sharddust reached them first, growing ever stronger as they descended. A gentle tickling of dust against skin quickly turned to an uncomfortable itch. The smells of the undercity grew thick in the gloom—sewage, cooking fires, roasting meat, molten metal, unwashed bodies. Muffled sounds echoed from all directions: the piercing ding of a chisel against rough Soulshard, the thud of crates and creak of floorboards. Somewhere nearby a Mage-powered machine whined. Voices of a hundred men and women gave a background hum, some shouting in warning or relaying orders, most just engaged in gentle conversation.

Through the haze, buildings appeared. Most were Mundane hovels, built using the round chitin shells of krilts. They grew over one another like infected pustules, an image not helped by the red dust staining their pale frame. Directly below, one building stood out simply because it looked like a building—rectangular, roofed in neat black tiles. An orderly intruder surrounded by haphazard boils.

They drifted towards the rectangular structure. Drothinius released Takket an inch above the Sharddust-coated granite roof tiles. Never before had Takket felt such relief at having his feet firmly planted in Sharddust.

Takket looked around. The roof was flat granite, buried under a layer of Sharddust that crunched underfoot. A corroded steel railing ran around the perimeter, piles of dust being blown under it with each gust. The red haze surrounded them on all sides, nearby Mundane houses merely misshaped shadows in the gloom. The roof's only other feature was a shed-sized brick protrusion to one end, sporting a heavy metal door, towards which Drothinius was already striding.

Following the Arcane, Takket squinted against the Sharddust scouring his face. The dust was almost as thick as it had been in the Crater Desert, and he could feel it scratching away in his sinus with every breath. It did, at least, provide some respite from the heat, covering the undercity in a cooling shade. That shade brought with it a dampness, the taste of mildew hanging heavy. Mould grew on every surface, an orange fungus spreading in defiance of the dust.

With a magical pull, Drothinius opened the steel door and ducked inside. Takket followed the Arcane and his wife into a small room, almost stumbling into a hole that filled most of the floor space. There were no stairs, no ladders, just a drop to the level below.

Of course, Takket thought. This was the entrance for Mages and Arcanes. Anyone who flew to the building could easily lower themselves down the gap.

A tug at his torso sent Takket's stomach groaning again, his feet rising from the floor and over the drop. Drothinius released him on the lower level. Takket mimicked the Arcane and stamped his feet on a metal grid to shed his Sharddust coating. They found themselves in a long hallway, grey granite lining the floors and walls alike, lit with gas lamps. This was far from the luxury of Varspire Tower, the walls unadorned, the lamps giving barely enough light to see. Sharddust coated the edges of the corridor, mingling with black and white ash. The smell was the strangest aspect of the hall: roast pork, mixed with an acrid hint of burnt hair.

At the far end of the corridor, a cast iron door opened to reveal an Arcane striding forward. She wore a black hooded robe, the hem and her leather boots coated in grey ash. A baggy silken scarf covered her neck, the very top of a Soulshard just visible between it and her collar. Black stains smudged her upper face, making her red eyes seem all the brighter.

She stopped in front of Drothinius to bow deeply. 'Arcane Drothinius. It is a pleasure to have such a distinguished guest. I'm Athika Hanaan, Prime Warden here. Welcome to Varspire Crematorium.'

Drothinius forced a smile. 'We've come to show Envoy Khantek here how we do things in Varspire. He has travelled a long way from the Imperium, so let's make sure he's welcome.'

Athika gave Takket a thin smile. 'Envoy, welcome to Varsen. I'm sure you'll be impressed. We've turned the criminal element into a boon for all faithful citizens. This way, please. We have been holding the condemned for your arrival, Arcane Drothinius.'

She turned and led the way back through the cast iron door, her footsteps thudding over the stone floor. After the doorway, she ushered them through to a balcony to one side.

'This is the Arcane observation booth—please do

make yourselves comfortable. I'll head down to the chamber right away, then we can bring out the first condemned.'

Takket stepped onto the balcony, which overlooked a circular pit of a room. Rough-hewn granite enclosed the chamber on all sides, the lower half blackened with soot. A metal grating ringed the outer wall, leading to a blackness below. Gas lamps circled the upper edge of the chamber, turned low to plunge the room into a sombre twilight. Across from their balcony stood a second, but where theirs was completed with elegant chairs and a table of refreshments, the far balcony was furnished only with a ring of iron bars that would have been at home in a prison cell.

Two doors faced each other on either side of the pit. The entire layout reminded Takket of the fighting arenas of old, where the condemned and reckless alike would fight to the death for the amusement of Arcanes. The image sent a chill down his spine.

An iron door to the balcony opposite slammed open and a handful of huddled Mundanes peered through. A mother with greying hair ushered her brood of five children onto the balcony, clutching a baby to her chest. All wore sleeveless cloth robes, grey dye stained red with Sharddust. Tears streamed down the faces of the woman and the older two children, while the younger three looked bewildered.

Athika emerged from one of the doorways below, trailed by a Scalist priest wearing a linen cloak that shifted from black near his feet to a bright red at his shoulders. Near the centre of the room, they came to a stop.

Shouts from the second doorway drew Takket's

attention. A mundane man, wearing only mottled brown trousers, was forced into the room. Around his neck, a steel collar was tightly wrapped. Two metal poles, ten feet long each, extended from the collar, pushed forward by a pair of Varsen soldiers. They manoeuvred the prisoner via this rigid leash into the centre of the room.

The prisoner screamed hysterically, alternating between desperate pleading, impossible threats and inventive curses. His yells cut off into a choke as the soldiers twisted their rods, tightening the man's leash. He fell to his knees, staring around in panic.

Athika's voice boomed through the pit. 'Relj, you have been found guilty and sentenced to immolation. The damage you have caused society will be repaid now. Fear not, your death shall benefit all of Varsen.'

She tugged her scarf over her lower face, red eyes regarding the man menacingly. He twisted, turning to stare up at his family on the balcony above. The stench of urine filled the room.

The priest's voice was calm, almost fatherly. 'The demons have guided your path in this life, but the angels still care for you. In the last moments, let go of your hate, your jealousy, your despair. Fill your mind with calm, clarity, joy, that you may be reborn into a better life, one that will lead you down the angel's path.'

'I love—'

But the man burst into flame. There was no scream, no pain. One moment a man knelt in the centre of the room, the next he was replaced by a pillar of fire. Droplets of water condensed around Athika, freezing into snowflakes, the Soulshard at her chest

176

glowing brightly. Shard and fire faded. Where the man had knelt, a pile of ash now lay, his metal collar a red-hot ring of steel suspended from the soldiers' poles. Jutting out of the soot was an uncut Soulshard, a large baton. A human rendered into a Shard to feed Varsen's economy.

Athika's Soulshard glowed again and the baton rose into the air and over to the balcony, where Drothinius grasped it.

'A gift, Arcane.' She bowed.

'Thank you.' Drothinius inspected the Shard, disinterested. The uncut red stone refused to glow at his touch. It would take a master craftsman hours of painstaking work to turn this into a usable Soulshard, chiselling out its faceted sides. 'But I do think this gift might be better appreciated by our good friend from the Imperium.'

He handed the Shard to Takket, who clutched it with both hands. Still warm. Still stinking of the man's death—burning hair, roasted pork. Takket felt sick. Unable to force himself to thank the Arcane for such a horrific gift, he merely nodded in response. He knew all Shards were produced by burning life in this way, and only human immolation had a chance of producing batons. He knew every Shard he had ever handled originated with a death. He knew this Shard was no different from the countless others that had passed through his hands, yet it still disgusted him. It was one thing to know technicalities of Shard manufacture, another thing entirely to see the murder committed.

'What was his crime?' Takket asked weakly.

Servants hurried into the room, sweeping the man's

ashes into the grated drains that surrounded the chamber.

Athika beamed with pride. 'Thievery.'

Takket shook his head. 'What?'

She thought for a moment. 'I can't recall the exact details. We get so many through here every day. I believe he was a Mage's servant who stole food from his master.'

'He was executed for stealing food?'

Insania gave Takket a patronising smile. 'Of course, our guest is from a land of lax laws. Here, we do not distinguish between criminal acts. Breaking the law is breaking the law. It is disobeying the orders set forth by the Arcane-lord. Any crime is treason. The price of betraying Varsen is immolation.'

Takket felt faint as he stared at the rock in his hand. Uncut, the Shard was rough to the touch, flickering only dimly through its matte exterior, like a smouldering log. Years of life, hopes, fears, joy and pain all resulted in this misshapen stone. This was the fate that awaited thieves in Varsen.

Thieves like Takket.

'Perhaps our guest would be more impressed by a show of patriotism,' Athika suggested. 'Next, we have a woman who has volunteered to give her life for the good of her family.'

'Why would anyone do that?' Takket asked, startled.

'She is dying,' Athika explained. 'She will go slowly, painfully, and for no reason other than the whims of demons. A burden on her family and friends. She has chosen the angel's path, the selfless path. In return, her family will receive Shard flakes worth half the value of the stone she produces.'

The Mundane onlookers on the opposite balcony had been replaced with another family, this one far larger. Three couples stood with a multitude of children. Some cried. Some gave bitter-sweet smiles. Some stared ahead in glazed disbelief.

The sweepers and soldiers withdrew from the room below. A moment later, the troops returned, helping an elderly woman stagger into the chamber. Her rough-spun dress hung loosely from her emaciated frame, her wispy hair the purest white. The two guards helped her sit on the ash-stained floor, giving far more care than Takket had expected.

'Kilana,' Athika said calmly, 'on behalf of all of Varsen, I thank you for this sacrifice.'

The priest followed on. 'You have followed the path of the angels in this life. I pray they see fit to recognise your selfless acts. Focus only on joy and accomplishment. I fervently pray that you be blessed and ascend to be reborn as a Mage in your next life.'

The elderly woman gave her family one final look, eyes tearing.

'I'm ready,' she croaked, closing her eyes.

Athika's Soulshard glowed brilliantly.

The woman became fire, then ash.

In the wake of the fading flames, another uncut shard lay in its bed of soot. This Shard, however, was hand-sized, less than half the length of the one Takket clutched.

'Just a rock?' Takket asked.

Athika nodded grimly. 'Only about a third of human immolations result in baton-sized Shards. Do not fear—her family will still receive half its value in compensation.'

A sob came from the opposite balcony. Half a rock's worth was a pittance compared to half a baton. For a family that size, it was the difference between months of food and mere weeks, between improving their home and simply patching its cracks. A grandmother's death, and all their family would receive was a few free meals.

The ashes were swept into the drain. The doors below opened for the next Mundane to be ushered in. Takket closed his eyes. He gripped the rock in his hands painfully, knowing he would never again be able to look at a Shard the same way.

Takket's foul mood persisted into the evening. Invited to a grand ball at Varspire Tower, he expected a fine place to further his cover story, make contacts, draw information. Instead, he found himself on the outskirts of the merriment. He could not stomach bowing to these people, making conversation while knowing full well where their power originated. Mages and Arcanes twirled above in pairs, clutching Soulshards to power their levitation. They spiralled in elaborate patterns to the sound of a choir, rising and falling in a dance made possible only by magic use. Each glowing Shard clutched in a dancer's hand represented a life lost, all to entertain these elites.

Takket found a quiet corner of the hall, behind an obsidian pillar, and watched the festivities. Large fires burned around the jade floor, replacing the heat Arcanes transferred into energy to keep themselves afloat. As with every major function in Varspire, lavishly appointed tables dotted the room, food and drink to fuel the distinguished guests. Woodsmoke mixed with the aroma of Varsen cooking and the freely flowing wine. The room flickered in the light of Soulshard chandeliers above. In the red glow Takket could see only the blood that had been spilled to manufacture the decorative lights. The charred meat smelled too similar to that demon-cursed pit in the crematorium.

'You're in my spot,' a voice called from nearby. Takket turned to see Hekaena striding over, her pace measured with the clack of her staff against the jade floor. *Not now.* Takket was in no mood to play nice with the abrupt woman, especially while she held that angel-forsaken Soulshard at the end of her staff.

'I wasn't aware it was claimed,' he said dryly.

'It is I who normally hides from these functions,' she replied. 'Are you not in the mood to be spouting pleasantries or taking part in the dance?'

Takket shrugged. 'It's not like my kind can take part in this.' He waved towards the airborne dancers.

Hekaena smirked. 'You really expect me to believe that the Imperium's envoy cannot afford to burn a few Shards to show off his abilities?'

'Mundanes don't burn Shards,' he retorted.

'You're a Mundane?'

'I thought everyone in Varspire was well aware of that particular disadvantage,' Takket grumbled. 'I've overheard more than a dozen whispered conversations questioning the Imperium's decision to send a humble Mundane to your court.'

'I don't keep up with court gossip,' Hekaena replied. 'I just assumed you were a Mage.'

'Simply a Mundane. My deepest apologies.'

She studied him in the ever-shifting light of her Soulshard as if looking at him for the first time. After a painfully long pause, she smiled. 'A Mundane representing the Imperium—how did that happen?'

Takket sighed. 'Oh you know, hard work, grit, luck. The only option for those of us who can't magic-away our problems.'

She barked a laugh. 'Not many would speak to a Varsen like that.'

Takket cursed himself. 'My apologies,' he stammered, suddenly all too aware that this woman had the power to have him executed. 'I did not mean offence.'

'None taken. It's about time someone at court actually spoke their mind. Though I do wonder, what happened to the sycophantic envoy I met at that banquet?'

His initial instinct was to make an excuse, feign illness. Criticising the crematorium, the core of Varsen's economy, would not go down well. Perhaps he could play off his bad mood as envy of Varsen's success.

No, he thought to himself. Hekaena had not responded like the other courtiers. This was the most open she had been—when he was curt, honest. He thought back to the dossiers, her work with Mundanes. It was time for a new approach.

'I was taken to the crematorium today,' he explained.

Her face softened with sympathy. 'Oh, of course. That would be...'

'Horrific,' he finished.

She nodded, glancing around the hall. 'I can

certainly understand how seeing fellow Mundanes die like that would be upsetting.'

He shook his head irritably. 'It doesn't matter if they were Mundanes or Mages or Arcanes—they were *people*. People harvested like crops. And their crimes? Stealing food. Lashing back at a guardsman. Failing to bow to an Arcane. The worst were the volunteers. It was made out to be a noble sacrifice, but the truth was far from noble. Their deaths were coerced. You tell an old man that the only way his family can afford to eat next month is if he dies, and of course he's going to "volunteer". These are nothing but executions with a prettier coating.'

She stared at him, vibrant red and silver eyes boring into his, seeming to search for something in his soul. She gave a grim nod. 'I'm afraid that is not even the worst of it.'

A shadow rounding the pillar interrupted her. They turned to see Ensellus silently crossing jade tiles.

'Hekaena,' he said hurriedly with that nasal voice of his. 'Is this man bothering you?'

She rolled her eyes. 'No, Ensellus. Not every conversation I have is painful, only those I have with you.'

Ensellus glared at Takket as he spoke to her. 'I do not like members of the royal family being isolated with a Mundane. Especially a foreigner.'

'Oh please,' Hekaena said, weary. 'You don't like most of what I do. As I've told you a thousand times over, I can take care of myself. I have this, do I not?' She raised her staff. 'You're the one who insisted I carry this thing around. If it can keep me safe in the depths of the undercity, it can keep me safe in my father's palace.'

Ensellus narrowed his eyes at Takket. 'The Mundanes of the undercity have no training. Who knows what abilities the Imperium gives its agents.'

'Enough,' Hekaena barked. 'I'll not have you dictate who I can and cannot talk to. I was enjoying a conversation with the Envoy here, and would like to continue. *Alone.* I'm sure there are spy reports that need your attention, or a servant that requires your needless questions.'

'Hekaena...'

She raised her chin. 'If you have a problem with my commands, I suggest you speak to my father.'

Ensellus relented with a bow. He met Takket's gaze as he turned to leave, red eyes filled with scorn. The pair watched him stalk away, his head arcing around like a ykkol cat searching for prey.

'Sorry about him,' Hekaena said once Ensellus was well out of earshot. 'He does not like me speaking to anyone he hasn't approved personally. And that list is short indeed.'

'He does seem...dedicated.'

'That's one word for it. Now, where were we?'

Takket sighed. 'I believe you were about to tell me what could be worse than murder for monetary gain.'

'Ah.' She grimaced. 'What you saw was horrid, I don't deny that. But that's not the end of the suffering. You saw the sting, the painful instant. To see true agony, you need to see the infection that's left behind.'

'Death seems relatively final to me.'

'For the deceased, yes. For their family, it's just the beginning. Those people only broke the law because it's so hard to survive as Mundanes here. Two parents

184

can barely scrape together enough flakes to keep their children fed. With one gone, what happens to the other? They have the same burden, but half the wages. It's never long before they are brought to the crematorium. Whether starvation drives them to steal, or frustration causes them to snap at an Arcane, they always end up convicted.

'Then their children become orphans. And orphans? In Varsen, they are just Soulshards in waiting. They either struggle on the streets, begging and pickpocketing, or they go to the orphanages. There, once they're old enough, most die, persuaded through fear or hunger or threats to volunteer themselves to the crematorium. Teenagers sacrificing themselves to give their younger siblings some meagre wealth. Those few who survive have no skills, no trade.'

Takket nodded grimly. 'So they struggle to make ends meet, and the cycle continues.'

'Exactly. This, all of this—' She waved a hand over the luxury that surrounded them, '—is built on the ashes of the Mundanes.'

Takket rubbed his face with frustration. 'And yet it continues. Soulshards made from destroyed families are burned for transport and industry and dancing.'

Hekaena regarded him thoughtfully, pity in those glorious eyes. 'You are either a genuinely good man, or a terrible envoy.'

Takket smirked. 'Can't I be both? I just feel so helpless.'

She bit her lip in thought. 'Do you really want to do something to help those broken families?'

'Of course.'

'Then come with me, tomorrow. I go down to the undercity most days. Help the Mundanes there. I'm building an orphanage—a real orphanage that will give children half a chance to break the cycle. A chance at a decent life.'

'I would be glad to help, but what can I do? I'm just a Mundane.'

'You would be amazed at what a difference a kind heart can make.'

He felt growing determination. He should be glad that the plot was progressing, that he was finally getting a chance to spend more time with Hekaena, but he could only think about those piles of ashes, those tearful families.

'I would be honoured.'

'Excellent, I will meet you at your embassy at noon tomorrow. We can do some real good here, Envoy.'

'Please, call me Khantek.'

She smiled fondly, placing a hand on his shoulder. 'Of course. Have a good night, Khantek.'

CHAPTER THIRTEEN

The gas lamps lit the jade-trimmed obsidian surface of the domed ceiling high above. Only a handful of functionaries clustered around the hall this early in the morning, conspiratorial voices a buzz in the background. Incense burned, ridding the room of the stagnant smell that accompanied much of the heart of Varspire Tower.

Takket traipsed over the well-worn jade rug to the throne dais. The vulgar chair radiated bloody light across the room, a memento to its murderous construction. Every Shard baton bound into its frame represented a life lost, a father who would never again hold his children, a sister never to grace a family's dinner table.

He forced his eyes away from the vile thing, and stared upwards. The central column of the spire towered dizzyingly, glowing blood-red in the light of innumerable Shards. Floors were marked in rings of balconies, windows and doorways. Specks drifted across the gulf, Mages traversing the structure, Soulshards glowing in hand.

At the peak of it all would be the royal chambers. Somewhere up there, his prize hung around Haddronius's neck. Yet having travelled across the world, conned his way into the heart of this Arcanedom, Takket felt no closer to the Pure Shard.

'Quite a view, is it not?' Innisel said. Takket turned

to see the elderly man striding across the hall, his white pleated hair draped over the shoulder of his black and green robes.

'Impressive indeed,' Takket replied with forced awe. 'I was hoping to find you here.'

'Well, found me you have. What can I do for you?'

'I wanted to discuss Akken, the servant you assigned to me.'

'I know who Akken is.' Innisel frowned. 'Is something wrong?'

'Not at all. I just really do not require his service.'

The frown deepened. 'Has he done something to offend you?'

'No,' Takket said, off-handed. He needed the servant gone. His suspicions that the man might be spying on him had only grown over the past few days. Documents moved. Papers disappeared, only to materialise a day later. Every time Takket had a hushed conversation, Akken would appear, dusting some clean object outside the door. Still, Takket could not directly accuse the man. He did not need Akken dismissed only to be replaced by a new agent more wary of discovery. 'It's simply that my two assistants can handle domestic chores around the embassy on their own.'

Innisel's eyes narrowed. 'I was under the impression that your two companions were diplomatic aides, not cleaners.'

'Well yes, but they are capable of doing both.'

'But they don't need to if Akken is there. Surely his presence can only be helpful, giving them more time to work with you instead of cleaning your laundry.'

'True, yet I cannot ask Varsen to pay wages of a

man who is not really required.'

'Are you implying Varsen cannot afford to employ a single Mundane servant?' Innisel asked, offended.

'Not at all. I just—'

Ensellus's nasal voice interrupted. 'What's going on here?'

Takket turned, the man's sharp features uncomfortably close.

'Ensellus.' Innisel nodded. 'We were discussing duty rosters. It seems Envoy Khantek is displeased with the servant he has been assigned.'

'Oh? And why would that be?'

Takket cursed the demons for this stupid scheme. He would have to try another tactic—before he made the situation worse.

'I'll be honest,' he lied. 'Having an extra servant is just causing me more work. I'm rather particular about filing systems, organisation. I may not keep my office tidy, but I know where ever document is, the location of every one of my notes. My aides understand my system. Akken does not. He seems to care about appearances more than practicalities. In his efforts to neaten the embassy, he keeps moving critical documents, making them harder to find. It's made all the worse by the sensitivity of some of those files.'

Innisel raised his eyebrows. 'You suspect he is tampering with important documents?'

'If that's the case,' Ensellus sneered, 'I can assign a troop of soldiers to monitor him.'

Demons, no. That was the last thing Takket needed. He took a breath. 'No, no. I'm sure the man is not dishonest. It's simply the inconvenience of having to search my office every time I need to remind myself of the details of a treaty, or the relation of a particular Arcane to the Varsen family.'

Innisel gave a patronising smile. 'It seems to me that you just need to instruct him better. I assure you— all Mundanes in Varspire Tower are well trained and will obey orders to the letter. Do not be afraid of giving him commands just because you are only a Mundane. He will still obey unquestioningly. Just make it clear to him what he is and what he is not to touch.'

'You are right, of course,' Takket said, admitting defeat. He was not going to convince Innisel to remove Akken, and if he kept pushing his luck, he was likely to have half a dozen soldiers loitering in the embassy. It was time to extricate himself before he dug this hole any deeper. 'I will have words with him today, make sure we are on the same page. Thank you for your time.'

'You are welcome,' Innisel said with the same patronising smile. 'Varsen can be a jarring experience for those from the Imperium, even for trained diplomats.'

Turning to leave, Takket met Ensellus's hateful expression. Innisel may have accepted the excuse of a foreigner too shy to confront a Mundane, but the security chief did not look convinced. Walking over the carpeted floor, Takket could feel the man's eyes boring into the back of his skull.

This meeting had been a disaster. Akken still had free reign to snoop through the embassy, and Ensellus would be watching Takket closer than ever.

Takket waited in the corridor outside the embassy

for Hekaena. Lingering inside would just increase the likelihood of a confrontation with Yelleck or Enara. He had spoken to them briefly, informed them of his meeting with Hekaena, but had made excuses to leave before they could pry any details. Now that he was finally making progress with the Varsen family, he did not want any reminders of his employers' lies.

Someone nearby was cooking lunch, the smell of charring meat carried through the air vents, allowing a brief respite from the stagnant air. Takket was growing accustomed to the smell, it was at least better than the Sharddust of the undercity. Often, he was woken by hints of frying krilt egg in the morning, as good an alarm as he had in his windowless room.

Hekaena rounded a corner, and he smiled broadly. Today she wore a maroon dress made of hard-wearing linen. The obsidian and gold staff in her hand tapped against the green carpet, the light of its Soulshard joining the glow of the hallway's gas lamps.

'Arcane Hekaena.' He bowed.

She tutted. 'Now, now, Khantek. If I'm to drop titles for you, then you must drop them for me. And no more bowing.'

He smiled. 'Sounds like a fair exchange...Hekaena.'

'Great. Shall we?'

He followed her through the winding corridors. Soldiers bowed low as the pair passed. Arcanes paused to nod respectfully to Hekaena. None so much as glanced at Takket.

'So,' Hekaena said. 'How are you finding our little city?'

'Other than the casual execution of humans for profit?'

She grimaced. 'Yes. Other than that.'

Takket had been asked the question a hundred times in the few days since he had arrived. Up till now, he had always answered with gushing platitudes, remarking on the scale of Varspire, the lavish food, the ingenious architecture. To Hekaena, he felt he should give a more honest assessment.

'Varspire is...a contradiction. Varsen accuses the Imperium of ostentation, yet throws regular extravagant parties, fills its halls with art.' He gestured towards the jade and obsidian sculptures along the walls. 'This tower is filled with Mages, burning Shards into dust constantly, yet is almost free of the red haze. The Mundanes below can't use Shards, yet drown in the dust. You say Mundanes are inferior, yet your corridors are protected by Mundanes bearing rifles.'

Hekaena smiled to a pair of soldiers guarding an ornate door, reinforcing his point. 'Yes. We say Varsen's major export is Soulshards, but in all honesty, I feel this city is best at producing hypocrisy. Strange that it has taken so long for an Imperium envoy to notice.'

'I believe my predecessors were better at holding their tongues.'

She chuckled. 'Then why are *you* so poor at diplomacy?'

'Perhaps it requires a Mundane's eyes to really see what's happening in this city.'

'Perhaps.' She smiled, pushing aside a glass door to a balcony overlooking the city. The midday sun dominated the clear sky, and filled the air with a dry heat. Just below the balcony, the Sharddust layer reflected the sunlight, casting a red hue over the host of towers rising from the haze. A strong wind blew from the north, but was too warm to offer much comfort from the sun's glare. It did, at least, bring fresh air to the stagnant hallways of Varspire Tower, even if marred with a hint of copper from the dust.

'Are you sure about this?' she asked. 'Walking the undercity is far from pleasant. And I don't mean the Sharddust. You cannot unsee what you'll experience down there.'

'I can't unsee what happened at the crematorium. If you say this can help those families, then what choice do I have?'

She studied Takket, then beamed. 'Then let's do some good together.'

She shifted her hand, releasing her staff's gold-lined obsidian haft to grip the Soulshard at its peak. The Shard responded to her touch with a brilliant glow.

'Try to relax,' she said. The pair ascended smoothly together. Hekaena seemed to take more care than Drothinius had as she manoeuvred them over the Sharddust layer. She pushed them north, just fast enough for the breeze to be pleasantly cooling.

'Are you doing alright?' she shouted over the wind.

'I'll be fine. Just a strange sensation—flying.'

'You were not flown around Indspire by Mages?'

'No.' Takket tried not to focus on the formless red clouds under his feet. He knew the tops of the misshapen houses would be just beneath the Shard layer, but his subconscious was convinced that nothing but an endless drop lay below. 'All Imperium cities are designed to be travelled on the ground. Streets. Carriages. Canals. Our simple joys.'

'And Indspire Tower itself? How do your dignitaries get to the upper levels?'

'Stairs, lifts. Hardly new inventions.'

She chuckled. 'The stagnant Imperium. Outsmarting us with stairs and streets.' She slowed them to a stop, eddies ripping across the haze below. 'We're here. Say farewell to the sun.'

They started to drop into the red gloom. The familiar scents of the undercity rose to greet the pair: Sharddust, decay, sewage, woodsmoke. Malformed buildings could be glimpsed through the haze, their chitin walls slopped carelessly into place. Takket peered at grooves on the outer walls, which Mundanes scaled to reach doorways built up the side of the structures. Holes had been drilled into the chitin, allowing light in and smoke out. The pinprick windows glowed orange from wood fires cooking the midday meal, bitter smells of boiling roots seeping from the bloated buildings.

Hekaena set them down on the street, or what passed for a street. Takket shifted his feet over the thick layer of Sharddust crunching over the bare bedrock. To one side, the road split and meandered into the all-consuming red dust between three of the grotesque housing piles.

Emaciated bodies lay in mounds of filth piled against the chitin walls. At first, Takket thought they were dead, corpses left to rot. To his horror, he saw signs of life: weak breathing, twitching arms. A few of the stronger homeless sat upright, empty clay bowls clutched in bony hands. He could not judge any of their ages, with their skin so taught, hair falling out, all caked in thick Sharddust. These were the poorest of the Mundanes, those who could not afford so much as a room in one of the hovels. Unemployed, yet too honest or stubborn to steal.

In the other direction, a large area was left free of buildings. Mundanes swept away the Sharddust between stacks of wood and chitin neatly arranged around the clearing.

One Mundane broke away from the others to hurry over, arms open, grinning madly.

'Hekaena,' said the grandfatherly man. His grey hair was as dishevelled as his beard, and his clothing was no finer, a drab grey cloak and worn moccasins. He stopped a pace away from Hekaena, not breaking into the hug that his arms promised, but still acting far less formal than Takket had come to expect.

'Rithdal,' Hekaena introduced, 'this is Khantek Fredeen, the new Imperium envoy. He's kindly offered to assist me today. Khantek, this is Rithdal. A local...magistrate.'

'That title's far too noble for me.' Rithdal turned friendly blue eyes to Takket. 'I'm just a cantankerous old man, loud enough for these dullards to have no choice but to listen. I organise folk for when Hekaena comes, get the capable to help, get everyone else out of her way.'

'A pleasure to meet you,' Takket said. Unsure how to greet a Mundane community leader, he bowed, eliciting a guffaw.

'Ha! That's a new one.' Rithdal grinned. 'Bowing to a Mundane. Only in the Imperium.'

'I'm a Mundane too,' Takket explained.

'Oh, I know. Don't think we've not heard of the Mundane envoy causing a stir up in the spires.'

Takket's surprise clearly amused Rithdal. 'You may not be able to see us up in those towers, but we see you. Mundanes fill Varspire Tower, cleaning toilets, holding plates, smoothing sheets. If one thing's true the world over, it's that Mundanes talk. Especially about anything that has the Arcanes grumbling into their wine. You're spoken of in drink houses from Towersfoot to Bridgehead. Got yourself quite the following.'

Hekaena smirked. 'Seems I'm not the only celebrity in the undercity today.'

Takket just bowed his head humbly. Greater notoriety could only hurt his efforts. More people talking about him meant more people watching. Rithdal was correct: Mundanes were everywhere in Varspire Tower, behind every curtain, in every side room. The invisible majority. It would take just one to overhear a scheme, see him skulking somewhere he did not belong, and it would be the talk of the town. Ensellus would certainly have sources in those Mundane taverns.

'Well,' Takket said, eager to change topic, 'we didn't come down here to exchange court gossip.'

'Indeed,' Hekaena said. 'Let's build an orphanage.'

Rithdal beckoned them onwards, setting off across the crunching Sharddust to the open area ahead. 'Right you are. We've done everything you said. Gathered the materials in piles for you. Cleared all debris. Even tried to sweep the dust, but the demons won't let the ground stay clean for long.'

'It's perfect.' Hekaena examined the stacked chitin, piles of wood and barrels of nails that stood before a clear expanse of bedrock. 'Well, let's begin. Do you have the plans, Rithdal?'

'Of course.' The man scurried away, returning moments later with a roll of paper. He spread it out over the floor, revealing a detailed pencil drawing of a domed building complete with measurements and notations. Rithdal pinned the corners with some dust-smoothed pebbles from his pocket.

Hekaena examined the diagram, then shifted her grip back onto her Soulshard. Its glow intensified, rays of light scattering off the surrounding red dust to form a glittering orb with Hekaena at its centre. A pile of chitin lifted from the ground, each carapace the height of a man, every section floating through the air like paper. They arranged themselves before the Arcane in a sweeping archway of shell. Nails flew from an oaken barrel, but instead of driving themselves into the chitin, they merely came to a rest underneath.

Takket shivered as a chill passed through the air, breath coming out in cloudy puffs as if on a winter morning. The nails began to glow red, then yellow. They melted together, forming a molten iron network that wrapped around the chitin, binding it together without so much as singeing the bone. Tendrils of molten metal drove themselves into the ground, securing the structure in place. The glow faded. An archway, large enough to walk through, now stood on the bedrock.

'Wow,' Takket breathed. The ground around Hekaena had frosted over.

Hekaena smiled. 'This is going to take too long if I keep having to move to draw on the heat around us, and we'll freeze if I stand in one place. I need another source of energy to transfer. Bring the wood over to me.'

Takket followed the stream of Mundanes who made their way over to a stack of wood. He hefted a large plank, struggling with its weight. Splinters dug into his palms from the decrepit log, the smell of mould thick from its damp surface. Only the finest of building materials for the Mundanes of Varspire.

At Hekaena's signal, Takket dropped the plank onto the dust by her feet. Once again, her Shard began to glow brightly and building materials took to the sky. Pale chitin plates interlocked to form walls, molten iron binding them in place. As Hekaena worked, the wood at her feet began to blacken and crumble to ash, consumed by an invisible fire. There was no light, no smoke, just a cloud of condensing steam billowing into the red sky.

Marvelling at the power of Arcanes, Takket hurried back over to the wood pile. As he struggled to lift another rotten log, a slim pair of hands grasped the far end. He looked up in surprise to see a girl, perhaps fifteen years of age. She wore a grey sleeveless tunic that stretched down below her knees. Mismatched patches and repairs littered the threadbare material, which looked as if it once formed a dress for a much younger girl. Her fair hair was cut short, rough clumps jutting out at haphazard angles, all caked in Sharddust.

She smiled shyly. 'Heard you came from the fancy towers just to help us. Least I can do is lend a hand.'

'Appreciate it.' Takket looked over his shoulder, backing towards Hekaena. 'I'm afraid I'm not as young as I once was.'

'Eh, we all have our faults.' She flashed a wicked grin as they dropped the log, and started back towards the pile. 'Name's Lyssa.'

'Pleasure to meet you, I'm Khantek Fredeen.'

'We all know you. It true you're from the Imperium?'

Takket chuckled, helping her with the next log. 'Yes. It seems I'm rather more famous than I thought. Do you often help with this sort of thing?'

'Yeah, course. Especially on this one. It's an orphanage, and I'm an orphan, ain't I? Oh, don't look at me like that. I'm fine. Doing this mostly for my sisters.' She nodded to a cluster of three girls, aged from around five to eight. Takket could see the family resemblance, the fragile noses, light hair. They were clad in similar rough-spun tunics, either too baggy or too small.

'Who looks after you?'

'I do,' Lyssa replied, defensive. 'I get jobs, time to time. Covering for people too sick to work. Hekaena helps us too, brings food or Shards. Keeps us going. Hoping I'll get a real job soon. Maybe working in a Magetower—those're the plushest gigs. Just want a good place for the girls to stay. A place like this.'

She nodded towards the growing structure. Where a short while ago there had been an empty space, the frame of a large complex was taking shape. Chitin attached alongside ribs of iron to form walls and floors of a large dome. Hekaena worked away, her brow creased with concentration.

'Well.' Takket dropped the plank. 'At this rate, your sisters will have a grand place to stay in no time.' He turned to Hekaena and spoke in a low voice. 'Thank you for this. It feels wonderful to actually do some good here.'

For once, he did not lie.

The darkening of the red haze signalled sunset, or as much of a sunset as the undercity would receive. The sun was alien here, some fabled object high above the Sharddust, bathing the landscape in a directionless glow.

Takket perched on an upturned barrel, slurping at the steaming bowl of soup in his hands. A sharp change from the scorched meats and sugared desserts of Varspire Tower, the soup was watery and bland. Root vegetables floated in its grey murk, boiled beyond recognition. Sharddust steadily dissolved into the liquid to stain it an ever more rusty brown. The soup tasted like copper, smelled of mildew.

Even the bowl was unimpressive, unpainted clay lumped together by untrained hands.

The meal was, however, appreciated. Takket had not exerted himself so much for months. He had pushed himself, trying to impress Hekaena with his dedication. Lyssa had matched his effort. The girl was an inspiration, probing him with questions of the Imperium, never once complaining or requesting a break. Whenever his hands cried at the pain of another rotten splinter, or his legs demanded he stop, he just had to look to the girl. This building was for her. Varsen had taken away her parents, but he would help build her a home.

An hour ago, the construction of the orphanage's shell was completed. Instead of an empty expanse, a bone-white dome now dominated the space before Takket, dark iron melding the sheets of chitin together. Hekaena had gone inside to plan how to add the furnishings, but that was a job for another day. The workers had drifted away, heading home to feed their families. Some locals brought out soup for those who had nowhere to stay. Lyssa and her sisters had eaten the meal hurriedly before disappearing into an alley for the night.

The last hours had been exhausting, but Takket felt content. Throughout the day, Hekaena had shot him smiles with increasing fondness. He was getting through to her. Moreover, he had done something to help these people. Whether or not he managed to steal the Pure Shard, his journey to the New World had at least eased some suffering.

Footsteps crunching over the Sharddust-coated bedrock drew Takket's attention. Rithdal approached, his movements strangely furtive. His hair had gathered dust throughout the day, turning from grey to a vibrant red. He glanced into the darkening gloom around them, then sat, uninvited, on a barrel alongside Takket.

'It's been great working with you,' Takket said. 'I look forward to returning.'

Rithdal shook his head, whispering urgently. 'I would love nothing more than to discuss work, but we don't have time. Hekaena will return shortly and I must speak to you in private.'

Takket frowned. 'Has something gone wrong?'

'No. Yes.' He sighed. 'It's about your...companions. Those who claim to be from the Free Circle.' Takket's blood turned to ice. Rithdal made a calming gesture. 'Don't fear. I'm Free Circle too. Or I should say, I'm *actually* Free Circle.'

'What are you talking about?' Takket glanced around him. His instincts told him to run, put as much distance between himself and the elderly man as possible, but flight was not an option. He had no idea how to navigate the undercity. Even caked in dust and damp with sweat, his velvet maroon robes marked him as an outsider. A rich outsider. If he found his way back to Varspire Tower without being mugged, he would still have to somehow explain himself to the door guards. Hekaena was his way back, and she must not discover his association with the Free Circle.

'The two who travel with you—Enara and Yelleck, I believe they go by now—they are not who they claim to be. They *were* part of the Free Circle, some time ago. Mage allies of ours. When we started to plan the theft of the Pure Shard, they became obsessed. They didn't want to wait for our chance. Weeks ago, they left for the Imperium, planning to murder Khantek Fredeen and replace him. Since you're here, I assume they succeeded, and you are not Khantek.'

Takket stared at the man, soup forgotten. He wanted to rush to Hekaena, make an excuse to leave before Rithdal had a chance to pass on his information, but he hesitated. Rithdal might be telling the truth. It would explain much about Enara and Yelleck.

'What do you want from me?' Takket asked quietly.

'We want you to continue. Carry out the theft. Work with Enara and Yelleck, they must not become suspicious. But when you're ready, alert *me*. The Free Circle fears that Enara and Yelleck have no interest in the welfare of Mundanes, perhaps they never did. They want the Shard for themselves. They want to become Arcane. Who knows what they will do if they ascend. People with that sort of ambition are never

202

happy. I fear they'll drag Varsen into a civil war, and in war, it's Mundanes that do the bleeding.'

'How do I know you're not just a rival Mage after the same thing?'

Rithdal reached into his pocket and pulled out a Shard flake the size of a thumbnail. It emitted barely any light, glimmering softly. Rithdal was no Mage.

A shadow approached through the haze. Rithdal rose to his feet, pocketing the flake.

'Please, think on what I've told you,' he said hurriedly. 'The people here need you.' He turned and beamed as Hekaena walked through the Sharddust, his tone shifting in an instant. 'Hekaena! We're so thankful for all you have done for us.'

She smiled fondly at the elderly man. 'A pleasure, as always. I'll return in two days to work on the interior. Can you have the materials ready in time?'

'For you, we'll find a way.' He grinned. 'I best be getting back before it gets too dark. Thank you again.'

He nodded respectfully and strode into the haze, his moccasins grating across the Sharddust that carpeted the bedrock. Hekaena turned to Takket with a kind smile, eyes smouldering in the darkening light.

'Come, let's go home.'

Instead of levitating him remotely as before, she held out a hand. He took it, returning her smile. As they rose into the darkening sky together, thoughts crowded Takket's mind. He had been right to distrust Enara and Yelleck. Now he had a real contact in the Free Circle, a Mundane to work with to pull off this heist. Feeling the warmth of Hekaena's soft palm against his, he knew he was closer than ever to the Pure Shard.

CHAPTER FOURTEEN

Even after soaking in a bathtub all morning, Takket could still smell the Sharddust on his skin. Once Hekaena had carried him back to Varspire Tower, he had spent the night in fitful sleep, haunted by images of those skeletal beggars lining the undercity. Throughout the morning he wondered what would happen to Lyssa. Would she find stable employment in a Magetower or factory, or would she end up starving on those dust-coated streets?

Steeling himself for a confrontation, he crossed the embassy's maroon carpeted foyer to Enara and Yelleck's room. He turned the brass handle and pushed aside the mahogany door. The room was smaller than his own, but no less grand. Brightly lit by gas lamps, and enclosed by a white marble wall, the room was furnished with mahogany chairs, tables and beds, the latter set with velvet sheets and duck down pillows. The air smelled musty, the two occupants cooped up together for too long in the windowless room.

Yelleck looked up from behind a desk strewn with papers. 'Our envoy arrives of his own volition,' he said dryly. 'What have we done to deserve this honour?'

'Ignore him.' Enara turned from a shelf of neatly arranged files. 'My brother is just worried that you intend to back out of our deal.'

'Justifiably worried,' Yelleck grumbled. 'You've barely spoken two words to us since we arrived.'

'I know.' Takket closed the door behind him in case Akken returned from lunch. 'I'm sorry. I've been busy keeping our cover story intact so we aren't taken to the crematorium before the week is out.'

Yelleck grunted. 'Well, we're still here. Have you made any real progress?'

'I have actually,' Takket replied. He informed them of the previous day's work down in the undercity, Hekaena's fond smile, the squeeze she had given his hand before parting.

'Sounds promising.' Enara sat on one of the high-backed chairs. 'Keep on working her. Any luck with Akken?'

'None,' Takket replied, though he was worrying less about the servant, who was probably spying on behalf of the Free Circle. Takket would need to ask Rithdal. 'For now, just keep an eye out.'

'We will,' Enara assured him. 'While you've been working on Hekaena, we've been setting things up at our end. When you're ready to take the Shard, we'll be prepared to lead the uprising.'

Takket grunted. He had no idea what they actually planned, but doubted it involved his survival. They would either kill him after taking the Shard, or leave him trapped for an infuriated Arcane.

Someone knocked at the door.

'Come,' Takket called.

Akken eased the door open silently—if the man was not a spy, he was missing his calling.

'Envoy.' He nodded respectfully. 'I am sorry to interrupt, but Arcane Hekaena Varsen is here to see you.'

Takket smiled smugly at Yelleck and turned

towards the door. He smoothed his maroon velvet robes, pushed back his still-damp hair and cleared his throat. Akken led him into the lobby.

Hekaena stood regally on the plush carpet, her Soulshard staff clutched in one hand. She wore an ivory dress, silk in place of her normal linen, sleeveless in the Varsen style. Her eyes sparkled under the Soulshard chandelier.

Akken bowed deeply. She gave him a dismissive wave. 'You may go.'

He nodded, scampering into the dining room.

'That's all it takes to get him to leave?' Takket grinned. 'I should have tried that days ago.'

She beamed. 'Khantek. How are you today?'

'Good. Legs aching after yesterday, but can't complain. I had a warm bath, a cooked breakfast and a night on a down-stuffed mattress. I doubt any of the other Mundanes received such luxury.'

'No, but no other Mundane volunteered to be in the undercity. You would be hard pressed to find anyone to go down into that grime without coercion or high wages. Trust me—I've searched for a long time. Unless there is a substantial weight in Shards offered, Mages and Arcanes like to stick to the towers. Even the Mundanes working as Magetower live-in servants rarely venture into the streets unless ordered.'

'As I said, it felt good to help those people. Thank you for the invitation.'

Hekaena smiled fondly. 'An invitation's the reason I'm here.'

'Oh? I thought Rithdal needed more time to arrange supplies before we return.'

'He does.' She chuckled. 'But I do like that "we"

part. You really want to go back?'

'Certainly. I didn't go down there as a one-off to balm my conscience. I plan to see this through. If you're going down, I will too. If I'm welcome, of course.'

'Help is always welcome, and I'm glad you plan on continuing. Ensellus came with me once. He said it was to protect me, but I think it was just to get into my good graces. When I asked him to return, he actually laughed in my face.'

'Charming,' Takket said dryly. 'Well, I for one look forward to going back. I can hardly complain about breathing Sharddust when the people down there can never leave it. Now, you mentioned an invitation?'

'Yes.' She smiled enigmatically. 'My father's weekly royal dinner is tonight, just his most trusted courtiers and immediate family. I would like you to attend.'

'I would love to,' Takket said honestly. He had hoped for the opportunity to speak to her in a more private setting, without being coated in dust and sweat. 'But am I allowed? I doubt I qualify as a trusted courtier.'

'No.' Her eyes gleamed. 'But I am. Father has been hassling me for years to invite a plus-one. I would like you to be my guest.'

'I would be honoured.' He smiled fondly to hide his satisfaction. A dinner with her family might not be the personal encounter he desired, but it was a start. He had gained her trust. If he could gain her heart, the Shard might just be within reach.

Only a handful of functionaries remained in the

shadowed throne room, hammering out last-minute deals in hushed tones. The nervous glances, the sly smiles, the discreet hand-offs—Takket had seen it all before, often orchestrating such meetings to further his heists. Some men would profit, some would fall to ruin, the only guarantee was that the common people would never benefit.

Hekaena waited by her father's throne, her ivory dress turned red in its dancing light. Takket ascended the stairs, smiling warmly.

'Good evening,' he said.

'Good evening, Khantek.' She returned his smile, then turned to the throne. 'Horrid, isn't it? It's a wonder why my sister wants so much to sit on it.'

'You wouldn't want to rule?'

'Angels, no. Father hasn't left the Tower in months. The Arcane-lord is kept busy here, settling disputes, adjusting laws, dealing with insipid dignitaries.'

'Insipid dignitaries like myself?'

She smiled. 'No, you are a rare exception. If more people in the Tower were like you, then I may have desired the throne. As it stands, I find the people of the undercity much more palatable.'

'I fully understand. Unfortunately, my job is to deal with people up here.'

'Well, today your job is only to endure the inner court.' She held out a hand. 'And good luck with that.'

He took her hand, her skin rough for an Arcane, calloused from her time in the Sharddust layer.

She gripped the Soulshard at the end of her staff, its light drowned out by the glow from the throne. Smoothly, she levitated them through the domed ceiling's circular opening and into Varspire Tower's main shaft.

Rings of flickering Shard light illuminated the vertical passage. Open doorways and balconies lined the shaft to allow Mages and Arcanes easy access to adjoining rooms. Through pristine windows he glimpsed libraries and guard stations, treasure vaults and art galleries, offices and luxurious apartments. As they ascended, the grandeur only increased. Glass-lined dining halls reserved for elites. Gilded homes of Arcanes. Observation decks appointed with imported mahogany furniture.

Even the air improved with altitude. The evening breeze whistled through unseen ventilation ducts, pleasantly cooling.

The ring of oppressive functionality of the guard quarters interrupted the majesty. Mages and Arcanes glared from balconies, Shards gleaming in hand. Braced between reinforced concrete buttresses, openings dotted the wall, there to allow Mages to hurl deadly objects at attackers while keeping them safe from return fire. No rifles, bayonets or swords could be seen. The veteran magic-users here had no need for such primitive weaponry.

They approached the top of the shaft, its ceiling a mosaic of jade and emerald, backlit by gas lamps. Hekaena brought them to a balcony on the penultimate level, just below the royal apartments. She pushed aside obsidian-encrusted doors with a flick of magic, then led him into an opulent dining room. Curved windows formed the outer wall, showing a breathtaking view of the city. The setting sun enhanced the Sharddust's red hue, making the haze glow like molten metal, Magetowers like spears of iron sinking into an endless cauldron.

Takket tore his gaze away from the city. The curved room occupied a quarter of the floor, nestled between the tower's outer wall and inner shaft. Jade patterned the floor, the walls carved obsidian embellished with emeralds. From the ceiling—jade sculpted into abstract angels—a Soulshard chandelier hung, emblazoning the room with red light. A table of gilded rosewood curved with the room, lined with matching chairs upholstered with green velvet.

Hekaena's siblings—Valena and Drothinius—and their spouses stood to one side with Innisel and Ensellus. A gaggle of children, immaculately dressed in sleeveless silk outfits, gathered near the windows. Ensellus crossed the jade floor, eyes burning with fury.

'This is a private function,' he barked at Takket. 'What gives you the right to be here?'

'My invitation,' Hekaena replied condescendingly. 'I am permitted to invite a guest to *my father's* table.'

Ensellus looked between her and Takket, struggling for words, finally giving up with a grunt before slinking into a corner.

Hekaena grinned. 'Well, inviting you tonight was worth it just to see that look on his face.'

'Irritating Ensellus is always a pleasure,' Takket replied softly. They joined the guests, exchanging pleasantries. Takket was regarded with a mix of curiosity and scorn, but they all kept their words polite. Ensellus remained silent, unable to say a kind word to a Mundane.

The conversation cut off as a white light dazzled the room. Takket turned to see Haddronius, his flowing robes the purest white, matching the Shard hanging from his neck.

Takket bowed low while the others dropped to their knees—even Haddronius's children had to supplicate themselves before the Arcane-lord.

'Rise,' the aged man rasped. He lingered by the door to study Takket.

'I have invited Khantek, Father.' Hekaena stood alongside Takket, laying a hand on his arm. 'If that is allowed?'

Haddronius considered, then smirked. 'Not my first choice to sit alongside you. Still, even an Imperium Mundane is better than an empty chair.'

The Arcane-lord trudged across the floor, back hunched, his every wrinkle accentuated by the steady light of the Pure Shard. He sat at the head of the table, apparently a signal for the rest to sit. Hekaena guided Takket to a chair alongside hers, his place left unset.

Mundanes entered through a jade-coated door on the far side of the room. Their leader noticed Takket and muttered a series of quick commands. Other servants flocked over and efficiently laid out a platinum dining set, before covering the table with pitchers of wine and steaming bowls of various sauced meats. The now-familiar fragrances of local spices and root wine suffused the air. The last plate was barely on the table before the Mundanes withdrew into the kitchen, the door swinging shut to cover the preparations for the next course.

Haddronius's Shard grew brighter and a selection of charred meats, dripping in sauce, flew onto his plate. Once he had finished taking his portion, the others gripped Shards. Skewers of vegetables drifted by hunks of meat and pitchers of wine, arranging themselves in front of the table guests.

Belatedly, Takket realised he was the only Mundane at the table, a fact that occurred to Hekaena at the same time.

'What would you like?' she asked.

Even after a week eating Varsen food, he could not name a single dish. Sauces ranged from yellow to brown. Meat sat in steaks, slices and cubes, their creature of origin obscured under a glazing of spice.

'I'll have the same as you,' he replied.

She gripped the Shard at the end of her staff—now resting against her chair—and levitated an assortment onto his plate. Pungent steam drifted from the meal, thick with exotic spices.

'Thank you.' He elected to start with the skewers, which tended to be less burned than the other offerings. Carefully gripping the small clean length of the wooden skewer, he took a bite. Lamb, coated in a bitter sauce. As the ubiquitous spice burned his tongue, he wondered if he would have any taste buds left by the time he left Varsen.

'I apologise for the poor organisation,' Innisel said from across the mountain of food. 'I believe you may be the first Mundane to eat at this table. We have not had to consider serving ladles since the children were taught to draw magic. I will have words with the chef, make sure we account for this in the future.'

'I don't think we need to concern ourselves with accommodating Mundanes,' Ensellus sneered. 'This is a one-off.'

'Is it?' Hekaena raised an eyebrow.

Ensellus shifted uncomfortably. 'Yes, surely. I understand the political advantage of inviting the new envoy to dinner, but you're not planning on inviting a new Mundane up here each week, are you?'

'Of course not.' Hekaena took a sip of her wine. 'That would be madness.' As Ensellus gave a reassured nod, she grinned. 'Now, inviting this particular Mundane is another matter entirely. I fully intend to invite him next week. He has helped me in the undercity far more than the rest of you.'

Takket and Hekaena shared a smile. Ensellus blanched.

Drothinius looked up, meat crammed into his cheek as he spoke. 'You actually went back into Varsen City, Khantek? Whatever for? Our crematorium visit filled my sinuses with enough Sharddust to last a year.'

Takket wiped some sauce from his chin with a silken napkin. 'It was that visit that inspired me to return. I felt I needed to do something to assist the families of those who were immolated. The sins of one should not harm their entire family.'

Ensellus narrowed his eyes. 'And you think it is an envoy's role to involve themselves in the internal workings of a foreign country?'

Takket smiled politely. He had anticipated this question. 'I may be a diplomat, but I am also a Unism Circlist. To us, all souls must be protected against jealousy, envy and rage. The more content people are when they die, the more likely they are to become angels—not demons—in their next life. To us, that goes for all people, not just Arcanes. As an envoy, it *is* my role to bring my culture's values and traditions to Varsen so that we may better understand one-another.' He smiled to Hekaena. 'Besides, the look on their faces makes breathing any amount of dust worthwhile.'

Hekaena reached over to give his hand a supportive squeeze. Ensellus looked ill. The other guests just watched with interest.

'Well,' Drothinius said, 'better you than me. If this means Hekaena will stop trying to guilt us into descending into that gloom, then I'm all for it.'

'Here, here,' Valena replied in a teasing tone. Haddronius just looked on from the head of the table, his face an unreadable mask.

As the evening progressed, the focus of conversation drifted away from Takket, onto the latest art exhibition arriving from the Imperium and plans for the next banquet. Throughout the meal, Hekaena edged ever closer to Takket. Judging by his glare, Ensellus had not missed her body language. Despite the man's murderous scowl, Takket found himself smiling. All night, Hekaena repeatedly sided with him, agreeing with him in debates and defending him from Ensellus's barbs. Her family seemed to grudgingly accept Takket's presence. If all went well, it would not be long before he stood alone in Haddronius's room, Pure Shard in hand.

Lightheaded from wine, overfull with liberally spiced meats, Takket stood by the balcony with the remaining partygoers. The children had levitated to the top floor an hour ago, leaving the adults to enjoy a nightcap of imported mountain whisky. Haddronius had been the next to leave. The ruler of Varsen had barely said two words all night, just glowering from the end of the room.

As Valena and her husband made their excuses,

Hekaena strolled over to Takket, laying a hand on his arm.

'You did well.' She squeezed supportively. 'Far better than my previous guests.'

'I'm glad,' Takket replied. 'Thank you for inviting me. It's nice spending time with you without having to duck flying building materials. Though, your father did not seem impressed.'

'Oh, that's just Father.' She smiled. 'Trust me—if he took a dislike, you would know. Come on, let's get you down to the Embassy. Don't want to leave you stranded up here.'

Ensellus appeared behind her. 'There's no need.' He glared at Takket. 'I have to go downstairs to take care of some things. I'll take the envoy.'

'It's really not a problem,' Hekaena said.

'Please.' Ensellus erased the scorn from his face. 'I must have a word in private with the envoy. I...wish to apologise for my past bluntness.'

'Oh?' Hekaena smiled. 'How unlike you. Well, in that case, be my guest. I'll see you tomorrow at noon, Khantek. Have a good night.'

She hesitated, then kissed him lightly on the cheek before retreating onto the balcony, disappearing into the central shaft amid rays of Shard light. Takket stood, speechless. This evening had gone far better than he had ever dreamed.

His mood evaporated at the sight of Ensellus's glare. 'Come.' The man grasped a Soulshard in his pocked, his voice absent of his supposed contrition. 'Let's get you home.'

Takket's ribcage lurched as the man levitated them roughly into the air and towards the balcony, almost clipping their heads against the doorway. They dropped down the shaft at startling speed. Soulshards, doorways, windows all blurred together as they rushed down, the air that roared by his ears growing more stagnant as they descended.

They came to a jarring halt just before they left the shaft. Takket's feet dangled far above the glowing throne. He turned to Ensellus, murderous intent in the man's eyes.

'Listen to me, Envoy,' Ensellus hissed. 'Whatever you're doing with Hekaena, it ends *now*. I don't care how, but I don't want to see you at a royal dinner again. I don't want to hear about your sojourns into the undercity. I don't want to see your hidden smiles.'

'Who she spends time with is up to her,' Takket said, defiant.

'I'm no fool.' Ensellus drew Takket closer, red eyes burning in the Shard light. 'An envoy from the Imperium, courting Haddronius's tearaway child. A perfect political coup, twisting the Arcane-lord's family to serve the Imperium's cause. At best, you bind yourself to a potential heir. At worst, you cause a national embarrassment that you'll exploit. An admirable plan. There's only one problem—Hekaena is better than you can ever hope to be. If she's going to settle down, it will be with someone worthy of her.'

Takket stared into the man's eyes, seeing something there, jealousy under the rage. All too aware of his precarious position, of the gulf between his feet and the hard stone floor, Takket knew he had to be careful. Still, Ensellus would not be cowed by weakness. Takket would be damned before he let this man derail his plans. It was time to poke the sabrebear.

'Someone worthy, like you?' he said disdainfully.

Ensellus's eyes widened, his face pale. With a scream of rage, he pushed Takket, releasing his magical grip.

Takket fell.

Air howled past, the red glow of the throne hurtling towards him. A few feet from the hard stones, Takket was caught by a magical pull. Ensellus floated down, gently depositing him on the obsidian dais.

'This is your last warning,' he snarled before stalking away. Takket knelt on the stone of the incense-filled room, panting, sweat beading across his forehead. He had assumed Ensellus would not dare attack a foreign envoy without proof of misdeed. No sane man would send two countries to the brink of war without his master's blessing. Yet that intensity, that jealous rage—if Takket continued to pursue Hekaena, he would face Ensellus's wrath.

CHAPTER FIFTEEN

Hand in hand, Takket and Hekaena descended through the layer of Sharddust. Takket was growing accustomed to the feel of the dust tickling his skin, its sharp scent, the orange hue of sunlight through the haze. For the past week, Hekaena had brought him to the orphanage every other day. He mostly spent his time hauling materials inside the building, always assisted by Lyssa. As the sun set, the work would stop. Takket would share a meal with the Mundanes, telling the younger children tales of the Imperium, of the mountaintops clear of Sharddust, the Mundanes who lived without fear of execution.

He had tried to question Rithdal about Akken, but could never get a private moment with the elderly man. Rithdal spent his time close to Hekaena, and Lyssa trailed Takket all day.

Hekaena and Takket landed on the bedrock street, the coating of Sharddust crunching underfoot.

Takket was struck by a rancid smell of blood.

The street was eerily quiet—the starving forms of the beggars were gone. Where once the nebulous buildings had been lined with the skeletal bodies and outstretched hands, now only filth and Sharddust remained. Dried blood stained the white chitin walls, soaked into the grime.

'Not again,' Hekaena whispered, tears in her eyes.

Rithdal hurried out of the swirling Sharddust, face

grim.

'It happened yesterday morning,' he panted.

'Demons below,' Hekaena muttered. 'How many?'

'Don't know.' Rithdal shrugged irritably. 'They landed at the orphanage. Spread out as far as Duxtown and Riverfront. Heard there were raids around the slaughter yards too—lot of beggars there subsisting on discarded gristle and marrow.'

'What's going on?' Takket asked.

Hekaena turned to him, eyes conveying a quiet rage. 'The purges. Whenever Shard production begins to drop off, the crematorium increases the payment for voluntary immolation. If that fails, they do *this*.' She swept a hand over the empty streets. 'They round up the homeless. Technically, in Varsen vagrancy is a crime—'

'And all crimes are punishable by death,' Takket finished.

'Exactly. If too few criminals are caught, they find another source. There's never a shortage of homeless in the undercity.'

Horrified, Takket surveyed the bloodied streets. Some must have chosen to resist—withered bodies against Mages and rifle-armed soldiers. This city was vile. The true blight of Varspire was not the stench of sewage in the undercity, not the muggers, not the choking Sharddust. No, the rot lived in the spires, looking down on the desperate and seeing only a resource.

Takket longed to leave. He had endured enough of forcing pleasantries with murderers, smiling at men and women who adorned themselves with Shards created from dead Mundanes. The sooner he took the

Pure Shard, the sooner he could put this entire continent behind him, go back to the Imperium where Mundanes were poor but still human. Where children were protected, not farmed.

The hair stood up on the back of his neck.

'Lyssa,' he whispered. 'Angels above, have you seen her?'

Rithdal made a placating gesture. 'She's fine—saw her yesterday. I checked on the girls myself after the purge. A local family took them in when it started, hid them from the soldiers.'

Takket breathed a sigh of relief. He would have to make sure the girls were cared for once he left. A portion of his reward would provide shelter, maybe see them leave Varspire for good.

Hekaena nodded grimly. 'I'm going to the orphanage. If we can get it up and running before the next purge, at least the children here will be safe.'

She strode into the haze. Takket moved to follow, but was stopped by Rithdal's call.

'Khantek...a moment?' The man waited until Hekaena could no longer be seen through the billowing red cloud. 'This, Khantek, is exactly why we need you. How close are you to carrying out the theft?'

'Close,' Takket replied. 'I believe Hekaena is falling for me. Once she gets me into the royal quarters, I'll only need to find a way into Haddronius's room at night. When I'm ready, I'll let you know.'

Rithdal nodded. 'Good work. You will be remembered for this, Khantek. Now, let's get to Hekaena before she misses us.'

'Wait.' Takket searched the gloom for eavesdroppers. 'I need to ask you. My servant, Akken, is he one of yours?'

Rithdal frowned. 'What do you mean?'

'I believe he's spying on me. I want to know if he works for you.'

'No,' Rithdal shook his head. 'He's not part of the Free Circle. If he's a spy, he's someone else's agent.'

Rithdal's words haunted Takket. If Akken was not working for the Free Circle, then for whom? Takket could not prepare for a heist with the man watching his every move.

His unease was not helped when Lyssa failed to appear. He had fretted for hours as he hauled rusting nails and damp wood, calming only when he glimpsed one of Lyssa's sisters outside the orphanage. Given the recent purge, Takket could not blame Lyssa for choosing to keep close to her siblings.

Hekaena's efforts took on an urgency. She worked throughout the day, wooden boards lifting, sheering into shape mid-air, then assembling into beds, chairs, desks, footlockers. The wood was the finest the Mundanes could cobble together, but was still rotten. The smell of mildew lingered on Takket's hands. Splinters dug into his palms.

By the time they had stopped for the day, the surrounding haze had darkened to a deep purple. Takket followed his normal ritual, collecting a bowl of watery stew to take into the orphanage. Bedrock still floored the building, coated in a layer of Sharddust that drifted through the door. The krilt-shell walls bowed and receded, lending a distinctly organic look to the corridors, the building materials resisting Hekaena's attempt to impose order. Molten iron entwined the chitin, an intricate glue holding the building together.

A flickering glow led him down the darkened corridors—not the impatient dance of Shard light, but the steady bounce of a weak fire. He ducked through an iron-edged doorway into a barren chamber. Soon, this room would become a dormitory for twenty children, but for now it remained unfurnished. A fire smouldered in the room's centre, damp wood reluctantly burning , filling the air with musty smoke.

The eyes of two dozen children twinkled in the firelight. Sullen faces brightened with grins.

'Khantek!' they cried in a disjointed chorus.

He sat cross-legged before the fire. 'So what will it be today? You lot want to hear about the marble buildings of Indspire? The mountaintop monastery of Green Grove? The red waters of the Thousand Isles?'

They responded with their usual burst of contradictory requests. Chuckling to himself, he took a spoonful of the watery broth—bland as ever. Some pale purple root floated in the bowl, a strangely large morsel for these Mundane soups. The woman who served this to him must have reached deep into the cauldron to give him the best they had to offer. He balanced the root on his spoon and took a bite, tasting the faint sweetness within.

'Alright, alright,' he said. 'Gather around, I'm too tired today to shout.'

The children settled in a broad semicircle around the fire, its light illuminating the excited expressions on their red-stained faces. One group stayed put, huddled in the far corner. Frowning, Takket recognised Lyssa's three sisters.

'Catta?' he called to the eldest. 'Don't you want to listen?'

Wordlessly, Catta ushered the younger two to stand. They plodded across the bare stone floor, dejected, then mechanically sat.

'What's wrong?' A weight grew in Takket's stomach. 'Wait...where's Lyssa?'

The younger two burst into tears. Catta, eight years old, met Takket's gaze with stony eyes, a hardness there that had no place in a child. She sniffed and forced out words devoid of emotion.

'Lyssa's dead.'

Takket stared in disbelief. 'What? No, Rithdal said you all survived the purge. You sheltered in someone's home.'

'We did.' Catta said, monotone. 'Lyssa saw how happy we were indoors. Said she didn't want us sleeping outside again. She...she volunteered herself to the crematorium.'

Catta tugged a small pouch from her dress pocket. Half a rock's worth of flakes. Enough for some decent meals. Nowhere near enough for a house. A paltry sum for blood money. A few flakes for a young girl's life.

The bowl slipped from his fingers, its lukewarm contents splashing over his robe. He barely noticed.

Lyssa was dead.

This was Varsen. It was sickness and pain. It was suffering and cruelty. It was hypocrisy and death. A land where an elite few built houses from the blood of the poor.

Tears blurred his vision. He wondered what Lyssa's Soulshard would be used for. Merely a rock— Arcanes would not be interested. It would fall into the hands of a Mage, being passed around in circulation before being burned for some pitiful purpose. Driving a carriage. Expanding a tower. Heating a bath.

He looked around the room, truly seeing the faces for the first time. All these children were orphaned by Varsen's pursuit of Soulshards. Few would survive to adulthood. Those who did would forever struggle to endure, scrimping and saving until through desperation they made the single mistake that would lead them to be immolated. Generation after generation burned alive.

This society was sick. The thin glorious coat of the Magetowers hid a festering heart. This could not stand. He would not let it. He would take Haddronius' Shard. Not for wealth. Not to become a hero. Not even for the Free Circle. No, he would take the Pure Shard for these children.

For the children, and for Lyssa.

'Children,' Hekaena called from the doorway behind Takket, 'I need to speak with Khantek alone. The other dormitory is ready. Why don't you go pick out beds.'

The youngsters filed out of the room, the smaller ones excitedly pushing to the door, while the teenagers gave Takket unsettled looks. He wanted to smile, give words of reassurance, but found none. For the first time in his life, he could not force a grin, could not hide his despair.

He stood and turned to Hekaena. Ever-shifting light from the Soulshard on her staff brightened the doorway. The staff disgusted him. Its Shard was a baton, formed from a living human. He wondered who it had been. A father foolish enough to steal from a

224

Mage? A mother wanting to provide for her children? A sister, looking to give her siblings a better life?

'How long have you been there?' he asked quietly.

'Long enough,' she replied with sympathy. 'I'm so sorry about Lyssa.'

'She was a good kid.' He struggled not to choke on the words. 'She didn't deserve this.'

'No one does.' She strolled over to him and lay a hand on his arm. He wanted to slap it away, to scream at her for pretending to care while using Shards, to demand she find a way to make amends to Lyssa's family. Instead, he took a calming breath. If he was going to steal the Pure Shard, he needed Hekaena to take him to Varspire Tower's peak.

'Thank you,' he said, the words bitter on his tongue. 'What you do for these children is amazing. You give them hope.'

'Thanks for coming with me. I may have built this shelter, but it's you who has given them hope. Don't think I haven't heard of the stories you tell. Learning of the Imperium, knowing that the entire world isn't this bad—that has inspired these kids.'

He forced a smile. 'Well, you build the houses, and I'll spin tales. We make a good team.'

Red sparkling eyes staring into his, she stepped close.

'I've searched for so long for someone who actually cares. Someone who sees what's going on here. Sees that something must be done.'

He gazed into those striking eyes. 'I promise you, I will do whatever I can to help these people. No matter how hard, no matter the cost, I will stop this suffering.'

She searched his face. He bared his honest

225

determination. His words were no lie. No matter the price, he would change Varsen.

Hekaena leaned close, kissing Takket, gingerly at first, then with firmness. He leaned into the kiss, wrapping stained hands around her linen dress.

The moment was ruined by a child's giggle. He peered over Hekaena's shoulder to see a cluster of children, half hidden behind the door frame.

Hekaena laughed. 'I think it's time we get back to the tower.' She took his hand, then whispered in his ear, 'We'll have more privacy in my quarters.'

The dawn light fell over Hekaena's sleeping form. She lay face down, partially covered by silken green sheets. Her long, dark hair sprawled over the duck-down pillow, the smell of her floral perfume still filling the room.

Takket perched naked at the edge of the bed. Her rooms were smaller than he had imagined, similar in size to his own. The decor was the standard Varspire finery: mahogany and rosewood furniture, inlaid with gold and gemstones. Obsidian tiled the floor. The jade ceiling was intricately carved into a scene that Takket suspected represented the creation of the first Soulshard. Or possibly a tree—it was often hard to tell with Varsen art.

The view, however, was breathtaking. A single curving sheet of Mage-blended glass formed the outer wall. Outside, the sun rose over the broken rocks of the horizon. The billowing Sharddust layer, so far below, sparkled in the dawn. Magetowers stood as dark sentries, knee-deep in the sea of red.

He dressed, careful not to wake Hekaena. Easing

open a golden door, he peeked into the circular foyer. The royal apartments circumscribed the upper floor, opening into a green-carpeted atrium. Gas lamps burned brightly above the jade and emerald mosaic ceiling, tinting the space a deep green. Wind whistled through air ducts disguised by impressionistic sculptures of Arcanes and angels, bringing a constant freshness. No railings barred the opening in the centre of the room—a circular void plunging into the tower's main shaft.

Haddronius's door was easy to spot—it stood alone on the far side of the foyer. Where the other doors were variations on engraved precious metals, Haddronius's circular door was hewn from a single massive block of jade, a Soulshard nestled in its centre.

Doublechecking that the other doors were closed, Takket ventured into the atrium. He wanted a closer look at the jade door, to see what security measures he needed to overcome. If he was lucky there would be no lock, but he doubted the Arcane-lord trusted his own children that much. Takket could break any standard tumbler. A combination lock would be harder, but he had cracked them in the past.

Reaching the round door, Takket found no visible lock. No keyhole, no bolt, no combination dial, not even a handle. The only blemish on the jade surface was the Soulshard—bright enough to be a baton, but laid end-on, only its cross-section visible. Takket touched the gem, pushed it, twisted it, but the shimmering Shard refused to budge.

Takket frowned. Perhaps the door was merely a distraction. He inspected the walls to either side for a hidden portal, a disguised handle, a discreet switch.

Nothing.

Chewing his lip, he turned to the circular opening in the foyer's centre. Varspire Tower dropped away below, the throne barely a speck fifty floors down. He needed time to explore this place, to watch Haddronius's comings and goings.

Suppressing a sigh, he crept back into Hekaena's perfume-suffused room. Haddronius's door was not his only obstacle—Akken was not working for the Free Circle. Before Takket proceeded any further in his plan, he needed to know whom the man served and how much he knew. Takket had been careless lately, not concerning himself with what Akken overheard. If the man knew of the planned heist, Takket could find himself walking into a trap.

He had to deal with Akken, and the kernels of a plan were growing in his mind. Returning to the bed, Takket sat alongside Hekaena. Her eyes cracked open. As she saw him, she gave a warm smile, replaced with a frown as her gaze dropped to his clothes.

'Good morning.' She yawned. 'Planning on slipping away?'

He chuckled. 'Oh yes. I normally go out the window but...' He looked out at the city far below. 'Ah well, there are worse places to be trapped.'

She rose from the bed to kiss him. He lingered with the kiss.

'As much as I would like to stay all day, I need to get to the embassy. An envoy's work is never done.'

'This doesn't count as improving international relations?' she teased.

'If only. My superiors would prefer trade deals,

extensions to anti-piracy measures, that sort of tedious thing.'

'Pity.' She stood, and threw on a dress from a mirrored cupboard. 'Well, let's get you down. I'm afraid this tower was not designed for Mundanes.'

'No.' He smiled. 'Do servants ever reach this floor?'

She pulled on a pair of green-dyed leather boots. 'The work parties are overseen by a Mage. They bring the Mundanes up and down.'

'Ah.' Demons below, that meant no secret passage to use as an escape route.

She made a half-hearted attempt at taming her hair before taking his hand and tugging him towards the foyer. Grasping her staff by the Soulshard, she pushed open the door and levitated them over the Tower's shaft.

The descent was smooth, much slower than his terrifying drop with Ensellus. His cloak fluttered in the breeze as they passed by level after palatial level. Bathed in natural light, the glimpses of apartments and vaults were all the more breathtaking. Precious jewels encrusted every wall, scattering the light in multicoloured patterns.

They dropped into the incense-heavy air in the throne room and Hekaena settled them on the green carpet. He tried to release her hand but she tightened her grip, stubbornly holding onto him as she led the way through the hallways. The few early risers dotting the corridor shot looks at the couple, ranging from curiosity to scandalised derision. Hekaena raised her head, defiant. She obviously did not care who knew of their budding relationship, but in those staring faces, all Takket could see were agents for Ensellus. If the man was angered at Takket's closeness to Hekaena before, now he would be murderous.

Hekaena stopped at the embassy's entrance. She held his unshaven face in her hands and kissed him firmly.

'I've got a meeting with some Mages this evening —someone needs to maintain the orphanage—but tomorrow I'm going back to the undercity. I hope you'll be coming?'

'I wouldn't miss it. Meet in the throne room at noon?'

'Can't wait.' Those red eyes lit up with joy and he found he could not help but smile back. She kissed him again and swept back down the corridor. He stared after her, watching her strong stance, her head held high.

He turned to the embassy. Akken stood inside, watching keenly.

'Shouldn't you be dusting my room or something?' Takket grumbled.

'Right away, sir.' Akken hurried up the stairs into Takket's room.

He had not intended it to be a command, but Takket could work with this. He followed the man at a measured pace. Inside the room, he found Akken remaking the unblemished bed. Pretending to ignore the servant's presence, Takket strode over to sit behind his desk. He leaned against the velvet backrest, the mahogany frame creaking.

Taking a fountain pen from the collection of writing devices, he selected a sheet of paper and began to compose a letter. He wrote hurriedly, casting glances at Akken as he worked, sheltering the document from the servant whenever the man peeked across the room. His writings were nonsensical—court politics mixed with meaningless codewords, phrased just right to be intriguing. Enough to keep a spy reading, but nothing so overt that he would bring the document immediately to his master. Takket finished with the line, *Akken, look to the darkened corner.*

Takket signed and folded the document. He locked it into the top desk drawer with a brass key. Opening a second drawer, he deposited the key inside, shutting it with enough force for the servant to hear.

Takket rose from his desk. 'Akken, Innisel explained to me that I must inform you of which items are off-limits. I'll make this clear. That desk is private. You are not to clean it. You are not to tidy it. You are not to go near it. Understood?'

Akken nodded, but his eyes wandered towards the desk with curiosity. Perfect. The trap was baited. Now Takket merely had to lie in wait.

CHAPTER SIXTEEN

Shard light from the hallway chandelier bled through the open doorway, barely illuminating Takket's room. The faint red glow played over corners of the wooden desk and outlined the bed. In the unsettled light, carved faces of angels leered from the ceiling. The room seemed alive, a restless creature twitching in its slumber.

The smells of cooking had died hours ago, leaving the air stagnant. Wind groaned through the ventilation shafts as if the tower struggled to breathe.

Takket's legs ached. He had been crouched in the shadowy corner of his room for hours. Boredom did not bother him—in his past he had certainly spent far longer loitering in shadows—but his body was ageing. His knees yearned to move, stretch, or at least shift where his weight pressed on the carpet. The plush material against his knee had grown uncomfortable. Still, he dared not stir. The slightest noise might alert his prey.

Hours ago, Enara and Yelleck had told Akken that Takket was out for the evening. The lie should be easy to believe—Akken knew of Takket's relationship with Hekaena. Besides, Enara and Yelleck were adept liars.

Out in the foyer, a door creaked, audible only due to the abject silence of the tower at midnight. Takket focused on his breathing, careful not to make a sound.

A shadow filled the doorway. Takket recognised

Akken's silhouette creeping into the room. Furtively glancing around, the man made straight for Takket's desk. A drawer scraped open, then thudded shut. A key rattled in a lock. Akken drew something onto the desk.

With a hiss, a match bloomed into flame, illuminating Akken's ageing features. He hunched over the desk, skimming the document. His frown deepened as he read the nonsensical script.

The man froze, then snapped his attention towards Takket's corner. With a smirk, Takket stood, joints popping.

'Light the desk lamp, before you burn yourself on that match, *Akken*.'

Hands shaking, Akken obeyed. The desk's gas lamp ignited, casting a weak pool of light over the study. Takket strolled to the edge of the glow, just close enough for Akken to make out his grim smile.

'Espionage is a serious crime, even in the Imperium,' Takket said calmly. 'Life imprisonment. Even death in some cases. Of course, here in Varsen, it hardly matters. A crime is a crime, and the only suitable punishment is death.'

The servant's eyes darted towards the door. Takket waited patiently for the man to realise escape was pointless. It would be the word of an envoy against that of a servant. Varspire needed no further proof to sentence a Mundane to death.

'Please,' Akken stammered. 'My son relies on my wages. His wife passed. He's got five children to feed. Can't do that on a Mundane's salary. I know you've been working with Arcane Hekaena in the undercity— I know you're a good man. Don't turn me in.'

Takket glowered. 'I don't want to hurt you, Akken.

Demons below, I've seen enough suffering here. But I can't let this continue.' He stepped forward and pointed at the paper. 'This time it was a ruse. Who knows what you'll read next. I'm not going to die because of your curiosity.'

'Not curiosity.' Akken collapsed onto the chair, defeated. 'I had my orders. You've been here long enough to know what happens to disobedient Mundanes.'

'I know.' Takket leaned forward on the desk, softening his voice. 'I know you were in an impossible situation and I want to help. To do that, I need to know *who* ordered you to spy on me.'

Akken gave a bitter laugh. 'I'll give you one guess.' 'Ensellus.'

'Who else?' Akken nodded, fingering the varnished tabletop. 'The paranoid demon-spawn wouldn't let a foreigner into Varspire Tower without keeping constant tabs.'

'You don't seem fond.'

'Of Ensellus? Only person fond of that man is himself. Demons below, all Arcanes are bad, but he's something else. You heard of the latest purge?'

Takket nodded. 'I saw...what was left.'

'Yeah. That was Ensellus's doing. He got pissed about the time you've been spending with Hekaena. Had me...find out where you two were going. Decided to vent his frustrations on the Mundanes you'd helped.' He sighed raggedly, rubbing his face. 'Angels above, I'm sorry I helped with that. I didn't have a choice.'

Takket should have felt fury. Guilt. Something. He just felt empty. The mahogany table creaked as he sat on its smooth surface. All those people dead, all

234

because of one man's spite. If Varspire was a diseased city, then Ensellus was the tumour at its core, the epitome of everything wrong with this land.

'Please,' Akken said, weary, 'don't turn me in. I beg you. I'll stop giving my reports. I won't tell that cursed man another thing.'

'No,' Takket replied. 'If you do that, he'll know you've been turned, or have become useless. Either way, I doubt you'll survive long. No, keep giving him reports, but run them by me first. We'll filter what he knows. That's far more help than you being replaced by another agent.'

Akken's shoulders sagged with relief. 'Angels above, thank you. I was right when I said you were a good man.'

'Don't tell him about any of this. If you need to give a report, tell him of me and Hekaena. I'm sure he'll find out soon enough anyway. At least that will keep his mind occupied.'

Akken nodded. 'I'm sure it will. Can...can I leave now?'

'Yes. Don't screw this up, Akken. I'm giving you a chance here, trusting that one person in this shit-hole of a city might actually be a decent human. Prove me wrong and we're both dead.'

'Thank you.' Akken stood shakily and tottered towards the door. He paused, leaning against its frame. 'Well, there's one thing that Ensellus was right about.'

'Oh?'

Akken smirked in the dim light. 'You *are* up to something. I just hope whatever you're scheming, that bastard ends up suffering from it.'

Takket simply nodded. Part of him knew he was

going soft. The old Takket would not have let a loose end hang around like this. It would just take one word to Innisel, and Akken would end up immolated for espionage. No second-guesses. No trial.

However, Takket knew he would not turn in the man. He had already seen far too much death.

Hekaena snored. Takket was not sure why that amused him so much, but he could not help but smile. It was not an obnoxious rasping or loud rumble, just a light crack at the top of her breath. Such an imperfection seemed far too unrefined for an Arcane. Too *human*. Still, Hekaena was the most human Arcane he had ever met.

Without disturbing her, he rolled out of the silken sheets. His earlier joke about slipping through windows had a great deal of truth—his youth had often involved sneaking out of women's bedrooms in the dead of night. Imperium high society may have been more accepting of Mundanes than Varsen, but few appreciated discovering that the charming Magelord from the south was nothing more than a Mundane thief.

By flickering Shard light, he threw on his velvet cloak. Hekaena's staff rested in its stand at her bedside. She had confirmed Enara and Yelleck's assertions that no magic-user ever touched a Shard while they slept, but all kept one nearby. They could grasp the Shard in mere moments to protect themselves against assassination, whether from rivals or rebellious Mundanes. Takket took a twisted delight in the thought of powerful Arcanes sleeping in the light of Shards, like frighten children with dim gas lamps to ward off night-time demons.

Silently, he crept across the plush carpet and eased open the door. He slipped into the foyer, the air fresh compared to Hekaena's room with its floral perfume and lingering sweat. A green glow filtered through the jade and emerald ceiling, contrasting the red Shard light emanating from the hole at the room's centre.

Giving that hole a wide berth, he crossed to Haddronius's door. The Shard at its centre radiated shifting light, but Takket could not tell if it was ornamentation—or something more. It certainly had the appearance of a lock, sitting proudly at the centre of the door, but it was like no device he had encountered in his career.

He probed around the Shard, pressing and twisting at the solid jade of the door to try to move some unseen switch. Putting his ear against the cold surface, he gently knocked, seeking a hollow that may have contained hidden machinery. Nothing. The door seemed solid, and thick. He abandoned his fleeting plan of chiselling a hole—breaking through would take days.

Expanding his search to the obsidian walls, he was again met with disappointment. Engravings of angels and demons were simply ornamental. Cracks between sections of obsidian refused to budge.

Irritated, Takket turned to the far side of the foyer. Haddronius's was not the only unique door. Far to the right stood a door marked by its simplicity. Where the apartments for the royal siblings were fronted with doors of gold, emerald and polished silver, this door was bland wrought iron.

Takket crept closer. A steady white light shone

through a keyhole, its light scattering off motes of drifting dust. He knelt to inspect the lock—a simple four-pin tumbler, like a hundred others he had picked.

He peered through the keyhole. Compared to the rest of this floor, the room beyond was stark. The walls were unadorned obsidian, floor and ceiling both worn hardwood. Bookcases lined the far wall, bowing under the weight of overstuffed files. No windows admitted starlight—the only illumination was the harsh glow of gas lamps.

A man strolled into view, holding an open file. As the figure sat at a plain desk, Takket recognised Ensellus's sharp features. The vile man studied the pages before him intently, leafing through the document before rising to search for another folder.

This was Ensellus's office.

The fact that the man was stationed next door to Haddronius made sense, but complicated any heist. The slightest noise and he would run to defend his master. He had to sleep at some point, but it was midnight now and Ensellus was still up and working.

Takket would have to find a way to bar this door. An Arcane would not be slowed for long by any barrier Takket could concoct, but even a few moments could make the difference between life and death.

Of course, there was no guarantee this was the solitary exit. Takket doubted the paranoid demon-spawn would allow himself only a single escape route. Without windows to dive out of, Ensellus would be vulnerable, easily cornered.

Unless there was a second egress.

A route between Ensellus's office and Haddronius's room. How else could the man reach his master's side quickly in an emergency?

Perhaps Takket had no need to get through the strange jade door. Perhaps he merely needed to find a way through Ensellus's office.

With a sigh, he turned from the door to return to Hekaena's room. Breaking into Ensellus's office required getting the man to leave Haddronius undefended. Tearing through the jade door with bare hands may have proven an easier task.

Before he could decide on a course of action, he needed more information. He needed to know if a route from Ensellus's room to Haddronius's existed. For that, he needed to study the building's plans. To get through the jade door, he had to understand the obscure security system. Only a Mage or Arcane would know of such things, and he doubted Hekaena would be accommodating in helping dethrone her father.

No, as much as he hated the idea, he knew who he had to turn to.

Enara and Yelleck.

The siblings' room was heavy with stagnant air and the odour of their bodies. Incense burned feebly in the corner, lending the stale room a hint of floral fragrance.

Takket sat on a velvet-upholstered couch opposite the siblings, who perched on matching chairs. He had just finished informing them of his progress with Hekaena, Akken's new loyalties, the seemingly impassable door.

The room descended into contemplative silence. The siblings had clearly been busy working on *something*. Files lay scattered over every surface. The low table between the couch and chairs was strewn with dossiers on the current political situation in the new world. Skimming over the documents, Takket found little of note. Kilroth was conducting military drills near Varsen's northern border. Octane and Santona border guards had exchanged rifle fire, killing two Mundane soldiers. Brekking had accused Medeth of sinking a cargo liner bound for Southreach. Normal posturing in a continent always on the brink of war. Arcanes spending Mundane lives for a few extra fields or advantageous trade routes.

'Well, let's start with the easy part.' Enara rose and crossed the maroon carpet to a pile of documents half hidden under the desk. She returned with a series of rolled sheets of paper and rifled through.

The woman set out a plan of the royal apartments on the low table's glass surface, shoving aside unwanted papers. Takket leaned forward to examine the diagram. It was incomplete, several measurements marked with question marks. Still, it corresponded to what he had seen of the floor. The royal apartments occupied wedges between the circular foyer and outer wall. One half of the floor was occupied by Haddronius's suite, divided into a bedroom, bathroom, private dining room and living quarters. Nestled between Haddronius's room and those of his children was an office simply labelled SECURITY. Ensellus's lair.

Yelleck grunted. 'There's no indication of a passage between Haddronius's room and the security office.'

'There's little indication of anything,' Takket grumbled. 'This is the best map you have?'

'Yes,' Yelleck replied. 'This is from the Imperium.

Believe it or not, Varsen doesn't release diagrams of their most protected haven. These are cobbled together from tours and servant reports.'

Takket examined the plan carefully. The dimensions of Hekaena's quarters seemed correct. The rest he could only guess at.

'I'm surprised the Imperium has not managed to do better than this,' he said. 'They've had angels-know-how-long to study this building.'

'True,' Enara said patiently, 'but I don't think the Imperium was as interested in breaking into the Arcane-lord's bedroom.'

'Great.' Takket leaned back on the too-soft couch. 'So there may or may not be a route from the security office to the bedroom. I'm not breaking into Ensellus's lair without a guarantee.'

'That we can't give you,' Yelleck said coldly.

'No,' Takket replied. 'That leaves the jade door. Have you heard of anything like it before?'

The siblings shared a look, no doubt wondering how much they could discuss without revealing their magical ability. This would be so much simpler if they had told him the truth. He still feigned ignorance of their deceit, not wanting to reveal his hand.

'We have come across something,' Enara said slowly. 'There are some references in the diplomatic notes of novel mechanisms made using Shards. Instead of drawing magic out of a Shard, some New World Arcane-lords found a way to harness the power, effectively *train* the Shard to cast on its own. Automating magic use.'

Takket frowned. 'So the Shard in the door might have been trained to open it on command?'

'Exactly. No doubt there is some physical bolt inside the door that the Shard pulls aside.'

'Fantastic,' Takket replied dryly. 'So how do I command the door to open?'

Enara grimaced. 'You can't. Every reference to these automated Shards says the same thing—they are tied to the bloodline of the Arcane who made them.'

'So I need a Varsen to open the door for me?'

'Yes. Well, you need Varsen blood. Shards respond to the blood of Mages and Arcanes. The blood is where the soul resides. The blood is what you need.'

'Not just any blood,' Yelleck interjected. 'You would need the dying blood of a Varsen.'

A chill descended over Takket. 'Why?'

Yelleck shot Enara a stern glance before continuing. 'My sister was right that it's the soul in the blood you need, but you can't just take a vial. The soul can't be split, and can't leave a living body. You need to kill the body, then the soul will be released into the blood, or enough of an echo to collect in a vial.'

Yelleck stood and strode to the desk. He returned and planted an object on the table. Takket stared in growing revulsion.

A dagger.

Its black leather sheath—elegantly gilded—and matching hilt could not hide the deadly intent of its curved blade. Hesitantly, Takket picked up the knife, drawing it from its sheath. The polished steel reflected a distorted image of Takket's face. Intricate engravings of demons toying with the living marred the reflection like an ugly scar.

'You want me to murder a Varsen?'

'Yes,' Yelleck said, eyes afire. 'You can't tell me

242

that you've never killed anyone in your line of work.'

'Of course I have,' Takket replied bitterly. Bungled escapes. Unfortunate witnesses. Untimely guards. Death came hand in hand with life in the underworld. He did not enjoy killing—he was not a psychopath, merely pragmatic. Still, something about this unsettled him deeply. 'You want me to kill Hekaena.'

'Is that a problem?' asked Yelleck.

'She's an Arcane.'

Yelleck smirked. 'I'm sure you can manage to kill a sleeping Arcane.'

'And if I don't strike a killing blow in one hit? I'm no assassin. All it takes is her getting a hand on a Shard and I'll be a stain on the wall.'

Enara looked up. 'What if she were sedated? Give us a few days, and I'm sure we can find something strong enough to knock out an Arcane—for a while, at least. Go have a private meal with her, slip some of the drug into her food, then there's no risk to you.'

'Seems like we have a plan,' Yelleck said, smug.

Takket nodded mutely, staring at the gleaming blade. Could he really kill for this Shard? Murder Hekaena? This would not be a mistake, a heat-of-the-moment thrust to save his life. This would be cold, calculated murder. He could not help but wonder if the Shard was worth it. If he was willing to become an assassin.

An image of Lyssa's smile flashed in his mind.

Yes, he thought. He would do anything to stop the injustice in this country. Even if it meant slitting Hekaena's throat.

Takket left the stuffiness of Enara and Yelleck's

room and entered the merely stale air the embassy foyer, dagger heavy in his cloak pocket. He felt sick. Was he actually contemplating assassination? He did not kill. Amateurs and thugs used violence. Real thieves used skill, ingenuity, deception. Perhaps he was nothing but a common knifeman, kin to those who broke knees to settle debts or preyed on lone farmsteads. As much as it disgusted him, to save children like Lyssa, he could wear any title, even *killer*.

Before committing to the plan, there was one other who might know about the strange lock. Akken. The man had worked in Varspire Tower for decades. Perhaps he had cleaned the royal apartments before, knew of a way to get into Haddronius's room without resorting to bloodshed. Enquiring might alert the servant to Takket's true plan, and he might run straight to Ensellus with the information. Still, if there was a chance to avoid violence, questioning the man was worth the risk.

He found the servant-spy changing the linens on Takket's bed. Easing shut the door behind him, Takket walked over.

'Akken,' he said quietly. 'I need to ask you about something. Something Ensellus can never know I mentioned.'

Akken froze.

'Have you ever been to the royal apartments?'

'Yes,' Akken replied slowly.

'Did you ever go inside Haddronius room?'

'Yes'

'How did you get in?'

Akken frowned. 'The Mage in charge of the work

party let us in.'

'The Mage was a Varsen?'

'Hmm? No. A Linthel, I think. One of the minor families in Varsen. She died a few years back in the last war against Kilroth.'

'So you don't need to be a Varsen to open Haddronius's door?'

Akken gave Takket a calculating look. 'You're wanting to get into Haddronius's room.'

With irritation, Takket realised there was no way to get the information he sought without revealing more of his plan. *Well,* he thought, *in for a grain, in for a flake.* 'Yes,' he admitted. 'I need to get inside. I've been told the door is tied to the Varsen bloodline.' He relayed Enara and Yelleck's information on the door, the need for blood, for death.

Akken let out a long breath. 'Well, I don't know where they've been getting their information, but it's demon-shit. As much as I'd like you to kill an Arcane, the blood doesn't need to be dying blood, just needs to be fresh. If all were too busy to let him in, the Mage would get a small vial of blood from one of the Arcane-lord's children. Doesn't need to be much, just a thimbleful. I asked about it once—he said there's some echo of the soul in the blood, lets the magic work. Demons know if that's true, but the vial would only be good for a day or so.'

'So there's no need to kill anyone?'

'Demons, no. Not like a Varsen was giving their life to open a door. Just a prick on the finger and a few drops. There's one other thing, though. Never bothered us, but if my guess is right, it's going to put a kink into whatever you're planning.'

245

'Go on.'

'Varsens are a paranoid bunch. Have been since they ascended. A bloodline-linked door is a good way to keep out most assassins, but won't help a damn against one of their own kids wanting to speed up the inheritance. They put in two more security steps. The corridor beyond the door is lined with Soulshards. Any Mage or Arcane makes the whole thing glow like the sun. That'll wake the dead, certainly the Arcane-lord.

'That still wouldn't stop a Varsen opening the door and sending in some poor Mundane with a rifle to do their dirty work. So the magic on the door has an added clause. The Mage said an alarm would be triggered if the door was opened "with ill intent", whatever that means. As I said, it never was an issue with us work parties. Don't think cleaning the Arcane's underwear counts as "ill intent", but I don't suppose you're planning on doing his laundry.'

Takket grunted noncommittally. 'I don't need to remind you not to tell anyone about this conversation.'

'You joking? Ensellus so much as suspects a Mundane of helping undermine his security, it's straight to the crematorium. If he learns I helped someone get into the Arcane-lord's room, he'll burn me himself.'

Takket nodded. 'Thank you. I need to think.'

'Just one thing,' Akken said quietly. 'Whatever you're doing, be careful.'

'I didn't know you cared,' Takket replied sardonically.

'About you? I don't. About the Mundanes of this city? Damn right I do. You get caught doing whatever it is you're up to, and you'll not be the only one who burns.'

'Believe me when I say it's the Mundanes of Varspire that I care about.'

Akken studied Takket. 'I believe you. Angels watch over you, Khantek.'

The servant strode from the room, leaving Takket alone with his thoughts. He collapsed onto the freshly made bed, the smell of perfumed soap suffusing the linens. Gripping his head in thought, he settled into the overt softness of the down-stuffed duvet and mattress. This room seemed too luxurious a place to be contemplating murder.

Akken's words were hopeful. No need for killing, just a few drops of blood. He could sedate Hekaena, take her blood, and break into Haddronius's room. Maybe thinking happy thoughts would get him through the outer door without triggering an alarm. Neat. Perfect.

Too perfect.

Takket could not shake the feeling that Akken was simply telling him what he wanted to hear. He had no guarantee that the man was not still working for Ensellus. Presenting a vial of blood while its owner still lived might trigger an alarm. It would be a decent way for the spy to dispose of Takket without risking his own neck—no one would believe the claims of an attempted assassination.

Did he believe the words of the confessed spy, or the pair that still lied to him every day? Did Akken's admission make him trustworthy, or simply incompetent?

Images of Lyssa bombarded Takket's mind, joined

by those of blood-stained walls, of emaciated bodies crying for sustenance, of families begging for loved ones in the crematorium.

With a hardening heart, he realised there was no choice. No matter how much he wanted to believe Akken, he could not risk the fate of so many innocents on the words of a lone spy. Only one path lay before Takket.

He would kill Hekaena.

CHAPTER SEVENTEEN

In Takket's pocket, the leaden weight of the dagger tugged at his fine velvet robes. A pair of glass vials in his other pocket counterbalanced the knife, one filled with a sedative, the other expectantly empty. The tools of his murderous plot.

Tonight, he would kill Hekaena.

Earlier in the day, he had alerted Rithdal. The Free Circle's Mage ally would be ready. To keep them out of the way, Takket had convinced Enara and Yelleck that he still had to lay ground work before executing the heist. The theft would be hard enough without their interference.

Entering the throne room, he forced a jovial expression, a mask to cover the guilt gnawing at his heart. Takket had spent a lifetime abusing trust. He stole heirlooms, relics, fortunes, all from the hands of those who called him 'friend'. It had never caused him much heartache. His victims always had an abundance of wealth. Their loss was only ever an inconvenience. Tonight though, he was using Hekaena's trust—her affection—to take her life.

Lyssa, he thought. The name had become a mantra. Whenever doubts crept into his mind, whenever guilt raised its ugly head, Takket remembered the young girl, the life destroyed by a cancerous society.

A society he could cure.

Yes, his plot was unpalatable, but inaction was

unconscionable. The life of one Arcane was a small price to pay for ending the suffering of untold millions.

Hekaena waited atop the dais, the light of her Soulshard mingling with that of her father's throne, bathing her in a glow as red as blood. She had changed her dress since their excursion to the undercity, her hard-wearing red robe replaced with a white silken gown.

He hurried up the stairs, hefting his wooden basket. Grinning as he reached her, he played the part of a smitten lover and kissed her in greeting. She wore the rose perfume he liked. He suffocated the pang of guilt with his mantra. Lyssa. Lyssa.

'You're in a good mood,' she said once he broke away.

'Of course.' A lopsided grin hid his inner turmoil. 'The orphanage is finally complete. I have a basket of the finest Imperium dishes to celebrate, and a remarkable woman to share it with.'

She smiled warmly. 'You're sweet. Your assistants managed to dig up Imperium food, then?'

'Yes. Took them a while but it's all here. Baked rustroot to start. Highland vegetable stew. A dessert of honeycake. And of course, a bottle of real mountain whisky.'

The food had taken Enara and Yelleck longer to acquire than the sedative. Takket was not sure if that reflected badly on his assistants or on Varspire.

'Sounds wonderful.' She grasped his free hand, her fingers more weathered than those of any Arcane he knew—of course, she spent more time in the Shard layer than any Arcane alive.

He repeated Lyssa's name over and over in his mind as they ascended the tower's shaft. The sights drifting by helped harden his heart. Individual balconies—ringed with golden rails and decorated with the finest sculptures—contained more wealth than a Mundane could ever hope to own. Jade and obsidian mingled together in ordered decoration, far removed from the bloated jumble of the undercity's buildings. In the baton-sized Shards lighting the shaft, he could see only the death from which they were born. Hundreds had died to illuminate this tower. Thousands more to construct this monument to Arcane vanity.

They reached the tower's summit, and Hekaena led the way into her room. Incense filled the space. Lavender. Imported all the way from the Imperium. A touch of home. A reminder of a more moral land.

Night had fallen over the city. Magetowers rose as tapering points of light, gas lamps and Shards alike shining through windows. Even the tallest building stood less than half the height of Varspire Tower. The only sign of life in the undercity was the feeble orange glow from wood fires burning deep within the Shard layer. The scene seemed removed, like a painting of some alien hive. Only the whistle of wind through the air vents linked this building to the world outside.

Takket set the basket down on the rosewood dining table and began to pull out the neatly wrapped dishes. Hekaena tore away the linen covers, releasing subtly fragranced steam. Compared to the past weeks of Indspire cooking, the Imperium food smelt bland.

'Where are the glasses?' Takket pulled the bottle of mountain whisky from the bottom of the basket.

Following Hekaena's directions, he strolled to a crystal drinking cabinet by the ornate wall. He found a pair of tumblers in the multitude of wine glasses, and uncorked the whisky.

'Forty-six years old,' Takket announced. 'This whisky was made the year I was born.' While he poured the auburn liquid, he plucked the vial of sedative with his free hand and broke the seal. Tucking it into his palm, he steadied Hekaena's glass. As the whisky flowed into the tumbler, he upended the sedative, the two dark brown liquids mixing seamlessly. A rudimentary sleight of hand, the kind he had practised in back alleys and taverns in his youth. Now used for a much more dire intent than conning drunks out of their flakes.

'Well, let's hope two good things were made that year.' Hekaena smiled, taking the offered glass. 'It seems to me that something this rare needs to be used in a toast. Any ideas?'

'To the children of Varspire.' Takket clinked his glass against hers. 'May the orphanage's opening be the first step to end their suffering.'

Hekaena raised her glass to her lips. 'To the children.'

They sipped. The oaky whisky burned his mouth. With none of the coppery tang of Varsen root wine, the taste brought Takket back home to the Imperium, the green fields of the highlands, the red waters of the Thousand Isles. He longed to return, but knew he could not leave Varspire until his duty was complete. Until the Mundanes were free. Until the Varsen family had been crushed.

Hekaena coughed. 'Strong.'

'Yes.' Takket smiled sympathetically. 'The whisky is distilled in the mountains above the Shard layer. If you're going to go to the effort of transporting barrels of alcohol down a mountainside, you'll be damn sure it's as strong as possible. Almost all Imperium drinks are this potent.'

'The Mundanes drink this?'

He shook his head. 'Rarely whisky, and never something of this vintage. The common folk do their best to emulate it, fermenting and distilling liqueurs from just about anything that grows. Tends to be sweeter than this, but tinged with Sharddust. Truth be told, this is the most expensive bottle I've ever bought. I suppose I was just waiting for the right person to share it with.'

Hekaena took another sip. Good. Takket had been worried she would dislike the stiff beverage, but knew he needed something powerful to obscure the sedative's taste. She might just be humouring him, forcing down the liquid for his sake. As long as she drank, he did not care.

They sat at the table and sampled the meal before them. Takket felt detached from his body, like a voyeur, watching the lie he had become. He laughed at the right times, spoke with a fondness he could not feel, caressed her hand with a devotion he had never known. He drank frequently, encouraging Hekaena to do the same. The alcohol numbed his senses as it extinguished hers.

By the time they had finished dessert, the sedative had taken hold. Hekaena yawned furiously, holding her head. She begged his forgiveness for being a poor host, suggesting he leave to avoid catching whatever virus afflicted her. He refused, murmuring sweet pleasantries as he helped her into bed. A few nonsensical words escaped her lips, her beautiful eyes flickering open, unfocused, before she finally slipped into a deep sleep.

Mechanically, he stood and quenched the gas lamps to plunge the room into darkness. By moonlight, he found his way back to the bed and sat beside Hekaena. Pushing down nausea, he reached into his pocket, feeling the leather hilt within, the gold embellishment on the sheath.

He drew the dagger.

Takket stared at the still-sheathed knife in his hands, anger rising. He hated this city, this fowl continent. He hated the casual disposal of Mundanes. He hated the suffering of those left behind. He hated the Shards used to light the corridors, the jade walls to hide the undercity, the incense to suppress the smell of Sharddust. More than anything, he hated that his only way to end such suffering was to commit murder.

He ripped the blade from its sheath.

The light of the twin moons played across the blade's engravings. Yelleck had picked it up in the Imperium, its origins reflected in the realistic depictions of angels and demons carved into the steel. It seemed fitting, a blade that had followed him from the Imperium, here to help him bring justice.

Takket turned to face Hekaena.

He raised the blade.

She lay peacefully on the covers, still in a white silken dress so fragile compared to the linen materials she favoured. Her hair lay scattered over the pillow, dishevelled and brittle from a day spent in the undercity. Gently, he touched her hand, feeling the roughness of a life serving those less fortunate than herself.

His arm refused to strike. He focused on her features, the pale light picking out the gentle rise and fall of her breath. Of all the Arcanes Takket had ever met, she was the kindest. Angels, she was the most caring person he knew. She was born to a life of luxury, but had spurned a pampered existence to help others. A lifetime spent helping the Mundanes of Varsen. How many houses had she built? How many lives had she saved? *She* was the true hero of the Mundanes.

With a silent scream, he lowered the knife to his lap. He could not kill Hekaena. The Mundanes of Varsen needed saving, true, but how could he help them by murdering their most ardent ally?

The leather hilt creaked as he tightened his grip. No, he could not kill Hekaena, but Varspire's Mundanes still cried out for an end to their agony. Hekaena's work in the undercity was a cooling flannel for the city's fever. Takket had to cure the underlying infection. He had to steal the Pure Shard.

Lifting her hand, Takket brought the knife against her skin. Delicately, he pricked the side of her finger, a small cut to accompany a dozen others from the day's hard work. He pulled the empty glass vial from his pocket, uncorking it to catch the blood welling from the wound.

A single drop broke free of her skin and splashed into the vial, darkening its crystal sides. He squeezed her finger, forcing more blood from the cut. Drop by drop, he filled the vial. When he had collected a thimbleful, he stoppered the bottle, tying the glass top in place with a steel wire.

Reverently, he pressed the wound to stop the flow. The mark left behind was barely noticeable. Perhaps she would never realise what he had done. Still, if Akken's words were correct, tonight Takket would slip into Haddronius's room and be gone by morning. If Akken had lied, then this night would be Takket's last. Either way, he would not have to answer to Hekaena.

The betrayal was minor compared to the murder he had originally intended, but guilt still gnawed at him. Hekaena would be heartbroken. Whether or not she admitted it to herself, she was in love with Takket. He felt sick for the pain he was causing her, but it could not be helped. Hers was not the first heart he had broken, and a heart seemed a small price to pay for revolution.

Turning his back to her, Takket crept to the door. He eased it open, then crossed the green-lit foyer to Ensellus's room. The door and curved handle may have been wrought iron, but it met the obsidian wall with a frame of black-painted wood.

Takket drew his knife, slotted it through the handle and pressed it into a join in the frame. The razor-sharp knife slid up to the hilt through two wooden sections with only the faintest creak. The hilt jutted from the frame, wedged between the door and the handle. It would stop Ensellus from pulling the door open, at least until he magically ripped it from its hinges.

It would have to suffice. Takket had a greater obstacle than Ensellus: Haddronius's door. He crept closer, examining the circular door's smooth jade surface, the Soulshard glowing at its centre. Unsure of

256

the meaning of Akken's 'of ill intent' warning, Takket tried to empty his mind. Having no thoughts surely counted as lacking ill intent.

Haltingly, he tugged the blood vial from his pocket and brought it to the Soulshard in the door's centre. The Shard gleamed brilliantly as if in proximity to a Mage. The groan of stone against stone reverberated through the jade door.

The door rolled open.

It barely made a sound as it disappeared into an alcove in the wall, revealing a long corridor coated in Soulshards. Dozens of batons. Hundreds. Their combined light matched the noon sun—he could only imagine their brilliance in the presence of an Arcane.

A shrill alarm pierced the air.

The ringing felt like needles driven into the skull. Haddronius and Ensellus would surely be startled awake. Demons, half the tower could hear the sound.

Disoriented by the din, he hurried back to Hekaena's room, flinging both incriminating glass vials into the shaft. They would shatter on the throne, a signal for Rithdal's Mage to flee. The heist had met disaster.

Ensellus's door slammed into the dagger, the wooden frame splintering as the handle rebounded, but it held. Takket eased Hekaena's door closed behind him. The sound of screeching metal and shattering wood resounded through the door, followed by something metallic clattering on hard stone.

Takket hurried away from rushing footsteps and shouts of alarm and into the darkness of Hekaena's room. She had not stirred, the sedatives far too strong to be overcome by an ear-splitting alarm. He hauled the covers from under her, then tucked her in. Throwing his clothes to the floor, he climbed in alongside.

He had barely finished when the door shook with a knock. A moment later it burst open, blinding light illuminating the room. Takket rose, not having to feign being disoriented by the brilliance.

'Hekaena?' Ensellus shouted from the doorway, Shard in hand, light radiating from an ethereal orb over his head.

'She's ill.' Takket slurred his words as though just awoken. 'She's not moved. What's going on?'

Ignoring him, Ensellus ran to Hekaena's side, checking her pulse. The air began to cool as the Arcane leached heat away to fuel his light. 'When did this happen?'

'This evening. She rapidly got tired. Is she alright?'

'She better be,' Ensellus snarled. 'There's been a security breach, perhaps an assassination attempt. I'm sealing this floor while we search the tower. You guard her with your life, Envoy. If anything happens to her, I'll skin you alive.'

Ensellus stomped out the room, slamming the door behind him. The lock rattled shut—Ensellus had trapped Takket. Or tried to.

In the ensuing silence, Takket gathered his thoughts. Enara and Yelleck had lied—for him to open the door, there was no need for Hekaena to die. He had nearly killed her for no reason. Demons, the blade had been in his hand. He found it hard to believe that the two Mages would have been mistaken about the workings of the magical door. No, they had seized the opportunity to have her murdered. But why? What would the siblings gain from Hekaena's death?

Akken, on the other hand, had been truthful. The small vial had worked, yet the alarm had triggered. Evidently, clearing one's mind was insufficient to bypass the protection against 'ill intent'. He needed more information, but had no allies to turn to.

The shouts and footsteps in the foyer had fallen silent. Takket dressed, then edged to the door. A glance through the keyhole revealed a deserted atrium. Haddronius's door had been resealed, but Ensellus's lay open, its handle lying on the floor by its shattered frame. The hole in the foyer's centre was sealed by a glistening sheet of steel.

No doubt, Haddronius was alert. He had no chance of stealing the Pure Shard tonight, but Ensellus's room was unguarded. There would never be a better time to search for a hidden passage. He tugged at the base of his pocket, removing a lock picking kit disguised as a gold embellishment of his cloak. He set to work, quickly picking Hekaena's simple lock, which seemed designed for privacy rather than keep out a determined thief.

Creeping across the circular hallway to Ensellus's office, Takket glanced at the wreckage of the man's door. It had been pulled open with enough force to rip the curved handle from the door, splitting the painted wooden frame. There was no sign of the knife.

Inside, the office was sparse. Only a simple desk, chair and bed occupied the floor space. Bookshelves lined the walls, each struggling with its burden of stacked folders. The only bare wall was the one behind the lone oaken desk—the wall shared by Haddronius's room.

Takket ran his hands over the flat obsidian wall, pushing at sections of the rock, prying at joints, twisting gas lamps, desperate to find a doorway.

Nothing.

The obsidian panels refused to budge. The gas lamps hid no switch. There was no route from Ensellus's room to Haddronius's. The only secrets this room contained were lined in the files along the walls.

Frustrated, Takket had just turned to leave when one folder caught his attention. In neat handwriting down its spine read the name *Envoy Khantek Fredeen.*

Curiosity overcame caution. He would never get another chance to find what information Ensellus had gathered. He hefted the thick folder to the desk. The first pages were filled with general information, the kind of dossiers Takket had read on Varsen courtiers. These gave way to pages filled with dates and times. Takket's every movement since arriving was noted down, all in the same small script. Meetings, meals, trips to the undercity, strolls through the tower—all fastidiously recorded. Angels above, during the royal dinner Ensellus had documented the length of time Takket had gone to the bathroom.

The methodical report was covered in coloured lines under certain activities. Any meeting with Hekaena was underlined in red. Little notes were scrawled into the margins.

Mundane sent as an insult? Perhaps show of submission.

Mundane nature confirmed by Hannig.

Physically healthier than age suggests. Potential physical threat. Assassin?

Interest in Hekaena continues. Attempt at gaining informant?

Hekaena situation becoming serious. Must intervene.

Clearly influencing Hekaena. Unknown motivation. Has ignored warning. Increase monitoring.

Still appears ignorant of role of his assistants— perhaps does not know of their loyalties.

Takket frowned. His assistants? Did Ensellus know they were Mages? Was he aware of the Free Circle's plan?

Replacing the folder, Takket searched the walls for a file on the Free Circle. Failing, he instead pulled down a file marked with Enara and Yelleck's names. Their file was much thinner than his own, the neat pages filled more with speculation than with day-by-day accounts.

One page drew his interest.

Strong evidence both are foreign agents. Not Imperium. Likely from Kilroth. Repeated meetings with known agent going by name of Rithdal. Objective unknown, but suspected to involve manipulating Envoy Khantek Fredeen. He appears unaware, but continues to associate with Hekaena. Kilroth clearly attempting to influence her. Will continue monitoring.

Kilroth? The land shared Varsen's northern border. Half of Varsen's recent wars were against them, fighting the Arcanedom they broke away from so long ago. Were Enara and Yelleck really working for

Kilroth, not the Free Circle? It made sense. The theft of the Pure Shard would make the Varsen dynasty vulnerable not just to a Mundane uprising, but to their neighbours.

Takket wanted to ruminate further, but the mention of Rithdal was too intriguing. Enara and Yelleck had never mentioned meeting—or even knowing—the elderly man, had no reason to. Either Ensellus was wrong, or they had been meeting the Mundane behind Takket's back. Yet, if they were Kilroth agents, why had Rithdal claimed they were ex-Free Circle?

Rithdal's file was easy to find, one of the largest on the shelves. The bookcase groaned as he lifted the folder. Takket dropped the leather-bound binder onto the desk with a thud. The first page was damning.

Rithdal—known Kilroth agent. Likely head of Kilroth spy network in Varsen. Keep under constant surveillance. Has ingrained self with Hekaena. Likely aims to destabilise Varsen family. Appears unaware of blown cover. Kill only if required. Surveillance has led to capture of multiple Kilroth agents.

Takket stared at the file. Rithdal was not part of the Free Circle. He was working with Enara and Yelleck. Demons below, if what this document claimed was true, he was their handler. Rithdal had first approached Takket shortly after he had started avoiding Enara and Yelleck. What if they had realised he had become suspicious and asked Rithdal to intervene?

Puzzle pieces clicked into place. They had been using him the whole time. This heist was never about freeing the Mundanes, never about giving the Shard to one more deserving. It was about shattering Varsen's power, opening the way for a Kilroth invasion without fear of a Pure Shard-wielding Arcane. Even if Takket was caught in the attempt, it could only benefit Kilroth —an Imperium envoy trying to break into Haddronius's room would inevitably ruin relations between the two countries. Perhaps precipitate intercontinental war. When the chance to have Hekaena assassinated landed in their lap, it was just the honey on the cake.

When he uncovered their lie on the airship, Takket had thought himself so cunning. He believed their plot had been ruined. In truth, they had merely exchanged their one ruse with another. He had been all too eager to believe Rithdal's hopeful lies.

All along, Takket had been part of their twisted scheme.

That night, Takket did not sleep. After returning the files to their shelves, he had scurried back to Hekaena's room to think. He was still determined to help the Mundanes of Varsen, but he would do so alone. All of his allies had turned to enemies. He was under no illusion that a Kilroth rule would be an improvement for the Mundanes of Varspire. The Arcanedoms of the New World barely varied by the extent to which they abused their underclass. When the invasion came, Mundane blood would run through the streets. Every word he had been fed by those cursed siblings had been a lie, meant to destroy the land he hoped to save.

Hekaena woke at dawn. Her motionless sleep had slowly given way to groans and pained twitches.

When her eyes finally cracked open, her face was ashen and beaded with sweat. Her floral perfume had faded—replaced with a feverish odour.

'What happened?' she croaked from cracking lips.

'You fell ill.' He handed her a glass of water, which she drank thirstily. 'I've never seen you so sick.'

'Can't remember being so sick,' she murmured. 'Think I could have slept through a storm.'

'In a way, you did,' he replied. 'There was some emergency last night, someone tried to break into your father's room.' She would find out soon enough, better he not appear to be keeping secrets.

'What?' She feebly attempted to rise. 'Is Father alright?'

Takket eased her onto the pillow. 'He's fine. Everyone's fine. Ensellus sealed the floor.' A knock came, followed by the sound of a key being turned. 'That's probably him now. You just rest. Whatever you have, it's clearly serious.'

She relented. Takket rose and crossed to the door, still wearing his cloak from the night before, his picks once again tucked into the recesses of his pockets. Instead of Ensellus, Takket found Innisel standing outside.

'Good morning, Envoy,' the old man said patiently. 'I was told I could find you here. I have a letter for you that arrived during the night. It was marked urgent, but I could not reach you until Ensellus ended the lockdown.'

Takket took the letter, still sealed with the elaborate mark of the Imperium. Before he had a chance to open it, Ensellus and two Mages levitated through the now-open hole in the foyer's centre, all three clad in green

Varsen military attire

'You'll be relieved in six hours,' Ensellus barked. The pair nodded and took positions either side of Haddronius's jade door.

'You're posting a guard?' Takket asked.

'Yes.' Ensellus narrowed his eyes at Takket. 'We were unable to catch the assassin. Until I find how they bypassed the door's security, it will be guarded at all hours. I trust you have no problem with that, Envoy?'

'Of course not.' Takket forced a smile.

'Good. And Hekaena?'

'I'm fine,' she croaked from the bed.

'She needs rest,' Takket explained.

Ensellus nodded curtly and strode into his office.

Innisel took a step back. 'I shall leave you in peace. Good day, Envoy.'

Takket closed the door, leaning back against its golden surface. Guards outside would make any further attempts at slipping into Haddronius's room impossible. Sighing, he broke the letter's seal, and hurriedly read.

Envoy Khantek Fredeen,

Her majesty Tessella Indel, daughter of Arcane-lord Venning Indel, heir to the Imperium, keeper of the angel's crown...

He skipped past the titles, which continued for a full paragraph.

...will be travelling to Varspire on the fifth day of Newroot. You will make all preparations to welcome

her and ensure her first visit to the New World is a
success.

It continued with detailed instructions, arrival times and dietary requirements, finally ending with the chief steward's elaborate signature. Takket folded the note, stomach sinking. Fifth of Newroot was just over a week away. The heir to the throne of the Imperium would surely recognise him as an impostor.

His time was running out.

PART III

CHAPTER EIGHTEEN

Takket pressed a damp cloth to Hekaena's brow. Throughout the day, he had tended to her. She groaned, she vomited, she shivered while wrapped in covers, dripped with sweat while naked. At times she was lucid, carrying out conversations in a cracking voice. These moments were few and far between, interrupting hours of delirium. Enara and Yelleck had made no indication of the severity of the sedative.

He should have learned to trust not a word they uttered.

He had no plan. No scheme for how to pull himself out of this mess. Everyone he had tentatively trusted had lied. Antellok. Enara. Yelleck. Rithdal. He cursed himself for accepting this job. His retirement had been secured. Right now, he could be sipping whisky on the porch of a Thousand Isles mansion. That was the dream. But it had only ever been a dream.

As much as logic told him that he should have never accepted Enara and Yelleck's offer—should have ran at the first sign of betrayal—part of him knew that he had to be here. If he had not journeyed to Varspire, there would be no end to Mundanes' suffering. If he had not come this far, he would never have met Hekaena.

His resolution had grown throughout the day. He would find a way to set things right, to free the

Mundanes.

Somehow.

With the jade door under constant guard, with no secret route to Haddronius's room, with no way around the alarm, the heist was slipping from his grasp. He needed time to plan, time to gather information, but the Imperium's letter had robbed him of that luxury. He had no idea how to carry out the heist, but he knew his next step. He would finally face the two who had dragged him into this quagmire, the two who had manipulated him into bringing a dagger to Hekaena's skin.

It was time to confront Enara and Yelleck.

Even after making up his mind, he found he could not tear himself from Hekaena's side. Every pained groan, every feverish nightmare, every body-wracking retch, was his fault. The one Arcane who showed an ounce of compassion, he had rewarded with suffering and betrayal. He made his choice to stay by her side.

A choice that was taken from him the next day.

Hekaena spent the night tossing and turning from fever, Takket from guilt. At dawn, there was a knock on the golden door.

Throwing on his crumpled velvet robe, Takket navigated the cluttered room. The air stank of stale sweat and mouldering food—he had shut the air vents to keep off the night's chill. To cover the window Takket had hung spare silken sheets, casting a cooling green gloom over the room. Discarded flannels, towels and half-eaten meals littered the floor. Whenever he had tried to clean, a cry of pain or nightmarish scream had pulled him to Hekaena's side.

He rubbed his face, tried to tame his hair. Grime

coated his skin, which had not seen a bath for two days. He could not offer himself such indulgence while Hekaena suffered.

Opening the door, he found Innisel standing alongside a wiry woman. She wore an immaculate white robe, greying hair pulled into a tight bun, eyes the brilliant red of an Arcane. She wrinkled her nose at the room's odour.

Innisel inclined his head. 'Has Arcane Hekaena recovered?'

'No.' Takket peered behind him into the dark room. Hekaena just groaned and rolled over.

'I should have been informed sooner,' the woman barked.

'This is Chief Physician Ennrella Varsen,' Innisel said. 'She will be taking over Arcane Hekaena's care.'

Takket felt a stab of selfish fear. A physician might discover that Hekaena had been poisoned.

'Is that necessary?' he asked feebly. 'She does seem to be improving.'

'Of course it's necessary,' Ennrella snarled. 'Arcanes rarely get ill. Whatever she has is serious, and must be treated. What are her symptoms?'

Takket relayed Hekaena's condition as the wiry woman pushed past him to Hekaena's side, ripping the sheet from the window to flood the room with harsh light. He did not hold back any of her illness— Hekaena would no doubt tell the woman everything in her next lucid moment. Part of him even wanted to tell the physician of the poison, but doing so would be signing his own death sentence.

'Was she anywhere unusual the day she fell ill?' Ennrella asked.

'She was in the undercity,' Takket explained. 'But that's not really unusual for her.'

The physician tutted. 'Exposure to so much Sharddust may have weakened her immune system. I'll take it from here. You must go.'

'Can't I stay?' Takket asked. 'I don't want to leave her like this.'

'I don't care what you want.' She glared at him, then turned back to her patient. 'If the Arcane-lord's daughter wants to frolic with Mundanes, that's her business, but I will not be subjected to your simple-minded musings. Out. *Now*.'

Takket turned to find Innisel still standing by the door.

'I will take you down,' Innisel announced. He hesitated, then gave a sympathetic smile. 'I'm sure she will be fine.'

The elderly functionary slipped a withered hand into his pocket, which immediately started to glow brightly. Takket's stomach lurched as his feet lifted from the ground. Innisel lowered them down the tower's central shaft faster than Hekaena had levitated Takket, but nothing close to the terrifying plunge with Ensellus.

As the fresh air whipped by, Takket focused on the matter at hand.

It was time to return to the embassy. It was time to face Enara and Yelleck.

Takket had wanted to change his clothes before facing the traitorous siblings, wanted a bath, wanted to feel more human. The demons had other plans. As he turned the corner into the maroon-carpeted embassy, he found Enara and Yelleck leaning against the marble pillars, expressions tense.

In three long strides, Yelleck crossed the hall to Takket. He seized Takket's arm and dragged him through the Shard-lit reception and into the embassy's dining room.

Enara slammed the door behind them. Takket shrugged out of Yelleck's grip, glaring at the man.

'What happened?' Yelleck snapped.

Takket ignored the question. 'There was no need to kill Hekaena.'

'What?' Yelleck blinked.

'The door opened with a few drops of her blood. She's alive, by the way. That "dying blood" bit of yours was demon-shit.'

Yelleck gave Takket a calculating look. 'What we told you was based on the best evidence we had. There are only a handful of references to such things in the documents. If you—'

'You can drop the act,' Takket hissed. 'I know damn well who you are.'

'What are you talking about?'

'This.' Takket fished his cloth flake-pouch from his belt and threw a handful of the dull red Shards at Yelleck's face. They brightened on impact. It was subtle, flakes being so weak compared to batons or even rocks. Still, it was clear enough under the dim glow of gas lamps ringing the room. 'You're a Mage. You both are.'

The room stilled. Takket held Yelleck's gaze, daring him to deny the truth.

'Fine,' Yelleck said. 'You were bound to find out soon enough. Yes, we are Mages. What difference does it make? We still want to change things, to help the Mundanes.'

'Just shut up,' Takket shouted. 'I know everything. I was in Ensellus's office. I read his files. I know you are both Kilroth agents. I know Rithdal is your handler. I know you just want to weaken the country for invasion.' He took a breath. 'I know you've been using me, but that stops *now*.'

Yelleck's face became murderous, his voice deathly quiet. 'You may want to be careful with your words. If we are what you claim, what's to stop us from just killing—'

His voice cut off as Enara laid a hand on his shoulder. She turned to Takket, calm. 'I could remind you that Ensellus is paranoid and probably thinks you are an agent from Octane sent to subvert the crown, but why bother. There's no point. What does it matter who we work for? Mundanes, Kilroth, whoever. Without the Pure Shard, Varsen *will* fall. Varsen's vaults are brimming with Shards. You'll get half. You'll go down in history as the world's greatest thief. Isn't that what you want? Isn't that why you came?'

'That may be why I came, but it's not why I'm still here. I've seen the suffering of the Mundanes. They must be free.'

Enara opened her arms wide. 'I don't see the problem. With the Pure Shard gone, the Mundanes will be free of Varsen's yoke.'

'And have it replaced with that of Kilroth?'

'I'm not saying we're from Kilroth,' Enara said carefully. 'But even if we were, surely anything would be better than Varsen rule. Yes, the other New World Arcanedoms execute Mundanes, but not on this scale, not like livestock.'

'Besides,' Yelleck said coldly. 'You need us as much as we need you, or have you forgotten? You can't just leave, and you can't escape Haddronius's floor without a Mage to catch you. Doesn't matter if you trust our motives. Without us, all you'll accomplish is a long fall and a sudden stop. We are your only option.'

Takket turned his back on them in frustration, trying to gather his thoughts. He had barely used this dining room since arriving in Varspire, preferring to dine alone or with Hekaena. Gas lamps burned around the walls, now turned low to plunge the room into twilight. A long, mahogany table dominated the space, a tidy golden band circumscribing its surface. Upholstered with red velvet to match the carpet, a dozen chairs flanked the table. Hints of the siblings' breakfast still lingered in the air: egg and fried krilt.

Perhaps they were right. Perhaps a Kilroth rule would be better than Varsen tyranny. It certainly could not be any worse. A slight improvement would still be an improvement. If even a single girl like Lyssa was saved, it would be a miracle. Still, he knew the transition would be bloody. But what had he hoped for? A Mundane uprising would end with blood flowing freely on all sides. Did it really matter who did the killing?

Sighing, he fingered the back of a nearby chair. The mahogany frame had been recently varnished, but he could still feel the underlying wear and tear. This chair was ancient. Its craftsmen long dead. The Mundane who felled the wood long forgotten.

However, Takket knew some facts about those

bygone Mundanes. This wood grew only in the Imperium. The Mundane woodcutter would have been paid a fair wage. The carpenter would have been lauded for his art. No person who had assisted in the construction would have feared purges. None had to choose between sacrificing themselves to a crematorium or seeing their child starve.

Varspire had to change. For that to happen, Takket needed aid. Try as he might, he knew he could not do this alone. Enara and Yelleck had been using him this whole time. It was time he started using them.

'The door was alarmed,' he said at last. 'Akken told me it only needed a few drops of blood to open, and that Hekaena did not need to die. He was right. He also warned that the door was protected with an alarm triggered if it's opened by someone with ill intentions. That's what happened. I managed to get out, but the whole tower was alerted.'

'That explains the security sweeps,' grumbled Yelleck. 'The tower was swarming with guards all night. They searched every corner, ransacked this place, hunting for something, someone.'

'Ensellus must not suspect you,' Enara said. 'Else we'd all be dead.'

'He knows you're with Kilroth,' Takket replied, bitter. 'He believes me to be your stooge. He seems certain your target is Hekaena, not Haddronius, so his focus is elsewhere. For now, we have a bigger problem.'

Yelleck grunted. 'Of course. Having that lunatic rip apart the tower isn't enough. What now?'

'Tressella Indel, the heir to the Imperium, is on the way here.'

275

Enara paled. 'What? When?'

Takket handed her the letter. 'Eight days from now.'

'She'll recognise you in an instant,' Enara said, aghast. 'Or rather, fail to recognise you.'

'So you see the problem.'

Yelleck began pacing, his leather boots scuffing over the plush carpet. 'We need to act before she arrives.'

'That's not going to be easy.' Takket sighed. 'Ensellus has posted a guard on Haddronius's door. Shifts of two Mages. The new ones arrive before the old depart...there's never an opening. And before you ask—no, I'm not going to take on two Mages with a knife.'

Yelleck tapped his chin. 'Perhaps you can get Hekaena to order them away.'

'Possibly,' Takket snarled. 'But only if she recovers. That demon-spawned sedative you gave me has all but crippled her. You forgot to mention that part.'

Yelleck sneered. 'Hardly seemed to matter. That plan was to kill her. The plan *you* decided against.'

'Thank the angels I did,' retorted Takket. 'If she had died, I would be ashes by now. And you alongside me. Of course that might have been your plan. Killing the child of Haddronius could only benefit Kilroth, right?'

Yelleck held Takket's glare. The bastards were never going to admit their true allegiance.

Enara stepped between them. 'Hekaena will be fine in a day or two. We're sorry we didn't tell you, but it really didn't seem to matter. The drug's after effects are pronounced, but short lived.'

Yelleck nodded. 'So all we need to do is wait a couple of days, get her to order the guards away, and you're home free.'

'Hardly,' Takket smirked. 'There's still the damned door and its alarm. Hekaena might be able to get the guards to leave for a short while, but they'll come running the moment that alarm is triggered. Another detail you missed out.'

'We didn't know about the alarm,' Enara replied. 'But it makes sense. Something to stop an assassin. Angels know how many times an heir has killed their parents throughout the eras.'

'I tried clearing my mind before opening the door.' Takket perched on the polished surface of the table, running his hand along the gold accent. 'Didn't help. The damned thing must still have known I intended on stealing the Shard.'

'Trained Shards can be very subtle,' Enara said. 'I don't think *you* can open the door.'

'Well I can't wait for Haddronius to open it, or he'll be wearing the Shard.' Takket scratched at the two-day-old stubble prickling his jawline. He sorely needed a shave. A bath. Sleep. 'Those few who visit him all come by appointment, when he's prepared. The work parties only enter when he's out.'

'So get Hekaena to open it for you,' Yelleck replied with a shrug. 'I'm sure you can convince her. A tour of her father's room? Sneaking in quietly at night as not to disturb him?'

Takket shook his head as he lay back on the table. The hard surface welcomed his exhausted body, his cloak's high collar forming a velvet pillow. 'Two problems there. First is the corridor after the door—it's built out of Shards. Haddronius sleeps in the room at its end. The glow's bright enough as is. If an Arcane or

Mage sets foot in that thing, it will glow like a gate to the underworld. That would wake even the heaviest sleeper.

'And if somehow Haddronius isn't stirred, what do you think Hekaena will do when I grab the Shard? Even if she doesn't have her staff with her, all she has to do is make it to that corridor and she'll have limitless power. She has feelings for me, yes, but those will fade the moment she realises what I've been planning this whole time. I've pissed off women before, but I've had the good sense not to rile an Arcane without being a hundred miles away.'

Yelleck's pacing stopped. 'There's a solution to both problems. Don't you see?'

The ice in his voice sent a shiver down Takket's spine. 'What are you talking about?'

'Kill Hekaena.'

Takket bolted upright, staring at Yelleck's cold face.

'Seems pretty obvious,' Yelleck continued. 'You need Hekaena to order away the guards, to open the door. Once the door's open, she's just a hindrance. Kill her. Slit her throat. Take the Shard while she bleeds out in the foyer. You'll be out of the tower before anyone finds the body.'

Takket felt the blood drain from his face. 'Why are you so determined to turn me into an assassin?'

'Why are you so determined to fail?' Yelleck stepped closer, glaring at Takket. 'We hired you because you were a man who could achieve the impossible. The person who stole the baton of Iggranious. The thief who talked his way into the Indspire vaults. Now after getting you here, giving you this cover story, risking our necks every demon-cursed day to assist you, we find you are a coward. A feeble man trembling at the thought of blood. What's the matter, Thief? Did she bat her pretty eyes at you?'

Takket rose to his feet, overcome with fury. Enara positioned herself between the two men, laying a calming hand on each of their arms.

'Please,' she said. 'Just take a breath. What my brother is trying to say—in his own blunt way—is that this is more important than one Arcane. No matter how you feel about her.'

'I don't—' Takket started before she cut him off.

'It doesn't matter. What matters is unseating the Varsen dynasty. I know you don't want to kill. No one does. But this is bigger than us. You've seen the suffering of the Mundanes. What would you sacrifice to put a stop to it?'

Takket's earlier vow returned to him. 'Anything,' he whispered.

Enara nodded, pride in her eyes. 'Exactly. That is what we need. It will hurt. It will cut you up inside. But it will be worth it. Her blood will save millions. Your pain will balm Mundanes all over Varsen.'

Takket felt sick, blinking back tears, but he knew she spoke the truth. He nodded weakly. 'She can still kill me with a thought.'

'Only if she has a Shard,' Yelleck said. 'When you're alone with her, put a knife to her neck. Take her hostage. Make her order the guards away. Force her to open the door. Then strike before she can move or shout in alarm. It's the only way. Time for you stop looking for an easy answer. This heist was never going to be bloodless.'

Takket could only nod, exhausted. His soul pulled in two directions. He had to help the Mundanes. He had to protect Hekaena. The more he thought, the more he realised those two drives were incompatible. The time had come to decide whether Hekaena meant more to him than every Mundane in Varspire. He gave a shuddering sigh, knowing there was only one answer.

He had to free the Mundanes.

Hekaena had to die.

CHAPTER NINETEEN

Takket did not have to force his smile at the sight of Hekaena. She stood in his room's doorway, a little unsteady, but looking far better than she had the previous day. Her black sleeveless linen dress made her look all the paler.

He hurried to her side. 'How are you?'

'Better.' Her voice cracked, but she retained her characteristic strength.

He drew her into an embrace. She smelled of perfume hastily dabbed over the acrid stench of strong soaps and tinctures. 'You had me worried.'

Hekaena pulled away with a fond smile. 'I'm fine, really. Thank you for looking after me. Angels know you did a better job than the physician. I don't think "bedside manner" is in her vocabulary.'

'Did she say what caused it?' he asked, nonchalant.

Hekaena shrugged. 'Some pathogen from the undercity. She claims I breathe too much Sharddust, advised me to stick to the tower for a few months. You can guess my response.'

Takket chuckled. 'I can imagine. It's good to see you back on your feet. Really good.'

'Feels good. I don't think I could have spent another minute in my room. That's sort of why I'm here. I agreed to go to Father's dinner tonight. Would you accompany me again?'

Takket grinned. 'I'd be delighted.'

'Great.' She led him by the hand, down the maroon-carpeted staircase to the embassy's foyer. 'I do want to see the look on Ensellus's face when he sees you.'

'Wouldn't miss it.' Takket could only hope that this evening would not end with death threats.

Hand in hand, they strolled along the winding corridors of Varspire Tower. The green carpets, obsidian walls and jade statues were all becoming familiar to Takket. Even the stagnant odour, mingled with exotic spices, began to seem normal.

'Innisel told me we have a royal guest arriving,' Hekaena said.

'Yes,' Takket replied with forced joviality. 'Quite unexpected. It's been some time since the last royal visit between our continents.'

Ahead, the arrival date loomed. Each day was one Takket could not afford to waste. Hekaena's illness had been a setback, bringing him ever closer to discovery and death. Still, some traitorous recess of his mind wanted him to fail. Wanted him to die, so that Hekaena may live.

As she squeezed his hand supportively, that recess grew louder.

'Might be a good thing.' Hekaena grinned. 'Maybe I can get Father to grant me permission to visit the Imperium in return. Perhaps with you as a guide.'

'I wouldn't have thought you'd want to leave the Varspire Mundanes.'

'Well, no. But seeing a land where the Mundanes don't suffer so terribly, that would be a wonder. I always hoped relations between our people would bring change here. So far, the angels have not obliged.'

Takket sighed. 'Truth be told, the Imperium would probably be much crueller if not for Circlist doctrine holding sway. Our Arcanes can be just as selfish, but they fear spreading too much misery, creating too many demons.'

'Perhaps we just need Circlism to spread here.' Hekaena flashed a conspiratorial smile.

Nervous, Takket smiled. 'Varsen adopting Circlist doctrine would make my masters very happy, but I doubt it's a popular topic here in court. If Ensellus suspected me of trying to convert the population, I don't even want to imagine his response.'

Hekaena chuckled mirthlessly. 'Unhealthy for you, no doubt. Ah well, we'll just need to change the country on our own then. The two of us against cruelty.'

'Sounds like a plan.' He smiled affectionately as they entered the throne room. The usual figures lingered at the edge of the hall, exchanging sealed envelopes and pouches of shards.

Hekaena levitated the pair into the Tower's main shaft. Wind howled through the ventilation ducts, a copper tang of Sharddust joining the fresh air. A dust storm was whipping up outside, winds blowing fast enough to carry errant grains of Sharddust up the tower's curving side. Tomorrow, Mundane servants would swarm the tower to eradicate the dust.

The smell of Sharddust faded—even the strongest winds could not carry the dust to this tower's peak. Hekaena deposited the pair in the dining room.

Takket's eyes were immediately drawn to the window-wall. The layer of Sharddust—normally a billowing haze a few storeys deep—now rose in great uneven sheets. Eddies ran up the side of Magetowers, launching the red dust skyward. Scarlet whirlwinds duelled between the spires, the scene backlit by the evening sun. Up here, it was mesmerising.

Down in the undercity, it would be hell.

Winds powerful enough to hurl dust into the sky would propel it through the lower city as an endless abrasive haze. Mundanes and animals alike would seek shelter in buildings, against boulders or in ditches. Ageing hovels would give way, walls would be scoured, greenery naive enough to sprout in the undercity would be flayed. There was no faint glow of wood fires—in these conditions, a naked flame could easily be blown into an inferno.

In the Imperium, such storms were rare, kept in check by mountain ranges and hardy forests. For Varspire, this was just the start of the storm season.

'Sister,' Drothinius called across the room. 'Glad to see you on your feet.'

Hekaena smiled and strolled to where Drothinius and Valena stood with their spouses. By the window, the children sat in a circle, playing a complex game with levitating sticks. In one corner, Innisel and Ensellus quietly conferred—the latter sneered at Takket.

Drothinius looked amused. 'And I see Khantek is joining us once again. It seems you are indeed to be a long-time addition to our dining.'

Valena gave a thin-lipped smile. 'Well, Hekaena, you always were fond of Mundanes. I just did not realise you were *this* fond.'

Before Hekaena could muster a rebuke, they were dazzled by white light reflecting off the curving window. Takket turned to see Haddronius gracefully drift through the doorway, his silken green robes fluttering. As everyone dropped to a knee, Takket bowed.

'Rise,' Haddronius croaked.

The Arcane-lord strolled across the room to the head of the curved table. The Pure Shard around his neck brightened as he magically pulled out his chair and sat. Takket followed Hekaena to their seats. This time, a place had been set for him.

Mundanes poured through the nearby doorway, laying out a steaming banquet with practised efficiency. The dishes had changed from the previous week, favouring larger cuts of meat and more of the bitter yellow sauce. Takket still could not put a name to any of it, but was beginning to identify the colours of those relishes less likely to burn his mouth.

After Haddronius had taken his selection, the table came to life, chunks of meat, skewers, pots of sauce, charred vegetables, all floating onto plates. This time, Hekaena needed no prompting, and filled Takket's plate with a selection matching her own. He was grateful to see she had favoured the milder orange sauces—she knew his difficulty with strong spice.

'Do you feel better, Daughter?' Haddronius barked, more accusation than parental worry.

'Yes,' Hekaena replied. 'Much better, thank you. Though I think due more to Khantek's doting over me than the physician's tinctures.'

Haddronius studied Takket in silence. He chewed thoughtfully on some fried krilt, wrinkled skin bouncing in time with his jaw. Unsure where to look, Takket held the man's gaze, staring into those small red eyes below the bushy and furrowed brow.

Haddronius washed his meat down with a sip of root wine. 'What do you intend with my daughter?'

Takket boggled. 'Excuse me?'

'You're sleeping with her.' Haddronius snapped. 'Is this some fleeting fancy? Some diplomatic move?'

Takket spluttered. He had not expected the question. Certainly not when surrounded by the intrigued eyes of the inner court. The entire table had fallen silent to regard him, expressions ranging from curiosity to mirth to disgust.

'No. Yes,' Takket stammered, gathering his wits. 'I mean, I am involved with your daughter. It's not a diplomatic move. It's not a passing fling.'

Hekaena smiled warmly. 'Oh it's not, is it?' she teased.

'Then what?' Haddronius's Pure Shard grew brighter as he dismembered some sort of roast fowl, ripping a leg free with magic.

Takket blushed, knowing he had to be careful. He needed to keep Hekaena on his side, but he could not forget Ensellus's warning. Any suggestion that he was serious with Hekaena would provoke further rage from that bitter little man. At the same time, implying that this was a mere dalliance would insult Hekaena— and her father.

Just one option gave him half a shot at taking the Pure Shard. He had to bind Hekaena closer to him. Angels willing, he would steal the Shard and flee before Ensellus exacted revenge.

He turned to her, forcing a shy smile as he stared into her vibrant eyes. 'I'm in love with Hekaena.'

She blinked in surprise, then squeezed his hand,

her face brightening with a smile that reached her eyes. 'And I'm in love with Khantek.'

Haddronius leaned back, sucking at a string of meat stuck in his teeth. 'You're a Mundane,' he said flatly.

'Yes,' Takket replied.

'You're not related to Arcane-lord Venning?'

'No.'

'This is not a move by the Imperium?'

'No.'

Cocking his head to the side, Haddronius examined Takket again, gnawing on a wing dripping with yellow sauce. He ran a hand steadily through his thin white hair. No one else moved. Even the children had paused their eating to watch the Arcane-lord. The only sounds were Haddronius's chewing and the wind's constant buffeting of the widow.

The man's red eyes turned to Hekaena. 'This man makes you happy?'

'He does, Father,' she said with conviction. 'More than anyone I've met. He shares my passion for helping the Mundanes. He's a good man.'

The Arcane-lord swished the root wine around his mouth, making infrequent sucking noises. Eventually, he swallowed, hammering the glass onto the rosewood table with finality.

'Fine,' Haddronius rasped. 'I have no objection to a marriage. I do not mean now, of course. Be sure. But if this man makes you happy, do what you will. Valena is inheriting. She has an Arcane heir in young Ithanius. The succession is secured. Even if all Khantek produces is Mundane children, the Varsen line will endure. Any Mundane children will carry your name, Hekaena, not Varsen. If you have children, of course.'

'You can't be serious,' Ensellus said. He realised his mistake a moment later and cowered from Haddronius's glare.

'*I* will make the decisions for *my* family. You are just here to keep them safe. If my daughter wants to marry this man, then I'll not hear a word against it.'

Ensellus muttered an apology, but narrowed his eyes at Takket. Hekaena was blushing furiously. Takket felt his own skin warm.

'Erm, thank you, Father,' she muttered. 'I don't think we're quite there yet.'

'I know,' Haddronius grumbled. 'I'm just giving my blessing now. I've made my decision. Just remember this, Envoy...Khantek. If you hurt my daughter, then no diplomatic tie, no threat of war, no foreign army will keep me from burning you alive.'

Takket nodded hurriedly. The corners of Haddronius's mouth twitched in what may have been a smile.

'Well.' Drothinius clapped twice. 'Seems Khantek will be a permanent feature at this table.'

'It will be nice to have more Imperium refinement,' his wife Insania said, giving Takket a measuring look.

Valena laughed tersely. 'A Mundane in the family —that will take some getting used to.'

'We're not getting married yet.' Hekaena buried her face in her hands, exasperated.

'Yet?' Takket teased.

She punched him in the arm, but could not hold back a grin.

Innisel cleared his throat, adjusting the pleated

white hair hanging over his shoulder. 'Of course, a foreign agent could not be allowed into the royal family. I'm afraid you will have to renounce all allegiance to the Indel Imperium.'

'Can we deal with the minutiae of getting married when there's actually a marriage to plan?' Hekaena asked, frustrated.

Drothinius clapped again. 'My dear sister is right. We have a royal visit on the way. That means we have a banquet to plan. Now, we greeted the envoy here with a roast krilt. We'll have to top that for the Imperium's heir. Innisel, do you think we can get a vrassashark in time for the arrival?'

'If we dispatch hunting airships now to spot for the harpoon barges, yes,' Innisel said patiently. 'But the creatures weigh a hundred tons. How do you plan on fitting it through the door to the banquet hall?'

'We could take out the windows,' Drothinius mused. The conversation turned to details of banquets, royal tours, military parades. Tessella's imminent arrival filled those around the table with excitement and trepidation. This was their one chance to show the future ruler of the Imperium that Varsen was a strong, worthy ally.

Takket met Hekaena's gaze, staring into those eyes, the silver flecks sparkling in a sea of red. He considered Haddronius's words. Marriage was on the table. A position as the spouse of an Arcane would assure him as much luxury as he could ever hope to achieve. With Hekaena, he could work from within Varspire to improve the lot of Mundanes. They could influence her family—maybe not Haddronius, but surely they could show Valena and her children the state of the undercity. No need for revolution or invasion, just a steady evolution to a better country.

Of course, it would involve a life of lies. Lying to the woman who loved him. Lying to everyone they met. Lying to any children. He had spent a lifetime deceiving others, but was he willing to spend the rest of his life in this lie?

Seeing the warmth in Hekaena's eyes, feeling the fondness in her touch, he sensed something inside stir. For the first time, he realised he had not been completely manufacturing his feelings. He really was coming to care for Hekaena. The thought of a life with her filled his heart with joy.

Yes, he thought. To spend a life with Hekaena and save the Mundanes, he would lie until his dying breath.

Haddronius said little else during the meal, seeming content to let his children arrange the details of the royal visit. He left immediately after dinner, pausing to give Takket a perfunctory nod.

Mundanes poured into the room, clearing the table under the watchful eyes of their Mage supervisor. The children disappeared to the upper level, levitating using Shards kept on necklaces or in pockets. Ithanea, Valena's Mage daughter, clutched two Shards in case she burned through one before reaching the upper floor. A puff of red dust floated down a short while later, a Shard having crumbled, its remains discarded.

The adults gathered around the window while the Mundane servants pulled chairs aside and laid out a selection of drinks. Takket wandered over, selecting a decanter of mountain whiskey and pouring the amber liquid into an intricate glass tumbler.

'Rather strenuous evening.'

Takket turned to see Antonius, Valena's husband, walking up behind him.

'You could say that again.' Takket offered the man his glass, which was taken gladly. 'I never expected to find myself in that situation.'

Antonius sniffed the whiskey and took a sip. 'I'm starting to feel lucky to not have been in the conversation where my marriage to Valena was discussed.'

Takket filled a new glass, and breathed in the oaky aroma. 'You weren't?'

'Angels, no. Valena and I had barely started courting. My parents were summoned to a private discussion with Haddronius. Three hours of wrangling later, they came out and announced I was to marry. So you're really considering this?'

'It's still far too early.'

'Of course, of course. You need to be certain. It's not an easy life, being married to a Varsen.'

Takket swallowed a mouthful of the burning liquid. 'But you're an Arcane. Surely it was not too much of an adjustment for you.'

Antonius gave a bitter laugh. 'Oh, more of an adjustment than it will be for you, I'm sure. An Arcane in Varspire is powerful, independent. Even lower ranked Arcanes working Shardrails or airships attract attention. Being from one of Varspire's great families, descended from the brother of the second Varsen Arcane-lord, I was always at the centre of things.'

'And now?'

'Now, I'm barely noticed. The Varsens eclipse

those around them. The day Valena and I swore our blood oath to honour each other for life, I stopped being an Arcane, and became her adornment.'

'You sound like you have regrets.'

Antonius shook his head. 'Not at all. I love my Valena. Raising our children has been the highlight of my life. No, I am more than happy. I just want you to know what's waiting. If you do marry Hekaena, you'll forever be in the background. Even more so, since you're a Mundane. She'll make all the decisions for you both. You'll not be seen as a true Varsen, just...an assistant. Make sure she is worth it.'

Takket gazed across the room to where Hekaena laughed with her siblings. He couldn't make out her words, but could tell from her half-smirk, her upturned eyes, that she was teasing her brother. Those eyes smouldered under the shifting light of the Soulshard chandelier.

'She's worth it,' he said quietly. He wondered at the truth in his words.

'Glad to hear it. Listen, if you need any help, just come to me. I know how hard it can be. It will be good to have another Varsen spouse to talk to.'

'What about Drothinius's wife?' Takket struggled for the name. 'Insania?'

Antonius chuckled. 'Oh, she's fine, just...intense. I think she's taken all the ambition she had for herself and is trying to cram it into her husband. Don't think Drothinius has noticed.' He shook his head. 'Oh, she's nice enough, but isn't as good at hiding her designs as she thinks. She'll probably warm to you, though. A marriage to a Mundane would put Hekaena forever out of the line to the throne. One less sibling for

Insania to try to chase off.'

Seeing Takket laugh nervously, Valena led her siblings over.

'What are you two conspiring about?' Valena asked.

Antonius gave her a peck on the cheek. 'Oh, just updating Khantek on court gossip. The Imperium may have prepared him for the role of an envoy. I'd like to make sure he survives the role as Hekaena's partner.'

Valena inspected Takket. 'Well, he's survived the undercity well enough so far. No doubt that's where Hekaena will be keeping him.'

Drothinius laughed. 'I feel sorry for you, Khantek. Those few Mundanes who land an Arcane look forward to a life of luxury. With Hekaena, you'll be spending as much time in the undercity as a... What's a Mundane job? Gutter cleaner?'

Hekaena rolled her eyes. 'The Mundanes don't have gutters—they would just clog with Sharddust.'

Drothinius grinned. 'My point exactly. An Arcane shouldn't need to know such trivialities. Is this really what you want, Khantek?'

Takket smiled broadly and took Hekaena's hand. 'Her devotion to the Mundanes is why I love her. I wouldn't sacrifice that for all the luxury in the world.'

'Good answer.' Drothinius looked between Takket and Hekaena, then smiled warmly. 'Well, Hekaena, it's honestly good to see you this happy. If Khantek's the cause of this joy, then I say keep him.'

'Indeed,' Valena said. 'I wondered if you would ever find someone. We should have known that it would take a Mundane to get your attention.'

Despite the thinly veiled barb from Valena, Takket

began to feel accepted. The siblings were not rejecting the idea of a marriage. Antonius seemed outright welcoming. Takket might be a Mundane, but they seemed to care only about Hekaena's happiness.

Perhaps this was the solution. Marry Hekaena. Show the Varsen rulers firsthand that Mundanes were not some skulking underclass but real speaking, crying, bleeding people. That might be enough to see change. Haddronius would die someday, passing the throne to Valena. If he had softened her view of Mundanes enough, she might be willing to relax the laws.

He could go further. Circlism had done wonders for the Mundanes of the Imperium. Hekaena was right when she said that spreading the faith here might cause real improvement. Takket had had a life's worth of experience in manipulating others—he would make a perfect missionary. Carefully timed words in the right ears could convert the future Arcane-lord.

The shift would be groundbreaking. Yes, the Arcanes would be dissatisfied, but the Mundanes would flock to Varsen. This could be the catalyst, Varsen's conversation spreading over the New World, bringing more far-reaching changes than the theft of a Pure Shard. Forget saving the Mundanes of a country, he could free a *continent*.

His thoughts were interrupted by a nasal voice behind him.

'Excuse me,' Ensellus said, uncomfortably close. 'I was about to retire for the night, but have some business in the lower tower. I would be more than happy than to escort Khantek down to the throne room on my way.'

Takket's blood turned to ice. He had not told Hekaena of Ensellus's threat. Looking into the man's angry, beady eyes, he knew he had made a mistake. The mention of marriage could be the final pebble to break the krilt's shell. Ensellus may, he feared, 'accidentally' drop Takket, find a way to worm his way into Hekaena's good graces once the envoy's mangled corpse was burned.

'There's no need,' Hekaena said slowly. Takket breathed a sigh of relief.

'I insist. There is no point in you taking him all the way down the shaft just to come back up again.'

'There's no point taking him down the tower at all,' Hekaena replied tersely. 'We were just about to return to my room.' Ensellus started to object, but she cut him off. 'No, I don't want to hear it. You heard Father—we have his blessing. Or shall I go knock on his door and inform him that his *bodyguard* is telling his own daughter who she can take into her room?'

Ensellus opened and closed his mouth, then turned with a frustrated grunt. 'Fine, I'll speak to the envoy another time.' The spiteful man stalked silently to the balcony, levitating up to his office.

Antonius shook his head. 'Don't worry, Khantek. He spoke the same way to me when I started to court Valena. Damn man wants the Varsen name as much as a Mage wants to ascend.'

'Well he's not getting it from me,' Hekaena grumbled.

'Urgh. You know what this means, dear?' Antonius asked Valena. 'He gave up on you, went for Hekaena. If she's now taken, he'll look for another. How long until he starts arranging a marriage with our little

Ithanea?'

'She's only eight,' Valena said flatly.

'This is Ensellus we're talking about.'

Valena grimaced. 'If he tries, I'll have him publicly gelded.'

'And that's why you're a good mother.' Antonius grinned and kissed his wife's cheek.

Hekaena chuckled. 'On that note, we best be going, before Ensellus puts that little mind of his to welding my door shut.'

They said their farewells and left the others drinking and badmouthing Ensellus. Takket smiled, his acceptance shown by how freely they discussed the intolerable security chief. He was part of their clique now, becoming a family member.

After levitating up to the royal floor and closing her door, Hekaena kissed Takket firmly. 'Thank you for putting up with that. You did well.'

He held her, smiling. 'I've been trained to deal with court politics. This was just...personal politics.'

'Did you mean what you said back there?'

He kissed her. 'Hekaena,' he said earnestly, 'I love you.' Managed to sound convincing.

She pulled him into a tight embrace, then stepped back. 'Excuse me for a moment.'

Hekaena gave him a grin and slipped away to the adjoining bathroom. Takket rubbed his hair, pacing. He was really considering this. Abandon the plan, achieve something greater. Instead of removing the Varsen line, he could infiltrate it, bring progress from the inside.

Catching a glimpse of himself in a mirror, he paused. He looked at the grey hairs tucked behind his ears. He looked at the wrinkles marring the edge of his eyes and down his clean-shaven cheeks. His appearance had fooled the entire court of Varsen. It could continue to do so for decades to come.

But it would not fool Tessella Indel.

The moment she arrived, she would identify him as a traitor. It would hardly matter if he wanted to steal the Pure Shard or convert the continent—either way, he would burn. Hiding himself during the Indel heir's visit would be challenging, but possible. However, she would not be the last Imperium visitor. If he renounced his supposed allegiance, they would send a new diplomat. Someone actually from Varsen's court.

Perhaps he could disguise himself. Something to disfigure his face, make him unrecognisable as either Takket or Khantek. But how? Fire was too difficult to control. Acid could work, but Varspire Tower did not have vats of the stuff lying around. An accident at a building site might be possible. It was a risk, but a broken cheek bone, shattered nose and scarred jaw might suffice. After the swelling, he would look different enough to pass off as having once been Khantek.

He sighed. Even that would not suffice. The replacement envoy would have been a co-worker of Khantek's, a friend. All it took was one slip, a wrong word, a difference tone of voice, and Takket would be exposed.

Bitterly, he shook his head. It was a wonderful fantasy—life here helping Hekaena save a continent—but it was merely a fantasy. Unworkable.

As Hekaena returned from the washroom, he smiled with genuine warmth. He was not willing to throw her life away, not unless he was backed into a corner. Thankfully, he already had the seeds of a germinating scheme—a scheme that might just allow him to steal the Pure Shard without harming Hekaena.

'I've had an idea.' He caressed her hands. 'This is becoming serious. I may be spending a long time in Varspire, but I've seen more of the undercity than this tower. I was thinking—could you give me a tour of the palace? No one like a local to show me around a new town.'

She beamed, having no idea she was stumbling into his trap.

'I'd love to.'

CHAPTER TWENTY

Takket luxuriated in his marble tub. Floral fragrances steamed from the water, oils suffusing his skin. He did not need to boil pails—Mage-powered boilers deep in the bowels of the tower provided hot water to the lower floors. The upper spire, of course, had no need for advanced plumbing. Mages and Arcanes would heat their own baths.

He shivered as he climbed from the tub. Through the ventilation ducts, the dying dregs of the dust storm blew the chill morning air. He had become accustomed to Hekaena effortlessly maintaining the temperature, touching her Shard to convert energy to cool or heat the air. Mages would steadily burn through Shards to retain comfortable conditions. As an Arcane, her one Shard had lasted a lifetime.

Takket dried himself on a linen towel, tucked it around his waist and ventured in search of clothing. A few steps into his room, he heard a noise in the corner. Curious, he turned.

Ensellus stepped out the shadows.

Towel dropping to the floor, Takket jumped back, tripped over the bed and sprawled across the carpet.

'What the demon-shit?' he exclaimed. 'What are you doing here?'

'I'm here for you, Khantek.' Ensellus stalked forward. Something flashed from the sleeve of his jet-black cloak.

299

A dagger.

Takket's dagger.

Scrambling back, Takket searched for a defensive weapon. He found only silken sheets, down-stuffed quilts and plush pillows. Hastening to his feet, he grabbed the first object he could find atop his mahogany dresser: a glass jar of incense. Its floral liquid sloshed as he hefted the container.

Ensellus looked amused. Takket could not blame him—right now he must look a pathetic specimen, a naked and ageing man, wielding a crystal jar as a weapon. This was not how Takket imagined this heist ending. Not how he imagined his death.

'Do you recognise this?' the man snarled.

'It's a dagger,' Takket said flatly. He could throw the jar. It might stun Ensellus long enough for Takket to wrestle away the knife. Of course, if Ensellus touched a finger to a Shard, Takket would be finished.

'Your powers of deduction are truly amazing. It's no wonder the Imperium put their trust in you. Do you recognise this particular dagger?'

'No,' Takket replied. Never before had he longed to see Enara and Yelleck in the doorway. They were only Mages, but they might be able to defeat Ensellus with the element of surprise.

'You should.' Ensellus stepped closer, holding the flat of the blade to Takket. 'See the engravings? The style is clearly from your homeland.'

'So? I can hardly be expected to track every object made in the Imperium.'

'But this isn't just any dagger. This dagger was found at the scene of the break-in last week. This dagger was jammed into my door. This dagger was part of an attempted assassination.'

There was a calmness to Ensellus's voice, not the rage Takket had expected. Perhaps the man was not here for murder. Takket pulled the duvet from his bed to cover himself, striving to regain his dignity.

'That would seem to be your problem, not mine.' Takket straightened, but kept his ad-hoc weapon ready in case the man lunged. 'What your citizens do with weapons in this country is your jurisdiction. If you want to object to the sale of arms, then this is hardly the correct place for trade negotiations.'

Ensellus smirked. 'Oh, this knife is your problem, but it will be best for both of us if we leave this out of the official record.'

'And why's that?'

'Because, you are going to do me a favour. You are going to break Hekaena's heart. You are going to spurn her. Leave her in tears. I don't care what lie you use, but the relationship ends. *Now*.'

'And why would I possibly do that?'

'Otherwise I'll have you burned alive.'

It was Takket's turn to smirk. 'You've made that threat before. The throne room? The fall?'

'What can I say? I believe in second chances.'

'Demon-shit,' Takket shouted, hopefully loud enough for Enara and Yelleck to hear. 'You know that threats are all you have. You heard Haddronius—he approves of my match with Hekaena. He's not going to let his...' He waved a dismissive hand at the man. '...underling dictate his family's life. You touch me, and your Shard will sit right alongside mine.'

Takket wanted to punch Ensellus's self-satisfied grin.

'Oh, that's where you are wrong, Envoy. You see, this dagger changes things. I can have a dozen soldiers swear they saw you holding it before the assassination attempt. I can have analysts testify it was recently forged, not an old import. I control the law here, Envoy. I will make Haddronius see you only as an assassin who used his daughter to breach his security. How long will his protection last once I put the right words in his ear?'

The man did not actually suspect Takket was involved in the break in. If not for the knife, Takket would have laughed—Ensellus threatened to frame Takket for a crime he actually committed. 'You would lie to your Arcane-lord, let the true assassin go unpunished, all to spite me?'

'Not to spite you. For Hekaena. I would do anything for her. Anything. Understand?'

'You're still spouting demon-shit,' Takket hissed. 'If you had that power, you'd have done it already.'

'Oh, believe me, I have considered it. But somehow I suspect even if you are proven to be an assassin, Hekaena would blame the man who ordered your execution. I would prefer for *you* to be the villain here. If you won't...' Ensellus shrugged. 'Then I'll have no recourse. Let me make this perfectly clear to you, Envoy. This is your final warning.'

Ensellus stormed towards the door and barged it open. Outside, Enara and Yelleck stood uncertainly on the stairs. Ensellus shoved past, almost knocking Yelleck from his feet. The siblings stared helplessly as the man marched down the embassy's marble-walled foyer.

'Thanks for the assistance,' Takket said dryly,

pulling the duvet comfortably around himself and setting down the incense jar.

'What was that about?' Yelleck asked.

'Just the kindly security chief wishing me well with a dagger. Thought he was going to kill me at first. Could have used some backup. A couple of Mages might have made a difference.'

'We didn't want to show our hand,' Enara said reassuringly.

'Helpful as ever,' Takket grumbled.

Yelleck glowered. 'You wouldn't have needed help if you hadn't delayed the theft. You know what you need to do.'

'Yes,' Takket replied. 'And it doesn't involve killing Hekaena.'

'Demons below, not this again.' Yelleck looked to the ceiling. 'We've been over this. Either you carry out the theft, or we all die. It's that simple. If not when Tessella identifies you, then when Ensellus frames you for your own botched break-in.'

'I *will* steal the Shard,' Takket retorted. 'I have a plan that doesn't involve killing anyone. Hekaena will let me in, voluntarily. No blood.'

'By all the demons, how are you going to do that?'

'Let me worry about the plan. Just make sure you're in position to catch me tonight.'

Yelleck considered, then gave a curt nod. 'Fine. If you insist on being spineless, then we'll try it your way. This had better work.'

'It will,' Takket assured him.

Yelleck turned towards the mahogany door. 'Good. Because if you fail, you will have only one final option. Cut Hekaena's throat.'

That afternoon, Hekaena had taken Takket on a grand tour of Varspire Tower. He was only interested in Haddronius's room, but could not afford to raise her suspicions, so he followed her itinerary.

The tour began at the base of the tower, with the Sharddust-stained corridors leading to the Mundane entrance—a heavily guarded doorway to the undercity. The storm had eased, but dust still blew past the lines of riflemen flanking the hallway. A handful of Mundanes braved the lower corridors, visiting the stuffy offices to apply for work as cleaners or riflemen, report crimes, or plead uselessly on behalf of a wrongly convicted family.

Most Mundanes avoided the tower at all costs. All it took was one wrong word, one missed bow, and they would end up in the crematorium.

The next level had contained the main barracks. Green-and-black uniformed men proudly presented themselves to Hekaena, Mage sergeants barking orders until the Mundane riflemen fell into neat lines. Marksmen had proudly displayed their skills, hitting targets at the end of long firing ranges. The soldiers were clearly excited to have a member of the royal family present. Takket went unnoticed.

Above the barracks lay the Varspire vaults: a dazzling collection of Shards, from sacks of splinters and grains through to rocks and row after row of batons. Takket had never seen such wealth in his lifetime. There was no need for gas lamps—the cavernous hall bloomed with light from a thousand Shards, the red light painfully bright as it danced across the obsidian walls.

Mages filled the surrounding rooms, a ring of magic-users ready to meet any thief with fire and death. They politely nodded to Takket.

Countless bureaucratic offices occupied the following floors. Minor functionaries toiled away behind stacks of paper. Messenger children ran down the hallways, carrying notes, orders and reports between the numerous departments. In guarded storerooms, ledgers tracked food shipments, soldier wages, factory output, naval positions and—of course —the constant tally of Varspire's Shards.

The couple had sauntered by the Imperium's Embassy, the only foreign consulate in Varspire. Diplomacy with Varsen's neighbours was handled by short-tempered ambassadors dispatched to deliver bribes and threats. When those failed, New World diplomacy was conducted by rifle volleys and magical projectiles.

Along the tower's main shaft, the wonders had refused to abate. Art galleries contained sculptures dating back to before the Devastation, including a clay urn that claimed to have been made in the Mundane era. A Scalist temple stretched up several floors, each filled with greater riches than the last. A bathhouse occupied one of the upper levels, its main pool built against the window-wall looking over the city.

Hekaena and Takket had dined in a gold-trimmed restaurant near the tower's peak. The head chef, an Arcane of some renown, had fawned over Hekaena, personally preparing his speciality dishes. The strips of krilt glazed in a sickly-sweet sauce had particularly impressed, spicy enough to add a sharpness without overpowering the meat. The chef had dusted off a bottle of root wine aged older than Takket himself. Decades encased in glass had mellowed the red wine, softening the taste of Sharddust the barest hint.

By the time Hekaena levitated them up the night-shrouded tower to the top floor, both were more than a little tipsy. They landed, laughing with excitement at having reached the end of their marathon tour. Either side of the jade door, two Mage guards gave the pair uncertain looks, but remained silent.

'Well, here we are,' Hekaena announced with an exaggerated bow. 'Thus ends your grand tour of Varspire Tower.'

'What about this floor?' Takket smiled playfully.

'Well, you've already seen my room.' She grinned at him, then turned to glare at the two guards. 'Oh, stop staring, you two.'

'What about the other rooms?' Takket nodded towards the jade door.

'Well,' Hekaena said thoughtfully, 'I suppose my brother and sister are out at that dinner party tonight. I can show you Drothinius's room. See how it compares to mine.'

Not the door Takket meant, but he followed her nonetheless. Drothinius's door was silver, polished to a mirror shine. Emeralds pitted its surface, scattering the jade-filtered light from the foyer. Hekaena knocked, then eased it open.

Drothinius's room was bathed in impatient red light from Soulshards, which ran in parallel strips along the ceiling, matching the Imperium-styled maroon carpet. Objects in the room were arranged in a clash of order and disarray. The black bedsheets were perfectly smooth, but overlaid with a dressing robe cast offhanded across the bed. Towels lay in perfectly square stacks on the rosewood dresser, or scattered over the floor. The mahogany desk was well-polished, but bore a drying ring of root wine.

'Cosy,' Takket said.

Hekaena smiled. 'Insania does her best. Drothinius has never been tidy. If it's not food, drink or something to make him laugh, he's not interested.'

'I'm guessing Mundanes clean the place.'

'Yes. Insania makes sure of that. Before her, Drothinius would often order the work parties away— hard to lounge around when someone's trying to sweep under your feet.'

'Lovely. Well, I must say, your room's neater.'

'Oh, you should see Valena's. Come on.' Hekaena beckoned and led the way back across the foyer. Valena's door was obsidian, streaked with jade. Hekaena opened it to a room lit under the steady glow of gas lamps. Inside, rosewood furnishings were bedecked with emerald insets. Every cloth, robe and perfume vial sat neatly in place, making the room seem more of a display-piece than a couple's home. Abstract Varsen sculptures loomed from the corners, angels and demons leering at each other with ruby eyes and exaggerated features.

'I didn't realise your sister was so religious.' Takket nodded to a snarling obsidian demon.

'Well of course. Scalism teaches that all effort should be made to give Arcanes a joyful life, so that they may become angels in the next. Anything that promotes my sister's happiness goes down well.'

Takket laughed. 'Well, it is certainly grand. I still prefer your taste in decor. Less...creepy.'

Valena smiled. 'Well, that's just about it. The children will be asleep, so let's not disturb them. I'm sure they'd be delighted to show you their rooms in the light of day.'

Takket turned to look at the jade door. 'What about your father's room?'

Hekaena frowned. 'He'll be asleep.'

'Well, then let's be sure not to wake him.' Takket flashed a mischievous grin.

Her frown deepened, then faded as she began to look excited. 'Alright. I suppose a peek can't hurt.'

As they approached the door, one of the Mage guards stepped forward to block the way.

'No one's to go into the Arcane-lord's room,' she said haughtily. 'Ensellus's orders.'

Hekaena glared at the woman. 'I'm Haddronius's daughter. Father has never had an issue with me visiting.'

'I can't speak for the Arcane-lord,' the Mage replied, 'but Ensellus's instructions were clear. No one opens this door.'

'Ensellus ordered you to disobey the direct command from a member of the royal family?'

'Well, not exactly,' the Mage stuttered.

'Then let me through. You know what? I think I've had enough of your glances. Go downstairs and guard the throne room.'

'But Ensellus—'

'Ensellus isn't here. Besides, I outrank him. I'm not asking—I'm issuing a command. Let me deal with your master. You have your new orders. Go.'

Hekaena glowered as the cowed guards dropped down the central shaft, Shards in hand.

'Wow,' Takket said. 'Remind me never to get on your bad side.'

'Always good advice.' She grinned. 'Now watch this. This door is really quite amazing. Only Varsens can open it, and an alarm is triggered by anyone with ill intentions towards the current Arcane-lord. It's kept the rulers of Varsen safe for generations.'

Takket whistled appreciatively. 'What exactly does "ill intention" mean?'

Hekaena shrugged. 'The magic is ancient, dating back to the founding of Varspire. Few Arcanes have ever will-cast into a Shard, and none pass on the secret. Too powerful. Too dangerous. You heard of the golem of the bloody glade? That was will-casting at work. The Shard makes a judgement, follows its original instructions to the best of its ability. In this case, I assume it would interpret any attempt to kill or harm the Arcane-lord as ill intent.'

'How does a Shard interpret anything? It's a rock.'

Hekaena gave a soft smile. 'Is it? They're called *Soul*shards for a reason. A soul, a consciousness—or at least the echo of one—trapped in this world, encased in a gem-prison. Mages and Arcanes tap the power of that soul when we cast, Mages creating or destroying energy, Arcanes moving it from one form to another. The only difference here is that the soul in this Shard was taught to cast its own magic.'

'How do you teach a soul to cast?'

'Talk to it, I suppose.' Hekaena grinned. 'As for how you communicate with a soul...well if I knew that, I could make these myself.'

Takket nodded. Using these Shards, drawing power from trapped souls, communicating with the dead—this was an alien world. All he could do was take Hekaena's word. 'Right, shall we see it in action?'

Hekaena nodded excitedly and turned to the door. She waved a hand over the Shard in the centre of the jade surface. The circular baton brightened in recognition. A muffled groan rumbled through the door, stone scraping against stone. Then, with barely a sound, the door rolled into a recess in the wall.

Blinking at the brightness of the Soulshard-coated corridor beyond, Takket peered through the doorway.

'Quite a sight, isn't it,' Hekaena whispered.

'Beautiful,' Takket agreed. 'How many Shards are here?'

'I don't know,' she replied grimly. 'A thousand, maybe? There were a lot of prisoners of war during Varsen's struggle for independence. The Mages and Arcanes were ransomed. The Mundanes...'

Takket shook his head. 'Can we have a look inside? I can't see anything beyond the corridor.'

'I don't want to wake Father.'

'We can be quiet,' Takket whispered playfully.

'I'm sure we can, but if I step foot in that corridor, the glow will surely wake him. And probably blind you.'

Takket nodded, his chest tightening. This was it. His opening. 'Could I go in alone?'

Hekaena laughed. 'You can't be serious.'

'Just a peek.' Takket kept his tone jovial. 'You've got me curious now—the most highly secured room in Varspire. I'd love to step inside. What harm could it do?'

'Well for one, Father will kill you.' She frowned. 'If he wakes up to a stranger in his bedroom, he's not

310

going to ask questions.'

'I'll be quiet, I promise.'

The frown deepened. 'Why are you so determined about this?'

Takket felt the situation slipping from his control. 'Not determined, just wondering how the Arcane-lord lives. Come on, I promise I'll be quiet. I'll be back before you know it.'

'Khantek, no,' she snapped, waving her hand over the wall, causing the door to roll back into position. 'I don't know what's got into you.'

'Sorry, just got carried away I guess. Too much root wine,' Takket said contritely. His words did nothing to calm her suspicious stare. The moment the stone locking mechanism rumbled back into position, Takket knew he had failed.

Throughout the rest of the evening, Takket tried to distract her, playing the role of the doting lover. His efforts eased the tension, but she kept casting unsettled glances his way.

Once she had fallen asleep, he sat in bed watching the sheets rise and fall with her every breath, listening to the gentle crack of her light snore, breathing in her lavender perfume. His heart ached as he looked down on her, the pale moonlight picking out her jawline, her twitching eyelids, her collarbone. He wanted to stay in this moment forever. He prayed to the angels to halt the approaching sunrise, just let him remain alongside Hekaena.

Such dreams were a fleeting fantasy, childish hopes born from failure. In his heart, he knew there was no way out. Unless he stole the Shard, he was going to die. The only path to the Pure Shard lay over

Hekaena's bloody corpse. There was just no other solution. He had a simple choice.

His life, or Hekaena's.

CHAPTER TWENTY ONE

Crossing the green carpet of Varspire's lower floors, Takket was assailed by the smell of a dozen breakfasts—fried meat, roasted cereals, fresh bread, seared vegetables. Mundanes littered the corridors, sweeping away errant wisps of dust that tumbled from ventilation ducts.

Hekaena had dropped him off in the throne room, her unsettled expression persisting. Asking to be allowed into Haddronius's room had shaken her trust. It had been a risk, but one he knew he had to take.

Anything to deny the simple truth.

Either he or Hekaena would die.

He stopped by a sculpture of the Angel of Southreach. The piece was exquisite, a single marble block carved into a bone-for-bone remake of the relic. The artist had captured the elongated limbs, the strangely ridged forehead, the not-quite-avian wings. This was Imperium art at its finest—the sculptor's skill demonstrated by how closely to reality they hewed the stone.

With unfamiliar sentimentality, Takket ran his fingers over the statue, feeling the grey imperfections marring the polished white surface. A small piece of home. It must have been carved in Southreach. Probably mined in the Hellik mountain range to the north of the city, famed for its vibrant-white marble. It would have travelled across the Imperium, circling to the Crater Desert to reach Portspire. There, it would have crossed the sea, finally arriving in Varsen with grand ceremony, following much the same route he had taken. Like him, it had become imprisoned in this demon-cursed city.

For so long, Takket had seen the Imperium only for its flaws. The inequality between Mundanes and those above. Cities built around the crumbling ruins of grand days long dead. The pageantry in the face of poverty.

Now, he longed to return to that continent, that paradise.

His home.

With a sigh, he turned from the statue and continued to stroll past steady gas lamps and gaudy pillars. Only in Varsen could the Imperium's faults seem like achievements to be lauded.

He turned the corner into the marble-walled Embassy, unsurprised to see Yelleck and Enara hovering nearby, inspecting one of the larger rubies embedded into a support column.

'Planning to settle for stealing a simple gem?' Takket grumbled.

Yelleck rushed over to grab Takket's arm. 'Keep your voice down.'

Takket let himself be dragged into the dining room. He collapsed into a plush chair left out from the siblings' breakfast. Half a slice of krilt-egg bread lay on a gold-rimmed plate. Idly, Takket picked up the leftovers and bit into the toasted slice.

Yelleck slammed a fist onto the table, making the cutlery bounce. 'Do you think this is a game? Do you think we brought you all this way so you could frolic with Hekaena?'

Takket glowered. 'She wouldn't let me in the room unattended. I tried, alright?'

'No, not alright.' Yelleck leaned close. His breath stank of tinnis spice. 'We waited all night, right beside the throne. Do you have any idea how dangerous that was? A couple of Mundanes, skulking about at night.'

'But you're not Mundanes.' Takket took a bite of the bread—still warm, though starting to dry. It was surprisingly bland, lacking the spices of most Varsen cooking. Judging from Yelleck's breath, these were Enara's leftovers.

'Exactly,' Yelleck hissed. 'So if they catch us, how long do you think it will take for them to realise that we're not the Mundanes we claim to be?'

The man narrowed his eyes, his face uncomfortably close. If this was his attempt at intimidation, Takket was not impressed. After Ensellus's death threats, Yelleck's efforts seemed amateurish.

Takket shrugged. 'Well if I'd barged my way into Haddronius's room, Hekaena would have just pulled me back. Maybe thrown me down the shaft. If you want me to dive off the top of the tower without the Shard, that I can do. If you want me to get you the Shard, you're going to have to be patient.'

Again, Yelleck's hand slammed down, toppling a glass. 'We wouldn't have to wait if you'd followed the plan in the first place.'

'If I'd followed the plan, Hekaena would be dead, and the three of us would be ashes.' The toppled glass rolled to the table's edge. Takket caught it deftly and set it back on the table, flatly eyeing Yelleck. 'Last night was a setback. I'll get the Shard.'

'And deliver it to us,' Yelleck said sternly.

'And deliver it to you.' Takket gave a patronising smirk.

'See that you do.'

Enara laid a hand on Yelleck's shoulder, staring him down until he backed away with a grunt.

'Please remember why we're doing this,' Enara said, calm.

Takket popped the last of the bread into his mouth. 'Well you're doing this for the glory of Kilroth.'

Enara sat beside Takket, leaning into the maroon velvet of her chair's backrest. 'Think what you will. If the Varsens lose that Shard, it can only benefit Varspire's Mundanes.'

'I'm sure the welfare of the undercity will be the top priority of an invading army,' Takket retorted sarcastically.

'Oh please,' Yelleck interjected. 'Fool yourself all you want, but you came here for infamy...riches. Both are now yours to take. Think back to when we first met. I remember that man, the greatest thief in the world, ready to achieve the impossible. What would he say to you now? What would he say to the man who had the Pure Shard of Varsen within his grasp, but held back to avoid spilling the blood of an Arcane?'

Probably would have called himself a demon-cursed fool. 'I've changed.'

'Good,' Enara said fervently. 'Great. You want to help the Mundanes—a laudable goal. Then stay. After the heist, don't return to the Imperium. Can you imagine what you could accomplish with the wealth of half of Varsen's vaults? You could change things here. Redefine this city.'

She was right. Takket had seen the treasury, the blinding glow of the stacks of Shards. More wealth than he could have imagined. He would be able to hire an army of Mage architects, have them transform the undercity. He could finance a thousand children like Lyssa, make sure they never knew the pain of hunger or the frigid cold of a night on the streets. Angels above—with that fortune, he could build an entire city, a place where no Mundane had to fear immolation.

Takket shook his head. The dream died. 'And I'm just supposed to take your word on the payment? After everything you've lied about?'

Enara grimaced. 'If we had told you the truth of our magical abilities, you would not have come here—no Mundane would trust a Mage.'

'And the whole Kilroth thing? Minor omission?'

'You're still trusting Ensellus on that?' Yelleck snarled.

Enara held out a placating hand. 'It does not matter who we work for—the Mundanes, Kilroth, the Imperium, the demons. Whoever our masters are, this theft will make you a hero of our cause. We will owe you an impossible debt, one we will handsomely repay. I swear it.'

Takket held her gaze, detecting not a hint of a lie. She was either telling the truth for once, or she was a better liar than Takket. Trusting the siblings again was tempting, rebuilding the world with his newfound wealth, saving Varsen.

All it would cost was Hekaena's life.

The bathwater was painfully hot. Staring into an ornate handheld mirror, Takket dragged a razor across his jaw. Enara's words rattled around his mind. Certainly, the man he had once been would curse his current actions as foolish, sentimental, weak. But Takket had his own words for his past self, the man who had thought only of riches and legacy. The man who had scorned his fellow Mundanes for not taking the wealth he had seized. The man who, without second thought, would have cut Hekaena's throat.

There was no foolishness in thinking beyond himself. No sentimentality in wanting to help those like Lyssa. No weakness in trying to protect Hekaena.

Finished shaving, he climbed from the tub and dried himself on a feather-soft towel. There was a lot of truth to Enara's words. If he had half the Varsen treasury, he would be able to reshape Varspire into something great. Still, he hesitated. He was not willing to throw his lot in with Enara and Yelleck, not without attempting to contact the real Free Circle. Surely an actual resistance organisation would better spend Varspire's fortune.

He slapped a musky aftershave on his freshly shaven cheeks, the sting focusing his mind. Wrapping himself in a red velvet dressing gown, he strode out of the bathroom.

Akken was remaking the bed. Takket had not actually slept here for days, but the servant religiously stripped and reset the bed every morning.

'I need a word with you.' Takket crossed the maroon carpet, pulling the brass handle to check the door was firmly shut.

Akken paused midway through stuffing a pillow

into a fresh cover. 'I get the feeling you're not wanting to discuss your laundry.'

'No.' Takket walked close to Akken so he could speak in a low voice. 'This is another conversation Ensellus cannot know about.'

Akken placed the pillow on the bed and waited.

'Have you ever heard of the Free Circle?'

Akken slowly shook his head. 'No. That a sect of Circlism?'

'It's the name of a Mundane resistance group. Or it might be.'

'Not heard of them. Sorry.'

Takket grimaced. 'Have you heard of any Mundane resistance groups? Any Mundanes struggling to overthrow the Varsens? Any Mages who support them?'

Akken considered Takket, running a hand through his long, greying beard. 'No. Nothing organised, at least. Plenty of grumblings or Mundanes snapping and trying to take a knife to their Mage masters. Never ends well.'

Takket's heart sunk. Had Enara and Yelleck fabricated the Mundane resistance as they had the rest of their story?

'But,' the man continued, 'I would be the last person to know. It's common knowledge that Ensellus has his agents throughout Varspire Tower. Any rebellious organisation with half a brain would give the tower's employees a wide berth.'

Takket sighed. 'Any idea where I could start looking?'

The servant shrugged. 'My guess? The Circlist temples would be your best bet. If anyone's got a shot at organising the disgruntled Mundanes, it's going to be the Cirlists. The main temple's out near the edge of Varspire City, under the wheat fields.'

'Thank you. Seems a good place to start.'

'Word of caution—it's a long walk, and you'll stick out on the streets.'

'I can put on cheaper clothes.'

'Won't help. Clean shaven means you've got a plush job high up in a tower. You carry yourself like a diplomat, not a Mundane. That's not to mention that you're talked about all over the city. Now some'll bend over backwards to help you—the Mundane from the Imperium, here to change the world. Others though, they're desperate. They'll knife you for your Shards without a second thought. My advice? Ask Hekaena to fly you there.'

Takket nodded. 'Thank you, Akken. I appreciate this.'

'Just watch yourself.' Akken smiled weakly. 'This path you're taking, it's going to be a bloody one.'

'I know.'

'Then I pray the angels watch over you, and the demons spite your enemies.'

Takket's door creaked open. He smiled as he saw Hekaena in the doorway, staff in hand, wearing her black linen dress.

'I was hoping you'd come by.' He strode across the room to place his hands on her bare shoulders. 'I wanted to apologise for how I was acting last night.'

'You already have,' she said flatly.

'I know. I just...I'm not sure what came over me. I think it's just this state visit—it's made me think of home. I never thought I'd miss it so much. For some reason, it got into my head that seeing Haddronius's room—seeing the seat of power of this place—would make the journey worthwhile. Stupid, I know.'

She studied him in silence, then slowly smiled. 'It must be hard to be so far from home.'

He sighed and walked over to sit on his desk. 'It is. Studying Varsen, its traditions, its formalities, its food, its politics...did little to prepare me for actually being here.'

She followed, giving a sympathetic smile he did not deserve. 'Can I do anything?'

He looked into her eyes, pretending to consider. 'Actually, yes. I've had a lot on my mind recently, and I really could use someone to talk it through with.'

'You can always talk to me.'

'I know, thank you. But this is a more...spiritual matter. The suffering here, the glorying of the Arcanes, the crematorium. I think I just need to speak to a priest. I've heard there's a Circlist temple in the undercity. Would...would you mind taking me?'

'Of course not.' Hekaena reached out a hand. 'There are quite a few, but the largest is probably the one you want. The head priest there is a good man. I've worked with him before—he always has ideas of how I can improve the undercity. I'm sure he'd gladly meet you.'

Takket took her hand and let her guide him to the Embassy foyer. They walked in companionable silence through the corridors. Takket had become used to the scandalised looks on the faces of the courtiers they passed, the whispers that followed in their wake. The tower was abuzz with their budding relationship.

Rumours of marriage ties with the Imperium circulated the lower floors. Arcanes in the spire tutted with consternation at the decay of the royal family. If the words bothered Hekaena, she gave no indication.

She opened a balcony door and stepped out under the cloudless sky. The Sharddust layer had settled after the storm. It would not be long before the wind would once again churn the dust into a hellish maelstrom. For now, the haze rested in an even layer that stretched to the broken rocks of the horizon.

Holding his hand, Hekaena gripped the Shard atop her staff and levitated the pair over the city. Takket watched the red haze billow just beneath their feet. Here and there, the dust was thin enough to catch a glimpse of the tallest Mundane hovels. The afternoon sun reflected off the sickly shell ceilings and bulbous walls.

The couple drifted by imposing Magetowers that reflected sunlight with their obsidian walls. As they moved further from Varspire Tower, the spires became smaller and less ornate. Mages and Arcanes preferred to build their homes close to the centre of government. These outlying structures were owned by the newer families of Varsen, struggling to carve out a niche in the cut-throat city.

They slowed as they approached one of the field platforms. The structure's granite supports held acres of freshly tilled farmland above the Sharddust. Toiling farmers looked up from their work ploughing grains into the soil, and squinted at the flying pair. The farm hands looked all the more curious as Hekaena descended into the churning Shard layer.

The undercity's krilt-shell buildings grew around

the stone supports like a fungus, using the granite to brace their precarious frames. Resting in the platform's shadow was a squat, ugly little building—grand by undercity standards. Whitewashed wooden beams linked walls of chitin in a rough circle, surrounding a central bowl filled with Sharddust. At the front of the building, a weathered wooden circle hung between two spires of rusting iron, a mockery of Southreach's temple.

Next to temple's doors coated in blistering paint, the pair landed in ankle-deep Sharddust. Takket turned, the dust crunching underfoot like powdery snow. Teams of Mundanes dragged carts through the bedrock streets. As one trundled close, Takket saw their load: mounds of dung, rotting food, dead birds, all cemented with Sharddust—fertiliser for the field platforms. A constant stream of the rickety wagons rolled by on the way to the platform's support. This stinking convoy was the closest the undercity had to a sewer, Mundanes hauling their own waste through the streets.

Hekaena led the way to the temple, pushing the doors aside with a wave of magic. Only the increased gloom differentiated the temple's interior from the street. Sharddust carpeted the floor, caught by a dozen drafts and blown through in the air. Situated so close to the nexus of the waste-carts, the smell was just as rancid. Light crept between gaps the boards of the ceiling, red rays cutting through the dust.

A man hurried down the curving corridor and bowed deeply to Hekaena. The greys in his otherwise black hair were stained red, his thin beard cut to his jawline. His auburn robes were so worn and

discoloured that it took Takket a while to realise that
the man was a priest. The robe's light staining of
yellow at the hem was an echo of the gold trim of the
Imperium's senior clergy.

'Arcane Hekaena,' the priest said. 'It's an honour
and a pleasure to see you again.'

'Stand,' Hekaena said wryly. 'You know how
uncomfortable bowing makes me.'

The man gave a weary smile. 'Bowing to Arcanes
is a habit dangerous for us to break, but for you I'll do
my best. How may I serve you today?'

'Not me. I've a friend here who could use some
spiritual guidance. This is Envoy Khantek Fredeen of
the Imperium. Khantek, meet High Priest Valco.'

'An honour,' Takket bowed.

Valco bowed lower. Both stood, laughed
awkwardly, then chorused, 'I'm no Mundane.'

Takket cleared his throat. 'You're still a priest.'

'A Mundane priest.'

'Still respected in the Imperium.'

'Ah, of course.' Valco smiled distantly. 'It's been so
long. What can I do for you?'

'I was looking for someone to talk to. In private.'

Hekaena smiled. 'I'll let you two go on alone. I'll
be here when you're ready to leave, Khantek.'

He nodded in thanks, then followed Valco down
the sharply curving corridor. Side rooms lined the
outer edge of the building, separated from the hallway
by hanging sheets, or—rarely—rotting wooden doors.
The air was moist in the platform's shadow, heavy
with mildew.

Valco opened the only painted door on the corridor
—red and cracked—and ushered Takket into a

claustrophobic office. Between the chairs, decaying desk and sagging bookcases, there was barely enough room for the two of them to stand.

After allowing Valco to navigate around him to get behind the desk, Takket sat in the unoccupied chair, tensing at its wooden frame's mournful creak.

'So, what did you wish to discuss?' Valco knitted his fingers together. 'I know we're not equal to the Circlist temples back home—here, we subsist on donations from Mundanes—but I assure you that I have as much knowledge of the angels and demons as any of my fellows in the Imperium.'

Takket picked his words carefully. 'It's not a spiritual matter, but one rather more...sensitive.'

Valco leaned back. 'What could be more sensitive than the beings that pull the strings of fate from outside the world?'

'Those that wield power here. Look, the questions I have are serious. Asking them may get me killed. May get you killed. But I feel I have to ask, for the good of every Mundane in this city.'

The priest stroked his beard in thought. 'You know, you are quite the topic of conversation among my congregation. The Mundane who represents the Imperium. The Mundane who shuns the spires to help those stuck in this murk. Rumour has it that you and Hekaena are closer than envoy and Arcane. The people like to whisper of a marriage between a Mundane and one of the royals, of the ramifications such an event would cause.'

Takket grimaced. 'If only it was that easy. But I *do* want to improve the lives of Mundanes in Varsen. I've seen their pain. I've seen the purges. I've seen the crematorium. It has to stop.'

Valco nodded slowly. 'In that case, ask your question. I'll answer as best I can.'

'Are there Mundanes in Varspire who want to fight for a fairer society? Is there a Mundane resistance?'

The room fell silent. The priest contemplated Takket. Noises from outside drifted through the high window carved into the shell wall—carts crunching through Sharddust, men groaning with exertion, a child's cry.

'Yes and no,' the priest answered at last. 'There are Mundanes who would fight for a better world. But no, there is no resistance. None are foolish enough to give voice to their thoughts. History is not well remembered in the undercity—few care of what happened fifty years ago, when tomorrow's dinner is in doubt. But there is one lesson all Mundanes know—every uprising, every time a Mundane has taken up arms against a Mage, every time one has sought to topple an Arcane dynasty, it has always ended in slaughter.'

'What if there was a way to weaken the Arcanes, to make them vulnerable?'

'Still not enough. Oh, the Mundane's might be persuaded to rise up. They'll cause a lot of noise, break into a tower or two, maybe spill the blood of some sleeping Arcane. Then they'll be routed. The Arcanes have more than just magic over us. They have hierarchy. Organisation. In the undercity, there are no leaders. No Mundane makes themselves known, or stands out from the crowd. To do so would attract attention, invite the next purge to descend on their heads. It's a wonder I've not been immolated yet, simply for being well enough known to pose a threat to those in the spires. I suppose I have Hekaena to thank for my survival.'

Takket nodded sadly. 'No doubt. She has a good heart. Why not lead an uprising yourself? If you're so well connected.'

Valco laughed mirthlessly. 'Oh, don't try to oversell my importance. Mundanes come to me to hear whispers of a better world across the ocean, to believe their next life could be as an angel, to be told how they are equal to the Mages and Arcanes. The other priests respect me because I distribute the alms we receive fairly. But follow me?' He shook his head. 'I'm no commander. No general. They'll see that before long. Then you'll have a million disjointed citizens, turning on each other as they claw at the Arcanes. I'm sure I can provoke a riot. But a revolution? Never.

'I'm sorry, Khantek, I really am. The Mundane resistance is a myth, told by drunks in taverns and widows comforting their children. In time, when Circlism grows, when Mages and Arcanes flock to our temples, maybe then we can right the injustices of society. Now? It's just our role to endure and pray to the angels for a better future.'

Takket nodded, weary. 'I had to ask. I had to try. Thank you for your time. I don't have to worry about you reporting this conversation to the authorities, do I?'

Valco laughed again. 'I don't feel like volunteering for immolation any time soon. I'll be staying away from the Arcanes.'

'Thank you.' Takket stood.

'You seem like a good man, Khantek. I don't know

why you're asking these questions. I don't know with what you found yourself involved. Just remember that it is by dying without regrets that we ascend to become angels. Don't allow yourself to travel a path that will lead you to torment on your deathbed, that will curse you to join the demon's ranks.'

With a heavy heart, Takket nodded and shoved open the door, the red paint flaking at his touch. There was no Mundane resistance, just another lie concocted by the siblings, that devious pair that were his final hope. He had to work with them if the Mundanes were to stand a chance at freedom, and that meant following their bloody plot.

Hekaena stood near the temple's entrance, surrounded by a gaggle of children. They laughed and clapped as she drew on her Shard, condensing snowflakes from the air and melting discarded pieces of iron into fantastic beasts. Takket leaned against the wall, watching her fondly.

He would regret it every day for the rest of his life if he failed to bring freedom to the Mundanes.

He would never forgive himself if he killed Hekaena.

CHAPTER TWENTY TWO

Takket spent the rest of the week paralysed by indecision. He frittered away the days helping Hekaena in the undercity, dining with her family, spending the nights by her side. Yelleck had given him a new dagger—one far less ostentatious—but it had remained hidden between the leather folds of Takket's boot. He could not bring himself to touch it. Could not bring himself to murder.

Nor could he convince himself to run. Escape would have been simple—ask Akken for some rough clothes, let his beard start to grow, cover himself in Sharddust, and venture into the undercity. He had enough Shards to buy passage to a port. Or he could just walk to the coast. Sign up on a ship and cross to the Imperium.

Yet each morning, he kept shaving his cheeks smooth. At the end of each day he spent in the undercity, he loyally returned to Hekaena's side.

The last evening had come and gone, lost in a blur of laughs and wine and passion. Takket lay, watching Hekaena contently sleep beside him, the moonlight highlighting the curves of her face, her parted lips. He knew he could never harm her, but the time for escape had slipped away. His mind turned to surviving the next few days.

He had to avoid meeting the Imperium's heir—a difficult task for an envoy. Still, he had a plan. While

Hekaena slept, he pulled on his robes, then tucked himself overly tight into the bed. He kept his head under the covers, his own humid breath trapped next to his face. Before long, sweat beaded on his forehead. By midnight, he was dripping.

Fitful dreams filled the night, nightmares fuelled by his self-induced fever. He had woken to the glare of the rising sun, numb from sleep deprivation, drenched in sweat, offended by the stink of his own unwashed body. He forced his muscles to spasm in a mock-shiver.

The movement roused Hekaena. Her initial smile gave way to horror as she saw his sweat-drenched face. 'Khantek! What's wrong?'

He rasped, 'Just a little unwell.'

'A little? You look awful.'

'Thanks.' He smirked.

'I'm serious. How do you feel?'

'I'm fine,' he mumbled. 'The state visit is today. I need to get ready.'

He pushed himself upright, let his arms shake, then fell back into bed.

'You're not going anywhere,' she said sternly.

'But—'

'No.' She laid a hand on his sweat-coated brow. 'I better get the physician.'

'Really, no need.' The physician might spot that Takket's illness was a fabrication. 'I'll be alright.'

'You don't look alright. Stay put. I'll be right back.'

Takket had never seen Hekaena so frantic. She threw on a dress—inside-out—and rushed barefoot towards the foyer. Seizing her staff, she threw open the door, leaving it ajar as she dropped down the shaft.

He would have to be convincing to fool a trained physician—or simply too disgusting to inspect closely. He was a Mundane. It should not take too much to persuade the healer that he was not worth the effort.

Steeling himself, he shoved his fingers down his throat. Bile erupted from his mouth, splattering across his sheets. His sinuses burned. Forget the physician—right now Takket wanted to be far away from his own stench.

Arguing voices drifted from the foyer, then the door burst open. Hekaena practically pushed Ennrella into the room, the chief physician looking tired, her grey hair a mess that tumbled by the shoulders of her white robe.

'...last time, I do *not* treat Mundanes,' Ennrella was saying.

'You treat the royal household,' Hekaena retorted. 'Khantek is a member of the royal household.'

'Not without a marriage or formal adoption he isn't.'

'He's my partner, and I am commanding you to take a look at him. Do not test me on this.'

With an over-dramatic sigh, Ennrella crossed the room, her nose wrinkling as she approached Takket. She stopped several paces away, making no attempt to hide her revulsion. 'He's sick.'

'Demons below, I know that. What's wrong with him?'

The physician made a cursory inspection from the foot of the bed. 'In all likelihood, he contracted the ailment that affected you last week.'

'So he's going to make a full recovery, like I did?'

'Perhaps.' Ennrella shrugged. 'You're an Arcane.

331

He's just a Mundane—weak immune system. A contagion that caused you such pain may well finish him.'

'Angels above.' Hekaena rushed to the bedside. Ignoring the vomit, she knelt to caress his sodden hair. 'What can we do?'

'Rest him. Keep him fed. Keep him drinking. I suggest we move him to the lower levels so other Mundanes can deal with this.'

'He's staying here,' Hekaena replied, firm.

'But, for the good of the Arcanes on this level—'

'No!' Hekaena glared at the woman. 'If this is as serious as you say, then moving him could do more harm than good, right?'

'Well—'

'Exactly. So he's staying here.'

Ennrella sniffed. 'I do hope you don't expect me to linger here with him, do you?'

The rage in Hekaena's eyes terrified Takket. 'I wouldn't expect you to have a conscience, no. Angel's forbid that a physician give a shit about someone without magical talent. I'll look after him. Get out.' The physician opened her mouth to object, but Hekaena bellowed louder, '*Get out.*'

Ennrella left in a huff, slamming the door.

'The visit,' Takket groaned. 'Tessella.'

'Don't even think of moving.' Hekaena's face softened. 'I'll greet her on the jetty myself. A royal welcome might just make up for an envoy's absence. I'll see to it that you're not disturbed.'

'You're far too good to me,' he replied honestly.

'Nonsense. You would do the same for me. You did, in fact, last week. Now it's *my* time to look after *you.*'

Shakily, he held out a hand to touch her cheek. 'Thank you.'

'You can thank me when you're on your feet. Now, the one thing that demon-cursed woman and I agree on is that you need food and water to keep your strength up. So, what breakfast would you like? I can get the head chef to whip up anything. Bet I can even twist his arm to do some Imperium dishes.'

Takket could only smile in response. Hekaena really was far too kind for this demon-infested continent.

Takket hunkered at the head of the bed, wrapped tightly in the down-stuffed quilt, and looked out of the glass exterior wall. A storm approached. The clouds mottling the sky raced west, sluggishly followed by the Sharddust layer. Small tufts of dust were caught by the air and carried across the cityscape like ocean waves. In the lee of Magetowers, turbulence sucked the haze into tight coils, which would stagger away from the spires a short distance then disperse.

Come evening, those coils would persist, Sharddust-filled tornadoes ripping across the city. The waves of haze would rise hundreds of meters into the air, obscuring all but the tallest towers. The viscous flow of the dust layer would become a torrent, battering the undercity. Mages and Arcanes would stay in their towers, disinterestedly watching the display of nature's wrath. Mundanes would cower for their lives.

Hell of a time for a state visit.

Hekaena had left an hour ago to prepare for Tessella's arrival. She had doted on him throughout the morning, bringing his favourite baked cereal loaf for breakfast, plying him with honey-flavoured hot water. She had changed the sheets using magic, even helped him to the bathroom.

Her first stop would have been the embassy to inform Enara and Yelleck of the change in plans. They would be livid. Most likely they were fuming already at Takket's failure to steal the Shard and his refusal to see them for the past several days. The news of his 'illness' would push them over the edge.

At first, he had worried that they would try to cut their losses at the news, kill Hekaena and flee. His fear dissipated as he thought of her past use of magic. She was not some spoiled spire-brat, only ever using her Shard to open doors or heat rooms. No, she practised her craft daily, moving houses, melting building frames, raising structures. With her Shard on hand, the two Mages would not stand a chance.

He did still fret over how long his ruse would last. The Imperium's heir may well insist on speaking to the envoy directly, despite his condition. Hekaena could realise Takket had no fever. The physician may, he knew, return in Hekaena's absence and take Takket to the embassy.

He sighed. Nothing he could do but sit and wait— have faith in his plan, faith in Hekaena's conviction. If the demons decreed that he would die here, pretending to shiver in soft sheets saturated in his own sweat, then at least he would be done with this city.

A messenger airship rounded a distant rock formation, a single oval speck in the distance. Two more followed, skimming over the Shard layer that blanketed Tellin River. Lethargic leviathans appeared minutes later, three immense airships navigating the broken landscape. Reluctantly, they turned their oblong air balloons and drifted directly towards Varspire Tower. A dozen small messenger ships played in their wake, flitting like bees around a hive.

The Imperium's flotilla had arrived.

Instead of descending, as would be expected with craft coming in to land, the three airships lifted further into the sky, their attendant messenger floats swarming behind. They were close enough now to make out the brilliant white paint coating the canvas air canisters and hanging cabins, a vibrant red band running down the centre of the airships.

As the ships crossed the outer edge of the city, great banners unfurled from their cabins. A hundred feet long, the banners draped below the craft, the lower edge surfing atop the Shard layer. The white and red banner of the Imperium was proudly displayed to all Varspire.

A flock of garricks broke free from the Shard layer as the three giant shadows passed over the undercity. Their wide, membranous wings flapped furiously to escape these strange invaders.

Takket marvelled at the central ship. Unlike the steel frames of most airship cabins, this was constructed from marble. Intricate statues of angels—three times the height of a man—smiled benevolently from the corners. From recesses in the stonework, Soulshards cast their shifting light. At the ship's prow, the statue of the first Arcane—Indel, founder of the Imperium—stretched out, the Bloody Staff he used to end the Devastation represented by Soulshards bound in gold.

The cabin was huge, far too heavy for the canvas of hydrogen gas to hold up alone. A team of Arcanes —or dozens of Mages—must have been working to keep the craft aloft. An extravagance only the Imperium would muster.

Close enough to see figures in the windows, the ship came to a rest before Varspire Tower. Ranks of soldiers littered the cabin's top level, gold armour contrasted by red cloaks. Ceremonial swords glittered at their hips—not sharp weapons, but elaborate decorations for the Shards held in their hilts. Every member of the Heir's Guard was an Arcane, ready to lay down their lives to defend the future ruler of the Imperium. This visit was as much a show of strength as a sign of friendship between two Arcanedoms.

The colossal ship dropped sedately towards the jetty at the tower's base, the giant banner retracting in time with its descent. Takket shifted to peer down to the widened base of the tower, the jetty barely visible just above the Sharddust layer.

A jade-green glow burst from the jetty, a hundred magic-users casting light towards the airship in welcome. In greeting the Imperium's heir, Varsen was holding nothing back. The reception Tessella would receive would make Takket's greeting seem insulting in comparison. An Arcane. A strong ruler. A show of strength. This visit was everything Varsen prized.

Turning to avoid its prow butting into the base of the tower, the airship came to a hover alongside the jetty. Takket could see nothing further—the few figures not obscured by the ship's magnificent canvas balloon were too distant to make out.

Hekaena would be down there to greet Tessella in

person, happily giving up her plans to make up for Takket's illness. Haddronius would await Tessella's arrival in the throne room—even the future ruler of the Imperium would have to journey to meet the Arcane-lord.

The rest of the Imperium's flotilla hovered near the tower's peak, the small messenger floats dancing between the two larger craft, all ardently watching over Tessella's airship. No doubt, they would be packed with staff and soldiers, ready to serve and defend the heir in this alien continent.

With a sigh, Takket turned from the window. This was it. Tessella Indel had arrived.

He was out of time.

The soft thud of the door woke Takket from his disturbed dreams. He felt sick with sleep deprivation. Even sweaty and uncomfortable he had quickly drifted off after the flotilla's arrival.

Blinking for focus, Takket peered to see Hekaena creeping across the carpet. The room was orange with the evening sun—he had slept longer than he had intended.

'Hey,' Hekaena said softly. 'How are you feeling?'

'Fine.' He shuddered.

She smirked, 'No, really, how are you?'

'Feels like I've got a dozen demons gnawing at my every joint.' He had to keep up this pretence for the length of Tessella's visit.

'No better at all?'

'Feel more nauseous. Does that count?' The sympathy on her face cut into his heart. 'It's not all that bad. Really. I made it to the bathroom by myself today. Twice.' The second time he had forced himself to vomit again, purposefully splattering over the jade-tiled floor. His stomach still burned.

'I know what will make you better—a nice bath. I know how much you like them.'

He smiled with affection. He could not remember ever telling her of his fondness of baths.

Slipping into the washroom, Hekaena turned on a tap, cold water pouring into the marble tub. While the bath filled, she strolled back to the bedroom to fetch her staff. The Shard at the staff's peak brightened at her touch. Takket felt the air around him chill as Hekaena drew energy from the room. Steam wafted from the tub.

'Alright.' Hekaena tested the water with her hand, then nodded in satisfaction. 'Let's get you in here.'

With a groan, Takket swung his legs out of the bed. Even with his illness being a mere fiction, a bath sounded wonderful right now. Grease covered his skin. His hair was damp with sweat. His own body odour turned his stomach whenever he focused on the stench. Hekaena, angels bless her, refused to show a hint of disgust.

As he stood on shaking legs, Takket was momentarily disoriented. He felt light. Looking over, he saw that Hekaena's staff still glowed brightly. She was levitating him, just a little. Not babying him, flying him across the room like an invalid, just enough to take the edge off what she thought were exhausted limbs. He marvelled at her compassion—wanting to help, but not wanting to cause embarrassment.

She was amazing.

He crossed the room, feet leaving damp tracks on

the soft carpet. Carefully, he lowered himself into the tub, completely submerging himself in the gloriously warm water. As he sat back up, he felt relief as the layer of sweat rolled down into the steaming tub.

Hekaena smiled and walked into the next room. 'Now, I didn't think you would approve of the soaps I have on hand, so I stopped by the embassy on the way back.'

She returned holding a glass bottle of bath oil. His oil, brought over from the Imperium. She poured a little of the red liquid into the tub, releasing its musky scent. He leaned back, feeling muscles loosen, a day's stress seeping from his body as the grime left his skin.

The engraved mahogany ceiling bristled with frost. Hekaena must have been drawing most of the heat from up high to keep the air around Takket relatively warm. The abstract representations of water animals now swam through a sea of ice crystals. Eel eyes bloomed with snowflakes, a vrassashark shining in its new silver coat.

Hekaena crouched beside the tub. 'Feel better?'

'Much.' Takket gently rubbed his limbs, kneading his muscles. 'Thank you for this. And for covering for me today. How was Tessella's arrival?'

Hekaena shrugged. 'Oh, you know. Grand. The Imperium trying to demonstrate its own magnificence. Varsen refusing to be topped on its own soil. The Imperium escorted Tessella to the throne room with a hundred gold-armoured soldiers, so we accompanied the escort with two hundred riflemen in their best greens. We had our choir, so they brought their finest string band. Father did his normal descending from on high. Tessella responded by levitating her—and all one hundred guards—to meet him. Between them, they were drawing so much energy that the room frosted over.'

Takket laughed. 'I bet your father's guards were happy with so many armed men in his presence.'

'Oh, Ensellus is apoplectic. All five hundred of the Heir's Guard arrived on those airships. Never seen the man so tense. Well, except for whenever he sees the two of us together.'

Takket grinned. 'What time's the feast?'

'Already started. Drothinius managed to get his vrassashark inside the banquet hall by only partially dismantling the outer wall. You should see the cursed thing—it's suspended from chains running the length of the hall. There's a team of Mage chefs working out a way to cook the beast.

'Of course, the Imperium anticipated such extravagance, and was not about to be outdone. One of those messenger ships was carrying a deepfang. Apparently, the Imperium's been hunting the oceans for one for months, caught it just before Tessella's departure. It's small, enough only for the most honoured guests, but I don't think anyone's even seen one for years.'

A knock from the bedroom. Hekaena grinned and hurried to answer the door. She returned with a covered silver tray.

'What's this?' Takket asked as she balanced it across the bath.

'Well, you might not be up for joining the banquet, but I see no reason why we can't have our own little feast.' With a dramatic flurry, she uncovered the tray. The rich aroma of root stew filled the room. Joining

340

the dish were plates of seafood in a white sauce, freshly baked honeycake, and a bottle of mountain whisky. 'I thought some more-familiar food might make you feel better. I chased down a chef to put this together for us. And I have it on good authority that mountain whisky is a well-known curative in the Imperium.'

'Oh yes. From Indspire to Southreach, nothing like a nip of whisky to chase away any disease the demons can concoct.'

'Excellent. Then let's get you better.'

He smiled warmly, breathing in as the smell of the meal mixed with the scents of bath oils. He was brought back home. A meal and a warm bath had always relaxed him. The stress of the day melted away. The heist did not matter. His fate did not matter. Everything he needed was in this room. Safety. Comfort. Hekaena.

In all his life, he had never met another quite like her. He had dined with nobility all over the Imperium, had drank with Mages and Arcanes, had laughed with Mundane whores and gambled with hardened criminals. He had seen the best and worst of mankind.

Hekaena stood apart from the rest. Her determination. Her kindness. Her loyalty. He knew now why he had refused to betray her, refused to flee, why he traded his every opportunity to survive this just for another day by her side.

He shook his head in amazement, lost in her silver-flecked red eyes. 'I love you, Hekaena,' he said.

He meant it with all his heart.

CHAPTER TWENTY THREE

Takket splashed frigid water over his face. Hekaena had been out all afternoon, so there was no one to provide heating. Washing had been painful, the icy sponge stabbing into his flesh. Gritting his teeth, he endured the torture. He would be damned if he would die coated in grime.

He dried himself and pulled on the fresh cloak that Hekaena had fetched. He smoothed the maroon velvet, tying the belt in an intricate knot. Ocean-scented oil smoothed back his hair. With a fresh razor, he trimmed his stubble. He left his boots—and that vile dagger— by the bedroom window. There was no need for violence.

In the polished mirror, he looked the image of Imperium pride. Sophisticated, cultured. It was a mask, like all his identities, but a comfortable mask. Perhaps the last he would ever wear.

Returning to the bedroom, Takket looked out into the tempest. Winds buffeted the tower, churning the Shard layer into a frothing soup. Only the peaks of the city's Magetowers peered above the haze. Dust devils ripped their way across the undercity. Far above, the Imperium's flotilla fought against the wind, which became more severe with altitude, but less turbulent, and free of abrasive dust.

At least the storm had driven away the worst of the stench that had filled the room. Takket had spent most of the afternoon cleaning, scrubbing the dried vomit from the green carpet, changing the sodden sheets, polishing the bathroom tiles. The room now stank of cleaning fluids, but was a dramatic improvement over the previous reek of a charnel house.

A floor below, comfortably above the storm and the coppery dust blasting through the vents at the tower's base, Haddronius entertained Tessella. Hekaena was with them, no doubt filling Khantek's role of envoy, settling nerves. Not easy with a dozen Arcanes and their guards crammed into the dining room.

Turning from the window, Takket perched on the bed, folded his hands in his lap, and waited. Hours passed, the room steadily darkening with the setting sun. Takket rose to turn on the gas lamps, bathing the room in a cool white glow.

The storm intensified.

The ceiling's air vents seemed to scream in agony, lending a horrid sense of life to the engravings. Benevolent smiles of angels became pained grimaces. A demon's mischievous grin became a shriek of terror. The windows shook with rage. The tower vibrated, the obsidian monument straining against the maelstrom.

Takket remained still.

Well into the evening, Hekaena returned. Shutting the golden door, she beamed.

'Sorry I'm late.' Hekaena hurried over. 'Tessella and Valena were comparing the merits of Circlism versus Scalism. It got quite...heated. Anyway, you're looking so much better.'

Takket flinched away as she stooped for a kiss. 'We need to talk.'

Her eyes darted around his face, her expression a mix of confusion and concern. 'What's wrong?'

With a shaking sigh he stood, pacing to the window. 'I've been going over and over this in my head, trying to find the right words. Try as I might, I don't think there are any. I have to tell you—I know—but it will just hurt us both.' His words flooded out. 'I keep wishing there was another way. I was tempted just to give up, but you deserve to know the truth. I still can't help but regret all I've done since Southport. You have to know how much this has cut me up inside.'

'Slow down.' Hekaena laid a caring hand on his arm. 'Take your time. You know you can tell me anything, Khantek.'

Unable to meet her gaze as he spat out the words, he screwed his eyes shut. 'That's just it. I'm not Khantek.'

He nervously checked for her reaction, her inevitable anger. Instead, she shook her head with a bemused smile. 'I really don't follow.'

'I'm not Khantek Fredeen,' he barked. 'I'm an impostor. A liar. A thief.'

Her hand dropped to her side. All amusement was gone from her voice, replaced with confusion. 'What are you talking about?'

'I'm not Khantek,' he repeated. 'The real Khantek is dead. Died en route to Varspire.'

Her head kept shaking. 'Do you mean you've changed? Every envoy acts the part their state requires. Angels—in their own way, every person is just playing a role.'

'I'm not speaking in metaphors. The envoy is dead.

344

Murdered. I saw his corpse.'

'Khantek, you're starting to scare me.'

'I'm not Khantek,' he snarled. Hekaena shrunk away. He took a deep breath and continued. 'My name is Takket. I'm a thief. I took Khantek's place. Lied my way onto the airship at Portspire. Lied my way into court. Lied to you. That's what I do, Hekaena. I'm a liar, a trickster. I'm good at it, too. Had you all fooled. Even Ensellus believes I'm the real Khantek.'

She blinked away tears. 'This isn't funny.'

'This is no joke. I'm a thief. Hired to infiltrate this tower. Hired to steal the Pure Shard of Varsen. To bring down your entire family.'

'Hired?'

'By Enara and Yelleck, my assistants. My employers. Or they were, I suppose. They want me to take away Varsen's power.'

She shook her head, growing ever more horrified. 'Why?'

'Because they're Kilroth Agents. They want to invade. I didn't know that at the time. Only found out a week ago. Too late. They claimed to be from the Mundane resistance, claimed to want to liberate the undercity.'

'No...why are you telling me this?'

'Because I still want to help the Mundanes.' He sighed bitterly. 'But I can't keep lying to you.'

'You don't seem to have had a problem with that so far.'

'That's before I realised...' His words faltered

'Realised what?' she pressed, horror hardening to rage.

'I really do love you, Hekaena. It's taken me a long

time to work that out, too long, but I've not lied about this. I *do* love you.'

She gripped her head, alternatively laughing and sobbing. Helpless, Takket stood. He wanted to comfort her. Demons—in the back of his mind, he was working out how he could backtrack, make all this out as some poorly considered jest.

It was no use. He had chosen this action. The damage was done. Now he had to see it through to the end.

She turned to him, the whites of her eyes red with tears, a pale shadow of her bright irises. 'This is why you asked to get into Father's room, isn't it. You wanted to steal the Shard. Demons below, you wanted *me* to be the one to open the door.'

Takket nodded grimly. 'A horrible, foolish longshot, I know, but it was better than the alternative.'

'What alternative?'

'Enara and Yelleck's new plan was for me to take you hostage. Force you to open the door.'

She barked a laugh. 'How were you going to take me hostage? Or are you a Mage on top of everything else?'

'No.' He shook his head. 'Those two are. I'm not. I'm just a Mundane.'

'Then how?'

Takket stared silently at his boots, which still rested by the window. Haltingly, Hekaena crossed the soft carpet. She lifted the black-dyed leather boots to the bed, then searched carefully through the darkened folds. It did not take her long to discover their deadly secret. With shaking hands, she withdrew a dagger. Compared to the knife Yelleck had first given Takket,

346

this was crude—an unadorned stiletto, the hilt wrapped in undyed leather.

Hekaena licked her lower lip, staring at the blade in disbelief. 'You were actually going to hold this up to me? When? When I was sleeping? After we had...' She shuddered.

'You see why I tried it another way. I never liked Yelleck's plan.'

'Some plan. As soon as you came to the Shard corridor, you'd be finished. You couldn't bring an Arcane down that without waking Father. Just because you had a blade to my neck, don't think he wouldn't crush your skull. He'd never surrender his Shard.'

'We knew about the Shard corridor.'

She shook her head. 'Then how did you plan on crossing it without waking Father?'

Takket just stared at the dagger. Hesitantly, she looked down at the blade, turning it over, testing the sharpened point. She flinched away, then raised a trembling hand to her throat.

'You were going to kill me.'

'No!' Takket said firmly. 'Yelleck wanted me to, but I wouldn't. Couldn't.'

'You still brought this dagger into our...*my* room.'

He nodded silently. There was no excuse. Deny it as he might, part of him had considered killing her. Nothing could absolve his betrayal.

Hekaena sunk onto the bed, cradling the knife in her lap. Her sniffing was drowned out by the roar of the ventilation shafts. Night had fallen, plunging Varspire into darkness. No wood fires burned in the undercity. The lights of Magetowers were smothered by the Shard layer. Even the flotilla lights were lost in heavy cloud. Staring at the window, Takket could see only his own distorted reflection, the curved glass making his features seem overly thin, sharp. Devious.

He turned away in disgust. Hekaena was staring at him.

'The Shard corridor,' she whispered.

'Sorry?'

'You said you knew of the Shard corridor, that you had planned for it. How did you know?'

Takket sighed, pushing down the instinct to lie. 'I opened the door before. The night the alarm sounded.'

'The night I was ill. But how...' She closed her eyes in disgust. 'I wasn't ill, was I.'

'No.' Takket blinked away tears of shame. 'I poisoned your drink. I didn't know how badly it would affect you. I didn't mean to hurt you.'

'No,' she scowled. 'You meant to abuse my trust, to rob Father of the one thing that holds this Arcanedom together.'

Numbly, he nodded.

She stood, pacing the green carpet in angry strides. 'Fine, *Thief*. How did you open Father's door? Who helped you?'

'You did.'

She stopped.

'I took a few drops of your blood. It was enough to open the door. Enara and Yelleck said I'd have to kill you for the blood to work, but I...couldn't.'

'And I suppose I'm meant to be grateful for you choosing not to murder me in my sleep?'

Takket sadly shook his head. He had no answers.

Hekaena rounded on him, glaring. 'And what was I during all of this? Just a way to get around my father's security?'

'At first. But then—'

'Then I was some added bonus? A bit of fun while you plotted my death? My family's demise? I *loved* you, Khantek.'

'I love you too.'

'You've a twisted way of showing it.'

Once again, Takket found himself speechless. What excuse did he have? That it had taken him a long time to realise how amazing this woman was, blinded while he manipulated her kind heart? That he was too far in denial to see that his feelings were real? That he was too slow to grow a conscience?

'Why?' she asked, almost pleading. 'Khantek. Takket. Whatever. Just tell me *why*. I understand your employers wanting to bring us down, but by every last angel—what did we do to you? Was all of this for money?'

'At first,' Takket admitted. 'That was before I came here. Before I saw the undercity. Before I *understood*. Before Lyssa.'

'And then?'

'And then it became about them. The Mundanes. Hekaena, I couldn't let it continue. I thought Enara and Yelleck were from a Mundane resistance group. They wanted to replace the Varsens with a benevolent ruler. One who would end the suffering. The immolations. The injustice. That seemed worth any price. Even...even your life.'

Hekaena narrowed her eyes. 'What changed?'

'I found that they weren't who they claimed to be. I thought I had located the real Mundane resistance, but Rithdal was lying about that.'

'Wait...Rithdal?'

'He's also working for Kilroth. It was in Ensellus's files. This group, they've been manipulating you for some time.'

Hekaena dropped back to the bed, pale. She shuddered. 'I expected Ensellus to keep secrets. You, I've only recently met. But Rithdal? I've known him for years. This whole time...I've been blind.'

Takket could only stare. No words of comfort came to mind. No rationalisations. He had hurt Hekaena. Now she sat alternately weeping and thumping her leg. Wanting to comfort her, he took a step forward, stopping short at her murderous glare. She needed solace, but none he could provide.

'What now?' Hekaena said at last. 'You want me to grant you a pardon? Beg my father to set you free?' Her voice dripped with scorn.

This was it. He had finished the painful task. Now came the impossible. 'No. I need you to help me steal the Pure Shard.'

She laughed. 'What? No, you can't be serious.'

'I am. It's the only way to help the Mundanes.'

'By what? Taking the Shard to Kilroth agents?'

'By taking the Shard to *you*.'

She blinked. 'What are you talking about?'

'Hekaena, there is no Mundane resistance. There never was. I searched the city. I tried to find alternatives, find a better solution than handing the Shard to Enara and Yelleck and hoping for the best. Maybe even getting it to the Imperium. I developed a thousand foolish schemes. But the answer was in front of me the whole time. You.

'You are the only Arcane who actually gives a shit

about the Mundanes. You care, Hekaena. You give up your time, your wealth, all to help the undercity. You build orphanages. You fund the sick. Comfort the children. You help every day. An Arcanedom under your rule would be a paradise.'

'I'm not the next in line,' Hekaena said, hesitant. Denial in her eyes. 'Valena will take over when Father passes.'

'You know Arcanedoms are not ruled by tradition and inheritance. They are ruled by the one Arcane who wields the Pure Shard. The invulnerable Arcane. The one with near-unlimited power. The one who—if needed—can level a city. Haddronius only rules because he is the Pure Shard's bearer. Valena will only inherit if he passes it to her on his death bed.

'Hekaena. Help me steal the Pure Shard. Take the throne. Bring an end to the suffering of Mundanes. Close the crematoriums. Divert funds away from balls and artworks and towers, and send them to the undercity. Have Mages build homes instead of monuments. Farm animals for Shards, not people.'

For a moment, he saw her temptation. She stared at him, contemplative. The hate and despair faded from her eyes, replaced with cold calculation, then hope. There was truth in his words. A rule by Hekaena was the best option to improve the lives of the Mundanes. The only option.

The moment passed.

'You're insane,' she said flatly. 'I'm not a thief, and certainly not a murderer. If you think I'd harm Father, then you don't know me at all.'

'But the Mundanes need—'

'I know what the Mundanes need,' she bellowed,

jumping to her feet. 'I've been here far longer than you. I've seen the worst they've had to endure. The difference between us? I actually help them. I know change isn't going to come by one quick theft. I've spent my entire life down there, bringing them hope.'

'And what have you achieved?' He regretted the words, but pressed on. 'You've built shelters. You've fixed plumbing systems. You've entertained children. But the crematorium is still open. The purges still occur. The Mundanes still live in terror. Your efforts are nothing more than sweeping dust away during a storm.'

'How dare you,' she snarled. 'I've done far more than you know. I've saved lives.'

'It's not enough,' he retorted, indignant. 'Mundanes starve. Families are shattered. Children die. I guess I was wrong about you actually wanting to bring justice. You just want to balm your conscience. The undercity is nothing but a hobby to you. You don't give a damn about the Mundanes.'

Her eyes burned with rage. 'How can you say that? After all we've done together.'

'Stop fooling yourself. You're just like the rest. Worse. At least they don't pretend to care about the undercity.'

Shaking with fury, Hekaena clenched her hands into fists. 'Demons take you. I live for Varspire's Mundanes.'

'How can you, while you wield that?' He gestured to her staff, which rested by the door, casting its blood-red light over the room. 'You know as well as I do—that baton came from a Mundane. A life ripped away, all so you don't need to climb stairs, so you keep your room comfortable, so you can levitate your demon-cursed food. Do you even know who it was? What they wanted out of life? What family they left behind?'

Hekaena wavered. 'Thisslae.'

'What?'

'Her name was Thisslae.' Hekaena's rage turned to weeping. 'She was Mother's hand servant. They had known each other since they were children. Shortly after Mother had me, Thisslae developed a tumour. Didn't want to wait for it to slowly strangle her. She asked for the crematorium. Begged for Mother's permission. Mother made sure her family was paid the full price of the baton. They still work in this tower.

'Mother was heartbroken. She wanted to keep something of her friend. Father had that staff made. Mother carried it every day for the rest of her life. When she passed, she left it to me.' Hekaena stared defiantly at Takket. 'Not what you were expecting? It's easy to demonise Arcanes, I'm sure. Easy to damn Father as some inhuman monster. You didn't see him weep when Mother died, or how he beamed with pride at the birth of his first grandchild. Every advisor argued that you should be banned from seeing me. He cared more for his daughter than those sycophants. He wants the best for our family. Wants happiness for me.

'No, I will not help you murder him. He's not perfect, but he's still human. Besides, if I was twisted enough to plan patricide, then the door's alarm would sound. Your plan is nothing more than a childish prayer for an easy solution.'

Her shoulders slumped. In his heart he yearned to walk over and pull her into an embrace. He longed to apologise, to beg her forgiveness, to find some way to make this right. He could only stare across the gulf between them, isolated.

'No,' she repeated dimly, 'I won't help you overthrow my father. Unlike you, I cannot stomach murder.'

Fear crept around his heart. Looking at her, he knew there was nothing he could say to change her mind. He had failed. His chance to save Varspire had been crushed. He had lost his opportunity to escape. He could only face whatever justice Hekaena saw fit.

'I should turn you over to Ensellus, or Father. Hardly matters—you'll burn either way.'

Takket's eyes fell to the dagger still in her hand. Her staff was across the room. She was an experienced Arcane, but not a brawler. He could disarm her easily. Cut her throat and run. But how to get down the shaft? Take her hostage? No, she would need a Shard to levitate, and then she could easily kill him with a thought. The window? The smooth, curving obsidian of the tower might just slow his decent into the undercity. It would hurt, but it was a chance.

He sighed. He needed to stop fooling himself. If he was capable of harming Hekaena, he would have done it by now. No, his last card had been dealt, his last die rolled.

'I can't give you to Ensellus or Father—I'm not a murderer.' Hekaena looked mournfully into his eyes. 'Or maybe some stupid part of me can't bring me to sentence the man I loved to death. But I can't stand the sight of you. This illness of yours, it was a ploy to avoid Tessella...?'

Takket nodded.

'Fine. I'll shelter you until she leaves. You can sleep on the floor—or in the bath, for all I care. The day she leaves, I want you gone. Understand? It doesn't matter how you get out, but you will get far from Varspire. I never want to see you again. I never want to hear another lie escape your lips. I never want to be reminded of how gullible I was to trust you.

'Congratulations, Thief. You fooled me. You've broken my heart. I hope, someday, you come to realise just what you've done. I hope the demons torment you for the rest of your life. I...I need to get out of here. I need to think.'

She turned and stormed from the room, seizing her staff on the way. The golden door slammed shut, leaving Takket with only the howling winds for company. His mind raced for other options, picking over his words, trying to find a sentence that he could have said better, a phrase that could have shaken her will.

None of it mattered. Takket had failed.

CHAPTER TWENTY FOUR

Two days later, Tessella embarked on a tour of the Arcanedom. For five days, she would visit the cities of Krannok, Veltan and Brixen, the obsidian mines along the Brakk Mountains, the star forts that held every border. She would visit fishing towns and battle sites, highland lakes and city temples, mountain passes and glittering caves—the pride of Varsen paraded before the Imperium's heir.

Her absence gave Takket a new opportunity, a final chance to salvage this disaster. First, he needed more information. At his urging, Hekaena had brought him down to the embassy—sick of the sight of him, she had needed little persuasion.

He crept across the maroon carpet, trying not to alert Enara and Yelleck to his presence. Climbing the stairs through the dancing light of Soulshards, Takket entered his bedroom. Relieved to see Akken dusting the mahogany armoire, Takket eased the door closed.

'Akken,' he said quietly. 'I need to speak to you.'

The ageing servant turned. 'I heard you were ill. Your friends next door have been throwing a fit.'

'They're not my friends.' He sighed, frustrated. 'Doesn't matter. I need your help again.'

Akken turned to stare flatly at Takket. 'Since you're asking me and not some young revolutionary, I take it your hunt for the Mundane resistance went poorly.'

'They don't exist. Or if they do, they're too well

hidden for me to find in a week. That's fine.' Takket shook his head irritably. 'I have a new plan. My last chance, but I need Hekaena's help.'

Akken frowned. 'Then why're you talking to me?'

'Because Hekaena hates me right now. For good reason.'

The elderly man narrowed his eyes. 'If you've done something to hurt her...'

'No. Yes. Look, Akken, I know you care about the fate of Varspire's Mundanes. Their only hope lies in Hekaena taking power.' He held up a hand to forestall questions. 'I really don't have time to explain. If you don't want any part in this, I'm out of options and you may as well report me to Ensellus now. Just please believe me when I say that this is for the good of every Mundane in the Arcanedom.'

Akken stroked his grey beard. Finally, he nodded. 'Alright. You didn't turn me in when you had a chance. I honour my debts. If nothing else, it sounds like you'll be pissing off Ensellus, and anything that aggravates that demon-spawn is fine by me. What do you need?'

'To see the records of those currently awaiting immolation.'

'Prisoners aren't held long...'

'I know. But I need those lists.'

'They'll be down in the Justice Office. Ground floor. The staff might take some persuading to release the documents.'

Takket grinned. 'Leave that to me.'

He crept back out of the embassy and set off towards the stairwell. Mundanes crowded the corridors, sweeping mounds of dust from the jade floors, scraping motes of the red powder from statues, and carrying crate after crate of Sharddust to be hurled into the undercity. The air was thick with the dust's coppery tang. The detritus would take all day to clean, hundreds of extra Mundanes drafted in with the promise of paid work. Takket wondered how many of these temporary servants would fall victim to the next purge.

The ground floor was chaos. Servants flowed from the stairwell towards the tower's Mundane entrance, bearing heavy loads of Sharddust. Inevitably, stray clumps of the red powder slipped between wooden slats, spilling over the floor and into the air. The Sharddust was chokingly concentrated, tasting as strong as in the undercity's streets. Teams constantly swept the dust, clearing the corridor just in time for the next batch of crates to mar it once again.

Near to the Mundane entrance, Takket found the Justice Office. It was far from the elaborate archives of the Imperium he was accustomed to, with their ornate bookcases neatly stacked with scrolls, all watched over by studious librarians. This office was a bland bureaucratic store house. Rows of steel bookcases packed with grey folders. Neat signs labelled each row by year. Thousands of folders. The paper record of every Mundane the state had murdered.

Takket walked up to a stocky administrator behind a rough wooden desk.

'Yes?' The man peered over his half-rim spectacles.

'I'm Envoy Khantek Fredeen of the Indel Imperium.' Takket drew himself straight. 'I require the records of all those criminals currently awaiting execution.'

The man adjusted his spectacles. 'Those are confidential.'

'I am the envoy from the Imperium. I have a duty to protect Imperium citizens, and I have it on good authority that one of our subjects has been sentenced to die. According to the Varsen-Indel Justice Treaty, the Imperium has a right to investigate any criminal charge raised against our citizens. Now are you going to obey the law, or do I have to speak to Chief Adjunct Innisel to find out why his bureaucrats are in breach of the treaty?'

With the deep sigh, the man pushed himself from his seat. 'I'll see what I can find. Wait here.' He sedately waddled down an aisle of folders.

Takket prayed to the angels for luck. He had referenced a real treaty, one of the innumerable documents he had perused on the journey to Varspire, but he had no idea whether an Imperium citizen actually was awaiting immolation. It was probable—Imperium migrants were common in Varsen, normally trade ship crews staying over between shifts—but nothing was guaranteed.

The bureaucrat returned, slapping a card folder onto the desk. 'Here it is. Tennik. Arrested for vagrancy. He tried to shelter in Varspire Tower instead of finding some suitable accommodation. Quite clear cut. He's scheduled for immolation this afternoon.'

'Thank you.' Takket grabbed the folder and headed for the door.

'Sir, you can't take that,' the man objected feebly, but Takket was already striding down the hallway.

He kept his pace brisk, though he doubted the man would bother giving chase. No, more likely he would lodge an official objection regarding Khantek's misconduct. It would hardly be the greatest stir Takket was to cause this day.

Fighting against the flow of servants, Takket ascended staircase after staircase to the throne room. On the way, he skimmed the document, the young man's death sentence written neatly and signed by a junior functionary.

Haddronius was nowhere to be seen, but Innisel stood near the throne, talking to some clerk.

Takket strode over to the pair, brandishing the folder in his hand. 'Adjunct. I have an urgent matter.'

The elderly man gave the clerk an apologetic smile and turned to Takket. 'Envoy. It is good to see you on your feet again.'

Takket raised the file. 'A boy, seventeen years old, has been sentenced to death.'

Innisel raised an eyebrow. 'A seventeen-year-old is a man in Varsen.'

'He's an Imperium citizen.'

'That doesn't protect him against Varsen justice.'

'No, but it does give me the right to appeal his case.'

Innisel gave a weary sigh. 'Such appeals would have to be lodged with the Arcane-lord himself. His next court session is in four days. You will have to wait until then.'

'Not good enough,' Takket replied. 'This boy will be dead by sundown.'

Innisel shrugged. 'There's nothing I can do.'

'But there is something *I* can do. As Envoy, I have the right to summon an emergency court session.'

Innisel groaned. 'Summon the entire court? Those

powers are meant for state emergencies.'

'The Imperium would consider the impending death of a child as an emergency.'

The elderly man pinched the bridge of his nose, shutting his eyes tight as if suffering from a migraine. 'I'm sure Tessella Indel will be most displeased when she returns to find you using our treaties so frivolously.'

'We can ask her when she gets back.'

'This really isn't the time. Bringing the accused from the crematorium, cancelling the arrangements of the entire court—'

Takket glared. 'Do I have the right to call a court session, or not?'

'You do...'

'Then arrange it. Now.'

With a roll of his eyes, Innisel relented, gripping his Shard to levitate himself up through the spire—no doubt to inform Haddronius that his lunch would be delayed.

Takket let' out a sigh. He was playing with the life of a young man, but it might be Varspire's last chance for justice.

The throne room was abuzz with impatient murmurs. Some of the Arcanes and Mages were excited, the nobility eager for any distraction. Most looked irritated at the disruption. None had a choice once Haddronius had proclaimed a general court gathering. It was unheard of for anyone but a Mundane to be executed for disobeying the Arcane-lord, but no one dared risk becoming the exception.

A commotion from the back of the room drew

Takket's gaze. Through the assembled crowd, a young man was shoved forward by long poles attached to a blackened steel collar. His brown eyes were wide. Patchy stubble dotted a face twisted with terror. Next to Takket, his captors brought him to a sharp stop.

'What's going on?' the lad squealed, eyes darting.

'Relax, Tennik,' Takket said, calm. 'It's going to be okay. I'm Envoy Khantek Fredeen. From the Imperium.'

'The Imperium?' The teenager grasped at his restraints. 'You here to help me?'

'Yes. I've taken note of your case. I'm going to ask the Arcane-lord for leniency.'

'Angels bless you.' Hopeful tears dampened the boy's cheeks. 'Thank you. Thank you so much. This is all a mistake. I shouldn't be here. Should have stayed home. You get me out of this, and I'm your man for life.'

Takket felt sick. He hated lying to the boy like this, but the lad's fate was sealed. Takket could only try to make his death matter.

On the dais, Haddronius's children stood beside the vacant throne. Valena and Drothinius glowered at Takket, muttering to each other—clearly galled by the envoy's audacity. Mundanes did not disturb Arcanes, and certainly never the entire court. Nearby, Hekaena stood, wearing a black linen gown, her face showing mixed emotions as she held Takket's gaze. Her staff added to the throne's brilliance, making Hekaena seem to glow with dancing light.

An angelic chorus heralded Haddronius's arrival. From the tower's shaft, the Arcane lord descended, his black silken robes contrasting with the blinding white of the Pure Shard around his neck. A rippling groan filled the room as the crowd fell to their knees. Tennik choked as he was dragged to the ground by his collar, his captors leaning against the poles as they knelt.

Takket bowed as the repulsive man landed on the throne's dais. Even with downcast eyes, Takket saw the change in the room's lighting. The moment the Arcane sat, the throne's shifting glow increased threefold. Silence hung over the room, Haddronius leaving the occupants to kneel for uncomfortable minutes until finally releasing them with a rasp.

'Rise.'

A hundred figures staggered to their feet, a few Shards glowing to aid elderly functionaries. Tennik remained on his knees, his collar painfully twisted to keep him still.

'Envoy,' Haddronius's voice echoed through the domed hall. 'It is agreeable to see you on your feet once more.'

'Thank you, Arcane-lord.'

Haddronius grimaced. 'Now, tell me why you have summoned my court. What peril plagues the Imperium?'

'One of its citizens is about to be wrongfully executed.' Takket held out a hand towards Tennik.

Haddronius's face hardened. 'Explain.'

'This man, Tennik, was born and raised in the Indel Imperium. He journeyed here on board a trade ship, bringing valuable imports to your Arcanedom. He agreed to join the crew of a barge travelling up the Tellin River, to deliver the goods directly to Varspire. He is but a boy, here to facilitate trade between our lands.'

'Then how did he end up chained in that collar?' Haddronius hissed.

'Alone in a foreign city, he did not know of any affordable boarding houses to spend the night. Given the warm climate, he elected to sleep outside. He knew nothing of the laws prohibiting vagrancy in Varsen. When the storm began to truly rage, he sought shelter in Varspire Tower. When he explained himself to the door guards, they arrested him. Without trial, without chance to speak in his defence, he was sentenced to death.'

Haddronius made an impatient gesture. 'And?'

'My lord, I ask for leniency. Surely you must believe this is not justice.'

'Do not presume to tell me what I believe,' Haddronius snapped. 'This man came to this country and broke my laws.'

'Laws he had never heard of.'

'That is his failing, not ours. It is up to visitors to learn our ways, it is not our duty to explain them to every last deckhand.'

'But he's an Imperium citizen, a valuable member of our society. Surely having his life thrown away for a mere mistake will only harm us.'

'Abandoning our laws will harm Varsen far worse. I will not make an exception just because you happened to read a file, Envoy.'

Takket pushed on, feigning determination. 'As Envoy of the Imperium, I must insist—'

'Enough,' Haddronius snarled, jumping to his feet. 'The Imperium does *not* get to insist on internal Varsen matters. The Imperium does *not* dictate to my court. You do *not* command me. This man, this whelp, this brigand, came to Varsen for profit. He had his chance to contribute, to pay for lodging. Instead he elected to spit in the face of our hospitality, of our laws, of everything Varsen stands for. No, Envoy, I will not betray my people to save one of your delinquents.' Haddronius stalked down the steps, his heavy footfalls echoing in the silence between his words. 'You say the Imperium, your fragile land, cannot afford the cost of this man's death? Then fine. For the sake of our alliance, I will see you justly paid.'

The Arcane-lord lashed a gnarled hand towards the kneeling boy. Takket jumped back as Tennik was replaced with a pillar of flame, painfully bright. The heat prickled at Takket's skin, forcing bystanders to shuffle back. The air filled with the disturbingly sweet smell of charcoal and roasting pork.

Leaving behind ashes over a singed carpet, the flames faded, the red-hot collar suspended in the drifting smoke. The pile of ash that was once a young man shifted, lances of red light breaking free. A Shard —a full baton—floated into the air and hovered before Takket.

'Take it,' Haddronius sneered. 'My gift to the Imperium. I hope it eases your pain.'

Hesitantly, Takket grasped the uncut gem. Still warm.

'Now,' Haddronius called over his shoulder as he ascended to his throne. 'Is there anything else with which you wish to waste my court's time?'

Sombrely, Takket shook his head. The Shard smouldered in his hand, casting dim red patterns over his robe.

'Then we are done here.' Pure Shard flaring bright,

Haddronius began to rise towards the shaft. 'Court dismissed.'

As the crowd began to drift away, Takket looked up to the dais. Hekaena stood there, staring at him, eyes tearing.

Takket was disgusted. His plan had worked perfectly. He had demonstrated Haddronius's callousness. Hekaena would surely see her father's true face now.

All it had cost was the life of a condemned boy.

The crowd bled away in clusters of silken robes and glowing Shards. Scandalised mutters were exchanged as functionaries gossiped about the strange events—a Mundane summoning the court, a plea for clemency, the Arcane-lord's direct intervention. Takket had just provided the Magetowers of Varspire with days of conversation.

Of course, all of this would be forgotten in a week. Either Takket would succeed, and a coup would be on everyone's lips—or he would fail, and they could all scoff at the Mundane who had dared infiltrate this obsidian hall.

Takket remained still as the room drained. The smell of roasting meat had given way to an acrid stench of burning wool. Belatedly, a servant had noticed that the carpet was smouldering and ran to stamp it out, smearing the boy's ashes into the woven strands. A cluster of Mundanes hurried to sweep the ash into dustpans. Supervisors arrived, tutting and taking measurements, mourning the cost of replacing the rug.

No one mentioned the boy's death.

366

The activity faded. The last servants scurried from the room. Takket was left alone with Hekaena, separated by a gulf of a few stairs.

She descended with caution, red eyes impossible to read. At the base of the stairs, she looked down at the baton in his hand. The prize for his success. The memento of how, when it suited him, he too could throw away a life.

Wordlessly, Hekaena seized Takket's hand, her staff glowing as she levitated them into the tower's shaft. Wind blew past their faces as they raced upwards, the taint of Sharddust fading with altitude. Takket was growing used to levitation, but this rapid ascend left him nauseous.

Mages and Arcanes stood in clusters on balconies or even hovered in the shaft, sharing conspiratorial whispers. They cast curious glances at the rising pair —no doubt the sight of Hekaena with the controversial envoy would fuel their excited conversations. Anything to distract from the monotonous wait for the Tessella's return.

Hekaena dropped Takket on the top level's foyer, then shoved him forward into her room. She slammed the door, turning to him, eyes glistening with tears.

'Did you know that was going to happen?'

His first instinct was to lie. Claim he was trying to make amends by saving a life. Claim he thought Haddronius would show mercy. Claim he had not furthered his goals in exchange for a young man's life.

But more lies would not sway Hekaena. It was time for truth.

'Yes.'

She slapped him, hard.

Takket staggered, but made no attempt to defend himself. She glared, shaking with fury.

'Why?'

'I had to make you see the truth. Make you see who your farther truly is.'

She shook her head. 'And the boy had to die?'

'He was already going to die.' Takket closed his hand around the Shard, feeling the stone's rough surface. 'If I did nothing, he would have been executed by sundown.'

'What would you have done if Father had spared him? Did you even consider that?'

He nodded. 'I would have left Varspire.'

'Demon-shit.'

'I'm not lying.' He held her gaze, trying to show the honesty in his words. 'If your father had shown mercy, that would mean there was hope. It would mean that he could be reasoned with, that he could see the Mundanes as people, not a resource to be plundered. I could have left then, safe in the knowledge that your conscience might rub off on him, and if not him, then Valena.'

Hekaena let out a shuddering sigh. She staggered to the bed and sat. Clutching her head, she looked over at him mournfully. 'But now...it means there is no reasoning with him. There never will be.'

'No,' Takket said quietly.

Letting her staff fall to the floor, Hekaena lowered her face into her palms. She did not weep, did not shudder or huddle into a ball, just sat in silent agony.

'So this is it,' she whispered. 'I have a choice of betraying my father, or condemning every Mundane in this city to suffering and death.'

368

Takket took a few hesitant paces towards her. 'It's not an easy choice, I know.'

'What do you know of this?'

'I had to choose between abandoning the Mundanes and betraying you.'

She scowled. 'That's not the same thing.'

'No, it's not. But it was a choice between failing countless innocents, and hurting the person I love.'

Hekaena raised her head to stare at him, thoughtful. The silence dragged. He could see the debate in her head, knew it well. Two impossible alternatives. Two nightmarish options. He had to have faith that she would choose the Mundanes over her father. He had to pray that she was stronger than him.

'I still don't trust you,' she murmured. 'Never will.'

'I know.' Takket sighed. 'I can't expect anything else.'

She shook her head bitterly. 'There's no way into Father's room. Those guards outside his door are permanent. Ensellus dropped by earlier, said he heard about my dismissing his men the other day. He's not happy. They now have orders only to leave by Ensellus's or Father's direct command. They won't obey me again.'

'We will find a way, together.'

She dropped back into silence. Takket ignored the growing sting on his cheek, focusing only on Hekaena. Her internal debate intensified. She chewed her lower lip in her turmoil, hard enough to draw blood.

'I'm not killing my father,' she said at last.

'But it's the only way.'

'I'm *not* killing my father.'

Takket suppressed a sigh. He could not blame her. He too had chosen his heart over his conscience. Despite everything, Haddronius was still her father, the man who had cared for her throughout her life. Takket had thrown away his plans for a woman he barely knew.

'But,' she said slowly, 'I cannot let this continue. I can't let boys like that—girls like Lyssa—die, discarded like cattle.' She blew out a long breath. 'I'll take the Pure Shard. I'll heal this diseased land.'

'I thought you said you weren't going to kill Haddronius.'

'I'm not.' She stood, crossing the room to stare defiantly into his eyes. 'I'll let Father retire in peace.' She held up a hand to forestall his objection. 'No. If we're doing this, we're doing this my way. No death. Not Father. Not Valena. No one. Understood?'

Takket nodded.

Hekaena stared at him, face filled with conviction. 'Good. Then we are agreed. We'll steal the Pure Shard. Together.'

CHAPTER TWENTY FIVE

In Hekaena's room, Takket and Hekaena shared a quiet meal. She had asked the head chef to prepare her favourite comfort food—charred mutton coated in a sauce as sweet as it was eye-wateringly hot. Takket endured the pain, simply grateful for the company.

Conversation was awkward. Hekaena brooded. Her decision to betray her father had not wavered, but had clearly made her miserable. Takket made a few attempts at cheering her. He would occasionally manage to raise a smile, distract her with some story of their work in the undercity, get a laugh at Ensellus's expense. She would relax, slipping back into her normal habits, those glorious eyes filling with humour. Then it would fade. Each time, he could pinpoint the moment she remembered his betrayal. The joy would leech from her eyes, her gaze falling to her plate or turning to the window, anything to avoid confronting the liar she had loved.

After the last morsel was scraped from the plates, silence filled the room. The wind had ceased howling through the engraved ceiling. The night sky was clear —no rain to batter the windows. Noiselessly, the gas lamps burned.

Hekaena was the first to speak. 'I can't believe it's come to this—betraying my family.'

'I'm sorry.' Takket could think of nothing else.

'Are you?'

Takket winced at the barb. He gave her question thought before answering. 'I'm sorry that you're in this situation. I'm sorry that I caused you so much pain. But honestly? No, I'm not sorry we are doing this. I am not sorry that we are going to help every single one of them.'

He jabbed a finger at the window. Wood fires burned again in the undercity, lending an uneven orange glow to the Sharddust, like a blacksmith's forge fading at the end of day. On the horizon, he could see the bobbing light of an airship, a drunken star in the night sky.

Hekaena examined him critically. 'You actually do care about them, don't you.'

'Yes.' Takket grimaced. 'That's one thing I didn't lie about.'

'Why did you need to travel to this continent? Why involve me? Why not just help Mundanes in the Imperium?'

Takket shrugged. 'In the Imperium, they're easier to ignore. Mundanes there live in poverty, sure, but nothing on this scale. Varsen's crematoriums are...something unbelievable. Something *wrong*. I guess it took seeing that—knowing Lyssa—for me to realise change has to happen. Whatever the cost.'

'Whatever the cost,' Hekaena echoed sadly.

Takket sighed, turning to the matter at hand. 'To help the Mundanes, we need to find a way through that door. A way to get rid of the guards.'

Hekaena nodded. 'Any ideas?'

'You sure they'll disobey your direct order?'

'Yes. Father gave his blessing to Ensellus's command. To leave their posts without Ensellus's

372

order would be treason.'

'I could pretend to take you hostage,' Takket offered. 'Force them to stand down.'

'You expect me to trust you with a knife at my throat?'

'You really think I would kill you after all of this? What good would it do me? Forget how I feel about you—it's *you* that needs to take power, *you* that can lead the Mundanes to a better future.'

She chewed her lip for a while, then shook her head. 'Doesn't matter anyway. Taking me hostage wouldn't work. They won't betray Father to save me. At best, they'll shout a warning. At worst, they'll crush your skull and simply hope you don't cut my neck in your death throes.'

'They would let you die to save Haddronius?'

'How long have you been in Varsen?' Hekaena scoffed. 'The gap between Arcane-lord and regular Arcanes is the same as that between Mages and Mundanes. Doesn't matter that I'm his daughter. They'd let me die a hundred times over to preserve Father. Angels, if Ensellus thinks one of Father's children was behind the break-in, he might have given those guards orders to cut down the first of us to approach.'

Takket sighed. 'So we need to find a way to get Haddronius or Ensellus to order them away.'

'Well, Father's out. There's no way to get him to dismiss the guards and then expect him to go meekly to bed.'

'That leaves Ensellus. So how do we convince your father's security chief to expose the Arcane-lord?'

Hekaena shrugged, idly tapping a silver spoon

against the table's immaculate wooden surface. 'He'll only do that if he believes the threat to Haddronius is gone, or if there's a greater peril that requires his attention.'

'Convincing him the danger's gone won't be easy. He threatened to frame me for the break-in, meaning he doesn't think I'm actually responsible.'

Hekaena grunted. 'So we can't just pretend you've left.'

'No. My guess is that he suspects that a Varsen is trying to assassinate Haddronius. Probably thinks you or one of your siblings is trying to supplant your father.'

Hekaena rose and paced to the window, staring into the dark cityscape. 'So he suspects the truth. The threat is from within the royal family.'

Takket nodded grimly. 'So it's going to be hard to persuade him otherwise. We need to find something to distract him, a more pressing threat.'

'How? The only thing more threatening to the Arcanedom than an assassin would be an invasion, or a full-blown Mundane uprising. I'm not inviting a foreign power to invade, and the Mundanes know better than to start a revolution.'

Takket sighed, striding along the far side of the bed from Hekaena. He stared out of the window, trying to make out the streets and buildings of the undercity. There seemed no pattern in the light of wood fires, just a diffuse orange glow throughout the dust layer.

'We don't need an actual invasion or uprising,' he said slowly. 'We just need to convince Ensellus that one's imminent.'

'Seems impossible. He has more information than

anyone. You've been in his office, seen his folders. He has spies everywhere. If they give no indication of an approaching threat, he'll dismiss any reports we fabricate.'

Takket turned to Hekaena with a grin. 'Then we best speak to one of Ensellus's spies.'

In the dust-coated basement of Varspire Tower lay the quarters of favoured servants. Most of the tower's staff lived in the undercity, but a lucky few—those with experience, skill, or who had ingratiated themselves with the court—were given rooms among these sunless corridors.

It was up to the residents to maintain the basement, sweeping away the dust that would constantly flow down the staircase. But by the end of long days of scrubbing, cooking and hauling, few of the Mundanes had the energy to carry yet more dust from the tower. As a result, it piled thickly here, Takket's feet crunching ankle-deep into the red powder. Each step filled the air with the metallic scent of Sharddust, overpowering the odour of watery stews boiling behind flimsy doors.

Gas lamps gave the only light, and these were few and far between, turned down to give the bare minimum orange glow. Thin doors let out sounds of the tower at night: overcrowded families laughing and arguing over one another. The dust, the gloom, the noise—only the lack of wind differentiated these halls from the undercity.

Takket and Hekaena came to Akken's door—a fragile thing made of the bark of some large root, imperfectly bound together with twine. Light crept through gaps in the boards. The door rattled at Takket's knock, seeming ready to shatter at a strong push.

Within the room, the sound of conversation silenced. The door creaked open just enough for a face to peer around. The man, about Takket's age, gave a wary look, his bushy eyebrows furrowing. Seeing Hekaena, the man widened his eyes. He dropped to his knees.

'Arcane,' he shouted, directing his voice back to his family.

The door swung open and Takket peered into the cramped room. A stove stood beside the door, on it a grey stew congealing within a fire-blackened steel pot. The rest of the room was occupied by mismatched chairs surrounding a worn table. Half a dozen Mundanes sprang up from the rickety furniture, children and adults alike scrambling to find a spare patch of ground on which to kneel.

'Rise,' Hekaena called out before the emaciated figures had quite managed to arrange themselves.

Haltingly, the Mundanes stood, but all kept their eyes downcast. The children nervously plucked at threadbare clothing, tugging at squares of cloth patching woollen tunics.

'We're, uh, here to see Akken,' Takket explained.

'Father's sleeping in the back,' the man replied. 'Please, this way.'

The man pushed aside a grey woollen cloth hanging over a doorway. The claustrophobic room beyond was filled entirely by three beds. On the furthest of the beds, Akken sat up, bleary-eyed.

'Father,' Akken's son said. 'Arcane Hekaena is here

to see you.'

Akken wrapped the woollen bedsheets around himself in a crude toga and knelt on the bed—there being no floor he could reach.

'Rise,' Hekaena said impatiently.

'Arcane.' Akken adjusted himself to a more comfortable position. 'How may I serve you?'

'We need a word.' Takket turned to Akken's son. 'In private.'

'Of course.' The man gave a small bow. 'I'll take the children for a walk. Fresh air will do them good.'

Takket nodded, though he had no idea where the Mundane planned to find fresh air. As the family was ushered out through the door, the remaining three occupants waited in silence.

A while after the door closed, Akken stood and picked his way around the beds. 'I take it that you two being here together means that you no longer hate one another?'

'No,' Takket replied with forced humour. 'She still hates me.'

Hekaena glowered. 'Takket said you might be able to help us.'

'Oh?' Akken looked between them, uncertain. 'I'll do anything I can, though I'm not sure why you'd need a servant.'

'We don't,' Takket replied. 'We need one of Ensellus's spies.'

'Ah.' Akken stroked his beard thoughtfully. 'Well, with the two of you together, I'm guessing this is not going to be some minor favour.'

'No.' Takket grimaced. 'We need the guards on Haddronius's door removed. At least for an hour or two.'

Akken let out a long breath. 'Demons, why do you need that? No. Wait. I really don't think I want to know.'

'I don't think you do,' Hekaena agreed.

Akken took a seat at the edge of one bed, gesturing to Hekaena and Takket to sit on its neighbour. They obliged, perched on the hard mattress, strands of straw sticking into Takket's thighs. The brown sheets stank of a decade of sweat, leading Takket to wonder what colour they had been when new.

'Well,' Akken said at last. 'It's not going to be easy. Did you have anything specific in mind?'

Takket nodded. 'Ensellus knows Enara and Yelleck are working for Kilroth.' Akken raised his eyebrows, but stayed silent. 'You could say you heard them talking about an impending invasion.'

Akken shook his head. 'I think there actually is one brewing, but he'll not withdraw guards from Haddronius's door unless there's trouble here in the city. An invasion's the border commanders' problem.'

'What about a Mundane uprising?' Takket asked. 'Ensellus also knows that Kilroth has agents in the undercity. You could tell him that my two assistants said something about staging a revolt. If it's aimed at attacking Varspire Tower, then surely he'll send every man to defend the lower floors.'

'Perhaps.' Akken plucked a grey hair from his beard, then scratched at his jaw. 'More likely he'll send them to make a perimeter outside—keep the rabble far from the tower. Would fit your plans anyway, I think.'

Takket smiled. 'Perfect.'

'No quite,' Akken clarified. 'Ensellus ain't going to

change guard orders based on what one old Mundane says. He'll need to see evidence. Fires. Calls from help from Magetowers. Crumbling admin buildings. He'll need a cursed riot before he'll dispatch every guard in the tower.'

Hekaena shook her head. 'There's no way the Mundanes will actually rise up. Even with my assurance, they know such an act would be suicide. It won't matter if they flee at the first sign of reprisal— the Arcanes will run them down through the streets.'

'Agreed,' Akken grunted. 'Sporadic attacks would give them a chance to get away, at least for a while. Fires started in the rail yard. Shards thrown out of Magetower windows to explode below. The crematorium set ablaze. That kind of thing. Easy to start, then run long before Arcanes arrive. But to get Ensellus thinking it's a city-wide emergency, the attacks would have to be widespread, and coordinated. Problem is, I don't know anyone who can get fifty Mundanes to act as one, let alone an entire city of them.'

Takket slapped his knee triumphantly. 'I just might. Hekaena, how would you like to go visit the Circlist temple again? I know a man who can start a riot.'

Takket felt a wave of vertigo as he and Hekaena flew over the moonlight-dappled Shard layer. This late into the night, the glowing pools of the undercity's wood fires were becoming rarer, extinguished as households went to bed. Large areas of the city became a black void, surrounded by distant Magetowers. The only proof of their motion was the air blowing past his face, heavy with a copper tang.

379

Hekaena held his hand, but the act seemed to be more habit than any real show of affection. There was no warmth in her touch, no loving caress of a thumb against his skin, just a rough grasp like a parent dragging a disobedient toddler.

By one of the large field platforms, they slowed to a stop and began to descend into the black clouds of Sharddust. Takket's heart pounded as his world became red. There were no nearby fires, and the Sharddust quickly obscured the stars. The only light source remaining was Hekaena's staff, casting its unsteady rays through the churning dust. Beyond their pool of bloody light, he could see nothing.

The touch of his boots against the ground startled Takket. They had landed on the street, thick Sharddust being kicked up with every step.

The air chilled as Hekaena produced a brilliant white light and sent it questing into the Sharddust to get their bearings. The light passed over a mound of garbage—wooden posts and broken krilt shells lying haphazardly over each other. With horror, Takket realised it was the remains of a building.

'Brought down by a storm,' Hekaena explained, mournful. 'This is why I spend so much time building more sturdy structures. The Mundanes construct hovels that are barely able to stand. Without magic, they can do no better with the materials on hand. Krilt shell just does not hold together well on it its own, and rotting wood makes a poor frame. Their buildings can handle weight, but not the shifting winds of a storm.'

'Would anyone survive this?'

She nodded. 'Some. Those near the surface, or lucky enough to get caught in a stable alcove.

Mundanes are practised at going over these wrecks, rescuing people, gathering reusable structures...burning the dead. Still, many would be wounded, often too injured to work.'

'And they would all be homeless,' Takket said grimly.

'Easy prey for the next purge...which often follows the storms. After all, Magetowers need their scuffed exteriors repaired.'

Takket's jaw tensed. 'We need to stop this.'

'Yes. The temple's this way.'

Following Hekaena's light, Takket left the pocket of cold air created by her magic use. The temple, at least, had survived the storm mostly intact. Thick Sharddust piled against the side that had faced the prevailing winds, and rough scaffolding had been thrown up beside one cracked wall, but the structure retained its basic shape.

Hekaena pushed the door, forcing it to open against the deep dust on the far side. She let her ball of light fade, the glow from her staff picking out the features of the deserted hallway. At least the lack of manure transports outside allowed the air to be more breathable than on his last visit—thick with copper, not human waste.

'Hello?' Hekaena shouted.

Takket followed as she wandered deeper into the structure, repeating her echoing call. Eventually, down the curving hallway, a door creaked open and a robed figure hurried out.

'Arcane Hekaena.' High Priest Valco dropped to his knees in the dust before her. 'This is most unexpected. I'm sorry for not answering sooner.'

'Stand,' Hekaena said, amused, 'and don't be ridiculous. It's the middle of the night—I would be concerned if you were not asleep.'

The ageing priest stumbled to his feet, brushing the dust from his robe. 'For you, I'm always happy to serve. But...something must be wrong, to call you here at this hour.'

'There is,' Takket said. 'Last time I was here, you told me that you had the power to start a riot. Is that still true?'

Valco licked his lips, nervously glancing between Takket and Hekaena.

'It's alright,' she assured him. 'I'm not here to arrest you. I need this riot. This city needs it.'

Valco did not look convinced. 'Why, may I ask?'

Hekaena closed her eyes, forcing out the words. 'I'm going to take my father's Pure Shard. I'm taking control of Varsen. I'm going to end the purges, close the crematorium, build real structures that won't collapse every few months. I'm going to change this city, this entire Arcanedom.'

'That...sounds fantastic,' Valco said dryly, eyes twitching. 'Too good to believe, to be honest.'

'Valco,' Hekaena persisted. 'You know me. You know the work I do in the undercity. You know how much I care for the Mundanes.'

He nodded slowly. 'That you do. But...it's one thing to build houses. Another to stage a coup. What changed?'

'This man did.' Hekaena gestured to Takket.

'Envoy Khantek?' Valco looked completely lost.

'Takket the thief.' Hekaena gave a grimace. 'It's a long story. Suffice it to say, he showed me that my efforts were not good enough, not by a long shot. This city needs change—not when Valena takes the throne, not in a decade, *now*.'

Valco ran a hand through his Sharddust-stained black hair. 'But what's this to do with a riot? The Mundanes love you, Hekaena. Some will die for you. But there's no way we can overpower your father.'

'We don't need you to,' Takket explained. 'We need a distraction. We have a way to get to the Pure Shard, but there are guards outside Haddronius's room. The only way they will move is if the head of security thinks there's an uprising.'

'It doesn't need to be real,' Hekaena added. 'We just need it to look convincing. Towers on fire. Shardrail yards collapsing. Government buildings attacked. But it needs to be all over the city, and all at once. I swear I will pardon everyone involved when I take power.'

'*If* you take power,' Valco grumbled.

'Yes,' Hekaena continued. 'It's a risk. Some might die. If this goes wrong, a lot of people will die, including myself.'

Valco smirked. 'If this goes right, a lot of people are going to die. No matter how careful they are, some Mundanes will be caught setting fires. Don't fool yourselves—there will be blood.'

'How much blood will there be if we do nothing?' Takket asked. 'If we let the purges continue, if we let children "volunteer" themselves to feed their siblings, if we let—'

'Alright, alright.' Valco made a placating gesture. 'You made your point. Just tell me this, Hekaena. Are you certain this will benefit the Mundanes of Varspire?'

'I am,' she replied, resolute.

Valco let out a shuddering sigh. 'Fine. If you were anyone else, I'd think you were mad. But if you say we need this...then I believe you. I can't make any promises, but I will start contacting my fellow priests. It's going to take a few days to get everyone together.'

'It needs to be before Tessella Indel arrives,' Takket said. 'This mustn't look like the Imperium is involved in any way.'

'Two days from now,' Valco offered. 'That's the best I can do. And, Hekaena, these people are going to be risking their lives for you. It might help if you come in person to the meeting. They worship you, and your presence might make all the difference.'

Hekaena nodded. 'Of course.'

Takket let out a breath. The other two began to finalise timings.

Two days.

Once the riots started, there would be no turning back. They would either succeed, Hekaena would sit on the throne and the Mundanes would be free—or they would fail and Hekaena, Valco, Akken, every good-natured person in this city, would be dead.

CHAPTER TWENTY SIX

Following Hekaena onto the balcony, Takket looked out over the uncovered city. That morning's deluge had been rare for Varsen, sheets of rain lashing over Varspire. The storm had been short lived, but intense enough to dissolve the Shard layer. Great red rivers flowed through the exposed undercity, torrents washing the Sharddust into the waters of the bloated Tellin.

Without the Sharddust to obscure his view, Takket could see the details of the Mundane's tumorous hives. Pale krilt-shell buildings rose in bulbous mounds, growing around the invasive neatness of Magetowers and field platforms. The rainwater had flooded through windows and spaces between wall panels, oozing from doorways, saturated in Sharddust. In depressions, the waters gathered, congealing as a thick mud. The entire city gave the impression of a diseased beast, gutted and bleeding out over the landscape.

Now, the red slurry baked under the afternoon sun. By nightfall, the trapped Sharddust would dry out, the mud cracking into a fine powder to be carried by errant gusts, re-establishing the Shard layer.

'It's time,' he said.

Hekaena nodded. 'Let's go change the city.'

With a small smile, she reached for his hand as they began their ascent. The ice in Hekaena's expression had begun to thaw over the past two days.

He caught her glaring at him less often, their conversations only occasionally breaking off into awkward silence. On some level, she seemed to be starting to understand his betrayal, see the impossible position he had found himself in—the choice between a loved one and a million innocent strangers—the situation in which she was now trapped.

He was still far from forgiveness. There were no more light-hearted laughs, no loving touches or stolen kisses. He still slept on the floor.

Despite it all—how close he had come to failure, how painful it had been, the depth of her new hatred— he was still glad to have told her the truth. It felt liberating, having someone with whom he could be open. At least they would face this final challenge together. If he failed, he would be standing alongside her at the end.

They flew lower than normal, just above the bulging buildings. Mundanes packed the streets, eager to make the most of the sun before the Shard layer engulfed them once more. In every direction the fallout of the recent gales was evident. Some buildings had survived with only light damage, a few krilt shells tearing free in the wind. Others now bore deep clefts in their bulbous forms where level after level had given way, tearing down entire sections. Many were simply destroyed, left as heaps of rubble and half-buried possessions.

Over it all, Mundanes teemed. On the peak of a misshapen mound of homes, a man hammered nails into a fresh krilt shell to cover a child's ceiling. At the weaving mill, a group of women erected a scaffolding of rotting planks to hold a decimated wall. Over the next rise, Mundanes picked through the remains of a large housing complex, digging out what little they could salvage. The items of value were dragged into the thickening red mud of the streets—piles of threadbare clothing, utensils hewn from chitin, chairs that looked as if they would shatter under a child's weight. The riches of the undercity.

Near the larger of the collapsed buildings were black stains—piles of charcoal and bone, half-corpses reaching out with charred hands. They were the mass pyres, built to deal with the bodies dragged from the ruins. Before the flames had a chance to finish rendering the remains to ash, the rains had extinguished the fire. A handful of Mundanes hovered nearby, critically inspecting the mess. They would have to wait until the piles dried out enough to be re-lit—the crematorium dealt only with the living.

Ahead stood the Circlist Temple. Sheltered by the field platform above, its walls had not been washed clean, and red still dusted its upper levels. The platform could not protect the building from the torrents of blood-red water that had flowed down the streets and smeared Sharddust like paint across the building's base.

Takket and Hekaena landed in the ankle-deep red muck by the doors. His leather boots stuck in the slurry, coming free with a squelch only after a great deal of strain. How the locals moved through this bog, Takket had no idea.

They trudged to the door, which Hekaena forced open, the mulch clinging to its wooden frame. Inside, they scraped their boots clean on a coarse rug left by the entrance—or as clean as they could manage on the filthy material. At least the hallway within was dry, the Sharddust powdering the halls having been spared the flood.

A young acolyte dropped to her knees before Hekaena.

'Arcane, it's an honour,' the girl breathed.

'Rise,' Hekaena replied. 'Hopefully we can soon abolish this horrid tradition.'

The girl stood, eyes fixed on the floor. 'The priests are waiting for you. This way.'

They were led through the dust-caked hallway, over to the rear of the circular building. There, the girl ushered them through an unpainted door into what passed for the temple's grand hall. Two dozen priests were packed into the cramped space, the room's worn dining table and chairs pushed aside to make room.

The priests varied in age, from their early twenties to some who looked at least sixty. Men and women, all wore similarly patched and fraying maroon cloaks. Most of their hair was still damp from the rain. They regarded Hekaena with mixed expressions.

To Takket's surprise, none bowed.

'Hekaena.' Valco pushed through the crowd. 'I'm relieved that you could make it. We mean no offence by standing—it just seemed fitting.'

'None taken.' Hekaena smiled. 'I've been telling you not to bow for years. Is everyone here?'

'Everyone's who's coming.' Valco nodded. 'I've not heard from the priests of Towersfoot or Bankton. They've most likely decided this is a trap, or simply foolhardy.'

Takket frowned. 'Do we need to worry about them divulging the plan to the authorities?'

'Demons, no,' Valco replied. 'They have no love for the Arcanes—present company excepted. Even if they did, they'd be signing their own death sentence. Anyone involved in this will burn if we fail.'

Hekaena nodded. 'Are those here ready?'

'They will be, once you speak to them.'

Hekaena steeled herself and climbed onto a table pushed against a wall. It groaned as she stood upon it to gaze at the crowd.

'Thank you for coming,' Hekaena called out. 'Today we have an opportunity to do something once thought impossible. Today we can right the injustices in society.'

A voice called out from the back, 'Or we could all die.'

Hekaena grimaced. 'Yes. This is not going to be easy, for any of us. But I promise you, this is for the good of all Mundanes.'

'I trust you, Hekaena,' said a woman near the front. She turned her eyes towards Takket. 'It's him that I doubt. The Imperium's involvement is more than a little troubling. How do we know this isn't a prelude to them retaking the New World?'

'Would that be such a bad thing?' another voice called from the side.

The room erupted into heated debate.

'At least the Varsens protect us. What can the Imperium do against a Kilroth invasion?'

'Even Kilroth rule would be an improvement—'

'My son was killed defending the border.'

'The Imperium could help us spread Circlism across—'

'Have you all forgotten the War of the Sixth

Shard?'

Not daring to pile more weight onto Hekaena's table, Takket climbed atop a nearby chair and whistled to silence the arguing priests.

'I understand your fears,' he shouted. 'But the Imperium has no part in this.'

The woman at the front snorted. 'Yet their envoy stands alongside the Arcane we would put on the throne.'

'I'm not the Imperium's envoy. I'm an impostor. A fraud. A thief hired to steal the Pure Shard.'

Consternation rippled through the crowd.

'That's hardly better,' the woman muttered.

'No,' Takket agreed. 'But Varspire changed me. I've seen the crematorium. I've seen the aftermath of the purges. I've seen only a fraction of your suffering, but I know that it must be stopped.'

Hekaena regarded him. 'He's speaking the truth. He confessed his role to me in order to give us this chance. He's risked his life to keep the dream of a moral Varspire alive.'

The priest did not look impressed. 'And what happens when we put Hekaena on the throne? We know of your relationship. You planning on marrying her? Is this just some scheme to put you alongside our head of state?'

Takket glanced at Hekaena, then cast his eyes towards the floor. 'No. I've burned that bridge. I don't know what will become of me once this is over. I'll leave that to your new government to decide. If you want to exile me, I'll go without resistance. If you want to immolate me—I deserve it. As long as the Mundanes here are free, I will die proud.'

Waves of whispers passed through the crowd. One by one, the priests looked placated.

'What about us?' another priest—a frail man swamped by his robe—called out. 'What about Circlism? You've called the Circlists to help you. It's our blood that's going to be spilled. If we fail, Haddronius will use this as an excuse to scour our doctrine from Varsen. Circlists are risking everything, yet last I heard you attend a Scalist temple. Do you intend to convert?'

Hekaena considered. 'I would love to promise you that, but I cannot make such an assurance. I was raised Scalist, as were all my siblings. I will make sure the laws no longer favour Scalism in Varsen. I will certainly hear out every argument you have for your doctrine. If you convince me, then I will gladly convert—openly. But I'm not going to simply pretend to in order to gain your support.'

Honesty. It still seemed unnatural to Takket, but Hekaena's words swayed the audience. More murmurs passed through the crowd, then a series of nods. There were no further questions.

Hekaena gave a small smile. 'I know what I'm asking of you is hard. Your parishioners will be taking an unheard of risk. If we fail tonight, my father's response will be widespread and merciless. I will not sugar-coat the truth—even if we succeed, Mundanes will likely die.

'But knowing that, I still ask you for your support. I ask not for myself, but for them.' She waved towards the building's wall. 'We all know what the Mundanes go through every day. We know how many will die if we do nothing. Every person here has lost someone to the crematorium—a friend, a sibling, a husband, a wife, a child. I know that if I did not take this opportunity to end that suffering, I could never again look myself in the mirror. Even if backing down now meant I could live in peace for the rest of my life, I would forever regret not taking action this day.

'Looking at you all now, I see that same conviction. We are going to do this. Together, we are going to change the world. For giving me this opportunity, I thank you from the bottom of my heart. You were right not to bow to me when I entered. No man or woman should be honoured by a fluke of birth.'

She glanced around at the faces. 'But you great people, you who have spent your lives bringing hope to the Mundanes, you who quiet their fears every day, you who will risk your skin tonight to save them. You are heroes. And if anyone should be bowed to, it's heroes.'

Astonished mutters as Hekaena dropped to her knees. She bent forward, supplicating herself on the table. Jaws dropped, stunned silence descending over the hall. An Arcane was bowing to Mundanes.

Varspire would be forever changed.

By the time Takket and Hekaena returned to Varspire Tower, the sun had set behind the rocky horizon. The last light of the dying day reflected off the obsidian spire. Lazy wisps of Sharddust rose from the blood-red streets, the Shard layer grudgingly covering the undercity.

Red footprints on the jade carpets as the pair walked the tower's winding corridors. Takket tried not to jump at shadows, tried not to see murderous intent

in the gaze of every passerby. Part of him feared that
Akken had betrayed them, that Ensellus knew of their
scheme, that a troop of guards would be waiting
around the next corner.

Turning into the embassy, Takket found no
soldiers, just Akken dusting the bejewelled marble
pillars. The greying man turned and bowed to
Hekaena.

'Rise,' she said instinctively.

'Doesn't seem like dusting is really required,'
Takket commented.

Akken shrugged. 'Keeps me busy.'

Beckoning the others to follow, the servant turned
and climbed the carpeted stairs to Takket's room. Once
Hekaena had closed the door, Akken gave the pair a
curt nod.

'It's done,' the servant said. 'I told Ensellus that I
overheard your two assistants discussing an uprising
planned for tonight. I dropped Rithdal's name—
someone I shouldn't know about—and that seemed to
convince the man. Security is on alert. Enara and
Yelleck are wanted.'

'Where are they?' asked Takket.

'Gone.' Akken shrugged. 'Something must've
spooked them. They fled before Ensellus could make
the arrest.'

Hekaena smiled uncertainly. 'That might actually
be good for us. If we're lucky, they've fled Varsen
entirely. One less complication.'

Takket grunted in agreement. 'And chasing them
will keep Ensellus busy long enough for the
Mundanes to get into position.'

'Speaking of which,' Akken replied warily, 'you

two best be getting upstairs. If Ensellus does sound the alarm, you can bet he'll seal off Haddronius's floor. Unless you intend on blasting your way through, you better be on the right side when that happens.'

'One thing first.' Takket looked around the room. 'Did you pick up my order?'

'Of course.' Akken strolled over to the bed and shouldered a large satchel. 'It's all here, plus some Shard grains I didn't spend.'

Takket swung the bag over his shoulder. 'I would say that you can keep the change, but if we succeed, we'll be able to give you a far more fitting reward.'

'And if you fail,' Akken added, 'I'll have no use for Shards.'

Hekaena nodded grimly. 'None of us will. Thank you for all you've done. Angels watch over you.'

Akken gave a tired laugh. 'It's you that'll be needing their help, I wager.'

They said their goodbyes, and left the servant pretending to dust. Walking through the obsidian-walled corridor, Takket felt a growing sense of finality. He gazed at the abstract jade statues, the finely engraved rosewood ceiling, the green-uniformed guards, knowing that this was the last time he would walk these halls as Envoy Khantek Fredeen. Come sunrise, he would be paraded through as either a liberator or a condemned traitor—assuming he still breathed.

Climbing the final staircase, they approached Haddronius's throne, that hateful altar. Takket wondered what Hekaena would do with it once she took power. Would she keep it for tradition's sake, mollifying the nobility? Would she dismantle the chair whose construction had caused the death of countless innocents, perhaps distributing the wealth to ease the poverty of the undercity? Or would she honour the memory of the fallen, ensure no one forgot the blood of the past, by displaying the monstrosity?

Whatever she decided, Takket knew she would act with the Mundanes at heart.

They ascended through the tower's central shaft, past Arcanes and Mages who joked and ate and schemed, all oblivious to the imminent reckoning. The guards at the barracks near the tower's summit appeared on edge, many shooting glances towards the windows. Good—Akken's words had been heeded.

In the top-level foyer, the jade door's guards looked impatient, clearly itching to move somewhere with a view over the city. Takket and Hekaena ignored them and entered her room.

Takket dumped the bag in her bathroom and unloaded the linen clothing within. He changed slowly, taking care as he pulled on the trousers, the mottled-grey tunic, the calfskin boots and fingerless leather gloves. He would stand out here among the immaculately dressed denizens of Varspire Tower, but that hardly mattered—being caught tonight would mean his death. At least now he would die in comfort.

He finished by transferring his lock-picking tools into his tunic's pockets, then hesitated, feeling a weight remaining in the bag. With a frown, he withdrew an object.

A dagger.

The unadorned steel blade was small, barely long enough to cause a fatal wound. It was a weapon designed for concealment, to be hidden and used only

395

if all other options failed. A thief's weapon. A paper note wrapped the blackened leather hilt. Takket unfurled it and read.

Blades against a Soulshards are weak, but they are a Mundane's only hope.
-A

Takket gave a small smile, the blade seeming far lighter than any Yelleck had given. It felt right as he tucked it into his boot. Now he would die comfortable and armed.

As he re-entered the bedroom, Hekaena smirked at his outfit. 'Didn't you get an assassin's costume for me?'

Takket adjusted his tunic, feigning indignation. 'We're thieves, not assassins. And no, it's probably best that you look...official. One way or another, soon you're going to have to face a lot of angry Arcanes.'

Hekaena grimaced, then turned to the window-wall. 'It will start soon.'

Takket crossed to her side. They stood shoulder to shoulder, both staring into the city below, but between them Takket could feel the impenetrable barrier—the barrier his lies had erected. He longed to reach for her hand, to pull her into an embrace, to whisper sweet nothings until her obvious torment lifted. But he knew that was impossible. His fleeting dream of a life with her shattered under the weight of reality. Instead he simply stood with her in uncomfortable companionship.

The sky slowly darkened, a few stars blinking into existence. The rains had left the Shard layer thinner than normal. A few of the tallest Mundane hovel-mounds reached above its surface, malformed islands in a faintly glowing sea.

The glow intensified as more and more cooking fires were lit. Those Mundanes who knew nothing of the coup carried out their daily routine. Those involved in the riot kept up appearances until the appointed hour, counting time on candles or the few mechanised clocks in the undercity.

The night dragged. Wood fires flickered to life, then faded into darkness. Scattered Shard lights drifted between Magetowers—Arcanes and Mages attending parties or returning home. A train pulled out of the Shardrail station, the lights of its carriages rapidly disappearing into the gloom. Half the city continued on, ignorant of what was about to transpire. The other half waited with impatience.

Hekaena was the first to spot a sign of the false uprising. 'There.'

A light bloomed in the undercity, an orange glow in the haze far larger than any cooking fire. Tongues of flame broke the Shard layer.

'The crematorium,' Hekaena whispered.

From the peak of a distant Magetower, a red glow plummeted—a Soulshard. As it impacted the tower's base, all of its stored energy was released in an uncontrolled burst of heat and light. The explosion vibrated through the city with a ripple of Sharddust.

At the Shardrail yards, more fire ripped into the sky. By the river, smoke billowed towards the stars. A nearby Magetower shuddered from some unseen blast.

A ringing pierced the air. Muffled shouts echoed through Hekaena's door. A metallic groan sounded through the floor. Some minutes later, down at the tower's base, a hundred lights spread out into the Sharddust—Mages and Arcanes setting up a perimeter.

Takket crept to the door, cracking it open an inch. The foyer was deserted, the shaft covered by a glistening metal disk.

Easing the door shut, Takket turned to Hekaena. 'It's time. Are you ready?'

She smirked. 'It's a little late for doubts. People are dying out there. We're committed.'

Takket crossed to her side. 'Whatever happens. I *am* glad I came here. I'm glad we have this opportunity. I'm glad I met you.'

Her face was impossible to read. 'Maybe someday I'll be able to say the same. Let's...let's just get this over with. The sooner we act, the sooner those Mundanes can stop risking their lives.'

Takket nodded and hurried to the door. They slipped into the foyer, passing under the backlit jade ceiling. Haddronius's door stood unguarded, Soulshard glowing brightly at its centre.

Hekaena hesitated. 'Be careful in there, alright? Father should have settled back asleep by now—he's always been a heavy sleeper. He'll be at the end of the corridor. The Pure Shard will be nearby—you won't be able to miss it. Don't let him touch to it, or any Shard, until you're back here. Understand?'

'You almost sound concerned about me.'

'This is about more than you. Everyone out there is counting on us.' She closed her eyes and sighed. 'But...no. Believe it or not, I don't want to watch you die. Be safe.'

Takket nodded with conviction. 'Get me inside, and I'll do the rest. We'll save this city, this country. I swear.'

Taking a deep breath, Hekaena waved a hand over the Shard. It brightened with recognition. Stone ground against stone within the locking mechanism, then the door began to roll open. No alarm. Takket grinned.

A grin that died when he saw what awaited him on the far side.

Ensellus.

CHAPTER TWENTY SEVEN

Takket backed away. Ensellus stalked forward, hands behind his back, smug grin on his face.

'I've been waiting for you.' The man's eyes were filled with murder.

'Ensellus? What are you doing here?' Hekaena stammered.

The man positioned himself between Hekaena and Takket. He waved a hand towards the wall, and the door rolled shut. 'Let's not wake the Arcane-lord. I told him there might be a threat. He's sleeping in his study, safe and sound. I'd hate for him to interrupt, perhaps show mercy.'

Hekaena frowned. 'How did you—?'

'The door?' Ensellus smirked. 'It only needs a Varsen to open. Anyone can close it. Really, you should have done more research before attempting an assassination.'

Hekaena shook her head. 'We're not—'

'Save it,' Ensellus snarled. 'I've been watching your little plaything, this envoy. I've seen the journeys you've been making to the undercity. Your clandestine meetings. I know a coup when I see one.' He leered. 'I would have gone to your father, but he's grown soft. The Haddronius I served with in the Great Southern War would have killed a Mundane who bedded his daughter, not welcomed him to dinner.'

'So what?' Hekaena asked, indignant. 'You plan on

400

killing me? Father will skin you alive.'

'I don't think so. Oh, he's always had a weak spot for you, Hekaena. Always valued what *you* want. Turned down political marriages because *you* did not approve. Suffered embarrassment again and again because *you* slummed with Mundanes. But now? He can't ignore this betrayal. The daughter who used an uprising to plan his assassination? No. He might not be able to bring himself to order your death, but he's not going to blame me for saving his life.'

Hekaena's hand went to the Shard at the end of her staff. Ensellus pulled his other hand from behind his back, brandishing his own baton-sized Shard.

'Do you really think you can best me?' Ensellus turned his back on Takket, staring down Hekaena. 'You use magic to build hovels and entertain children. I've fought in wars. I've faced down battle-trained Arcanes on every border. You stand no chance.'

Hekaena's face hardened. 'I'm no pushover.'

Ensellus laughed. 'We'll see. At least this will be interesting. Oh, and don't worry—once you're dead, I'll make sure your pet envoy suffers for leading you down this path.'

Their hands shot out, Soulshards gleaming brilliantly. The space between them shifted, strange rents appearing like air above a sun-scorched plateau. A vibration filled Takket's ears, an otherworldly moan at the edge of his hearing. Motes of dust flicked back and forth between the two Arcanes, tossed around in a magical battle Takket could barely see, let alone comprehend.

The air chilled as both combatants drew in heat to fuel their mystical struggle. Takket stood by, helpless.

He was just a Mundane. The moment Ensellus sensed him closing, the Arcane would lash out. Hekaena could defend herself against the magical bombardment, stilling Ensellus's attacks. If Takket interfered, he would be snapped in half by a simple thought.

Takket shifted, the sound of his own footsteps sounding distant, distorted. The combatants were dampening all sound. Neither wanted to wake Haddronius, to have their fatal duel interrupted.

In the cooling air, his breath came out in misty puffs. Deep in the recesses of his mind, he had a sense of the energy snapping around the room, the massive forces straining against each other. Distortions filled the space between the two Arcanes as reality frayed. The air became acrid, strange chemical emissions forming in the tortured atmosphere. Takket's shivered, a primal dread seizing his heart.

Ice crystallised over the foyer, fractal patterns building across the obsidian walls, snow frosting the jade and emerald ceiling. Takket shivered. The green light filtering from above seemed to darken, shadows with no source dancing across the floor. The Arcanes were draining their surroundings. Unable to move away, they were feeding on every last ounce of power.

Looking over Ensellus's shoulder, Takket saw Hekaena's face—the image of determination. Both combatants were entirely focused on victory, both perfectly matched.

It would not last long. Eventually, the room would become completely drained, the Arcanes unable to take more heat from the air without freezing themselves to death. They would be forced to burn their Shards, turning them to dust for a final burst of power.

Then, Hekaena would die.

Both Arcanes held only a single baton, but Ensellus stood by the jade door, and the Soulshard at its centre. Once their Shards were burned, Ensellus had only to stretch a hand to the door and he could burn the Shard, tear apart the unarmed Hekaena. This was a battle of attrition that Ensellus would win.

Takket struggled to find options. He was a Mundane. His only weapon was the short dagger tucked into his boot. He could throw it, but Ensellus was already deflecting a hundred light magical blows from Hekaena, the small knife would be knocked aside with ease. A lunge would carry more force, take more effort for Ensellus to push away, but it would not be enough to overcome the Arcane. Takket had no hope of killing the man.

He froze. Hekaena did not need an assassin.

Just a distraction.

With a hardening resolve, Takket crouched, drawing the blade from his boot, feeling the soft handle, the balanced weight. He braced himself, like a ykkol cat lining up a kill. Staring at Ensellus's back, he sized up his prey.

Then pounced.

With all his strength, he lunged forward into that orb of frantic air surrounding the Arcanes. His skin itched—then pain lashed his body as he threw himself into the supernatural fray. The tip of his blade pieced the green silk of Ensellus's robe and tore through skin and muscle to impact a bone.

Agony wracked Takket's body.

An unseen force launched him across the foyer. A hard surface rammed into his back—the ceiling. In his ribs, something gave. The floor ripped towards him, smashing into his face. The crack of his skull against the stone floor seemed oddly distant. Dazed, he dropped the knife. Blood darkened the tip where it had entered the vile man.

Only half an inch deep.

Takket had barely nicked his target. Pain lancing through every joint, he looked up to see his failure. His muscles cried out, every breath a torture. He could barely move, and had managed only to irritate Ensellus.

But it gave Hekaena her chance.

She took advantage of Ensellus's distraction, burning her Shard in a last desperate burst of energy. Ensellus could not counter in time. He was shredded. His chest flew left, his hips right. His head smashed against the ceiling, legs shattering on the floor. The air settled, formless red globs of Ensellus dripping over the foyer.

It was over.

Sharddust drained through Hekaena's fingers, her decapitated staff collapsing to the floor. Without its Shard, the obsidian and gold shaft was nothing more than a garish bauble. Sucking in agonised breaths, Takket watched as the staff rolled into a wet chunk of something that had once been Ensellus.

Hekaena recovered first, running to Takket's side.

She knelt beside his crouched form. 'Are you alright?'

He nodded, the act sending jolts of pain through his neck. 'Broken rib, I think. I'll be fine.'

'That was a risk,' she said sternly. 'He could have killed you.'

With her help, Takket struggled to his feet. 'I know.'

She looked into his eyes. 'Thank you.'

He gave a slight smile at the warmth in her voice. For a moment, he was transported back two weeks, to before he had told her the truth, to when everything seemed right. To when her gaze had held only love. Those faded days where he had actually contemplated staying, to find a way to spend their lives together. Those days were gone.

Part of Ensellus sluiced off the ceiling, slapping into the floor nearby. Takket's attention snapped back to the present.

'If Father heard the fight...' Hekaena started.

'Then we're dead. There's nothing we can do but push on.'

Hekaena slowly nodded. 'Ensellus said Father's in his study. Turn left at the end of the corridor. It's through two sets of doors, on the far side of the living room. The Pure Shard will be with him, probably a pace or two from his bed.'

Takket nodded. 'I'll be back as soon as I can. Best if you wait here—I don't want some stray Shard light waking him.'

Hekaena crouched by Ensellus's shredded arm, prying the intact Shard from his dead fingers. 'When you take the Shard, try to pick it up using the chain— don't touch it directly. It's been nearly two thousand years since a Mundane held a Pure Shard. I don't want you to burn it by accident.'

Takket nodded. 'Good plan. We've not come this

far just to turn me into a Mage.'

She gave smile, a hint of admiration in her eyes as she waved her hand over the jade door. 'Angels be with you.'

The door rolled to the side, revealing the blindingly bright corridor. Taking a breath, Takket crept forward. His calfskin boots made no sound on the Shards that covered the floor. He squinted against the light emanating from every surface of the hallway, the faceted Shards giving dangerously slick footing. Takket briefly wondered how the elderly Haddronius managed to make it down the corridor each day without tripping, then smirked as his own idiocy—the man would just levitate.

The combined light of the hallway's Shards illuminated Haddronius's bedroom. There was no sign of the Arcane-lord or the Pure Shard—Ensellus had told the truth. Takket picked his way over the lush green carpet, moving away from the white silken bed, around rosewood armoires and looming jade statues. Spiced incense burned nearby, the sharp smell strong enough to give Takket a headache.

Carefully, he twisted a golden handle and eased open the whitewashed door. Light from the corridor flooded into the living room, giving a clear view of its opulence. Jade and obsidian lined every piece of furniture—the couches, the table, the drinks cabinet, the compulsory statues of angels and demons glaring from the corners.

Ensuring he made no sound, Takket closed the door behind him, creeping through the darkness. As he passed the table, he caught a whiff of a half-finished meal—root wine and charred meat.

White light on the far side of the room guided him. He came to its source: a keyhole piercing a stone door. Takket tried the cold handle—locked.

Reaching into his tunic pockets, Takket retrieved his picks. He scraped the inside of the lock, counting tumblers—five. This would be a challenge. With his only light source being the white glow filtering through the partially-blocked keyhole, Takket relied on feel alone. He took one tumbler at a time, gently tapping it into position, then jamming it to the side, wincing at every rattle, every muted screech of metal against metal. All it would take was one sound loud enough to wake Haddronius and this would all be over. Takket would die. Hekaena would be executed. The Mundanes would be slaughtered.

The final tumbler clicked into placed and the lock rotated. With an agonising creak, the door swung open. Haddronius's study was illuminated by the Pure Shard. The constant white light cast distorted shadows over the jade walls. Haddronius lay on a bed that had been placed at a strange angle, wedged between a rosewood desk and a corner cabinet. The silk-sheeted bed must have been placed recently—the Arcane-lord might deign to stay in his study for safety, but he would certainly not go without luxury.

Haddronius let out a beautiful sound: a snore—he still slept. Takket's gaze fixed on the desk, the source of light, the Pure Shard. It lay on the leather-topped surface, its silver chain draped towards the sleeping Arcane.

One careful foot at a time, Takket approached the desk, his boots silent against the velvet carpet. The only sounds in the room were Haddronius's steady

407

breaths and the occasional whistle of wind through the ceiling vents. Heeding Hekaena's warning, Takket kept his hand well away from the Shard, lifting the silver chain. Gingerly, he raised the white crystal from the desk, sending shadows dancing over the walls.

He had the Pure Shard.

Haddronius did not stir. As fast as he dared, Takket retreated to the safety of the living room. He pushed the door shut, then hurried across the lush carpet to the bedroom. Heart racing, he ducked into the Shard-lined corridor. Each nearly-silent step seemed deafening to his ears, every floorboard's creak painfully loud.

Hekaena's gaze dropped, eyes full of amazement as she stared at the Shard. Haltingly, she took it from his extended hand. The Shard glowed painfully bright at her touch, filling the foyer with an even white light.

'You did it,' she whispered.

'*We* did it.'

She nodded distantly, laying the chain around her neck, the Shard settling onto her chest. She had access to one of the most valuable objects in existence. She now stood as the most powerful person in the Arcanedom.

Hekaena was the Arcane-lord.

The fact dawned on her at the same time. They stared at one another in silent astonishment. He gazed into her silver-flecked red eyes, seeing the hope there, the fear, the dreams, the nightmares. The strength. Under her control, Varsen would be forever changed. The crematorium would close. The purges would stop. The suffering of Mundanes would at last end.

They had accomplished the impossible. He had stolen the core of a country. He had freed an entire

Arcanedom. He was a hero.

A blast punctured the air.

Debris flew down the Shard corridor—
smouldering wood and carpet, shattered furniture, and
ash. The grey dust billowed, catching the frantic light
of a thousand Shards.

Hekaena and Takket stood, stunned, staring into
the swirling mass. A silhouette moved in the cloud,
then another. Muffled voiced muttered, then footsteps
pounded across Haddronius's carpet.

'Father,' Hekaena breathed. She took off into the
swirling maelstrom. The corridor reacted to her
presence, every Shard shining in newfound brilliance
as she passed by, the combined light agonising.

After only a moment's hesitation, Takket followed.
He coughed at the dust-filled air. The stench of
burning wool mingling with woodsmoke tainted every
breath.

In Haddronius's bedroom, the epicentre of the blast
was revealed to be a gaping hole, which led to the
devastated dining room on the floor below. The table
where Takket had shared meals with the Varsen family
was cracked in half, grey wafts of smoke rising from
its ruin.

Through the shattered door to the living room,
Takket sprinted after Hekaena. They crashed into
Haddronius's study a moment too late. The Arcane's
bed was engulfed in a pillar of fire, the heat stinging
Takket's eyes. As the flames faded, Takket saw two
figures standing by the pile of ash and smouldering
silk where Haddronius had lay. Eyes adjusting, Takket
recognised the assassins.

Enara and Yelleck.

The Mages turned to Hekaena, self-satisfied expressions on their faces.

'Thank you for all you have done,' Yelleck said, smug. 'Did you think we were fools, that we wouldn't realise what you were up to? Avoiding us? Meetings in the undercity? The Mundane riots were a nice touch, by the way. It would have been better if you had given us the Shard, but Kilroth will settle for Haddronius's death.' She turned towards Hekaena with a sick grin. 'Let this be a lesson for you, Usurper—never underestimate Kilroth's resolve. Our sacrifice will go down in history, as will your part in this. Thank you. We could not have accomplished so much without the two of you.'

With a scream of rage, Hekaena flung a hand towards the pair, the Pure Shard around her neck glowing intensely. The two Mages made no attempt to defend themselves—there was no point. She was an Arcane, now armed with a Pure Shard. They were powerless to prevent her from igniting their bodies.

Tears flowed freely down Hekaena's cheeks. She did not give them the quick death they had allowed her father, not the rapid immolation that would form a Shard. No, she let the flames linger, to take their time wrapping their bodies, charring their skin, scorching their lungs. Agonised screams echoed through the tower, chilling Takket to the core.

Finally, the pained pleas ceased. The blackened husks slumped to the floor. The room stilled.

Hekaena let out a sob and staggered the few paces to the smouldering ash that had been her Father's bed. Disgusted at his own stupidity, Takket followed, stepping over Enara and Yelleck's bodies. They had used him one final time. He had given them a far greater prize than Hekaena's death. He had disarmed the Arcane-lord, exposed him to their assassination. Yet more diplomacy of the New World playing out in blood and fire.

Unsure how to comfort Hekaena, Takket laid a hand on her shoulder. She did not react, just crouched there, shaking before the pile of ash, illuminated by the white glow of her stolen Shard—the Shard that had cost her her father's life.

Takket frowned, eyes drawn to the smoking pile. White rays broke the surface of the black ash. Unthinkingly, Takket reached into the pile, feeling something warm from its core, something faceted. With shaking hands, Takket drew the object out, its white light dazzling. Haddronius's fiery death had been rapid enough to form a Shard. But not just any Shard.

A Pure Shard.

He could feel the crystal drawing him in. Some distant power wanted to meld with his essence. In that instant he knew all he had to do was accept, allow the Shard's energy to fuse with him, and his world would be forever changed. No longer a Mundane, he would be a Mage, elevated to the upper ranks of society. The first Mundane to burn a Pure Shard for two thousand years, he would be a legend. A valuable asset to any Arcanedom. It was an enticing future.

A future he refused.

Too many had suffered for his ambition, his dream of legacy. Hekaena had lost too much to his self-interest. For him, this Shard would be a minor boon. For her, it could reshape the world. Not since the

Second Imperium Era had an Arcanedom possessed two Shards. This would make Varsen a world power, and allow Hekaena to change the entire continent.

He held out the Shard. Hesitantly, she took it, looking up at him with a distant expression. She nodded once in gratitude.

The door burst open. Valena and Drothinius rushed inside, their spouses a few paces behind, all bearing Shards. They paused to take in the scene—the charred assassins, the ash at the heart of a collapsed bed frame, the Pure Shard around Hekaena's neck and the other in her hand. They stared in disbelief, tension rippling through the room as they realised the implication. Valena frowned, horrified, her inheritance stolen. In her eyes, Takket could see the temptation to attack. Valena would fall, even if the other three Arcanes helped, so long as Hekaena could bring herself to kill her own siblings. Hekaena had balked at the idea of harming one family member. Could she really murder her brother and sister, even in self-defence?

Takket had to spare her that choice, that pain.

'The Arcane-lord is dead,' he called out. 'Assassinated by Kilroth agents. Kneel to your new Arcane-Lord, Hekaena Varsen.'

The others hesitated. Takket dropped to his knees. It was all they required. One at a time, they each fell into a reverent bow.

The room echoed a response.

'All hail the Arcane-lord.'

EPILOGUE

From the top of the central dais, Takket looked out over the packed throne room. Arcanes and Mages crowded the space, nobles and guards, accountants and pilots, functionaries and commanders. Crammed behind the magic-users, filling every last inch of the room, were countless Mundanes. In the early hours of the morning, after bringing Takket down the tower, Innisel had spread Hekaena's first command—the call to court. Not just for dignitaries, but for all who could attend, Mage and Mundane alike.

The humid air hummed with a thousand contradictory rumours. Haddronius was dead. Haddronius had fought off an assassin. Hekaena had murdered him. Hekaena had saved his life. Valena was Arcane-lord. Valena had been killed. Kilroth was behind it. Kilroth had been conquered.

A few rumours had started about a new Pure Shard. Most of the conversations focused on the advantage this would give Varsen, of the golden age it could usher in, how the Arcane-lord could pursue war with any rival, able to burn the second Pure Shard, level a city, and still be able to hold onto power.

The wiser courtiers saw something deeper. A handful knew the truth. The Pure Shard had come from Haddronius's immolated corpse. It seemed a one in a million event, the thirteenth Pure Shard in all history being formed by one man's death. A fortuitous event, proof of the angels' favour.

Takket's stomach twisted. What if it was not a coincidence? Haddronius might be the first Arcane in history to be immolated. Hundreds had died in wars, sure, most killed by other magic-users, but Arcanes seldom used fire when simply puncturing someone's torso took much less effort. Those who did die by flame would have resisted, fighting to cool themselves, extinguish the fire, slowing their death. None died unarmed, meekly accepting fate like Mundanes in the crematorium. None left Shards.

Until now.

Plants produced Shard splinters and grains. Insects produced grains and flakes, small animals, flakes and gems, large beasts, gems and rocks, humans, rocks and batons. Perhaps Arcanes produced Pure Shards when immolated. Perhaps it was not a one-in-a-million occurrence, but a reproducible event. Perhaps Pure Shards could be manufactured.

The utmost sacrifice would be required, Arcanes willing to be executed, but for centuries society had been sending Mundanes to their deaths. How much of a change would it be to extend that to Arcanes? For the creation of the most powerful objects on the planet, any price would be paid. Arcanes on their death bed might volunteer as Mundanes did now, granting their heirs endless power.

It could lead to a new golden age—over time every last Mundane could ascend, forming a culture of Arcanes, a classless world. Or it could lead to a power struggle more destructive than the Devastation, hundreds of Arcane-lords, wielding their Shards, dragging both the Old World and New into endless war, levelling cities, killing millions.

A choir's call snapped Takket from his reverie. Looking up, he saw Hekaena descending from the shaft. She had adapted her necklace overnight, and the silver chain now bore both Pure Shards against her collarbone. She wore her simple black linen dress, the one she favoured in the undercity. After landing in front of Takket, she stood regally before the crowd.

He fell to his knees. After a moment's delay, the crowd mirrored his action, a thousand Arcanes, Mages and Mundanes crammed into the hall, all pledging allegiance to Hekaena.

Takket had no idea what was in store for the new Arcane-lord, but he was certain she had taken the throne at the dawn of history's most turbulent era.

ACKNOWLEDGEMENTS

First of all, I would like to thank Laurence King. His mentorship has turned me into the writer I am today. Without his patient advice, editing and proof reading, none of this would be possible.

Thank you to Neil Rankin, who put designed the covers. His work is absolutely stunning, unique and professional. I could not be happier with how they came together.

A big thank you goes to my parents, for always encouraging my writing from the days when it was just paper stapled together to make books, all the way through to now.

I would also like to thank all of my other beta-readers—Charlotte, Fiona and Michael. Thank you for putting up with some very rusty work and giving invaluable feedback.

Most of all, I would like to thank my wife, Emma. Without her help, support and constant encouragement, I would have given up a long time ago.

The Blind Shaper

by K. J. T. Carr

Now available on Kindle

Heart pounding, Harsen hurried through the branching sandstone corridors. The wraps over his face trapped his breath in his beard. It felt uncomfortably hot, but discretion was necessary. What he planned to do was illegal, dangerous—and, as far as Triumvirate were concerned, the worst of all possible sins.

He averted his gaze as he made his way through the thinning crowd, all too aware of how the pure white of his wraps stood out against the dull cream of their cheap linens. He was a wealthy man, here in the impoverished lower levels of the city of Trident.

Earlier that evening, he'd been far more content. He had been eating Calm wafers in his study, happily idling away the last days of the annual break before he had to return to lecturing. He'd greeted the knock at his door with irritation, expecting some early student trying to get into his good graces or a colleague looking for advice in planning their course. Instead, he had found a man looming on the other side of the door, his body wraps extending up to cover his head, leaving only a thin strip for the eyes. It was not overly rare for the more devote followers of the Three to completely cover their faces in this way, protecting their skin against sinful blemishes, but it was strange for such people to call on Harsen.

'The Reformists need your help, Harsen,' the man said, shouldering his way into the room.

'Excuse me?' Harsen stammered, the Calm Glyph from the wafer still dulling his senses.

'Shut the door,' the man commanded with such authority that Harsen obeyed unthinkingly. 'Good. This is urgent. We need a Scribe, a skilled Scribe. You are the best we know.'

'What are you talking about?'

The man shook his head irritably. 'We know you spend all your free time shut away here, but even you must be aware of what's going on in the city. People are dying every day from illnesses Glyphs can cure. Those who are caught with life-saving Glyphs are flayed. Those few Scribes brave enough to help are hunted by the tribunes. We—the Reformists—have had enough. We won't stand by while the Triumvirate's dogma condemns innocents to suffer. We've begun stepping in, saving those lives that can be saved, protect those willing to fight for justice. We have resources. We have a wise leader. What we need are Enscribers.'

Harsen gave a bark of a laugh. 'Who put you up to this? Ikkaro? I hardly find this sort of thing a joking matter.' Harsen's laugh faded as the man just stared at him, unflinching. This was no joke. 'Enscribing is illegal. Enscribers can be put to death.'

'Made illegal by the same people who use your Pain Glyphs to torture confessions out of the innocent.' Harsen flushed, hating being reminded of his greatest mistake—the discovery of that Glyph.

'The fact that people are flayed alive for Enscribing is all the more reason for you to join us. Can you honestly stand by in a world where saving a child's life merits a death sentence? People are dying, Harsen.'

'And? People die all the time. The elderly man across from me passed away last month. Two weeks ago, a man drowned in the currents of the North canal. Their deaths don't mean I should join these... Reformists.'

'The deaths I speak of are different, and you know it.'

'Why?'

'Because they are deaths *you* can prevent. I'm not speaking figuratively here. A woman is dying right now of wasting fever. The physicians have given up on her. She won't see the morning without an Enscribed Heal Glyph. You could save her, Harsen.'

Harsen shook his head, slowly at first, then more strongly, with anger. 'No. No. I tried to help when I was attempting to discover a new Glyph. Instead, I unleashed Pain. If I try again, I know I'll just end up fumbling into something far worse.' He paused to sigh. 'I can't help this woman, and I'm certainly not going to risk being flayed alive trying to save a stranger.' He pulled open his door and gestured for the man to leave.

'What if she wasn't a stranger?'

Something about the man's tone sent a shiver down Harsen's spine. 'What do you mean?'

'The woman I speak of... I'm sorry to say this, Harsen... She's Sillana.'

On hearing his sister's name, Harsen's world had come apart. He wasn't sure if it was guilt or hope that drove him to wrap his face and venture into the bowels of the pyramidal city. It had been almost a full year since he had seen Sillana. He'd not even heard she was ill, let alone on her death bed.

By the time he had approached her home, his guilt had only grown. The corridors narrowed on these lower levels, the floor turning scuffed and dirty. Bright Glyphs on the walls were of poorer quality, lending the area an oppressive gloom. Even the air tasted foul, the ventilation struggling so far from the surface.

Now, he stood before Sillana's door, staring at the cracked woodwork, his hand raised but refusing to knock. If he went in there, he would have no choice. He was weak. He knew that if he saw his sister dying, he'd be driven to save her, no matter the cost. This was his last moment of clarity, his last chance to turn away.

He sighed, taking a step back.

It had been two nineyears since he had discovered Pain, but he still felt the sting of that failure. His greatest mistake, his moment of outstanding incompetence, that day had changed his life—and that of far too many others. Since then, he had pulled away from the world, accepting his stipend and teaching students. He'd made this decision long ago for a good reason. His short sightedness had cost the world enough already. He would not risk causing another disaster.

He turned from the door and took a step to walk away when he was stopped by a cough coming through the thin wood. It was a pitiful thing, more a gasp than a real cough, but he could hear his sister's voice behind the sound, fading. He took in the surrounding squalor. While he had lived in wealth as one of the handful of Scribes to discover a Glyph this generation, his sister had toiled in the lower levels of the city, eking out a living making fishing nets. She had refused his offers of ink, always too proud to accept his wealth, even after her husband had died. Despite her refusal, he knew there was more he could have done. She may not have wanted money, but she had always welcomed a visit from him. He had allowed those to become too few and far between.

He closed his eyes as another weak cough reached him. He couldn't leave her like this. He hurriedly placed two thin plates the Reformist man had given him a few paces from the door in either direction. They were almost invisible in the gloom, the Loud Glyphs hidden on the underside. If stood on, they would break, a last-ditch warning if anyone approached. The only people coming down the corridor at this early hour of the morning would be tribunes.

He turned back to Sillana's door and knocked with determination.

'It's unlocked,' came the whispered reply.

The door creaked as it opened. As he peered into her humble, triangular apartment, his heart caught in his throat. Sillana lay on the bed she had shared with her husband, looking so small in its scuffed reed frame. He could barely recognise his sister. Her cheeks were sunken, her skin dry and wrinkled. She looked as if she had aged forty years since he last saw her. She turned her head towards him, the very motion seeming to cause her agony.

'Harsen,' she said with a pained smile. Of course she would recognise him with his face almost entirely covered, while he would have passed her in the corridor without a second glance. Once more, his stomach twisted with guilt.

'Sillana,' he said, easing the door shut and crossing over to her bedside. Up close, she looked no better. The cheap Bright Glyph on the wall only served to highlight every last wrinkle and sunken feature. This deep within the city, no natural light would reach her, only the failing glow of the Brights. Even her bedcovers looked ill, stained as they were from days of fever. The smell of sweat and excrement that suffused the room was almost unbearable. The Reformist contact had not lied—Harsen's sister was dying.

'Should have known they would send you,' Sillana murmured. 'They shouldn't have involved you.'

Harsen hushed her. 'I'm going to help. I'm here for you.'

A single tear ran down his sister's cheek. 'Thank you.'

From his satchel, Harsen pulled out a small reed pen and inkwell, uncorking the latter with gloved hands and setting it to one side of his sister's bed. He then pulled back her wraps, exposing her collar bone. The Heal Glyph would have a stronger effect the closer it was to her heart. He wetted the reed pen in the ink and leaned over his sister, pen a hairsbreadth from her skin.

'Are you certain?' he asked. His love for his sister battled against a lifetime of being told this very act was the worst of all sins. They said Enscribing stained the soul. Was he about to doom her for all eternity?

'Please,' she whispered. It was all he needed for the love to win out.

He visualised the Glyph, Heal. He pictured the outer triangle that enclosed all Glyphs, then three gentle curves that made Heal. He held it in his mind, focusing on every detail, the angle of every curve, the thickness of every stroke. He projected the image onto Sillana's skin and began to Scribe. He started at the lower right corner, carefully drawing out two of the three sides in perfectly straight black lines with his pen.

'It'll have to be a brittle Glyph to have a hope of being strong enough,' he explained as he worked. It took a lot of practice to be able to maintain the image in his mind while Scribing, let alone carry out a conversation at the same time, but these days it came naturally to him. 'It will only activate once we cut it, breaking the Glyph, but it will be very powerful when it does. Even so, we'll probably need more than one. I'll try to put them somewhere you can hide easily. Don't worry. Everything's going to be fine.' Even saying the words, he wasn't sure whether he was speaking to his sister or to himself. 'I'll use a quick-fading ink, but it will still take a nineday or so to disappear. Don't show it to anyone. Don't see the same physicians ever again. Move out of the city, if you can. Aunt Rissa has that rice farm in the southern end of the Ithsmus. She'll take you in.'

Sillana nodded mutely as he continued to spread the ink over her flesh. It was strange, Scribing on skin. The texture felt so different from paper, smoother, softer. As alien to him as it was, it didn't feel like a sin. Seeing the relieved smile build on his sister's face, he knew he had made the right decision.

Harsen Scribed the final stroke, the last edge of the

outer triangle. The completed Glyph flashed brightly for a moment as it sealed, the brilliance of the light indicating how close he had come to Heal's perfect form. He allowed himself a small smile of his own. He'd always been a precise Scribe.

'Now we just need to break it. I won't cut deep, but this may still sting.'

He took the knife he used to sharpen his pen from his satchel and held it over the Glyph on his sister's skin. He met her eyes, impressed by the determination he found there. Even on death's door, she exuded strength. He tried to mirror her resolution, forcing his hand to push the knife down, applying enough pressure to cut the outer edge of the Glyph. As soon as he did so, the black ink flashed a blinding white. The change on his sister was instantaneous, her taut muscles relaxing, skin growing less pale, lips turning away from their sickly purple.

'It worked,' he said, vision blurring with tears.

'Of course it did,' she replied, already sound healthier. 'You always were the best Scribe I knew.'

Harsen shrugged away the compliment, re-inking his pen and readying to Scribe another Heal next to the first. 'We'll need more to beat this. Four should do it, five would be safe. The later ones you'll need to break yourself in the morning to make a full recovery. I'll be back tomorrow evening to see how you're doing. I can always-'

He trailed off as a *crack* sounded from outside— the Loud Glyphs he'd placed.

'The corridor should be empty,' Sillana said, her renewed strength only adding to the fear in her voice.

'Tribunes,' Harsen whispered, throwing himself at

the door and slamming the bolt closed. He stepped back as the door shook violently. Someone was on the far side, trying to break through. If they were tribunes, the rusting hinges wouldn't last long.

He ran back to his sister and threw his inkwell and pen into his satchel before hurriedly covering the broken Glyph on her skin.

'The cooker shares its vent with my neighbours.' Sillana pointed to one corner of the room. 'You can escape through there.'

'You're coming with me,' Harsen demanded.

'No, she replied firmly. 'I can't move. You can't carry me and escape tribunes. You know that. You tried to save me, Harsen. It's my turn to save you. I'll slow them. Go. *Now*.'

Harsen wanted to argue, wanted to drag her out with him, wanted to fight the tribunes, wanted to do something, anything. But it was hopeless. He couldn't stand up to tribunes, couldn't carry her with them in pursuit.

He had failed her.

He ran across the room with an anguished cry. Throwing open the shutter at the back of the cooker, he crawled through the small opening, the heat from the Glyphs below the covering under him made him grit his teeth. He rolled out the far side, running between the next house's occupants, ignoring their startled cries. He barged open their flimsy door and sprinted into the winding tunnels that ran between the homes in the lower levels of Trident.

The tunnel before him was dimly lit with only a handful of Bright Glyphs spread along its length, all of dubious quality. As he sprinted away, he heard

426

shouts from behind, some angry, some fearful. Furniture crashed as the shouts intensified, the sound of reedwork chairs being smashed echoing after him. He focused on the end of the tunnel, where it branched into two at one hundred and twenty degree angles. If he could just get down one before the tribunes saw him, he might just lose them in the maze of alleyways.

Only a few more paces.

The door crashed open behind him and an angry shout drove out all thoughts of an easy escape.

'Halt, in the name of the Triumvirate.'

The order only spurred him to run all the faster, but he knew fleeing would only delay the inevitable. Tribunes had access to the best Glyphs in the known world—he'd probably made some used by the very soldiers behind him. Their armour weighed less than a feather, and they could increase their speed just by swallowing one of the nines of Glyph tablets kept in holsters on their belts. No, he could not outrun them. He could Scribe better than almost anyone, but that required patience. A quick scribble would be useless. Given enough time, he could erect an impassable barrier, or create an inferno that even their Engraved armour could not withstand, but time was a commodity he severely lacked. He could hear the soft footsteps of their leather boots closing behind him.

Then he saw it—salvation. A section of wall made of a different colour from its surrounds. He grinned, ripping the knife from his satchel and digging it into the corner of the discoloured wall. With a scrape, the clay panel came away, shattering by his feet. Behind it, a Strength Glyph carved into the wall was revealed. A structure like the city of Trident could not be made out of any known material, let alone the sandstone that formed the majority of its walls. Instead, it relied on Glyphs, as everything did in this world. Glyphs to lighten the top beams, to allow some to flex and some, like the one before him, to be strengthened to hold up many times more weight than it had any right to.

He slammed his knife at the Glyph, chipping at one of carved lines that made up its encompassing triangle. Again and again he thrust his knife into the wall, battling against the unnatural strength of the Engraved sandstone. His efforts were rewarded with a tiny gash marring one of the lines. It wasn't much, barely visible in the poor lighting, but it was enough to break the persistent Glyph. The wall flickered with a strange light for a moment as the power of the Glyph disintegrated. A moment later, a low groan sounded from the wall.

He sprinted away as the tribunes rounded the corner behind him. For a moment, he thought that the wall might hold, that the tribunes would catch him, that his failure would be complete.

Then, with a deafening crack, the wall shattered.

The sandstone, now as weak as nature had intended, was unable to support the weight of the towering city above it. With a spray of stone and dust it came down, blocking the tunnel with rubble.

It would take the best Shapers in the city many ninedays to undo Harsen's destruction, and he gave a momentary thought to anyone unlucky enough to be on the level above, but the city had been designed to withstand such failures. It may not cause lasting damage, but it was enough to stop his pursuers.

To better fit in when he rejoined the main

corridors, he dusted off his wraps, freeing those around his head, all the while tormented by thoughts of his sister. He had tried, actually tried, to help her and all it would bring her was an even more painful end. That was how things were in Trident—the best of intentions were turned to ash under the heel of the Triumvirate.